BURIED ANGELS

Camilla Lackberg is a worldwide bestseller renowned for her brilliant contemporary psychological thrillers. Her novels have sold over 12 million copies in 55 countries with translations into 37 languages.

www.CamillaLackberg.com

Also by Camilla Lackberg

The Ice Princess
The Preacher
The Stonecutter
The Stranger (previously titled *The Gallows Bird*)
The Hidden Child
The Drowning
The Lost Boy

CAMILLA LACKBERG

Buried Angels

Translated from the Swedish by Tiina Nunnally

HarperCollins*Publishers*

HarperCollins*Publishers*
77–85 Fulham Palace Road,
Hammersmith, London W6 8JB

www.harpercollins.co.uk

Published by HarperCollins*Publishers* 2014

1

ISBN: 9780007507498

Set in Meridien by Palimpsest Book Production Ltd,
Falkirk, Stirlingshire

Printed and bound in the United States

'If one man can display so much hatred, imagine how much love all of us together could show.'

They had decided to renovate their way out of the grief. Neither of them was sure it was a good plan, but it was the only one they had. The alternative was to lie down and slowly pine away.

Ebba ran the scraper over the outside wall of the house. The paint was coming away easily. It had already started to flake off in big chunks, so all she had to do was help it along. The July sun was so hot that her fringe was sticking to her forehead, which was damp with sweat, and her arm ached because it was the third day in a row she'd carried out this same monotonous, up-and-down motion. But she welcomed the physical pain. The worse it got, the more it muted the ache in her heart, at least for a while.

She turned around and looked at Tobias, who was working on the lawn in front of the house, sawing boards. He seemed to sense that she was watching him, because he glanced up and raised a hand in greeting, as if she were an acquaintance he was meeting on the street. Ebba felt her own hand respond with the same awkward gesture.

More than six months had passed since their life had been shattered, but they still didn't know how to react to each other. Every night they would lie in the double bed with their backs turned, terrified that some involuntary touch might release something that they wouldn't know how to handle. It was as if the grief filled them to the point there was no room for any other feelings. No love, no warmth, no empathy.

Guilt, heavy and unexpressed, separated them. Things would have been easier if they could have defined it and worked out where it belonged. But it kept shifting back and forth, changing strength and shape, constantly attacking from new directions.

Ebba turned back to the house and continued scraping at the wall. Under her hands the white paint came off in big pieces, revealing the wooden boards underneath. She stroked the wood with her free hand. This house seemed to have a soul in a way that she'd never noticed anywhere else. The small terraced cottage in Göteborg had been almost new when she and Tobias had bought it together. Back then she had loved the fact that the whole place had shone so brightly, that it was so untouched. Now all of that newness was a thing of the past, and this old house with all its flaws was better suited to her present state. She thought again about the leaky roof, the boiler that regularly needed a good kick to get it started, and the draughty windows that made it impossible to keep a lighted candle on the windowsill. Rain and wind also swept through her soul, mercilessly blowing out the candles that she tried to light.

Maybe her spirit would be able to heal here on Valö. She had no memories from this place, and yet it was as if they knew each other, she and this island. It was just opposite Fjällbacka. If she went down to the dock, she could see the small coastal town spread out across the water. At the base of the steep granite cliff the little white buildings and red boathouses were lined up like a string of beads. The sight was so beautiful that it almost hurt.

Sweat was running down her forehead, stinging her eyes. She wiped her face on her T-shirt and squinted up at the sun. Seagulls were circling overhead. The birds called and shrieked to each other, their cries mixing with the sound of motorboats moving through the strait. She closed her eyes and let the sounds carry her away. Away from herself, away from . . .

'How about taking a break to go swimming?'

Tobias's voice broke through the background noise, startling her. She shook her head in confusion, but then nodded.

'Sure, let's do that,' she said, climbing down from the scaffolding.

Their bathing suits had been hung up to dry in back of the house. Ebba peeled off her sweaty work clothes to put on a bikini.

Tobias was faster, and he waited for her impatiently.

'Ready?' he said and then led the way down the path to the beach. The island was quite large and not as barren as many of the smaller islands in the archipelago of Bohuslän. The path was lined by leafy trees and tall grass, and Ebba stomped hard on the ground as she walked along. She had an intense fear of snakes, which had grown worse since she saw a viper basking in the sun a few days ago.

As they started down the slope towards the water, she couldn't help thinking about how many children's feet had walked this path over the years. The place was still called the summer camp, even though it hadn't been a summer camp for children since the 1930s.

'Watch your step,' said Tobias, pointing to several tree roots sticking up from the ground.

His concern, which should have warmed her heart, felt almost suffocating, and she made an exaggerated effort to avoid the roots. After another few metres, she felt rough sand under her feet. Waves were lapping the long shoreline, and she tossed her towel on to the beach and walked right into the salty water. Seaweed rubbed against her legs and the sudden cold made her gasp for breath, but she quickly adapted to the chill. Behind her she could hear Tobias calling her name. Pretending not to hear, she kept on going. When the bottom fell away beneath her, she started swimming, and with only a few strokes she reached the bathing platform anchored a short distance from shore.

'Ebba!' Tobias shouted from the beach, but she continued to ignore him and grabbed hold of the ladder. She needed some time to herself. If she lay down and closed her eyes, she could pretend that she was shipwrecked out on the wide open sea. Alone. With no need to pay attention to anyone else.

She heard him ploughing through the water, getting closer. The bathing platform rocked as Tobias climbed up, and she squeezed her eyes tighter in order to shut him out a little longer. She wanted to be alone, by herself. Not the way things were now. She and Tobias were both alone, but together. Reluctantly she opened her eyes.

Erica was sitting at the table in the living room, which looked as if a bomb had blown toys all over the room. Cars, dolls, stuffed animals and dress-up clothes were scattered everywhere. Three children, all under the age of four, were the primary reason why the house looked as it did. But now that she had some time to herself without the children, she had, as usual, given priority to her writing instead of tidying up the house.

When she heard the front door open, she glanced up from her computer and caught sight of her husband.

'Hi. What are you doing here? Weren't you going over to see Kristina?'

'Mamma wasn't home. Typical. I should have called first,' said Patrik, kicking off his Crocs.

'Do you really have to wear those things? How can you drive with them on?' She pointed at the loathsome footwear which, to top it off, were a neon green. Her sister Anna had given them to Patrik as a joke, but now he refused to wear anything else.

Patrik came over to her and gave her a kiss. 'You're so beautiful,' he said, and then headed for the kitchen. 'Did the publishing house get hold of you, by the way? It must have been important – they even tried my mobile.'

'They wanted to know if I could attend the book fair this year, as I promised. I still can't make up my mind.'

'Of course you must go. I'll take care of the kids that weekend. I've already made arrangements to take those days off.'

'Thanks,' said Erica, but in her heart she was irritated with herself for feeling so grateful to her husband. After all, didn't she always have to take over when his work called him away at a moment's notice, or when their weekends, holidays, and evenings were interrupted because his job couldn't wait? She loved Patrik more than anything, but sometimes it felt like he hardly noticed that she had to bear most of the responsibility for their home and the children. She had a career too, and quite a successful one at that.

She often heard people say how amazing it must be to make a living as a writer. To be in charge of her own schedule, to be her own boss. That always annoyed Erica. Much as she loved her work and realized how fortunate she was, it wasn't as easy as everyone seemed to think. Freedom was not something she associated with being an author. On the contrary, when she was writing, it consumed her 24/7. Sometimes she was envious of people who went off to work, put in their eight hours, and left

7

it all behind them as soon as they set off home. She could never put her work aside, and with success came demands and expectations that had to be combined with her life as the mother of young children.

But it was hard to claim that her work was more important than Patrik's. He protected people, solved crimes, and helped to make society function better, while she wrote books that were read as entertainment. So she put up with the fact that she was usually the one who drew the short straw, even though it sometimes made her feel like screaming.

With a sigh she got up and went to join her husband in the kitchen.

'Are they asleep?' asked Patrik, taking out the fixings for his favourite sandwich: flatbread, butter, caviar, and cheese.

Erica shuddered, knowing his next step would be to dunk the sandwich in a cup of hot chocolate.

'Yes, for once I managed to get them to take a nap at the same time. They had a good play session this morning, so all three of them were worn out.'

'Great,' said Patrik, sitting down at the kitchen table to eat.

Erica went back to the living room to fit in a little more writing before the children woke up. Stolen hours. That was all she could count on these days.

She was dreaming of fire. Horror etched on his face, Vincent was pressing his nose against the windowpane. Behind him she saw the flames shoot up, higher and higher. They were getting closer to him, singeing his blond locks as he screamed soundlessly. She wanted to throw herself at the glass, shattering it so she could rescue him from the flames that threatened to engulf him. But no matter how she tried, her body refused to obey.

Then she heard Tobias's voice. It was filled with reproach. He hated her because she couldn't save Vincent, because she was standing there watching as he was burned alive right before their eyes.

'Ebba! Ebba!'

His voice made her try again. She had to run forward and break the glass. She had to . . .

'Ebba, wake up!'

Someone was tugging at her shoulders and forcing her to sit up. Slowly the dream faded. She wanted to hold on to it, throw herself into the flames, and maybe for one brief moment hold Vincent's little body in her arms before they both perished.

'You have to wake up. Fire!'

Suddenly she was fully awake. The smell of smoke prickled her nostrils, making her cough so hard that her throat hurt. When she looked up she saw that smoke was billowing through the doorway.

'We have to get out!' shouted Tobias. 'Crawl underneath the smoke. I'll follow you. I'm going to see if I can put out the fire.'

Ebba rolled out of bed and dropped to the floor. She could feel the heat of the floorboards against her cheek. Her lungs were burning, and she felt so terribly tired. How could she possibly manage to move? She wanted to surrender, to sleep. She shut her eyes and felt a heavy lethargy spread through her body. She would rest here for a moment. Just sleep for a while.

'Get up! You have to get up!' Tobias's voice was shrill, rousing her from her torpor. He wasn't usually scared of anything. Now he was yanking on her arm, hauling her on to all fours.

Reluctantly she began crawling forward. Fear had begun to take hold of her too. With every breath she could feel more smoke filling her lungs, like a slow-acting poison.

But she'd rather die from smoke than from fire. The thought of her skin burning was enough to make her move faster as she crawled out of the room.

All of a sudden she got confused. She ought to know which way the stairs were, but it felt as though her brain had stopped functioning. The only thing she could see was a thick grey fog. Panicking, she started crawling straight ahead, so that at least she wouldn't get stuck in the smoke.

As she reached the stairs, Tobias raced past, holding a fire extinguisher in his hands. He ran down the stairs in three bounds, as Ebba stared after him. It was like in her dream – her body no longer seemed willing to obey her, and her joints refused to move. Helplessly she stayed where she was, down on all fours, as the smoke got thicker and thicker. She was coughing again. One fit of coughing followed another. Her eyes were running, and her thoughts shifted to Tobias, but she didn't have the energy to worry about him.

Again she felt an overwhelming urge to give up. To disappear, to rid herself of the grief that was tearing her apart, body and soul. She felt that she was on the verge of fainting, so she lay down, resting her head on her arms, and closed her eyes. Everything around her was soft and warm. A great lethargy again came over her, welcoming her. It meant her no harm, it wanted only to receive her and make her whole.

'Ebba!' Tobias was pulling on her arm but she resisted. She wanted to be carried off to that beautiful, quiet place she was heading towards. Then she felt a slap on her face, a blow that made her cheek sting. Shaken, she pulled herself up and looked into Tobias's face. His expression was both worried and angry.

'The fire's out,' he said. 'But we can't stay here.'

He made an attempt to pull her up, but she pushed

him away. He had taken from her the one opportunity for rest that she'd had in a long time. Furious, she pounded her fists against his chest. It was a huge relief to let loose all her rage and disappointment, and she kept on striking him as hard as she could, until he finally caught hold of her wrists. Gripping them tight, he drew her towards him. He pressed her face against his chest, held her close. She could hear his heart beating fast, and the sound made her cry. Then she let him lift her up. He carried her out, and when the cold night air filled her lungs, she let go and sank into a daze.

FJÄLLBACKA 1908

They arrived early in the morning. Her mother was already up with the little ones, while Dagmar still lolled in bed, savouring the warmth under the covers. That was the difference between being her mother's real child and one of the bastard kids that she cared for. Dagmar was special.

'What's going on?' shouted her father from the bedroom. Both he and Dagmar had been awakened by an insistent pounding on the door.

'Open up! It's the police!'

Then whoever it was evidently lost all patience because the door was torn open, and a man wearing a police uniform stormed into the house.

Frightened, Dagmar sat up in bed, trying to hide behind the blankets.

'The police?' Her father came into the kitchen, fumbling to button up his trousers. His sunken chest was sparsely covered with grey hair. 'If you'll just let me put on a shirt, I'm sure I can straighten everything out. There must be some misunderstanding. This is the home of respectable people.'

'Does Helga Svensson live here?' asked the policeman. Two more officers were waiting behind him. They had to stand close together because the kitchen was cramped and filled with beds. At the moment they had five young children living in the house.

'My name is Albert Svensson and Helga is my wife,' said Pappa. By now he had put on his shirt and was standing there with his arms folded.

'Where is your wife?' There was a note of urgency in the policeman's voice.

Dagmar saw the worried furrow that had appeared on her father's brow. He was so easily upset, her mother always said. Delicate nerves.

'Mamma is in the yard out back. With the children,' said Dagmar. Only now did the policemen notice her.

'Thank you,' said the officer who had done all the talking. He turned on his heel and left the room.

Her father followed close behind. 'You can't come storming into the home of decent people, scaring the life out of us. You have to tell us what this is all about.'

Dagmar threw off the bedclothes, set her feet on the cold kitchen floor and dashed after them, wearing only her nightgown. She came to an abrupt stop behind the men. Two of the officers were gripping her mother by the arms. She was struggling to get free, and the men were straining with the effort to hold on to her. The children were shrieking, and the laundry that her mother had been hanging on the line had fallen off in all the commotion.

'Mamma!' cried Dagmar, running towards her.

Then she threw herself at the legs of one of the policemen and bit him in the thigh. He screamed and let go of Helga, turning around to punch Dagmar so hard that the child fell to the ground. In surprise, she sat there on the grass, her hand pressed to her stinging cheek. In the eight years of her life, no one had ever hit her. She'd seen her mother give the children a swat now and then, but she had never raised a hand to Dagmar. And for that reason her father had never dared strike her either.

'What are you doing! Did you hit my daughter?' Helga kicked out at the men in fury.

'That's nothing compared to what you've done.' The policeman again gripped Helga's arm. 'You are accused of killing a child,

13

and we have the right to search your house. And believe me, we plan to make a thorough job of it.'

Dagmar watched as her mother seemed to collapse. Her cheek still felt as if it was on fire, and her heart was racing in her chest. All around her the children were screaming as though it was Judgement Day. And perhaps it was. Because even though Dagmar didn't understand what was happening, the expression on her mother's face told her that their world had just been torn apart.

'Patrik, can you head out to Valö? A report's come in of a fire out there, and they think it might be arson.'

'What? Sorry, but what did you say?'

Patrik was already getting out of bed, clasping the phone between ear and shoulder as he pulled on his jeans. Still bleary with sleep, he glanced at the clock. Seven fifteen. For a second he wondered what Annika was doing at the station so early in the day.

'There's been a fire on Valö,' Annika repeated patiently. 'The fire brigade was called out early this morning, and they suspect it might be arson.'

'Where on Valö?'

Erica turned over in bed. 'What is it?' she murmured.

'Police business. I have to go out to Valö,' he whispered. For once the twins were sleeping past six thirty, so he didn't want to wake them.

'It's out at the summer camp,' said Annika on the phone.

'Okay. I'll take the boat and head out there. I'll ring Martin. He's on duty today too, isn't he?'

'That's right. I'll see you both back at the station later on.'

Patrik ended the call and put on a T-shirt.

'What's happened?' asked Erica, sitting up in bed.

'The fire brigade thinks someone has set a fire over at the old summer camp.'

'The summer camp? Someone's trying to burn it down?' Erica swung her legs over the edge of the bed.

'I promise to tell you all about it later,' said Patrik with a smile. 'I know it's one of your pet projects.'

'What a strange coincidence that someone would try to burn down the place now, just when Ebba has come back to live there.'

Patrik shook his head. He knew from experience that his wife liked to get herself mixed up in things that were not her concern. She was always jumping to outlandish conclusions. It was true that occasionally she turned out to be right – that much he had to admit – but sometimes she also made a real mess of things.

'Annika said they suspect arson. That's all we know at this stage, and it might not be arson at all.'

'But still,' said Erica. 'It's odd that it should happen now. Can I come with you? I was planning to go out there anyway to have a little talk with Ebba.'

'And who's going to take care of the kids? Have you thought about that? I think Maja's still too young to heat up the formula for the boys.'

He kissed Erica on the cheek and then raced downstairs. Behind him he heard the twins start to cry, right on cue.

Patrik and Martin exchanged only a few words on their way out to Valö. The suggestion that this could be arson was both unsettling and hard to believe. As they approached the island and surveyed the idyllic setting, it seemed more unlikely than ever.

'It's so beautiful out here,' said Martin, lost in admiration as they walked up the path from the dock where Patrik had tied up the boat.

16

'You've been out here before, haven't you?' said Patrik without turning around. 'At least that one Christmas.'

Martin muttered something in reply. He didn't want to be reminded of that fateful Christmas when he had been drawn into a family drama on the island.

A large expanse of lawn stretched out before them. They stopped to look around.

'I have some wonderful memories of this place,' said Patrik. 'We used to come here on school outings a few times a year, and in the summertime when I was at sailing camp. I've kicked a lot of balls across that lawn. And played a lot of games of rounders.'

'I know. Who hasn't been to camp out here? Strange how it's always been called the summer camp.'

Patrik shrugged and started up the path towards the house. 'I suppose the name stuck. It was only a boarding school for a short time, and nobody wanted to name the place after old man von Schlesinger who lived here before.'

'Oh, right. I've heard about that lunatic,' said Martin, cursing as a branch slapped him in the face. 'Who owns the place now?'

'I assume the couple who live here own it. After what happened in 1974, it's been administered by the local council, at least as far as I know. Too bad that the house has been allowed to fall into such disrepair, but it looks like they're starting to fix it up.'

Martin peered up at the scaffolding that covered the entire front of the building. 'They seem to be putting a lot of work into it. I hope the fire didn't cause too much damage.'

They made their way to the stone stairway that led up to the front door. The Fjällbacka Volunteer Fire Brigade were gathering up their equipment, going about their work in a calm, methodical manner. They must be sweating buckets in those heavy uniforms, thought Patrik.

The heat was already oppressive, in spite of the early hour.

'Hi!' Östen Ronander, chief of the fire brigade, came over and nodded a greeting. His hands were black with soot.

'Hi, Östen. So what happened here? Annika said you suspect the fire might have been deliberately set.'

'It certainly appears that way. But we're not qualified to make that judgement, from a technical point of view. We're hoping that Torbjörn will get here soon.'

'I phoned him on our way over, and they expect to be here in . . .' Patrik glanced at his watch, 'about half an hour.'

'Good. Want me to show you around, in the meantime? We've tried not to disturb anything. The owner had already put out the flames with a fire extinguisher by the time we arrived, so we've just made sure that nothing is still smouldering. There wasn't really much else we could do. Take a look over there—'

Östen pointed to the front hall. On the other side of the threshold the floor was scorched in a strange, irregular pattern.

'Must have been some sort of flammable liquid, don't you think?' said Martin, peering at it.

Östen nodded.

'I'd say somebody poured the liquid under the door and then ignited it. Judging by the smell, I reckon it was petrol, but I'm sure Torbjörn and his boys will be able to tell us for sure.'

'Where are the people who live here?'

'They're sitting out back, waiting for the medics, who unfortunately have been delayed because of a traffic accident. They both seem to be suffering from shock, and I thought they could use some peace and quiet. I also thought it would be best if we didn't let them tramp about inside the house before you had a chance to secure any evidence.'

'Good thinking.' Patrik patted Östen on the shoulder and then said to Martin. 'Shall we go and have a talk with them?'

Without waiting for a reply he headed towards the back of the house. As they turned the corner they spotted a few pieces of patio furniture a short distance away. The chairs and table were shabby, as if they'd been subjected to years of all kinds of weather. Sitting at the table were a man and a woman, both in their mid-thirties, looking lost. When the man caught sight of Patrik and Martin, he stood up and came to greet them, holding out his hand, which was hard and callused, as if accustomed to working with tools.

'Tobias Stark.'

Patrik and Martin introduced themselves.

'We don't understand what happened. The firemen said something about arson. Could that be right?' said Tobias's wife, who had come over to stand next to her husband. She was slender and petite. Even though Patrik was only of average height, she barely reached to his shoulder. She seemed delicate and fragile, and she was shivering in spite of the heat.

'That's not necessarily true. We don't yet know anything for certain,' said Patrik, wanting to reassure them.

'This is my wife Ebba,' Tobias told them. Then he wearily rubbed a hand over his face.

'Why don't we sit down?' said Martin. 'We'd like to hear a little more about what happened.'

'Sure, we can sit over there,' said Tobias, pointing to the patio furniture.

'Who discovered the fire?' asked Patrik when they were seated. He was studying Tobias, who had a dark patch on his forehead. Like Östen, his hands were black with soot.

Noticing the direction of Patrik's gaze, Tobias glanced down at his hands. It appeared he hadn't realized until now how dirty they were. He spent a few moments wiping his palms on his jeans before he answered the question.

'I did. I woke up and noticed a strange smell. As soon as I realized that there was a fire downstairs, I tried to wake Ebba. It took a few minutes because she was sound asleep, but finally I managed to get her out of bed. Then I ran to get the fire extinguisher. There was only one thought in my mind: to put out the fire.' Tobias spoke so fast that he was out of breath, and he had to pause for a moment.

'I thought I was going to die. I was absolutely convinced of it,' said Ebba, picking at a cuticle. Patrik gave her a sympathetic look.

'I took the fire extinguisher and sprayed it like crazy at the flames in the front hall,' Tobias went on. 'At first nothing happened, but I kept on spraying, and all of a sudden the flames went out. But there was still a lot of smoke. There was smoke everywhere.' Again he had to stop to catch his breath.

'Why would anyone . . . I don't understand,' said Ebba vaguely, and Patrik suspected that Östen was right: she was in a state of shock. That would also explain why she was shivering as if she were freezing. When the medics arrived, they were going to have to pay special attention to Ebba and also make sure that neither she nor Tobias was suffering from smoke inhalation. Many people didn't realize that smoke could be deadlier than the actual fire. Drawing smoke deep into the lungs could have consequences that didn't show up until later.

'Why do they think the fire was deliberately set?' asked Tobias, rubbing his face again. Patrik assumed that the man hadn't had much sleep.

'As I said, we don't know anything for sure at the moment,' he replied evasively. 'But there are certain indications. I don't want to say more until the technical experts have been able to confirm our suspicions. Did either of you hear any noises in the night?'

'No. As I mentioned, I didn't wake up until the fire was already burning.'

Patrik nodded towards a house a short distance away. 'Are the neighbours at home? Would they have noticed if there were any strangers about?'

'They're on holiday. We're the only ones on this part of the island.'

'Is there anybody who might want to do you harm?' Martin chipped in. He often let Patrik take charge of the questioning, but he always listened attentively and watched the reactions of the people they were interviewing. And that was just as important as asking the questions.

'No. Not as far as I know.' Ebba shook her head.

'We haven't lived here long. Only two months,' said Tobias. 'This house belonged to Ebba's parents, but it was rented out for years, and she hasn't been back until now. We decided to fix up the place and make something of it.'

Patrik and Martin exchanged a quick glance. The story of this house and Ebba's family was well known in the area, but this was not the right moment to bring it up. Patrik was glad Erica hadn't come with him. She wouldn't have been able to restrain herself.

'Where did you live before?' asked Patrik, even though he could make a good guess, based on Tobias's distinctive accent.

'Göteborg, born and bred,' said Tobias.

'And no old quarrels to settle with anyone back there?'

'We've never quarrelled with anyone in Göteborg – or anywhere else, for that matter,' said Tobias curtly.

'So what made you decide to move here?' asked Patrik.

Ebba stared at the table as she fingered the pendant that hung on a chain around her neck. A lovely little angel made of silver.

'Our son died,' she said, tugging so hard on the angel that the chain bit into her neck.

'We needed a change of scene,' said Tobias. 'This house had been allowed to fall into disrepair, and nobody cared about it any more. We saw it as a chance for us to start over. I come from a family of innkeepers, so it seemed the natural choice to set up in business, open a bed-and-breakfast. In time, we hope to get conference-goers to stay here.'

'Looks like you've got a lot of work ahead of you,' said Patrik, staring at the big house with the peeling paint. He purposely chose not to ask about their deceased son. The pain on their faces was too obvious.

'We're not afraid of working hard. And we'll keep at it as long as we can. If we run out of steam, we can always hire some help, but we need to save money. It's going to be tough to make a go of it financially.'

'So you can't think of anyone who might want to hurt you or your business?' Martin persisted.

'Business? What business?' said Tobias with a sarcastic laugh. 'But no. As I already told you, we can't think of a single person who would do something like this to us. That's not the kind of life we lead. We're just ordinary folk.'

Patrik thought for a moment about Ebba's background. Not many ordinary folk had that sort of tragic mystery in their past. Fjällbacka was rife with wild rumours about what had happened to Ebba's family.

'Unless . . .' Tobias cast an inquisitive glance at Ebba, who didn't seem to understand what he was hinting at. With his eyes fixed on her, he said, 'The only thing that comes to mind is the birthday card.'

'Birthday card?' said Martin.

'Ever since she was little, on every birthday Ebba has received a card from someone who simply signs the card "G". Her adoptive parents never found out who was sending those cards. And the cards kept on arriving, even after Ebba moved away from home.'

'And Ebba has no idea who they're from?' asked Patrik before he realized that he was speaking as if she wasn't present. He turned to her and repeated the question. 'You have no idea who has been sending these cards to you?'

'No.'

'What about your adoptive parents? Are you sure they don't know anything?'

'They haven't a clue.'

'Has this "G" ever tried to get in touch with you in any other way? Or threatened you?'

'No, never. Nothing like that, right, Ebba?' Tobias reached out as if to touch his wife, but then he let his hand drop back on his lap.

She shook her head.

'Torbjörn is here,' said Martin, gesturing towards the path.

'Good. In that case we'll stop now and let the two of you rest. The medics are on the way, and if they feel you ought to go to the hospital, I think you should do that. These kinds of things need to be taken seriously.'

'Thanks,' said Tobias, standing up. 'Let us know if you find out anything.'

'We'll do that.' Patrik cast another worried glance at Ebba. She still seemed to be enveloped in a bubble. He wondered how the tragedy of her childhood had shaped her, but then he pushed that thought aside. Right now he needed to focus on the job at hand. And that meant determining whether they were dealing with an arsonist.

FJÄLLBACKA 1912

Dagmar still didn't understand how it could have happened. Everything had been taken from her, and she was utterly alone. No matter where she went, people whispered ugly words behind her back. They hated her because of what her mother had done.

Sometimes at night she missed her mother and father so much that she had to bite the pillow to stop herself sobbing aloud. Because if she did that, the horrid witch she lived with would beat her black and blue. But she couldn't always hold back her screams when the nightmares got so bad that she woke up drenched in sweat. In her dreams she saw the chopped-off heads of her mother and father. Because in the end both of them had been beheaded. Dagmar had not been present to see it happen, but the image had been burned into her mind.

And sometimes images of the children also hounded her dreams. The police had found the bodies of eight infants when they dug up the earthen floor in the cellar. That was what the witch had said. 'Eight poor little children,' she said, shaking her head, whenever anyone came to visit. Her friends would then turn to glare at Dagmar. 'The girl must have known about it,' they said. 'Even as young as she is, surely she must have realized what they were doing, don't you think?'

Dagmar refused to be cowed. It didn't matter whether that was true or not. Mamma and Pappa had loved her, and nobody wanted those dirty, squealing little kids. That was why they had wound up with her mother. For years she had worked so hard, yet the only thanks she ever received for taking in all those unwanted children was that people ended up demeaning her, jeering at her, and then they killed her. The same thing had happened to her father. He had helped Mamma bury those children and for that reason people said that he too deserved to die.

Dagmar had been sent to live with the witch after the police took her parents away. No one else was willing to have her, not the relatives or any friends. No one wanted anything to do with her family. The angelmaker from Fjällbacka – that was what people had started calling her mother the day those little skeletons were found. Now people even sang ballads about her. About the murderer who had drowned the children in a basin, and about her husband who had buried them in the cellar. Dagmar knew those songs by heart. Her foster mother's snotty-nosed kids sang them to her whenever they got a chance.

None of this mattered to her, because she was still her parents' little princess, and she knew that she had been both wanted and loved. The only thing that made her tremble with fear was the sound of her foster father's footsteps approaching across the floor. At those moments Dagmar wished that she could have followed her mother and father into death.

✤

Josef nervously ran his thumb over the stone that he was holding. This meeting was important, and he wasn't about to allow Sebastian to ruin things.

'Here it is.' Sebastian pointed at the drawings that he'd placed on the conference table. 'Here's our vision. A project for peace in our time.' He said the last phrase in English.

Josef sighed to himself. He wasn't convinced that the local council representatives would be impressed with fancy phrases in English.

'What my partner is trying to say is that this is an amazing opportunity for Tanum to do something for peace. An initiative that will bring the area a great deal of prestige.'

'Sure, peace on earth is a good thing. And financially it's not such a daft idea, either. In the long run, it should increase tourism and create new jobs for the people who live here, and you know what that means.' Sebastian held up his hand and rubbed his fingers together. 'More money for the whole area.'

'Yes, but above all it's an important peace project,' said Josef, resisting the urge to give Sebastian a kick in the shins. He'd known this would happen when he accepted Sebastian's money, but he'd had no choice.

Erling W. Larson nodded. After the scandal over the renovation of the Badhotel in Fjällbacka, he'd found himself out in the cold for a while, but now he was once again involved in local politics. This sort of project would show that he was still a force to be reckoned with, and Josef hoped that Erling would realize this.

'We think it sounds interesting,' said Erling. 'Could you tell us more about how you envision the whole thing?'

Sebastian took in a breath as he prepared to speak, but Josef beat him to it.

'This is a little piece of history,' he said, holding out the stone. 'Albert Speer purchased granite from the quarry in Bohuslän for the German Reich. He and Hitler had grandiose plans to transform Berlin into the world capital of "Germania", and the granite was supposed to be shipped to Germany for use in construction.'

Josef stood up and began pacing back and forth as he talked. In his mind he heard the stomping boots of German soldiers. The sound that his parents had so often told him about in horror.

'But then the war turned,' he went on. 'Germania never evolved beyond a model that Hitler fantasized about during his last days. An unfulfilled dream, a vision of stately monuments and edifices that would have been built at the cost of millions of Jewish lives.'

'How awful,' said Erling, showing little concern.

'The shiploads of granite never left Tanum—'

'And that's where we come in,' Sebastian interrupted Josef. 'We were thinking that from that granite we could make peace symbols that could then be sold. It would bring in a lot of money, provided it's done properly.'

'And we could then use the money to build a museum devoted to Jewish history and Sweden's relationship to Judaism. Including our purported neutral position during the war,' Josef added.

He sat down, and Sebastian put his arm around his shoulders. Josef had to stop himself from shaking off his arm. Instead he mustered a strained smile. He felt just as phoney as he had during those days on Valö. Even back then he'd had nothing in common with Sebastian or his other so-called friends. No matter how hard he tried, he knew he'd never be able to enter the upper-class world that John and Leon and Percy came from. Nor did he want to.

But right now he needed Sebastian. It was his only hope of realizing the dream he'd had for so many years: to pay homage to his Jewish heritage and make public what he knew about the assaults that had been carried out, and were still being levelled against the Jewish people. If that meant he had to sign a pact with the devil, then he'd do it. He hoped that over time he'd be able to end his association with Sebastian.

'As my partner here was saying,' Sebastian continued, 'it'll be a really great museum, and a pilgrimage destination for tourists from all over the world. And all of you will get the credit for backing this project.'

'Doesn't sound half bad,' said Erling. 'What do you think?' He turned to Uno Brorsson, his second-in-command on the council, who in spite of the heat was wearing a checked flannel shirt.

'It might be something worth considering,' muttered Uno. 'But it depends how much we're expected to contribute. Times are hard.'

Sebastian gave him a big smile. 'I'm sure we can reach an agreement. The main thing is that there's enough interest to move forward. I'm personally investing a large sum in the project.'

Right. But you're not about to tell them what your terms are, thought Josef. He clenched his jaw. All he could do was silently go along with whatever was offered and keep his eye on the goal. He leaned forward to shake hands with Erling. Now there was no turning back.

A small scar on her forehead, scars on her body and a slight limp were the only visible traces of the accident eighteen months ago. The accident when she lost the baby that she and Dan were expecting, and when she herself almost died.

Inside, it was a different matter. Anna was still feeling broken.

She hesitated a moment at the front door. Sometimes it was hard to be with Erica and see how everything had worked out for her. Her sister bore no scars from what had happened, and she had lost nothing. Yet it also did Anna good to see her. The wounds inside Anna twinged and ached, but the time she spent with Erica somehow helped them heal.

It was probably just as well that Anna hadn't realized how long the healing process would drag on. If she'd had any clue, she might never have emerged from the automatonlike state she'd landed in after her life shattered into a thousand pieces. Recently she'd joked to Erica that she was like one of the old vases she used to handle when she worked for an auction house. A vase that had fallen to the floor and broken, then been laboriously glued back together. From a distance it appeared whole, but as you got closer, the cracks became painfully obvious. But as Anna rang Erica's doorbell, she realized it wasn't really a joke. That was her situation now. She was a broken vase.

'Come in!' shouted Erica from somewhere inside the house.

Anna went in and kicked off her shoes.

'I'll be right there. I just have to change the twins' nappies.'

Anna went into the kitchen, which was so familiar to her. This house had belonged to their parents, and she knew every nook and cranny of it. Several years ago the house had prompted a quarrel between the two sisters that had almost destroyed their relationship, but that was in a different time, a different world. These days they could laugh about it and talk about 'LWL' and 'LAL' – 'Life With Lucas' and 'Life After Lucas'. Anna shuddered. She had vowed to think as little as possible about her ex-husband Lucas and what he'd done. He was gone now. All that remained were the only good things he'd ever given her: the children, Emma and Adrian.

'Want something to eat?' asked Erica as she entered the kitchen, carrying a twin on each hip. The boys' faces lit up when they saw their aunt. When Erica set them down on the floor, they ran towards Anna and tried to climb into her lap.

'Take it easy, there's plenty of room for both of you.' Anna lifted the boys up and then looked at Erica. 'That depends on what you've got.' She craned her neck to see what Erica had to offer.

'How about Grandma's rhubarb cake with marzipan?' Erica held out a cake covered with cling wrap.

'Are you kidding? Who could say no to that?'

Erica cut two big slices of cake and put them on a platter that she set on the table. Noel immediately launched himself towards the platter, but Anna managed to pull him back just in time. She broke off a little chunk of cake for each of the twins. Noel happily stuffed the whole piece in his mouth while Anton carefully nibbled at one corner as he gave her a big smile.

'They're so different,' said Anna, ruffling the hair of the two towheaded boys.

'You reckon?' said Erica sarcastically, shaking her head.

She poured the coffee and set Anna's cup down, making sure, as usual, that it was out of the twins' reach.

'Are you doing okay, or should I take one of them?'

she asked, noticing that Anna was trying to juggle the children, the coffee cup and the cake all at once.

'No, I'm fine. It's lovely to hold them close.' Anna nuzzled the top of Noel's head. 'So where's Maja?'

'She's glued to the TV. Her new great love in life is Mojje. At the moment she's watching "Mimmi and Mojje in the Caribbean". I think I'm going to puke if I have to listen to "On a Lovely Caribbean Beach" one more time.'

'Adrian is obsessed with Pokemon right now, and it's driving me crazy too.' Anna cautiously sipped her coffee, afraid of spilling it on the squirming eighteen-month-old toddlers sitting on her lap. 'What about Patrik?'

'He's at work. Suspected arson out on Valö.'

'Valö? Whose house?'

Erica hesitated before answering. 'The summer camp,' she said, unable to keep the excitement out of her voice.

'Oh, how awful. It always gives me the creeps when I think about that place and the way they disappeared into thin air.'

'I know. I've tried to do a little research about it, off and on. I thought I could turn the story into a book if I found out anything. But there's been nothing much to go on. Until now.'

'What do you mean?' Anna took a big bite of rhubarb cake. She'd also been given her grandmother's recipe, but she rarely baked. Practically never, in fact.

'She's back.'

'Who?'

'Ebba Elvander. Although her last name is Stark now.'

'You mean that little girl?' Anna stared at Erica.

'Exactly. She and her husband have moved to Valö, and apparently they've started renovating the place. And last night somebody tried to burn it down. That makes me wonder.' Erica had given up trying to hide her enthusiasm.

31

'Couldn't it be a coincidence?'

'Of course it could. But I still think it's odd. The fact that Ebba comes back and suddenly things start to happen.'

'Only *one* thing has happened,' Anna pointed out. She knew how quickly Erica's imagination could jump to conclusions. How her sister had ever managed to write a series of carefully researched and substantiated books seemed both a miracle and a mystery to Anna.

'Okay, okay. One thing,' said Erica, waving her hand dismissively. 'I can hardly wait until Patrik comes home. Actually, I wanted to go with him, but I didn't have anyone to take care of the children.'

'Don't you think it would have seemed a bit strange for you to show up with Patrik?'

By now Anton and Noel had grown tired of sitting on Anna's lap. They climbed down on to the floor and dashed off to the living room.

'Well, I was thinking of going out there to talk to Ebba one of these days,' said Erica, refilling their coffee cups.

'I can't help wondering what happened to that family,' said Anna pensively.

'Mammmmaaaaa! Get them out of here!' Maja cried shrilly from the living room. Erica got up with a sigh.

'I knew it was too good to be true. This is what happens all day long. Maja is forever getting cross with her brothers. You have no idea how many times I have to intervene each day.'

'Hmm . . .' said Anna, watching Erica as she hurried out of the room. She felt a pang in her heart. Personally she could have done with a little less peace and quiet.

Fjällbacka had never looked better. From the dock outside the boathouse where he sat with his wife and in-laws, John had a view of the entire harbour entrance. The glorious weather had enticed more sailing enthusiasts and tourists than usual, and scores of boats were moored close together along the pontoon dock. He could hear music and laughter coming from inside the vessels, and he was surveying the lively scene as he squinted into the sunlight.

'It's too bad that debate is at such a low level in Sweden today.' John raised his wine glass and took a sip of the nicely chilled rosé. 'People pay lip service to democracy and say that everyone has the right to be heard, but we're not allowed to express our views. It's as if we don't exist. What everybody forgets is that we were elected by the people. A sufficient number of Swedes showed that they harbour a deep mistrust of the way things are being handled. They want change, and we've promised them that change.'

He set his glass down and went back to peeling shrimp. A big plate of unpeeled shrimp was still awaiting his attention.

'I know. It's terrible,' said his father-in-law, reaching for the bowl of shrimp and grabbing a handful. 'If this is truly a democracy, we need to listen to the people.'

'And everybody knows that lots of immigrants come here purely to take advantage of the social benefits,' interjected his mother-in-law. 'It would be fine if all these foreigners were prepared to work and contribute to society. But I have no desire to see my tax money used to support those parasites.' She had already begun to slur her words.

John sighed. What idiots. They had no idea what they were talking about. It was the same with most voters: they were nothing but sheep, oversimplifying the problem, unable to see the big picture. His in-laws personified the ignorance that he loathed, and here he sat, stuck with them for a whole week.

Liv stroked his thigh in an attempt to calm him. She knew what he thought about them, and she mostly agreed.

But Barbro and Kent were still her parents, and there wasn't much she could do about that.

'The worst part is the way they're moving into all areas these days,' said Barbro. 'A family just moved into our neighbourhood, and the mother is Swedish, but the father is an Arab. I can't begin to imagine how awful it must be for that poor woman, the way Arabs treat their wives. And I'm sure the children will be bullied in school. Then they'll get in trouble with the police, and she'll end up regretting that she didn't marry a Swedish boy instead.'

'You can say that again,' said Kent, attempting to take a bite of a huge shrimp sandwich.

'Can't you let John have a rest from politics for a while?' said Liv, her tone mildly reproachful. 'He spends enough time discussing the immigrant issue in Stockholm, day in and day out. He deserves a break when he's over here.'

John gave her a grateful look as he paused to admire his wife. She was perfect. Silky blonde hair swept back from her face. Classic features and clear blue eyes.

'Sorry, sweetheart. We weren't thinking. We're just so proud of what John is doing, and the position that he has achieved. All right, let's talk about something else. How's it going with your little business, by the way?'

Liv eagerly began recounting all the difficulties she'd been having with the customs department, which seemed determined to complicate her business affairs. She was constantly dealing with setbacks to deliveries of the home furnishings that she imported from France and then sold through her online shop. But John knew that her interest in the shop had been dwindling. She was devoting more and more time to party politics. Everything else seemed unimportant in comparison.

The seagulls were hovering lower over the dock, and he stood up.

'I suggest we clear things away. Those birds are getting

34

a little too close for comfort.' He picked up his plate, walked out to the end of the dock, and tossed the shrimp peelings into the sea. The gulls swooped down to catch as many as possible. The crabs would take care of the rest.

He stood there for a moment and took a deep breath as he stared at the horizon. As usual, his gaze settled on Valö, and as usual the anger began smouldering inside him. Fortunately his thoughts were interrupted by a buzzing sound in his trouser pocket. He swiftly took out his mobile, casting a glance at the display before answering. The call was from the prime minister.

'Tell me, what do you think about those cards?' asked Patrik as he held the door open for Martin. It was so heavy that he had to give it a shove with his shoulder. Tanum police station was built in the 1960s, and the first time that Patrik set foot in the bunker-like building, he'd been overwhelmed by the dreary appearance. He'd since become so accustomed to the dirty yellow and beige of the furnishings that he'd ceased to notice the complete lack of comfort or appeal.

'It all sounds very odd. Who would go on sending anonymous birthday cards every year?'

'Not totally anonymous. They were signed "G".'

'Well, that makes it even more peculiar,' replied Martin, and Patrik laughed.

'What's so funny?' asked Annika, peering at them through the glass panes of the reception area.

'Nothing in particular,' said Martin.

Annika swivelled about in her desk chair and scooted over to the doorway of her small office. 'How'd it go out there?'

'We need to wait and see what Torbjörn can find out, but it does appear that someone was trying to burn down the house.'

'I'll make some coffee and we can talk.' Annika headed down the hall, shooing Patrik and Martin ahead of her.

'Have you told Mellberg?' Martin asked as they went into the kitchen.

'No, I didn't think it necessary to say anything to Bertil. He's got the weekend off, after all. No point bothering the boss yet awhile.'

'You have a point,' said Patrik, sitting down on a chair next to the window.

'So here you all are, having a nice chat over coffee, and you didn't think to invite me.' Gösta was standing in the doorway, looking sullen.

'You're here? But it's your day off. Why aren't you out on the golf course?' Patrik pulled out the chair next to him so Gösta could sit down.

'Too hot. Thought I might as well come in and write up a few reports, then I can spend a couple of hours out on the course another day when it's not so hot that you could fry an egg on the pavement. Where have you guys been? Annika mentioned something about arson.'

'That's right. It seems somebody poured petrol or some other accelerant under the front door and then ignited it.'

'Good Lord!' Gösta took a Ballerina biscuit and carefully separated the two halves. 'Where did this happen?'

'On Valö. The old summer camp,' said Martin.

Gösta gave a start. 'The summer camp?'

'Yes. It's a bit odd. I don't know whether you heard, but the youngest daughter – the one who was left behind when the whole family disappeared – has come back and taken over the place.'

'Right. There have been a lot of rumours about that,' said Gösta without lifting his gaze from the table.

Patrik gave him a puzzled look. 'You were here then, you must have worked on the case, right?'

'Yes, I did. That's how old I am,' Gösta told him. 'I wonder why she'd want to move back there.'

'She mentioned something about losing a son,' said Martin.

'Ebba lost a child? When? What happened?'

'They didn't say anything else about it.' Martin got up to fetch some milk from the refrigerator.

Patrik frowned; it wasn't like Gösta to show concern. But he'd seen this happen before. Every veteran police officer had an unsolved case that he couldn't get out of his mind. An old investigation that he kept brooding over, constantly mulling it over, trying to solve the mystery before it was too late.

'So that case stood out for you?'

'Too right. I'd give anything to know what happened on that night before Easter.'

'I'm sure you're not alone in that,' interjected Annika.

'And now Ebba is back.' Gösta rubbed his chin. 'And somebody tried to burn the place down.'

'Not just the house,' said Patrik. 'Whoever lit that fire must have known, maybe even counted on the fact, Ebba and her husband were asleep inside. It was sheer luck that Tobias woke up and was able to put out the fire.'

'A bizarre coincidence, no doubt about it,' said Martin.

He jumped when Gösta slammed his fist on the table.

'It's no coincidence!'

His colleagues stared at him in surprise, and a stunned silence descended over the kitchen.

'Maybe we ought to take a look at the old case,' Patrik said at last. 'Just to be sure.'

'I can show you what we have,' said Gösta. His gaunt, greyhound-like face had regained its eager expression. 'Every so often I take out the files and go through them again, so I can easily dig them out.'

'Okay, do that. Then we'll help you review the evidence.

Maybe we'll come up with something new if we approach the case with fresh eyes. Annika, could you get out everything you can find in the files about Ebba?'

'Leave it to me,' she said as she began clearing the table.

'We should probably also check out the finances of Mr and Mrs Stark. And see whether the house on Valö is insured,' said Martin, casting a cautious glance at Gösta.

'Are you saying they did it themselves? That's the stupidest thing I've ever heard. They were inside when the house started to burn, and it was Ebba's husband who put out the fire.'

'It's still worth investigating. Who knows, maybe he set the fire but then had regrets. I'll make a few enquiries.'

Gösta opened his mouth to say something but changed his mind and stomped out of the kitchen.

Patrik stood up. 'I think Erica has quite a bit of information too.'

'Erica? Why's that?' Martin stopped mid-stride.

'She's been interested in the case for a long time. It's a story that everybody in Fjällbacka knows, and considering what Erica writes about, it's understandable that she would take a keen interest.'

'So find out what she knows. The more information, the better.'

Patrik nodded, although he was feeling a bit hesitant. He knew what would happen if he allowed Erica to get involved in the investigation.

'Sure, I'll have a talk with her,' he said, hoping that this wouldn't be a decision he'd come to regret.

Percy's hand trembled slightly as he poured two glasses of his best cognac. He handed one of them to his wife.

'I simply don't understand what they're thinking.' Pyttan downed her drink in several swift gulps.

'Grandfather would be turning over in his grave if he knew about this.'

'You've got to solve this somehow, Percy.' She held out her glass, and he didn't hesitate to refill it. It was still only early afternoon, but somewhere in the world it was past five o'clock. And if ever there was a day that called for strong drinks, this was it.

'Me? What am I supposed to do?' His voice rose to a falsetto, and he was shaking so badly that half the cognac splashed over the rim of Pyttan's glass.

She pulled her hand away. 'Watch what you're doing, you idiot!'

'Sorry. I'm sorry.' Percy sank down on to one of the big, worn armchairs in the library. They heard a ripping sound, and he realized that the upholstery had split. 'Bloody hell!'

He jumped up and began kicking the chair in rage. All around him everything was falling apart. The whole manor was on the verge of collapse, his inheritance had been used up long ago, and now these revenue agency bastards were claiming he had to fork over a large sum of money that he didn't have.

'Calm down.' Pyttan wiped her hands on a napkin. 'There must be some way to work this out. But I don't understand how all the money can be gone.'

Percy turned to stare at her. He knew how frightening that thought was, but he felt nothing but scorn for her.

'*How all the money can be gone*?' he shouted. 'Do you have any idea how much you spend each month? Have you no clue how much everything costs? All the travelling, the dinners, the clothes, handbags, shoes, jewellery, and God knows what else you buy?'

It wasn't like Percy to shout in this way, and Pyttan shrank from him in alarm. Then she sat studying him for a while, and he knew her well enough to surmise that she was weighing her options: deciding whether to fight back or try to soothe him. When her expression abruptly softened, he knew that she'd decided on the latter.

'Darling, let's not start quarrelling about something as trivial as money.' She straightened his tie and then tucked in his shirt, which had been pulled up out of his trousers. 'All right. Now you look like my elegant lord of the manor again.'

She pressed close, and he felt himself starting to relent. She was wearing the Gucci dress today and, as usual, he was finding it hard to resist her.

'Here's what we're going to do. You phone the accountant and go through the books again. Things can't be that bad. I'm sure you'll find it reassuring to discuss the situation with him.'

'I need to talk to Sebastian,' murmured Percy.

'Sebastian?' said Pyttan, wincing as if she'd swallowed something foul. She glanced up at Percy. 'You know that I don't like you spending time with that man. Because then I have to entertain his insipid wife. Those two simply have no class. I don't care how much money he has, he's an utter boor. I've heard rumours that the fraud authorities have been keeping an eye on him for a while. They've yet to come up with any proof, but it's only a matter of time. We shouldn't have anything to do with him.'

'His money is as good as anyone else's,' said Percy.

He knew what the accountant was going to say. There was no money left. It was all gone, and in order to get himself out of this bind and to save Fygelsta, he needed capital. Sebastian was his only hope.

They had been taken to the hospital in Uddevalla, but everything seemed fine: there was no sign of residual smoke in their lungs. Now that the first shock had subsided, Ebba felt as though she'd awakened from a strange dream.

Finding herself squinting in the dim light as she sat at her desk, she turned on the lamp. Now that it was summer, dusk crept in slowly, and she invariably sat straining her eyes for a while before realizing that she needed more light.

The angel she was working on was proving intractable, and she struggled to attach the loop. Tobias couldn't understand why she made the jewellery by hand instead of having it manufactured in Thailand or China, especially now that a lot of orders were coming in via the web shop. But then the work wouldn't seem as meaningful to her. She wanted to make each piece of jewellery by hand, put an equal amount of love into every necklace that she sent off. Weave into the angels her own sorrow and her own memories. Besides, she found it soothing to do this sort of work in the evenings, after spending a whole day painting and hammering and sawing. When she got up in the morning, every muscle ached, but while she worked on her jewellery, her body would relax.

'I've locked up the house from top to bottom,' said Tobias.

Ebba gave a start. She hadn't heard him come in.

'Damn it,' she swore as the loop fell off, just as she had almost put it in place.

'Don't you think you should take a break from all that tonight?' said Tobias cautiously, coming to stand behind her.

She could feel him hesitating about whether to put his hands on her shoulders or not. In the past, before what happened to Vincent, he would often massage her back, and she had loved his firm yet gentle touch. Now she could hardly stand to have him touch her, and there was a risk that she would instinctively shake off his hands and hurt his feelings, and then the distance between them would grow even greater.

Ebba tried to fasten the loop again, and finally managed it.

'Does it really matter whether we lock up the house?' she said without turning around. 'Locked doors didn't seem to stop whoever it was trying to burn the place down last night.'

'What else can we do?' said Tobias. 'And you could at least look at me when we're talking. This is important. Somebody tried to burn the bloody house down, and we have no idea who it was or why. Doesn't that scare you?'

Slowly Ebba turned to face him.

'What should I be scared about? The worst has already happened. Locked or unlocked doors, it doesn't matter to me.'

'We can't go on like this.'

'Why not? I did what you wanted. I've moved back here, agreed to your grand plans to renovate this dilapidated old mansion and then live happily ever after in our island paradise while the guests come and go. I've agreed to everything. What more do you want?' She could hear how cold and unrelenting she sounded.

'Nothing, Ebba. There's nothing I want.' Tobias's voice was every bit as cold as hers. He turned on his heel and left the room.

FJÄLLBACKA 1915

Finally she was free. She'd found a situation as a maid on a farm in Hamburgsund, and now she'd be able to get away from her foster mother and those odious children of hers. Not to mention her foster father. His nightly visits had become more frequent the older she got and the more her body developed. After she had her first monthly period, she'd lived in constant terror that a baby would start to grow inside of her. A child was the last thing she wanted. She had no intention of being one of those frightened girls, their faces swollen from crying, who came and knocked on her mother's door, holding a screaming bundle in their arms. Even as a young girl she had despised them, their weakness and their air of resignation.

Dagmar packed up her few possessions. She had nothing left from the home of her real parents, and here she'd acquired nothing of any value to take with her. But she was not about to leave empty-handed. She slipped into her foster parents' bedroom. In a box under the bed, way back against the wall, was the jewellery that her foster mother had inherited. Dagmar lay down on the floor and pulled out the box. Her foster mother was in Fjällbacka, and the children were playing in the yard, so no one was around to disturb her.

She opened the lid and smiled with satisfaction. There were enough valuables here to give her some semblance of security for a while, and she was glad that it would pain the witch to lose these inherited jewels.

'What are you doing?' demanded her foster father from the doorway, making her flinch.

Dagmar had thought he was out in the barn. Her heart pounded wildly for a moment, but then she felt a great calm come over her. Nothing was going to ruin her plans.

'What does it look like I'm doing?' she said, taking all of the jewellery out of the box and stuffing the pieces in her skirt pocket.

'Are you out of your mind, girl? Are you stealing the jewellery?' He came a step closer, but she held up her hand.

'That's right. And I'd advise you not to try and stop me. Because if you do, I'll go straight to the county sheriff and tell him what you've been doing to me.'

'You wouldn't dare!' He clenched his fists, but then the frown on his face relaxed. 'Besides, who would ever believe the Angelmaker's daughter?'

'I can be very convincing. And rumours will start to spread faster than you can imagine.'

His face clouded over again, and he seemed to hesitate, but she decided to help him out.

'I have a suggestion. When my dear foster mother discovers that her jewellery is missing, you'll do everything you can to calm her down and convince her to forget all about it. If you promise to do that, then I'll give you a little extra reward before I leave here.'

Dagmar went over to her foster father. Slowly she raised her hand, placed it on his genitals, and began rubbing. The farmer's eyes soon took on a glazed look, and she knew that she had him in her power.

'Do we have a deal?' she said, slowly unbuttoning his trousers.

'We have a deal,' he replied, placing his hand on top of her head and pressing it down.

The diving tower at Badholmen loomed as majestically against the sky as it always had. Erica cast aside the image of a man gently swaying from a rope attached to the tower; the last thing she wanted was to be reminded of that awful event. As if trying its best to distract her from such dark thoughts, the small islet of Badholmen was sparkling like a jewel in the water off Fjällbacka. The youth hostel out there was very popular and often fully booked during the summer, and Erica could understand why. The location and the old-fashioned charm of the building made an irresistible combination. but today she wasn't really able to enjoy the view.

'Is everybody here?' Feeling her stress levels mounting, she looked around her, counting the children.

Three rambunctious figures wearing bright orange life-jackets were capering about on the dock.

'Patrik! Maybe you could help out a little here,' she said, catching hold of the big collar on Maja's life-jacket as her daughter dashed past, running dangerously close to the edge of the pier.

'Then who did you think is going to start up the motor?' Patrik threw out his hands, his face flushed.

'If you get the kids into the boat first, before they fall into the water, then you can start the motor.'

Maja was squirming like a worm to get loose, but Erica had a good grip on the loop of her collar and held on tight. With her free hand she grabbed Noel, who was chasing after Anton on his chubby little legs. Now at least there was only one child running wild.

'Here, come and get them.' She hauled the boisterous children towards the wooden *snipa* boat tied up at the dock. Clearly annoyed, Patrik climbed up on to the deck to grab Maja and Noel. Then Erica spun around and hurried after Anton, who had taken off in the direction of the little stone bridge between Badholmen and the mainland.

'Anton! Stop!' she shouted, but he carried on regardless. Despite his best efforts though, Erica caught up with him in the end. Shrieking hysterically, he struggled to break free as she carried him back to the boat.

'My God, why on earth did I think this would be a good idea?' she said as she handed the sobbing Anton to Patrik. Perspiration running down her face, she untied the mooring line and jumped into the boat.

'It'll be better when we get out on open water.' Patrik turned the ignition, and for once the motor started up on the first try. He leaned over to untie the aft mooring line as he used his other hand to keep the boat a safe distance from the next vessel at the dock. It was no easy task to make their way out into the harbour. The boats were crowded together, and if they hadn't had rubber fenders, neither their own boat nor their neighbours' would have been able to avoid damage.

'I'm sorry about snapping at you,' said Erica as she sat down after getting the children to settle on the floor of the boat.

'I've already forgotten all about it,' Patrik shouted, slowly shoving the tiller away from him, which made the boat swing around with the aft towards the harbour and the bow facing Fjällbacka.

It was a radiantly beautiful Sunday morning, with a clear blue sky and mirror-smooth water. Shrieking gulls circled overhead, and when Erica looked around, she noticed that people were eating breakfast on several of the boats in the harbour. No doubt plenty of people were also still in bed, sleeping off the booze they'd consumed the night before. Saturday nights involved a good deal of drinking for the visiting youths. I'm glad those days are past, she thought and then glanced with much greater tenderness at the children who were now sitting quietly in the boat.

She went over to stand beside Patrik, leaning her head on his shoulder. He put his arm around her and kissed her cheek.

'By the way,' he said suddenly. 'When we get there, remind me to ask you some questions about Valö and the summer camp.'

'What do you want to know?' asked Erica with interest.

'I'll tell you later, when we have a bit of peace and quiet,' he said, giving her another kiss.

She knew he was doing this to tease her. She was itching to know more, but she controlled herself. Silently she raised her hand to shade her eyes as she gazed at Valö. As they slowly chugged past, she caught a glimpse of the big white house. Would they ever find out what happened out there so many years ago? She hated books and movies that failed to answer all the questions in the end, and she could hardly bear to read about unsolved murders in the newspapers. When she'd started digging into the Valö case, she'd found out nothing new, despite searching long and hard for an explanation. The truth was as hidden as the house, which was now out of sight behind the trees.

*   *   *

Martin paused for a moment with his hand in the air before pressing the doorbell. He soon heard someone approaching inside, and he had to fight back an impulse to turn around and leave. The door opened, and Annika stared at him in surprise.

'Martin? What are you doing here? Has something happened?'

He forced a smile. But Annika was the wrong person to try to fool, and that was essentially why he'd come to her house. Ever since he'd started at the station, she'd been like a substitute mother to him, and right now she was the one he wanted to talk to.

'Well, you see, I . . .' That was all he could manage.

'Come in,' said Annika. 'We'll go in the kitchen and have a cup of coffee. Then you can tell me what's on your mind.'

Martin stepped inside, took off his shoes, and followed her.

'Sit down,' she said, and with a practised hand she began putting scoops of coffee grounds in the filter. 'Where are Pia and Tuva?'

'They're at home. I said I was going for a walk, so I have to get back soon. We're thinking of heading out to the beach.'

'Ah. Sounds nice. Leia loves to swim too. We were out at the bathing beach earlier today, and we could hardly get her out of the water when it was time to come home. She loves the water, that girl. Lennart just went off with her so I could catch up on some cleaning.'

Annika's face lit up when she talked about her daughter. It was almost a year now since she and her husband Lennart, after many years of sorrow and grief, had been able to bring home their adopted daughter from China. These days everything in their lives revolved around Leia.

Martin couldn't imagine a better mother than Annika. She had such an air of warmth and concern, and she always made him feel secure. Right now he would have liked nothing more than to lean against her shoulder and let loose the tears that were threatening, but he restrained himself. If he started crying, he might never stop.

'I think I'll get out a few buns.' She took a bag from the freezer and put two buns in the microwave. 'I baked yesterday, and was planning to take some over to the station.'

'I hope you realize that it's not part of your job description to keep us supplied with treats,' said Martin.

'I don't think Mellberg would agree with you about that. If I were to study my employment contract more carefully, I'm sure the small print would read: Supply the Tanum police station with homemade baked goods.'

'My God, without you and the bakery, Bertil wouldn't last a day.'

'I know. Especially since Rita put him on a diet. According to Paula, they're eating nothing but whole-wheat bread and vegetables at Bertil and Rita's flat lately.'

'I'd like to see that.' Martin burst out laughing. It was nice to laugh, and some of the tension he was feeling started to ease.

The microwave dinged, and Annika put the warm buns on a plate and then set two cups of coffee on the table as well.

'All right now. Help yourself and then tell me what's bothering you. I could see something was wrong earlier today, but I thought I'd let you talk about it in your own good time.'

'It might not be anything, and I don't want to bother you with my problems, but . . .' Martin noticed with frustration that sobs were already rising in his throat.

'Don't be silly. That's why I'm sitting here. Now tell me.'

Martin took a deep breath. 'Pia is sick,' he said at last, hearing how the words echoed off the walls in the kitchen.

He saw Annika's face turn pale. This was probably not what she was expecting. He rotated the coffee cup between his hands and started over. Suddenly the words came pouring out.

'She's been feeling tired for a long time. Actually, ever since Tuva was born, but we thought nothing of it. It just seemed a normal response after having a baby. But Tuva is almost two now, and Pia hasn't been feeling any better. In fact, it's getting worse and worse. Then Pia noticed several lumps in her neck . . .'

Annika's hand flew to her mouth, as if she understood where this conversation was going.

'And a few weeks ago I went with her to see a doctor, and I could tell at once what he suspected. She got an immediate referral to see a specialist in Uddevalla, and we went there so she could have some tests. And now she has an appointment with an oncologist tomorrow afternoon to hear the results, but we already know what they're going to say.' Tears began rolling down his face, and he angrily wiped them away.

Annika handed him a paper napkin. 'Go ahead and cry. It usually helps.'

'It's so unfair. Pia is only thirty-three, and Tuva is still a baby, and I've Googled the statistics, and if it's what we think, the odds aren't very good. Pia is being incredibly brave, but I'm such a bloody coward, and I can't bear to talk to her about all this. I can hardly stand to see her with Tuva or even look her in the eye. I feel so damned useless!' He could no longer hold back the tears. He leaned over the table, burying his head in his arms and sobbing so hard that his whole body shook.

Annika put her arm around his shoulders and pressed her cheek against his. She didn't say a word, just kept stroking his back. After a while, he sat up, turned towards her, and crept into her arms. Annika gently rocked him, the way she would have rocked Leia if she'd hurt herself.

They had been lucky to find a table at the Café Bryggan. All of the outdoor seating was taken, and Leon watched as one shrimp sandwich after another was served. The location near Ingrid Bergman Square was perfect, with tables along the entire wharf, all the way out to the water.

'I think we should buy the house,' said Ia.

He turned to gape at his wife. 'Ten million kronor isn't exactly small change.'

'Did I say it was?' She leaned forward to straighten the blanket on his lap.

'Leave the damn blanket alone. I'm sweating to death.'

'You're not supposed to catch cold. You know that.'

A waitress came over to their table, and Ia ordered a glass of wine for herself and mineral water for Leon. He glanced up at the young girl.

'I'll have a large beer,' he said.

Ia gave him a reproachful look, but he merely nodded at the waitress. She reacted in the same way that everyone he met always did, making an exaggerated effort not to stare at the scars from the burns. When she left, he gazed out at the water.

'It smells just the way I remember,' said Leon. His hands, covered with thick scar tissue, rested in his lap.

'I still don't care for this place. But I'll learn to like it if we buy the house,' Ia said. 'I have no intention of living in some hovel, and I don't plan to be here all summer. A couple of weeks a year should be sufficient.'

'Don't you think it's unreasonable to buy a house for ten million if we're only planning to use it a couple of weeks a year?'

'Those are my conditions,' she said. 'Otherwise you can stay here alone. And that won't work, will it?'

'No. I realize that I can't manage on my own. And on the rare occasions I forget, I can always count on you to remind me.'

'Do you ever think about all the sacrifices I've made for your sake? I have to put up with your crazy whims, and you never consider how I feel. And now you want to come here. Aren't you a little too burnt to be playing with fire?'

The waitress brought the wine and the beer, setting the glasses on the blue-and-white checked cloth. Leon took several swigs and then ran his thumb over the cold glass.

'Okay, do whatever you want. Call that estate agent and say that we're going to buy the house. But I want to move in as soon as possible. I hate staying in a hotel.'

'Great,' said Ia without enthusiasm. 'If we have that house, I'm sure I can stand being here a couple of weeks a year.'

'You're so brave, darling.'

She gave him a dark look. 'Let's just hope that you don't regret this decision.'

'A lot of water has gone under the bridge,' he said calmly.

At that moment he heard someone behind him gasp with surprise.

'Leon?'

He flinched. He didn't have to turn his head to recognize that voice. Josef. After all these years, there stood Josef.

Paula gazed out across the glittering fjord, enjoying the heat. She put a hand on her stomach and smiled when she felt the kicking.

'Okay, I think it's about time for some ice cream,' said Mellberg, getting to his feet. He cast a glance at Paula and wagged his finger at her. 'Don't you know that it's not a good idea to expose your stomach to sunlight?'

She stared at him in astonishment as he headed for the kiosk.

'Is he pulling my leg?' said Paula, turning to her mother.

Rita laughed. 'Bertil means well.'

Paula muttered to herself but got out a shawl to cover her stomach. Leo dashed past, totally naked. Johanna quickly caught up with him.

'Bertil's right,' she said. 'The UV rays can cause pigment changes, so you should also slather your face with sunblock.'

'Pigment changes?' said Paula. 'But my skin is already brown.'

Rita handed her a bottle of factor 30 sunblock. 'I got lots of brown spots on my face when I was pregnant with you, so don't argue.'

Paula obeyed, and Johanna rubbed some on her own fair skin.

'Well, you're lucky,' she said. 'At least you don't get sunburnt.'

'I just wish Bertil would take things a little easier,' said Paula, squeezing a big blob of sunblock into the palm of her hand. 'This morning I caught him reading my pregnancy magazines. And the day before yesterday he brought home a bottle of Omega-3 oil for me from the health food store. He read in some magazine that it was good for the development of the baby's brain.'

'He's so happy about the whole thing. Leave him be,' said Rita. For the second time she began smearing sunblock on Leo from head to toe. He had inherited Johanna's ruddy, freckled skin, and he burned easily in the sun. Paula wondered absentmindedly whether the

53

baby would have her colouring or that of the unknown donor. It didn't matter to her. Leo was their son – Johanna's and hers – and she hardly ever thought about the fact that anyone else had been involved. The same would be true of this baby.

Her thoughts were interrupted by Mellberg's happy shout. 'Ice-cream time!'

Rita fixed him with a stern glare. 'I hope you didn't buy any for yourself.'

'Only a tiny Magnum. I've been so good all week.' He smiled and gave Rita a wink, in an attempt to get her to relent.

'Nothing doing,' she said calmly, taking the ice cream away from him and tossing it into the rubbish bin.

Mellberg muttered something.

'What did you say?'

He swallowed. 'Nothing. Not a word.'

'You know what the doctor said. You're in the risk group for heart attacks and diabetes.'

'One Magnum isn't going to do me any harm. A man's got to live a little once in a while,' he said, handing out the other ice cream bars that he'd bought.

'Another week of holiday left,' said Paula, closing her eyes to the sun as she ate her Cornetto.

'I really don't think you should go back to work,' said Johanna. 'The baby's due soon. I'm sure you could take sick leave if you talked to the midwife. You need to rest.'

'Stop right there,' said Mellberg. 'I heard what you said. Don't forget that I'm Paula's boss.' He pensively scratched his thinning grey hair. 'But I agree. I don't think you should be working either.'

'We've already discussed this. I'll go crazy if I just sit around at home, waiting. Besides, things are pretty quiet at the moment.'

'What do you mean by quiet?' Johanna stared at her.

'This is the most hectic time of the whole year, with drunks and everything else.'

'I mean that we don't have any big investigation in progress. The usual summer break-ins, et cetera – I can handle those in my sleep. And I don't need to go driving around. I can stay at the station and take care of the paperwork. So quit fussing. I'm pregnant, not sick.'

'We'll see how things go,' said Mellberg. 'But you're right about one thing. It's actually nice and quiet at the moment.'

It was their wedding anniversary, and Gösta had brought fresh flowers to put on Maj-Britt's grave, just as he did every year. Otherwise he wasn't very good about tending to the grave, but that had nothing to do with his feelings for Maj-Britt. They'd had many happy years together, and not a day went by that he didn't miss her. Of course he had grown used to his life as a widower, and his days were so regimented that sometimes it felt like a distant dream when he thought about how he'd once shared the small house with someone else. But the fact that he'd got used to life alone didn't mean that he liked it.

He squatted down and touched the letters etched into the headstone, spelling out the name of their little boy. There were no photos of him. They'd thought that they had all the time in the world to take pictures of him, and it hadn't occurred to them to take any photos right after the birth. And when he died, no pictures were taken. That just wasn't done. He understood that they handled things differently these days, but back then a person was supposed to forget and move on.

Have another child as soon as you can. That was the advice they were given as they left the hospital in shock. But that was not to be. The only child they'd ever had was the girl. The lass, as they called her. Maybe they ought to have done more to keep her, but their grief was still too great, and they didn't think they'd be able to give her what she needed, except for a brief time.

It was Maj-Britt who had finally made the decision. He had tentatively suggested that they should take care of the girl, that she should be allowed to stay. Maj-Britt had replied: 'She needs siblings.' And so the little girl had disappeared. They never spoke of her afterwards, but Gösta hadn't been able to forget her. If he had a one-krona coin for every time he'd thought about her since then, he'd be a wealthy man today.

Gösta got up. He'd pulled out a few weeds that had sprouted up, and the bouquet of flowers looked lovely in the vase. He could hear Maj-Britt's voice so clearly in his mind: 'Oh, Gösta, what nonsense. Wasting such gorgeous flowers on me.' She had never believed that she deserved anything out of the ordinary, and he wished that he had thrown caution to the wind and spoiled her more often. Given her flowers when she could actually enjoy them. Now he could only hope that she was up there some-where, looking down, and that the beautiful flowers made her happy.

FJÄLLBACKA 1919

The Sjölins were having another party. Dagmar was grateful for every occasion that they celebrated with a party. She needed the extra income, and it was marvellous to have the chance to see up close all those rich and beautiful people. They lived such wonderful and carefree lives. They ate good food and drank copiously, they danced, sang, and laughed until dawn. She wished that her own life was like that, but so far she would have to settle for waiting on those more fortunate, basking in their presence for a short while.

This party seemed to be something special. Early in the morning she and the other staff had been taken over to an island off Fjällbacka, and all day long boats had shuttled back and forth, bringing food, wine, and guests.

'Dagmar! You need to fetch more wine from the root cellar!' shouted Mrs Sjölin, the doctor's wife. Dagmar hurried off.

She was anxious to stay on good terms with Mrs Sjölin. The last thing she wanted was for the woman to start keeping an eye on her. If that happened, Mrs Sjölin would soon notice the glances and affectionate pinches her husband kept giving Dagmar during their parties. Sometimes he went even further, if his wife excused herself and retired to her room. By then the rest of the revellers would be too drunk or preoccupied with their own merriment to care about anything else going on around them.

After those occasions, the doctor would slip Dagmar a little extra when the wages were handed out.

Quickly she plucked up four bottles of wine and dashed back up the steps with them. She was hugging them close to her chest when she ran right into somebody, and the bottles fell to the ground. Two of them broke, and Dagmar realized with anguish that the cost would most likely be deducted from her wages. Tears began rolling down her cheeks as she stared at the man in front of her.

'Forgive me!' he said, but the Danish words he spoke sounded strange.

Her distress swiftly turned to anger.

'What do you think you're doing? Don't you know you can't stand in front of a door like that?'

'Forgive me,' he repeated. 'Ich verstehe nicht,' he said in German.

Suddenly Dagmar knew who he was. She had collided with the evening's guest of honour, the German hero, the pilot who had fought bravely during the war. But after Germany's stinging defeat, he had been making his living by flying in air shows. Everyone had been whispering about him all day. He'd apparently made a home for himself in Copenhagen, but it was rumoured that some scandal had now forced him to come to Sweden.

Dagmar stared at him. He was the most handsome man she'd ever seen. He didn't seem to be as drunk as many of the other guests, and his gaze was unwavering as he looked into her eyes. For a long moment they stood there, staring at each other. Dagmar lifted her chin. She knew she was beautiful. She'd had this confirmed so many times by men who ran their hands over her body and panted words in her ear. But never before had she been so pleased with her own beauty.

Without taking his eyes off her, the pilot bent down and began picking up shards of glass from the broken bottles. Carefully he carried them over to a little grove of trees and tossed them to the

58

ground. Then he set his finger to his lips, stepped into the root cellar and brought out two more bottles. Dagmar smiled gratefully as she went over to take the bottles from him. She happened to glance down at his hands and discovered that he was bleeding from a cut on his left index finger.

She gestured to show that she wanted to have a look at his hand, so he set the bottles on the ground. It was not a deep cut, but it was bleeding heavily. With her eyes fixed on his, she put his finger in her mouth and gently sucked away the blood. His eyes widened, and she saw the familiar look as they glazed over. She moved away and picked up the bottles. As she turned and walked back to the guests, she could feel his eyes following her.

Patrik had gathered his colleagues to discuss the case. It was important that Mellberg be brought up to date. He cleared his throat. 'You weren't here over the weekend, Bertil, so I'm wondering whether you heard about what happened.'

'No, tell me,' demanded Mellberg, looking at Patrik.

'On Saturday there was a fire out at the summer camp on Valö. There are indications that it was started deliberately.'

'Arson?'

'We haven't had it confirmed yet. We're waiting for the report from Torbjörn,' said Patrik. He hesitated for a moment before going on. 'But there's enough evidence to indicate that we should keep working on the case.'

Patrik pointed to Gösta, who was standing at the white-board, holding a marker in his hand.

'Gösta has taken out the files on the family that disappeared on Valö. He—' Patrik began before being interrupted.

'I know the case you're talking about. Everybody knows that old story. But what does it have to do with this?' said Mellberg. He leaned down to pet his dog Ernst, who was lying under his chair.

'We're not sure.' Patrik was already feeling tired. He always had to run things past Mellberg, who was officially in charge of the station, although in practice he was more than willing to let Patrik assume full responsibility. So long as he could take full credit when the case was solved. 'We're going into the investigation without any preconceived notions. But it does seem very strange that this should happen just as the sole surviving member of the family, the daughter, returns to the island for the first time in thirty-five years.'

'They probably set the house on fire themselves. To get the insurance money,' said Mellberg.

'I'm looking into their finances,' said Martin, who was sitting next to Annika. He seemed unusually subdued. 'I should have something to report by tomorrow morning.'

'Good. I'm sure that will solve the mystery. Most likely they found out it was going to cost too much to renovate that old eyesore, so they decided it would make more sense to burn it down. I saw a lot of that during my days in Göteborg.'

'As I said, we're not going to lock ourselves into any specific theory at the moment,' said Patrik. 'Now I think we should let Gösta tell us what he remembers.'

He sat down and nodded for Gösta to begin. What Erica had told him during their boat trip through the archipelago was fascinating. Now he wanted to hear what Gösta could tell them about the old investigation.

'I'm sure that all of you are familiar with the case, but if you don't mind I'll start from the beginning.' Gösta looked around, and everybody seated at the table nodded their agreement.

'On 13 April 1974, the night before Easter Sunday, somebody rang the police in Tanum and told them to come out to the boarding school on Valö. The caller hung up before explaining what had happened. The old police

61

chief took the call, and according to him, it was impossible to tell whether the informant was male or female.' Gösta paused for a moment as in his mind he was carried back to that time in the past. 'My colleague Henry Ljung and I were told to head out there and find out what was going on. Half an hour later we arrived on the scene and found something strange. The table in the dining room was set for Easter lunch and the food had been partially eaten, but there was no trace of the family that lived there. The only person present was a one-year-old girl, Ebba, who was toddling around all alone. It was as if the rest of the family had gone up in smoke. As if they'd stood up in the middle of the meal and vanished.'

'Poof!' said Mellberg. Gösta gave him a withering glare.

'Where were all the pupils?' asked Martin.

'Since it was the Easter holiday, most of them had gone home to their families. Only a few were still on Valö, and they were nowhere in sight when we arrived, but after a while five boys turned up on a boat. They said they'd been out fishing for a couple of hours. During the following weeks, we questioned them intensely, but they didn't know anything about what happened to the family. I talked to them myself, and they all said the same thing: they hadn't been invited to the family's Easter lunch, so they'd gone out fishing instead. When they left, everything was perfectly normal.'

'Was the family's boat still tied to the dock?' asked Patrik.

'Yes. And we went over the island with a fine-tooth comb, but there was no trace of them.' Gösta shook his head.

'How many people are we talking about?' Against his will, Mellberg's curiosity had been aroused, and he was leaning forward to listen.

'There were two adults and four children in the family.

One of the children was little Ebba, of course. So the adults and three children disappeared.' Gösta turned to write on the whiteboard. 'The father, Rune Elvander, was the headmaster of the school. He was a former military man, and it was his idea to establish a school for boys whose parents set high standards for education, combined with strict discipline. First-class teaching, character-building rules, and invigorating outdoor activities for well-to-do boys. That was how the school was described in the brochure, if I remember correctly.'

'Jesus, that sounds like something out of the 1920s,' said Mellberg.

'There have always been parents who long for the good old days, and that was exactly what Rune Elvander offered,' said Gösta, and then resumed his report. 'Ebba's mother was named Inez. She was twenty-three years old at the time of her disappearance, significantly younger than Rune, who was in his fifties. Rune also had three children from a previous marriage: Claes, who was nineteen; Annelie, who was sixteen; and Johan, who was nine. Their mother, Carla, died a year before Rune remarried. According to the five pupils, there seemed to be a number of problems in the family, but that was all we managed to get out of them.'

'How many pupils were attending the boarding school when they weren't away on holiday?' asked Martin.

'It varied a bit, but about twenty. In addition to Rune, there were two other teachers, but they'd gone home for Easter.'

'And I assume they had alibis for the time the family disappeared, right?' Patrik said, looking at Gösta.

'Yes, they did. One of them was visiting relatives in Stockholm to celebrate Easter. At first we were a little suspicious of the other teacher, because he kept making excuses and didn't want to tell us where he'd been. But it turned out that he'd gone off with a boyfriend to some sunny holiday destination, and that was the reason for all the secrecy. He didn't want anyone to find out that he was gay. He'd been so careful to hide the fact at school.'

'What about the students who'd gone home for the holidays? Did you check up on all of them?' asked Patrik.

'Every single one of them. And their families confirmed that the boys had spent Easter at home and hadn't been anywhere near the island. And by the way, all of the parents seemed pleased with the effect that the school was having on their children. They were extremely upset that they wouldn't be able to send them back to the boarding school. I had the impression that many of the parents considered it bothersome having the boys at home even for the holiday.'

'Okay. And you didn't find any physical evidence to indicate what might have happened to the family?'

Gösta shook his head. 'Of course, we didn't have the equipment and the expertise that's available today, so that factored into the technical investigation. But everybody did the best they could, and there was nothing. Or rather: we found nothing. But I've always had a feeling that we missed something, though I could never put my finger on what that might be.'

'What happened to the little girl?' asked Annika, whose heart went out to any child in trouble.

'There were no living relatives, so Ebba was placed with a foster family in Göteborg. As far as I know, they later adopted her.' Gösta paused for a moment, looking down at his hands. 'I have to say that we did a good job. We investigated every possible lead and tried to form some idea of a motive. We poked around in Rune's past but found no skeletons in the closet. We knocked on doors all over Fjällbacka, to find out if anyone had seen anything out of the ordinary. We tackled the case from every imaginable angle, but never made any headway. Without proof, it was impossible to work out whether they'd been murdered or kidnapped or had simply left voluntarily.'

'Fascinating,' said Mellberg, clearing his throat. 'But I still don't understand why we need to revive this old case. There's no reason to complicate matters unnecessarily. Either this Ebba and her husband set the fire themselves, or some kids decided to get up to mischief.'

'Don't you think it seems to involve more sophisticated planning than the sort of thing a bunch of bored teenagers would do?' said Patrik. 'If they wanted to burn down a building, it would be a lot simpler to start a fire in town than to go out to Valö in a boat. And as we mentioned, Martin is looking into whether this might have involved insurance fraud. But the more I hear about the old case, the stronger my gut feeling is that the fire is connected to what happened when that family disappeared.'

'You and your gut feelings,' said Mellberg. 'There's nothing concrete that points to a connection. I know that you've been right a few times in the past, but in this instance, I reckon you're way off the mark.' Mellberg got up, clearly pleased at delivering what he considered the truth of the day.

Patrik shrugged, letting his boss's remarks roll right off him. He'd long since stopped taking Mellberg's opinion into consideration. In fact, he'd never really bothered with Mellberg's view. So he assigned the various tasks to his colleagues and ended the meeting.

On his way out of the room, Martin pulled Patrik aside.

'Could I have the afternoon off? I know it's short notice, but . . .'

'Sure, of course you can if it's important. What's it about?'

Martin hesitated. 'It's a personal matter. I'd rather not talk about it just now. Is that okay?'

There was something in his tone of voice that stopped Patrik from asking any more questions, but he was hurt that Martin didn't want to confide in him. He thought they had formed such a close relationship during the years they'd worked together that Martin should feel comfortable telling him if anything was wrong.

'I can't talk about it,' said Martin, as if he guessed what Patrik was thinking. 'So is it okay if I leave after lunch?'

'Of course. No problem.'

Martin gave him a faint smile and turned to go.

'But I'm here if you want to talk,' said Patrik.

'I know that.' Martin hesitated, but then headed off down the hall.

As she made her way down the stairs, Anna already knew what she'd see in the kitchen. Dan would be sitting at the table, wearing an old bathrobe and deeply engrossed in the morning newspaper, holding a cup of coffee in his hand.

When he saw her come into the room, his face lit up.

'Good morning, sweetheart.' He reached out for a kiss.

'Good morning.' Anna turned her head away. 'I have such bad morning breath,' she said apologetically, but the damage was done. Dan got up without a word and went over to the dishwasher to put his cup inside.

Why did it have to be so damned hard? She was always saying and doing the wrong thing. She wanted things to be good again, back to the way they used to be. She wanted to re-establish the natural relationship that they'd had before the accident.

Dan busied himself washing up the breakfast dishes, and she went over to put her arms around him, leaning her cheek against his back. But the only thing she felt in his tense body was frustration. It spread to her, making her desire for closeness disappear, at least for now. It was impossible to say whether the occasion would present itself again.

With a sigh she let go of Dan and sat down at the kitchen table.

'I need to get back to work,' she said, picking up a slice of bread and reaching for the butter knife.

Dan turned and leaned against the counter with his arms folded.

'What kind of work?'

Anna hesitated before saying, 'I'd like to run my own business.'

'That's a great idea! What sort of business? A shop? I could check around to see what's available.'

Dan gave her a big smile, but somehow his eager response dampened her own enthusiasm. This was her idea, and she didn't want to share it. She couldn't explain why.

'I want to do this myself,' she said, noticing the sharp tone of her voice.

The joy instantly vanished from Dan's face.

'Sure, go ahead,' he said, going back to clattering the dishes.

Shit, shit, shit. Anna silently cursed herself, clenching her hands into fists.

'I've been thinking about opening a shop. But I'll need to do all the furnishing myself, go sourcing antiques, and things like that.' The words spilled out as she tried to recapture Dan's attention. But he was making a lot of noise, washing the glasses and plates, and he didn't respond. His back seemed rigid and unforgiving.

Anna set the slice of bread down on her plate. She'd lost her appetite.

'I'm going out for a while,' she said, getting to her feet and heading out of the kitchen to go upstairs and get dressed. Dan still didn't say a word.

*   *   *

'How nice that you could join us for a spot of lunch,' said Pyttan.

'A pleasure to come over here and see how the other half lives.' Sebastian laughed and gave Percy such a hard slap on the back that he coughed.

'Well, you're not exactly living in poverty.'

Percy smiled to himself. Pyttan had never made it a secret what she thought of Sebastian's ostentatious mansion with the two pools and tennis court. The house may have been smaller in size than Fygelsta manor, but it was much more lavish. 'Money can't buy taste,' Pyttan used to say after they'd visited, turning up her nose at the gleaming gilded frames and the enormous crystal chandeliers. Percy was inclined to agree.

'Come and sit down,' he said, ushering Sebastian to the table that had been set for lunch out on the terrace. At this time of year Fygelsta was unbeatable. The beautiful park stretched as far as the eye could see. For generations it had been meticulously tended, but it wouldn't be long before it would fall into neglect, just as the manor had done. Until he had worked out their finances, they would have to make do without gardeners.

Sebastian sat down and leaned back in his chair, his sunglasses pushed up on his forehead.

'Some wine?' Pyttan held out a bottle of first-class Chardonnay. Much as she disliked the thought of asking Sebastian for help, Percy knew that his wife would do her utmost to support him now that the decision had been made. It wasn't as if they had any other option.

She filled Sebastian's glass. Oblivious to the fact that it was her prerogative, as the hostess, to welcome her guest before he started eating, Sebastian immediately launched himself at the appetizer. He shovelled in a big forkful of shrimp salad with dill and began chewing with his mouth open. Percy saw Pyttan turn away in disgust.

'So you're having a little problem with your taxes, is that right?'

'Yes, it's a mess. I don't know what to say.' Percy shook his head. 'Nothing seems sacred any more.'

'How true. It doesn't pay to work in this country,' said Sebastian.

'No, things were different in Pappa's day.' Percy began eating his food, after first giving Pyttan an enquiring glance. 'You'd think people would appreciate the fact that we've put so much work into taking care of this cultural monument. It's a piece of Swedish history, and our family has borne the brunt of preserving it, and we've done it with honour.'

'True. But times have changed,' said Sebastian, waving his fork. 'The winds of social democracy have been blowing for a long time now, and it doesn't seem to help that we've got a conservative government. Nobody's allowed to have more than his neighbour. If you do, those bastards will take away everything you own. I've been through it all myself. Had to pay a lot in back taxes this year, but luckily only on what I have here in Sweden. You've got to be smart and put your assets abroad, where the tax authorities can't get their hands on everything you've worked so hard to acquire.'

Percy nodded. 'Indeed. Naturally. But so much of my capital has always been invested in the manor.'

He wasn't stupid. He knew full well that Sebastian had exploited him over the years. He'd often allowed Sebastian to borrow the manor for meetings with his customers for hunting parties, or for entertaining his countless mistresses. He wondered whether Sebastian's wife suspected anything, but that was none of his business. Pyttan kept him on a tight rein, and personally he would never dare try something like that. But he wasn't about to criticize how other married people behaved.

'Still, you must have got a sizeable inheritance from your old man?' said Sebastian as he held up his empty wine glass towards Pyttan. Without revealing so much as a hint of what she was thinking, she picked up the bottle and filled his glass to the brim.

'Yes, but you know . . .' Percy shifted uncomfortably on his chair. He had a deep aversion to discussing money. 'It costs a fortune to keep the place running properly, and the cost of living keeps going up. Everything is so expensive nowadays.'

Sebastian grinned. 'The cost of living is definitely on the rise.'

He was blatantly scrutinizing Pyttan, from her costly diamond earrings to her Louboutin high heels. Then he turned to Percy.

'So what is it you need help with?'

'Well . . .' Percy hesitated, but after casting a glance at his wife, he gathered his courage. He had to resolve the situation, otherwise he'd have to start investigating other options. 'You see, it's a matter of a short-term loan.'

A weighty silence followed, but it didn't seem to bother Sebastian. A little smile played over his lips.

'I have a suggestion,' he said then. 'But I think we should discuss it alone, just the two of us, as old classmates.'

Pyttan was about to protest, but Percy gave her a stern look, which was unusual for him, so she didn't say a word. His eyes met Sebastian's and the words flew soundlessly between them.

'That would probably be best,' he said, lowering his gaze.

Sebastian smiled broadly. Once again he held out his glass to Pyttan.

It was too hot to be climbing about on the facade when the sun was at its zenith, so during the middle of the day they worked indoors.

'Shall we start with the floor?' asked Tobias as they stood in the dining room.

Ebba tugged at a loose scrap of wallpaper and a big piece came off with it. 'Wouldn't it be better to do the walls first?'

'I'm not sure the floor is going to hold. A lot of the boards are rotting in places. I think we should fix that before we do anything else.' He pressed his foot down on a floorboard, which gave way under his shoe.

'Okay. We'll do the floor,' said Ebba, putting on her protective glasses. 'How do we go about it?'

She wasn't afraid of hard work, and she was perfectly willing to put in as many hours as Tobias. But he was the one who had experience of this type of thing, and she had to rely on his expertise.

'A sledgehammer and a crowbar should do the trick. I'll take the sledgehammer and you can use the crowbar, okay?'

'Fine.' Ebba reached for the tool that Tobias handed her. Then they got started.

She could feel the adrenalin flowing, and she noted with pleasure the burn in her biceps when she stuck the crowbar in the gaps between the planks and pulled up the wood. As long as she pushed her body to its limit, she didn't have to think about Vincent. When the sweat poured out and the lactic acid filled her muscles, she was free for a brief time. She was no longer Vincent's mother. She was Ebba, who was fixing up her inherited property, who was breaking it apart and then renovating it.

Nor did she think about the fire. If she closed her eyes, she was reminded of the panic, the smoke stinging her lungs, the heat that made her realize how it must feel to be burned alive. And she remembered the wonderful feeling of finally surrendering.

Then with her eyes fixed straight ahead, and using

more strength than was necessary to loosen the rusty nails from the underlying joists, she forced herself to concentrate on the task at hand. But after a while thoughts began crowding in. Who would want to hurt them and why? As she worked, the questions kept whirling through her mind, leading nowhere. She couldn't think of anyone. They were the only ones who might mean to harm themselves. She had often thought that it would be better if she was dead, and she knew that Tobias had thought the same about himself. But everyone they knew had showed them nothing but compassion. There was no ill will, no hatred, only sympathy for what they'd been through. At the same time, there was no escaping the fact that somebody had been sneaking around in the dark, trying to burn down the house with them inside. Unable to drive the thoughts from her mind, she stopped to wipe the sweat from her forehead.

'It's too damned hot in here,' said Tobias, slamming the sledgehammer against the floor, making small pieces of wood fly in all directions. He'd taken off his T-shirt, fastening it to his carpenter's belt.

'Watch out that you don't get something in your eye.'

Ebba studied his body in the sunlight flooding through the dirty windows. He looked exactly the same as when they first got together. A lean, sinewy body which, in spite of all the hard manual labour, never seemed to acquire any muscles. She, on the other hand, had lost her womanly curves over the past six months. Her appetite had completely disappeared, and she must have dropped more than twenty pounds. She didn't know for sure, since she never bothered to weigh herself.

They worked for a while in silence. A fly buzzed angrily against a pane, and Tobias went over and threw the window wide open. Outside there wasn't a breath of wind, so it gave them no relief, but the fly was able to slip out and they were rid of the constant buzzing.

The whole time they were working, Ebba was aware of what had once been. The history of the house was in its walls. She pictured all the children who had come out here to spend the summer at camp, for the sake of fresh air and good health, as it said in the article in an old issue of *Fjällbacka-Bladet* that she'd found. The house had had other owners too, including her father, but it was mostly the children that she thought about. What an adventure it must have been to leave their parents behind and come out here to stay with children they didn't know. Sunny days and swimming in salt water, rules and regulations mixed with games and commotion. She could hear their laughter but also their cries. The article had mentioned a report of abuse too, so maybe everything hadn't been so idyllic. Sometimes she wondered whether the cries came only from the summer camp, or whether her own feelings about the house had got mixed in with other memories. There was something alarmingly familiar about those cries, but she had been very young when she lived here. These memories, if that was what they were, had to belong to the house itself, not to her.

'Do you think we'll be able to manage?' asked Tobias, leaning on the sledgehammer.

Lost in her own thoughts, Ebba jumped at the sound of his voice alongside her. He grabbed the T-shirt hanging from his belt and used it to wipe his face. Then he looked at her. She didn't want to meet his eyes. Instead, she gave him a furtive glance as she continued to work on a board that was refusing to come up. He made it sound as if he was talking about the renovation, but she realized that his question encompassed much more than that. And she had no answer for him.

When she didn't reply, Tobias sighed and picked up the

sledgehammer again. He banged it against the floorboards, groaning with every blow. A big hole was starting to take shape in the wooden floor in front of him. Again he raised the sledgehammer. Then he slowly lowered it.

'What the . . .? Ebba, come and see this!' he said, motioning her over.

Ebba was still working on the stubborn plank, but her curiosity got the better of her.

'What is it?' she said, going over to him.

Tobias pointed down in the hole. 'What does that look like?'

Ebba squatted down to see better. She frowned. A large dark patch was visible where the floor had been removed. Tar was the first thing she thought, but then she realized what it might be.

'It looks like blood,' she said. 'Lots of blood.'

FJÄLLBACKA 1919

Dagmar was smart enough to realize that it wasn't solely because of her skill as a waitress and her beautiful face that she was hired to work at parties given by the wealthy. There was never anything very discreet about the whispering that went on. The host couple always saw to it that everyone at the table immediately knew who she was, and on this occasion she once again felt the eyes of the sensation-seekers fixed upon her.

'Her mother . . . The Angelmaker . . . Executed . . .' The words flew through the air like tiny wasps and their sting hurt, but she had taught herself to keep a smile on her face and pretend not to hear.

This party was no exception. As she walked past, the guests would put their heads together to murmur and give small, telling nods. One of the women put a hand to her mouth in fright and openly stared at Dagmar, who was filling her glass with wine. The German pilot observed with apparent astonishment the commotion she was causing, and out of the corner of her eye she saw him lean towards the woman seated next to him. The woman whispered something in his ear. Her heart pounding, Dagmar waited to see his reaction. The German's expression changed but then his eyes glittered. Calmly he studied her for a moment before he raised his glass to her. She smiled back and felt her heart beat even faster.

The sound level at the large outdoor table rose as the hours passed. Darkness began to fall, and although the summer evening was still warm, some of the guests withdrew to the rooms inside where they continued their drinking. The Sjölins were generous with the liquor, and the pilot also looked as if he'd had a good deal to drink. With a slightly trembling hand, Dagmar had refilled his glass several times. Her reaction surprised her. She had met a lot of men, and a number of them had been quite handsome. Many had known exactly what to say and how to touch a woman, but none of them had caused this sort of vibrating sensation in her abdomen.

The next time she went over to serve him, his hand brushed against hers. No one seemed to notice, and Dagmar did her best to appear unperturbed, although she did thrust out her bosom a bit more.

'Wie heissen Sie?' he said, gazing up at her, his eyes bright.

Dagmar gave him a puzzled look. Swedish was the only language she knew.

'What's your name?' slurred the man sitting across from the pilot. 'He wants to know your name. Tell the pilot, there's a good girl, and then maybe you'd like to come over here and sit on my lap for a while. And find out how a real man feels . . .' He laughed at his own joke and patted his fat thighs.

Dagmar wrinkled her nose in disgust and turned back to the pilot.

'Dagmar,' she said. 'My name is Dagmar.'

'Dagmar,' repeated the German. He pointed with an exaggerated gesture at his own chest. 'Hermann,' he said. 'Ich heisse Hermann.'

After a brief pause he raised his hand to touch the back of her neck, and she felt the little hairs on her arms stand on end. He said something else in German, and she turned to the fat man sitting across the table.

'He says that he wonders what your hair looks like when it's

76

loose.' The man again laughed loudly, as if he'd said something enormously funny.

Dagmar instinctively put her hand up to her hair, which was gathered in a bun. Her blonde hair was so thick that she never managed to fasten it properly, and a few stray locks were always coming loose.

'He'll just have to keep on wondering. Tell him that,' she said, and turned to go.

The fat man laughed and uttered several long sentences in German. The pilot didn't laugh, and as she stood there with her back to him, she felt his hand again touch the nape of her neck. With a tug he pulled out the comb and her hair came tumbling down her back.

Her posture rigid, she slowly turned to face him. For a few moments she and the German pilot stared at each other, accompanied by the fat man's roar of laughter. Between them a tacit understanding arose, and with her hair still loose, Dagmar walked up towards the house where the hooting and howling of the other guests shattered the peace of the summer night.

♣

Patrik was crouching down next to the big hole in the floor. The planks were old and rotting, and it was obvious that the floor needed to be replaced. So what they'd found underneath was all the more surprising. He felt an uneasy lump forming in the pit of his stomach.

'Good thing you called us immediately,' he said, without taking his eyes off the hole.

'It's blood, isn't it?' Tobias swallowed hard. 'I don't know what old blood looks like, and it might be tar or whatever. But considering . . .'

'It does appear to be blood. Could you ring the tech team, Gösta? They need to come out here and take a closer look at this.' Patrik stood up, grimacing when he heard how his joints creaked. A reminder that he wasn't getting any younger.

Gösta nodded and moved a short distance away as he tapped in a number on his mobile.

'Do you think there's something else . . . underneath there?' asked Ebba, her voice quavering.

Patrik realized at once what she was hinting at.

'It's impossible to say. We're going to have to rip up the rest of the floor to see what we can find.'

'It's true that we could use some help with the

renovation, but this wasn't exactly what we had in mind,' said Tobias with a hollow laugh. No one else laughed.

Gösta finished his phone call and came back to join them. 'The techs can't come out here until tomorrow. So I hope you can stand to leave things the way they are until then. Nothing must be touched. You can't do any cleaning or tidying up.'

'We won't touch anything. Why would we do that?' said Tobias.

'This is my chance to find out what happened,' said Ebba.

'Maybe we could sit down somewhere and have a little talk.' Patrik backed away from the section of the floor that had been removed, but what he'd seen was already burned into his memory. For his part, he was convinced that it was blood. A thick layer of congealed blood, no longer red but dark with age. If his theory was right, it had to be more than thirty years old.

'We can sit in the kitchen, that's nice and neat,' said Tobias, making a move to show Patrik the way. Ebba stayed where she was, along with Gösta.

'Are you coming?' Tobias turned to his wife.

'You go ahead. Ebba and I will join you in a minute,' said Gösta.

Patrik was about to say that it was Ebba, above all, that they needed to talk to. But he glanced at her pale face and realized Gösta was right. She could use a moment to herself, and there was really no hurry.

Describing the kitchen as nice and neat proved to be an overstatement. Tools and paintbrushes were scattered everywhere, and the worktop was hidden beneath piles of dirty dishes and the remains of breakfast.

Tobias sat down at the kitchen table.

'We're actually neat-freaks, Ebba and I. Or rather, we were,' he corrected himself. 'Hard to believe when you see things in this state, isn't it?'

'Renovating is hell,' said Patrik, sitting down on a chair after first brushing off a few breadcrumbs.

'It doesn't seem so important to keep everything neat and clean any more.' Tobias looked towards the kitchen window. It was covered with dust, as if a veil had been drawn across it to hide the view.

'What do you know about Ebba's past?' asked Patrik.

He could hear Gösta and Ebba talking in the dining room, but he couldn't make out what they were saying, although he tried. Gösta's behaviour surprised him. Back at the station, when he had dashed into Gösta's office to tell him what had happened, his colleague's reaction had also seemed completely out of character. But then Gösta had closed up like a clam, remaining silent all the way out to Valö.

'My parents and Ebba's adoptive parents are good friends, and what happened in her past has never been a secret. So I've known for a long time that her family disappeared without a trace. I don't think there's much more to know, is there?'

'No. The police didn't make any progress with their investigation, despite putting in a lot of time and energy. It remains a mystery why they simply disappeared.'

'But maybe they've been here the whole time.' Ebba's voice made them both jump.

'I don't think they're lying under the floor,' said Gösta, pausing in the doorway. 'If someone had damaged the floorboards in any way, we would have noticed. The planks were completely untouched, and there was no trace of blood either. It must have seeped in between the boards.'

'Well, I want to know for sure that they're not under there,' said Ebba.

'The techs will inspect every millimetre when they get here tomorrow. You can be sure of that,' said Gösta, putting his arm around Ebba.

Patrik stared. Normally when they were out on a job, Gösta made very little effort. And Patrik couldn't recall ever seeing him touch another person.

'Right now you need some strong coffee.' Gösta gave Ebba a pat on the shoulder and went to turn on the coffee maker. As the coffee began dripping into the pot, he stood at the sink and washed a few cups.

'Why don't you tell us what you know about what happened here.' Patrik pulled out a chair for Ebba.

She sat down, and he was struck by how thin she was. Her T-shirt seemed much too big, and her collarbone was clearly visible under the fabric.

'I don't think I can tell you anything that people around here haven't already heard. I was barely a year old at the time, so I don't remember. And my adoptive parents know only that someone called the police to report that something had happened. When the police arrived, my family were nowhere to be seen, and I was here all alone. This was on the evening before Easter. That's when they disappeared.' She pulled out the pendant that was hidden under her T-shirt and began tugging on it, just as Patrik had noticed her doing the day before. It made her seem even more fragile.

'Here.' Gösta set a cup of coffee in front of Ebba, and poured one for himself before sitting down. Patrik couldn't help smiling. Gösta was his old self again.

'How about some coffee for the rest of us?'

'Do I look like a waiter?'

Tobias got up. 'I'll do it.'

'Is it true that you were left all alone when your family disappeared? That you had no living relatives?' asked Patrik.

Ebba nodded.

'Yes. My mother had no brothers or sisters, and my maternal grandmother died before I turned one. My father was much older, and his parents had died long ago. The only family I have is my adoptive family. And in one sense, I've been very lucky. Berit and Sture have always made me feel like their very own daughter.'

'There were a few boys from the school who were staying here over the Easter holiday. Have you ever been in contact with any of them?'

'No, why would I do that?' Ebba's eyes looked huge in her thin face.

'We've had nothing to do with this place until we decided to move here,' said Tobias. 'Ebba inherited the house when her biological parents were declared dead, but after that it was rented out several times. Periodically it stood empty. That's actually what prompted us to get started on the renovation. Nobody was taking care of the house. Only the most basic repairs have been done.'

'I think we were meant to come here and tear up the floor,' said Ebba. 'There's a reason for everything.'

'Really?' said Tobias. 'For everything?'

But Ebba didn't reply, and when Tobias followed Patrik and Gösta to the door, she was still sitting at the table in silence.

As they left Valö behind, Patrik was pondering the same question. What would they do if the techs confirmed that it was blood under the floor? The statute of limitations had expired. Too much time had elapsed, and there were no guarantees that answers could be found this long after the event. So what was the reason behind this discovery? Patrik's head was filled with uneasy thoughts as he steered the boat homeward.

The doctor stopped talking and utter silence descended over the room. The only sound that Martin heard was the beating of his own heart. He looked at the doctor. How could he seem so unaffected by what he'd just said?

Did he give people this sort of news several times a week? And if he did, how could he stand it?

Martin forced himself to keep breathing. He felt as if he'd forgotten how. Every breath demanded a conscious act, a specific instruction to his brain.

'How long?' he managed to say.

'There are several different types of treatment, and the field of medicine is constantly making progress . . .' The doctor threw out his hands.

'But what's the prognosis, statistically speaking?' asked Martin, trying to remain calm. He would have liked to launch himself across the desk, grab hold of the doctor's coat, and shake the information out of him.

Pia didn't say a word, and Martin still couldn't look at her. If he did, everything would fall apart. Right now all he could do was focus on the facts. Something tangible, something he could grasp.

'It's difficult to be precise. There are so many factors that play a role.' The same apologetic expression, his hands raised in the air. Already Martin detested that gesture.

'Answer me!' he shouted, practically jumping at the sound of his own voice.

'We'll start treatment immediately, and then we'll see how Pia responds. But considering how the cancer has spread, and how aggressive it seems to be . . . well, we're talking about six months to a year.'

Martin stared at him. Had he heard right? Tuva wasn't yet two years old. She couldn't possibly lose her mother. Things like that didn't happen. He started shaking. It was oppressively hot in the small room, but he was so cold that his teeth were chattering. Pia put her hand on his arm.

'Calm down, Martin. We need to stay calm. There's always a chance that the prognosis is wrong. And I'm going to do whatever it takes to . . .' She turned to the doctor. 'Give me the best treatment you have. I plan to fight this.'

'We'll admit you at once. Go home and pack a bag. A room will be arranged for you.'

Martin felt ashamed. Pia was being so strong while he was on the verge of collapse. Images of Tuva whirled through his head, from the moment of her birth to early this morning when she had snuggled with them in bed. Her dark hair tousled, her eyes lively with laughter. Would that laughter be silenced now? Would she lose her joy, her faith that everything was good and that the next day would be even better?

'We'll make it through this.' Pia's face was ashen, but there was a determination in her expression, which he knew was a sign of her great tenacity. And she was going to need all the resolve she could muster for the most important fight of her life.

'Let's go pick up Tuva from Mamma's place and go out for coffee,' she said, standing up. 'We can talk in peace and quiet after she has gone to bed. And I need to pack. How long should I plan on being away from home?'

Martin slowly got to his feet, although his legs felt as if they might buckle at any moment. It was so typical of Pia to think of the practical details.

The doctor hesitated. 'Just pack enough things for a while.'

He said goodbye and then left to see his next patient.

Martin and Pia stood in the corridor for a moment. Silently they reached out to hold hands.

'You give them juice in their bottles? Aren't you afraid it'll be bad for their teeth?' Kristina cast a disapproving look at Anton and Noel, who were sitting on the sofa, each holding a bottle.

Erica sighed heavily. Her mother-in-law meant well, and she had actually improved of late, but sometimes Kristina really got on her nerves.

'I've tried giving them water, but they refuse to drink it. And they need fluids in this heat. But I've diluted the juice quite a bit.'

'Well, it's up to you,' sniffed Kristina. 'I've given you my opinion. Patrik and Lotta were only given water, and that worked out fine. They didn't have a single cavity before they left home, and the dentist was always complimenting me on their beautiful teeth.'

Erica bit her tongue as she stood in the kitchen, cleaning up, well out of Kristina's view. Her mother-in-law was tolerable in small doses, and she was wonderful with the children, but these half-day visits tested Erica's patience to the limit.

'I think I'll put a load of washing in the machine, Erica,' said Kristina loudly and then continued talking, as if to herself: 'It's easier if you pick up things a little at a time and keep the place tidy, then you don't end up with piles of clutter. Everything should have its place. You need to put it all away when you're done with it, and Maja is big enough to tidy up after herself. Otherwise she'll turn out to be a spoiled teenager who never moves away from home and who expects to be waited on, hand and foot. You know my friend Berit? Well, her son is almost forty, but he's never . . .'

Erica stuck her fingers in her ears and leaned her forehead against one of the kitchen cupboards. She quietly pounded her head against the cool wooden surface, praying for patience. A firm tap on her shoulder made her jump.

'What are you doing?' Kristina was standing next to her, with a fully loaded laundry basket at her feet. 'I was talking to you, but you didn't answer.'

With her fingers still stuck in her ears, Erica tried to come up with a plausible explanation.

'I'm having . . . trouble with pressure in my ears.' She

pinched her nose and blew hard. 'It's been bothering me a lot lately.'

'Oh my,' said Kristina. 'That's something you need to take seriously. Have you checked to make sure it's not an ear infection? Children are forever bringing home illnesses when they go to day-care. I've always said that day-care centres are not the best solution. In my day, I stayed home with Patrik and Lotta until they started middle school. They didn't need to go to day-care or stay with a babysitter for even a single day. And they were never sick. Our doctor was always praising me because they were so—'

Erica cut her off mid-flow. 'The kids haven't been there for weeks, so I don't think the day-care centre is the culprit.'

'If you say so,' replied Kristina, looking hurt. 'But at least you know my opinion. After all, who is it you call whenever the children are sick and the two of you have to work? I'm the one who always has to step in.' She tossed her head, picked up the laundry basket, and left the room.

Erica slowly counted to ten. There was no denying that Kristina often helped out, but they certainly paid a high price for it.

Josef's parents were both over forty when his mother received the highly unexpected news that she was pregnant. Having long since accepted the fact that they'd never have any children, they had arranged their lives accordingly, devoting all their time to the small tailor's shop in Fjällbacka. Josef's arrival changed everything. Although they felt great joy at the prospect of a son and heir, they also felt a great weight because of the responsibility of passing on their heritage, through him.

Josef lovingly studied the photograph of them, which he kept in a solid silver frame on his desk. Behind that photo stood framed pictures of Rebecka and the children. He'd always been the centre of his parents' lives, and they would always be at the centre of his. That was something his family had to accept.

'Dinner will be ready soon,' said Rebecka as she cautiously entered his study.

'I'm not hungry. You go ahead and eat,' he said without glancing up. He had much more important things to do than eat.

'Can't you join us? Now that the children are home to visit?'

Josef looked at her in surprise. She usually never insisted on anything. Annoyance surged within him, but then he took a deep breath. She was right. These days the children seldom came home.

'Okay, I'll be right with you,' he said with a sigh, closing his notebook. It was filled with ideas about how to shape the project, and he always carried it with him in case inspiration struck.

'Thank you,' said Rebecka. Then she turned on her heel and left.

Josef followed. In the dining room the table had already been set, and he noticed that she had used the good china. She had a slight tendency to be ostentatious, and it seemed to him absurd to go to such lengths just for the children, but he made no comment.

'Hi, Pappa,' said Judith, kissing his cheek.

Daniel stood up and came over to give his father a hug. For a moment Josef's heart filled with pride, and he wished that his own father could have seen his grandchildren grow up.

'Let's sit down before the food gets cold,' he said, taking his seat at the head of the table.

Rebecka had made Judith's favourite dish: roast chicken with mashed potatoes. Josef suddenly realized how hungry he was, and it occurred to him that he'd forgotten to have lunch. After murmuring grace, Rebecka served the food, and they began eating in silence. After assuaging the worst of his hunger, Josef put down his knife and fork.

'How's it going with your studies?'

Daniel nodded. 'I got top marks on all the exams during the summer course. Now it's a matter of landing a good trainee position in the autumn.'

'And I love my summer job,' Judith interjected. Her eyes were bright with enthusiasm. 'You should see how brave the kids are, Mamma. They have to endure all those difficult operations and radiation treatments and everything else imaginable, but they never complain and they never give up. They're incredible.'

Josef took a deep breath. The success of his children did nothing to quell the uneasiness that was his constant companion. He knew that there was always a little more they could give, that they could reach a little higher. They had so much to live up to, so much to avenge, and it was his duty to ensure that they did all they could.

'What about your research? Do you still have time for that?' He fixed Judith with a piercing stare and saw how the eagerness was extinguished from her eyes. She wanted him to acknowledge her and offer some words of praise, but if he gave the children the impression that what they were doing was good enough, then they'd stop making an effort. And he couldn't let that happen.

He didn't wait for Judith to reply before he turned to Daniel. 'I talked to the course instructor last week, and he said that you'd missed two days of class. Why was that?'

'I had stomach problems,' said Daniel. 'I don't think they'd have been too pleased if I'd sat there in the lecture hall, throwing up into a paper bag.'

'Are you trying to be funny?'

'No. That's my honest answer.'

88

'You know that I can always find out if you're lying,' said Josef. His knife and fork were still sitting on his plate. He'd lost his appetite. He hated the fact that he no longer had control over his children the way he had when they lived at home.

'I had stomach problems,' Daniel repeated, lowering his eyes. He too seemed to have lost his appetite.

Josef hastily rose to his feet. 'I need to get back to work.'

As he retreated to his study, he thought they were probably glad to be rid of his presence. Through the door he could hear their voices and the clatter of china. Then Judith laughed, a loud, carefree laugh, sounding as clear as if she were sitting next to him. All of a sudden he realized that the children's laughter, their joy, always became muted whenever he entered the room. Judith laughed again, and it felt like a knife turning in his heart. She never laughed like that around him, and he wondered whether things could have been different. At the same time, he had no idea how that might have been accomplished. He loved them so much that it caused him physical pain, but he could never be the father they wished for. He could only be the father that life had taught him to be and love them in his own way, by carrying on his heritage through them.

Gösta was staring at the flickering screen of the television. He could see people coming and going, and since he was watching *Midsummer Murders*, no doubt somebody was being murdered. But he had lost interest in the plot some time ago. His thoughts were somewhere else entirely.

On the coffee table in front of him was a plate with two open-face sandwiches. Skogaholm rye bread with butter and salami. Generally that was all he ever ate at home. It took too much effort and it was too depressing to cook for only one person.

The sofa he was sitting on was getting old, but he didn't have the heart to get rid of it. He remembered how proud Maj-Britt had been when they brought it home. Several times he had caught her running her hand over the smooth, floral upholstery as if petting a kitten. He was barely allowed to sit on it during that first year. But the little lass had bounced and slid all over it. Laughing, Maj-Britt had held her hands as she jumped higher and higher on the groaning springs.

Now the upholstery was worn smooth, with big holes. In one place, next to the right armrest, a spring was sticking out. But he always sat on the left-hand side. That was his place, while the other side had belonged to Maj-Britt. In the evenings during that summer, the little lass had sat between them. She'd never seen a TV before, so she shrieked with delight whenever it was on. Her favourite programme had been the puppet show *Drutten and Gena*. And she could never sit still as she watched; she would squirm with sheer pleasure.

No one had bounced on the sofa in a very long time. After the lass disappeared, it was as if she took part of the joy with her, and many silent evenings followed. Neither of them could have imagined that regret could hurt so much. They'd thought they were doing the right thing, and when they realized that they'd made the wrong decision, it was too late.

Gösta gazed vacantly at Inspector Barnaby, who had just discovered yet another body. He picked up one of the salami sandwiches and took a bite. It was an evening like so many others. And it would be followed by so many more.

FJÄLLBACKA 1919

It would not do for them to be seen in the servants' sleeping quarters, so Dagmar waited for a signal from him to withdraw to his room. Earlier she had made up the bed and tidied the room for him, not knowing that she would long so fervently to slip between those lovely cotton sheets.

The party was still in full swing when she received the signal she'd been waiting for. He was a bit unsteady on his feet, his blond hair was dishevelled, and his eyes glazed with drink. But he was not so intoxicated that he couldn't slip her a key to his room. The brief touch of his hand made her heart race; without meeting his eye she hid the key in her apron pocket. At this stage no one would notice if she left. The hosts and the guests were all too drunk to care about anything besides refilling their glasses, and there were plenty of other servants to see to that.

Yet she still paused to glance around before unlocking the door to the large guest room, and when she stepped inside, she stopped with her back to the door and took several deep breaths. The mere sight of the bed with the white sheets and the elegant coverlet made her tingle all over. He could arrive at any moment, so she dashed into the small bathroom. Quickly she smoothed her hair, took off her servant's clothing, and washed under her arms. Then she bit her lips and pinched her cheeks to make them rosier, since that was the fashion among the city girls.

When she heard the door handle turn, she hastened back into the room and sat down on the bed, wearing only her slip. She draped her hair over her shoulders, fully aware of how glossy it looked in the pale light of the summer night coming through the window.

She was not disappointed. When he saw her, his eyes opened wide, and he swiftly shut the door behind him. He studied her for a moment before he came over to the bed and placed his hand under her chin, lifting her face. Then he bent down and their lips met in a kiss. Cautiously, as if wanting to tease her, he slid the tip of his tongue between her parted lips.

Dagmar responded passionately to his kisses. She had never experienced anything like this before. It felt as if this man had been sent by some divine power to unite with her and make her whole. For a brief moment everything went black before her eyes, and images of the past were conjured up in her mind. The children who were placed in a basin, with a weight on top until they stopped moving. The policemen who rushed in and seized her mother and father. The tiny bodies that were dug up in the cellar at home. The witch and her foster father. The men who had groaned on top of her with their breath stinking of liquor and cigars. Everybody who had used her and derided her – now they would be forced to bow and ask forgiveness. When they saw her walking beside this blond hero, they would regret every word they had ever whispered behind her back.

Slowly he pulled her slip up over her stomach, and Dagmar raised her arms above her head to help him take off the garment. She wanted nothing more than to feel his skin against hers. She undid the buttons on his shirt one by one, until he finally tore it off. When all of his clothes were in a heap on the floor, he lay down on top of her. Nothing more separated them.

As their two bodies joined, Dagmar closed her eyes. At that moment she was no longer the Angelmaker's daughter. She was a woman whom fate had finally blessed.

He'd been preparing for weeks. It had proved difficult to get an interview with John Holm in Stockholm, but since the politician was coming to Fjällbacka on holiday, Kjell had managed to persuade him to give up an hour of his time for a profile article to be published in *Bohusläningen*.

Kjell was sure that Holm would know of his father, Frans Ringholm, who had been one of the founders of the Friends of Sweden, the party which Holm now led. The fact that Frans was a Nazi sympathizer was one of the reasons that Kjell had distanced himself from his father. Shortly before Frans died, Kjell had come to some measure of reconciliation with him, but he would never share his father's views. Just as he would never respect Friends of Sweden or its newfound success.

They had agreed to meet at Holm's boathouse. The drive to Fjällbacka from Uddevalla took almost an hour in the summer traffic. Ten minutes late, Kjell parked on the gravel area in front of the boathouse, hoping that his tardiness would not cut into the hour he'd been promised for the interview.

'Take a few pictures while we're talking, just in case there's no time afterwards,' he told his colleague as they got out of the car. He knew this wouldn't be a problem.

Stefan was the newspaper's most experienced photographer, and he always delivered, no matter what the circumstances.

'Welcome!' said Holm as he came to meet them.

'Thanks,' said Kjell. He had to make a real effort to shake Holm's hand. Not only were his views repulsive, but he was also one of the most dangerous men in Sweden.

Holm led the way through the little boathouse and out on to the dock.

'I never met your father. But I understand that he was a man who commanded respect.'

'Well, spending a number of years in prison does have that effect.'

'It can't have been easy for you, growing up under those conditions,' said Holm, sitting down on a patio chair next to a fence that offered some protection from the wind.

For a moment Kjell was gripped by envy. It seemed so unfair that a man like John Holm owned such a beautiful place, with a view of the harbour and archipelago. To hide his antipathy, Kjell sat down across from the politician and began fiddling with the tape recorder. He was well aware that life was unfair, and from the research he'd done, he knew that Holm had been born with a silver spoon in his mouth.

The tape recorder started up. It appeared to be working properly, so Kjell began the interview.

'Why do you think you've now been able to secure a seat in the Riksdag?'

It was always a good idea to start off cautiously. He also knew that he was lucky to catch Holm alone. In Stockholm the press secretary and other people would have been present. Right now he had Holm all to himself, and he was hoping that the party leader would be relaxed seeing as he was on holiday and on his own turf.

'I think the Swedish people have matured. We've become more aware of the rest of the world and how it affects us. For a long time we've been too gullible, but now we're starting to wake up, and the Friends of Sweden has the privilege of representing the voice of reason during this period of awakening,' said Holm with a smile.

Kjell could understand why people were drawn to this man. He had a charisma and a self-confidence that made others willing to believe what he said. But Kjell was too jaded to fall for that sort of personal charm, and it made his hackles rise to hear Holm's use of 'we' when referring to himself and the Swedish people. John Holm certainly did not represent the majority of Swedes. They were better than that.

He continued with the innocent questions: How did it feel to enter parliament as a member? How had he been received? What was his view of the political work being done in Stockholm? The whole time Stefan circled around them with his camera, and Kjell could imagine what the pictures would show. John Holm sitting on his own private dock with the sea glittering in the background. This was a far cry from the formal photos that usually appeared in the newspapers, showing him wearing a suit and tie.

Kjell cast a quick glance at his watch. They were twenty minutes into the interview, and the mood he'd set was pleasant, if not exactly warm. It was now time to start asking the real questions. During the weeks that had passed since his request for an interview had been granted, Kjell had read countless articles about Holm and watched numerous clips of televised debates. So many journalists had made a poor job of it, barely scraping the surface. On the rare occasions they did slip in a probing question, they were invariably fobbed off with a self-assured response that was riddled with erroneous statistics and outright lies that they never thought to challenge. Such shoddy

95

work made Kjell ashamed to call himself a journalist. Unlike his colleagues, he had done his homework.

'Your budget is based on the huge savings which, according to your party, the country will achieve if immigration is halted. To the tune of seventy-eight billion Swedish kronor. How did you arrive at that figure?'

Holm gave a start. A furrow appeared between his eyebrows, signalling a slight annoyance, but it swiftly disappeared, to be replaced by his usual smile.

'The numbers have been carefully substantiated.'

'Are you sure about that? Because quite a few people have been saying that your calculations are wrong. Let me give you an example. You claim that only ten per cent of those who come to Sweden as immigrants actually get jobs.'

'Yes, that's correct. There's high unemployment among the people that we allow into Sweden, and that places an enormous economic burden on our society.'

'But according to the statistics I've seen, sixty-five per cent of all immigrants in Sweden between the ages of twenty and sixty-four have jobs.'

Holm didn't reply, and Kjell could practically see his brain working overtime.

'The figure I have is ten per cent,' he said at last.

'And you don't know how that number was derived?'

'No.'

Kjell was beginning to enjoy the situation. 'According to your calculations, the country would also save a great deal because the cost of social services would be lowered if immigration was stopped. But a study of the period from 1980 to 1990 shows that the tax income contributed by immigrants greatly exceeds state expenditure on immigration.'

'That doesn't sound at all credible,' said Holm with a wry smile. 'The Swedish people can no longer be fooled by such fraudulent studies. It's common knowledge that immigrants take advantage of the social service system.'

'I have a copy of the study right here. Feel free to hang on to it and go through it at your leisure.' Kjell pulled out a sheaf of papers and placed them in front of Holm.

He didn't even glance at them. 'I have people to attend to stuff like that.'

'I'm sure you do, but they don't seem to read very well,' said Kjell. 'Let's consider how much it would cost to implement your proposals. For instance, the universal military service you want to institute – what would that bill run to? Shouldn't you be able to list all the costs so we can see what they are?' He slid a notepad and pen over to Holm, who glanced at them with an expression of distaste.

'All the numbers are included in our budget. You can look it up.'

'So you don't have them memorized? Despite the fact that your budget figures are the core of your policy-making?'

'Of course I have a thorough understanding of the finances.' Holm shoved the notepad away. 'But I have no intention of sitting here and jumping through hoops.'

'All right, let's forget about the budget figures for the time being. Perhaps we'll have occasion to come back to them later.' Kjell rummaged in his briefcase and took out another document, a list that he'd compiled.

'In addition to a stricter immigration policy, you want to work towards instituting more severe sentences for criminals.'

Holm stretched as if to ease the muscles in his back.

'Yes. It's scandalous how lenient we are here in Sweden. Under our proposed policies, criminals will no longer get away with a mere slap on the wrist. Within the party itself we've also set a high standard, especially since we're fully aware that historically we've been linked to a number of . . . well, undesirable elements.'

Undesirable elements. That was certainly one way of expressing it, thought Kjell, but he purposely didn't comment. It sounded as though he was on his way to getting Holm precisely where he wanted him.

'We've got rid of all the criminal elements on our parliamentary rosters, and we're putting into practice a zero-tolerance policy. For instance, everyone has to sign an ethics oath, and all legal convictions, no matter how far they date back, must be revealed. No one with a criminal past is allowed to represent the Friends of Sweden.' Holm leaned back, crossing his legs.

Kjell let him feel secure for a few more seconds before he placed the list on the table.

'Why is it that you don't make the same demands of people who work in the party's government offices? No less than five of your co-workers have a criminal background. We're talking about convictions for domestic abuse, intimidation, robbery, and assault on a civil servant. For example, in 2001 your press secretary was convicted of kicking an Ethiopian man to the ground at the marketplace in Ludvika.' Kjell pushed the list closer, so that it was right in front of Holm. An angry flush was now visible on the party leader's throat.

'I don't take part in the job interviews or day-to-day operations in the offices, so I can't comment on this issue.'

'But since you're the one who's ultimately responsible for staff hired by the party, shouldn't this matter end up on your desk, regardless of whether or not you're in charge of the practical details?'

'Everyone has the right to a second chance. For the most part, we're talking about youthful sins.'

'A second chance, you say? Why should your staff members deserve a second chance when the same doesn't apply to immigrants who commit a crime? According to your party, they ought to be deported as soon as they're convicted.'

Holm clenched his jaw, giving his face an even more chiselled look.

'As I said, I'm not involved in the hiring process. I'll have to get back to you on this.'

For a few seconds Kjell considered pressing Holm further on this point, but time was running out. At any moment Holm might decide that he'd had enough and terminate the interview.

'I have a few personal questions as well,' Kjell said instead, referring to his notes. He'd actually committed to memory all the questions that he wanted to ask, but he knew from experience that it had an unsettling effect on the person he was interviewing if he seemed to have everything in writing. The printed word evoked a certain respect.

'You've previously stated that your involvement in immigration issues started when you were twenty years old and two African students attacked and beat you. They were studying for the same degree as you were at the university in Göteborg. You reported the incident to the police, but the investigation was abandoned, and then you had to see those students every day in class. For the rest of your university years, those two sat and jeered at you, and by extension, at Swedish society as a whole. The latter is a direct quote from an interview you gave *Svenska Dagbladet* this past spring.'

Holm nodded solemnly. 'Yes, that was an episode that had a strong impact on me and shaped my view of the world. It was a clear demonstration of how society functions and how Swedes have been demoted to second-class citizens while an indulgent attitude is shown to those we've been naive enough to welcome here from the rest of the world.'

'Interesting.' Kjell cocked his head. 'I've checked up on this incident, and there are several things that are a bit . . . odd.'

'What do you mean?'

'First, there is no such report in the police files. And second, there were no African students enrolled in the same degree programme as you. In fact, there were no African students whatsoever at Göteborg University when you were studying there.'

Kjell watched as Holm's Adam's apple rose and fell.

'You're wrong. I remember the whole thing quite clearly.'

'Isn't it more likely that your views stem from the place where you grew up? I have information indicating that your father was a fervent Nazi sympathizer.'

'I can't comment on what my father's views might have been.'

A quick glance at his watch showed Kjell that he had only five minutes remaining. He felt a mixture of annoyance and satisfaction. The interview hadn't produced any concrete results, but it had been a pleasure to knock Holm off balance. And he wasn't planning to give up. This was merely round one of the fight. He was going to keep digging until he found something that would bring John Holm down. He might need to meet with him again, so it would be better to wind up the interview now with a question that had nothing to do with politics. He smiled.

'I understand that you were a pupil at the boarding school on Valö when that family disappeared. I wonder what really happened back then.'

Holm glared at him and then abruptly got to his feet. 'The hour is up, and there are a lot of things demanding my attention. I assume that the two of you can find your own way out.'

Kjell's journalistic instincts had always been good, and

Holm's unexpected reaction pushed his brain into over-drive. There was something related to this topic that Holm didn't want him to know about. Kjell could hardly wait to get back to the editorial office and start poking around to find out what it might be.

'Where's Martin?' Patrik looked at his colleagues seated around the table in the station's kitchen.

'He called in sick,' said Annika, sounding evasive. 'But I have his report on what he found out about the finances and insurance.'

Patrik glanced at her but didn't ask any questions. If Annika didn't want to tell them what she knew, they'd have to resort to torture to get anything out of her.

'And I have the old investigative materials here,' said Gösta, pointing at several thick manila folders on the table.

'That was fast,' said Mellberg. 'It usually takes ages to find things in the archives.'

There was a long pause before Gösta replied. 'I had them at home.'

'You keep archival materials in your house? Are you out of your mind, man?' Mellberg jumped up from his chair, and Ernst, who had been lying at his feet, sat up with his ears pricked. He barked a few times but then decided that everything seemed calm enough, and he lay back down.

'Once in a while I review the files, and it got to be too much trouble, running to the archives every time. Besides, it's just as well I already had the files out – otherwise we wouldn't have them here now.'

'How bloody stupid can you be!' Mellberg went on, and Patrik could see that it was time to intervene.

'Sit down, Bertil. The important thing is that we have access to the material. We can discuss any disciplinary measures later.'

Mellberg grumbled something but reluctantly complied. 'Have the techs started work yet?'

Patrik nodded. 'They're breaking up the entire floor and collecting samples. Torbjörn has promised to contact us as soon as he knows anything.'

'Can anyone tell me why we should be wasting time and resources when the statute of limitations has already expired?' said Mellberg.

Gösta glared at him. 'Have you forgotten that somebody tried to burn the place down?'

'No, I haven't. But I don't see any reason to believe that one case is linked to the other.' He pronounced each word with exaggerated care, as if trying to provoke Gösta.

Patrik sighed again. They were both acting like kids.

'You're the one who decides, Bertil, but I think it would be a mistake not to look a bit closer at what the Starks discovered yesterday.'

'I'm aware of your opinion in the matter, but you're not the one who has to answer to the higher-ups when they want to know why we're squandering our meagre resources on a case that is past its expiry date.'

'If it's connected to the arson, as Hedström thinks, then the disappearance of the family is relevant,' Gösta stubbornly insisted.

For a moment Mellberg sat in silence. 'Okay, then we'll spend a few hours on it.' He gestured for Patrik to continue.

Patrik took a deep breath. 'All right. Let's start by looking at what Martin found out.'

Annika put on her reading glasses and peered at the report. 'Martin didn't find any discrepancies. The summer camp is not heavily insured – quite the contrary. So the Starks wouldn't get a large sum in the event of a fire. As far as their personal finances are concerned, they have a lot of money in the bank from the sale of their house in Göteborg. I assume that the money is going to be used for the renovation and all their daily expenses until they get their bed and breakfast up and running. In addition, Ebba has a business registered in her name. It's called My Angel. Apparently she makes angel jewellery in silver and sells the pieces online, but the income is negligible.'

'Good. We won't drop that aspect of the investigation entirely, but at least it seems we can rule out insurance fraud. Then we have yesterday's discovery,' said Patrik, turning to Gösta. 'Could you tell us how the house looked when the police searched it after the family disappeared?'

'Sure. You can also see for yourselves – here are the original photographs,' said Gösta, opening one of the file folders. He took out a stack of yellowing photos and handed them around. Patrik was surprised. In spite of their age, the pictures of the crime scene were of excellent quality.

'In the dining room there were no clues as to what happened,' said Gösta. 'The family had begun to eat their Easter lunch, but there was absolutely nothing to indicate any sort of struggle had taken place. Nothing was broken, and the floor was clean. Take a look if you don't believe me.'

Patrik did as he said, studying the photos carefully. Gösta was right. It was as if the family had simply stood up in the middle of lunch and left. He shivered. There was something ghostly about the table with the half-eaten food still on the plates and the chairs neatly pushed into place around the table. The only thing missing was the people. And the discovery under the floorboards cast a whole new light on the scene. Now he understood why Erica had devoted so many hours to trying to find out what was behind the mysterious disappearance of the Elvander family.

'If it's blood, can we determine whether it belonged to the family?' asked Annika.

Patrik shook his head. 'That's not my field of expertise, but I doubt it. I reckon the blood is too old to do that kind of analysis. About the best we can hope for is confirmation whether it's human or not. Besides, we have nothing to compare it with.'

'Ebba is still alive,' said Gösta. 'If the blood came from Rune or Inez, maybe they could work up a DNA profile and see if it matches Ebba's.'

'Possibly. But I think that blood breaks down very quickly, and too many years have gone by. Regardless of the results of the blood analysis, we need to find out what happened on that Easter weekend. We need to transport ourselves back in time.' Patrik set the photographs on the table. 'We'll have to read through all the interviews that were done with people connected to the boarding school and then have another talk with them. The truth is out there somewhere. A whole family can't simply disappear. And if it's confirmed that we're dealing with human blood, then we have to assume that a crime was committed in that room.'

He glanced at Gösta, who nodded.

'Yes, you're right. We need to transport ourselves back in time.'

Some people might find it strange to have so many photographs on display in a hotel room, but if so, no one had ever mentioned it to him. That was the advantage of living in a suite. Everybody assumed that a person with so much money might be a little eccentric. And his appearance gave him the opportunity to do as he liked without caring what anyone thought of him.

The photos were important to him. The fact that he always kept them on show was one of the few things that Ia was not allowed to meddle in. Otherwise, he was in her power, and he knew it. But what he had once been and what he'd accomplished were things that she could never take away from him.

Leon rolled his wheelchair over to the chest of drawers where the photos stood. He closed his eyes and for a brief moment allowed himself to be carried back in his mind to the places shown in the pictures. He imagined the desert wind burning his cheeks and how the extreme cold made his fingers ache. He had loved the pain. 'No pain, no gain' had always been his motto. Now, ironically enough, he lived with pain every second of every day. Without gaining a single thing from it.

The face that smiled back at him from the photos was beautiful – or rather, handsome. To say it was beautiful implied that it was a feminine face, which was misleading. He radiated manliness and strength. A bold daredevil, longing to feel adrenalin rushing through his body.

He stretched out his left hand which, unlike his right hand, was whole, and picked up his favourite photograph, taken at the top of Mount Everest. It had been an arduous climb, and several members of the expedition had been forced to drop out at various stages. Some had given up before starting. That sort of weakness was incomprehensible. Giving up was not an option for him. Many had shaken their heads at his attempt to reach the summit without oxygen. Those with an understanding of what was involved said that he'd never succeed. Even the expedition leader had begged him to use oxygen, but Leon knew he could do it. Reinhold Messner and Peter Habeler had done it in 1978. Back then it was also considered impossible; not even the native Nepalese climbers had managed it. But he'd made it to the summit of Mt. Everest on the first attempt – without oxygen. In the photograph he was smiling broadly, holding the Swedish flag in one hand, with the colourful prayer flags behind him. At that moment he was on top of the world. He looked strong. Happy.

Leon carefully set the photo down and picked up the next one. Paris to Dakar. Motorcycle division, of course. It still bothered him that he hadn't won. Instead he'd had to settle for placing among the top ten. He realized this was an amazing accomplishment, but for him first place was the only thing that counted. It had always been like that. He wanted to stand on the first-place podium, no matter what the endeavour. He ran his thumb over the glass covering the framed photo, holding back a smile. If he smiled, one side of his face tugged unpleasantly, and he hated that feeling.

Ia had been so scared. One of the competitors had been killed at the very start of the race, and she had pleaded with him to pull out. But the accident merely increased his motivation. It was the sense of danger that drove him, the realization that his life could be taken from him at any moment. Danger made him love what was good in life all the more intensely. The champagne tasted better, the women seemed more beautiful, the silk sheets felt smoother against his skin. His wealth was more valuable if he stood to lose it. Ia, on the other hand, was afraid of losing everything. She loathed the way he laughed at death and gambled for high stakes at the casinos in Monaco, Saint-Tropez, and Cannes. She didn't understand the rush he felt whenever he lost big, only to win it all back the following night. On those nights she couldn't sleep. She tossed and turned in bed while he peacefully smoked a cigar out on the balcony.

In his heart he had actually enjoyed her distress. He knew that she loved the life he could offer her. She not only loved it, she needed and demanded it. That was what made it so exciting to see her expression whenever the roulette ball landed in the wrong slot. He would watch her bite her cheek, trying not to scream out loud when-ever he bet everything on red and it came up black.

Leon heard the sound of a key in the lock. Gently he set the photo back on the chest of drawers. The man on the motorcycle gave him a big smile.

FJÄLLBACKA 1919

It was a marvellous day to wake up to, and Dagmar stretched her limbs like a cat. Now everything was going to be different. Finally she'd met someone who would silence all the talk and make the laughter stick in the throats of all those gossiping women. The Angelmaker's daughter and the hero pilot – that would certainly give them something else to chatter about. But it would no longer have any effect on her, because they would be going off together. She didn't know where, but that didn't really matter.

Last night he had caressed her as no one had ever done before. He had whispered so many words in her ears, words that she couldn't understand, but in her heart she knew they were promises about their shared future. His passionate gasps had made desire spread through her whole body, and she had given him everything she possessed.

Dagmar slowly sat up on the edge of the bed. Naked, she went over to the window and opened it wide. Outside the birds were chirping, and the sun had just come up. She wondered where Hermann was. Had he gone to fetch breakfast for them?

In the bathroom she carefully performed her morning ablutions. She would have preferred to keep the scent of him on her body, but at the same time she wanted to be as fragrant as the most beautiful rose when he returned. And she would soon smell his scent again. She had a whole lifetime to breathe in his scent.

*When she was finished, she lay back down on the bed to wait,
but he was taking his time and she felt her impatience grow.
The sun had climbed higher in the sky, and the chirping of the
birds was starting to seem annoyingly loud. Where had Hermann
gone? Didn't he know that she was waiting for him?*

*Finally she got up, put on her clothes, and left the room,
holding her head high. Why should she care if anyone saw her?
It would soon be clear what Hermann's intentions were.*

*The house was very quiet. Everyone was in bed, sleeping it
off, and no doubt they wouldn't be up for a few more hours.
The guests didn't usually appear until eleven. But there were
sounds coming from the kitchen. The staff were up early,
preparing breakfast. The party-goers always had a ravenous
appetite when they finally awoke, so the eggs had to be boiled
and ready, the coffee made. She peeked into the kitchen. No,
Hermann wasn't there. One of the cooks saw her and frowned,
but Dagmar tossed her head and pulled the door closed.*

*After searching the house, she headed towards the dock. Could
he be having a morning dip? Hermann was so athletic. He'd
probably gone down to have an invigorating swim.*

*She walked faster and then began to run down to the shore.
Her feet seemed to fly over the grass, and when she reached the
dock, she smiled as she gazed out over the water. But her expression soon turned solemn. He wasn't there. She took one more
look around, but Hermann was not in the water, and there were
no clothes tossed on the dock. One of the boys who worked for
the doctor and his wife came sauntering towards her.*

*'Can I help you, miss?' he said, squinting into the sun. When
he got closer and saw who she was, he laughed. 'Well, if it isn't
Dagmar. What are you doing down here at this time of day? I
heard that you didn't sleep in the servants' quarters last night
because you were enjoying yourself elsewhere.'*

*'Be quiet, Edvin,' she said. 'I'm looking for the German pilot.
Have you seen him?'*

Edvin stuck his hands in his trouser pockets. 'The pilot? Is that where you were?' He laughed the same scornful laugh. 'Did he know that he was going to bed with the daughter of a murderer? Maybe foreigners like him find it exciting.'

'Shut up! Answer my question. Have you seen him this morning?'

Edvin paused for a long time before replying. He stared at her, looking her up and down.

'Maybe we should get together sometime, you and me,' he said at last, taking a step closer. 'We've never really had a chance to get to know each other.'

She glared at him. Oh how she despised these odious men, without class or sophistication. They had no right to touch her with their filthy hands. She deserved better. She deserved a nice life, that was what her mother and father had told her.

'Well?' she said. 'You heard the question.'

He spat on the ground, then looked her right in the eye, unable to hide his glee as he said:

'He left.'

'What do you mean? Where did he go?'

'He got a telegram this morning about a flying job. He caught a boat out of here two hours ago.'

Dagmar gasped for breath. 'You're lying!' She wanted to punch Edvin right in his sneering face.

'You don't have to believe me,' he said, turning away. 'But he's gone.'

She gazed out over the water in the direction that Hermann must have departed, and she swore that she would find him. He would be hers, no matter how long it took. Because they were meant to be together.

❖

Erica felt a twinge of guilt even though she hadn't actually lied to Patrik, she just hadn't told him the whole truth. Last night she had wanted to discuss her plans with him, but she couldn't find the right moment. And besides, he was in such a peculiar mood. When she'd asked about his day, he had avoided telling her anything and they'd ended up spending the evening in silence in front of the TV. So she'd worry about it later when she had to explain where she'd been.

Erica sped up and turned the boat to port. She thought with gratitude of her father, Tore, who had taught his daughters to steer a boat. It was an obligation, he always said, to know how to handle a boat if you lived near the sea. And if Erica was being honest, she was better than Patrik when it came to docking, even though she let him do it, for the sake of peace in the house. Men had such fragile egos.

She waved to one of the Coast Guard boats heading towards Fjällbacka. It seemed to be coming from Valö, and she wondered why it had gone out there. But she quickly dismissed the thought as she focused on docking the boat, elegantly sliding it up to the wharf. To her surprise she was feeling nervous. After devoting so much time to the story, it felt a little strange to be meeting one of the main characters in real life. She picked up her handbag and jumped ashore.

It had been ages since she'd been out to Valö. Like most natives of Fjällbacka, she associated the island with camps and school expeditions. She could almost smell the grilled pigs-in-a-blanket on skewers as she walked among the trees.

As she drew close to the house, she stopped in surprise at the feverish activity going on there. Standing on the steps was a familiar figure, waving his arms about. She started walking towards him, picking up her pace until she was practically jogging.

'Hi, Torbjörn!' She waved and finally caught his attention. 'What are you lot doing out here?'

He stared at her in astonishment. 'Erica? I could ask you the same question. Does Patrik know you're here?'

'I don't think so. But tell me what you're doing.'

Torbjörn seemed to be considering how much to tell her.

'The owners made a discovery inside the house yesterday, when they were working on the renovation,' he said at last.

'A discovery? Did they find the family that disappeared? Where?'

Torbjörn shook his head. 'I'm afraid that's all I can tell you.'

'Could I come in and have a look?' She started to climb the steps.

'No, I'm sorry. I can't let anyone come in. We can't have unauthorized people running around while we're working.' He smiled. 'I assume you've come to see the couple that lives here. They're out back, in the yard.'

Erica retreated. 'Okay,' she said, unable to hide her disappointment.

She walked along the side of the house, and when she

112

turned the corner, she saw a man and a woman who seemed to be about the same age as herself. They were staring at the house, their expressions grim. They were not talking to each other.

Erica paused for a moment. She'd been so full of enthusiasm and curiosity that she hadn't given any thought as to how she would explain the purpose of her visit. But her hesitation lasted only a few seconds. It was part of her job, after all, to ask nosy questions and root around in other people's secrets and tragedies. She had long ago conquered her own doubts, and she knew that afterwards many of the family members had liked her books. Besides, it was always easier when the incident, as in this case, had happened in the distant past. Usually by this time the wounds had healed and the tragedies had begun to be transformed into history.

'Hi!' she called, and the couple turned to look at her. Then the woman gave her a smile of recognition.

'I know you. You're Erica Falck. I've read all your books, and I love them,' she said. Then she abruptly fell silent, as if embarrassed at being so forward.

'Hi. You must be Ebba.' Erica shook her hand. It felt so vulnerable in her grasp, but the calluses on the palm bore witness to how hard she'd been working on the renovation. 'I'm so glad you like my books.'

Still a bit shy, Ebba introduced her husband, and Erica shook hands with him too.

'Perfect timing,' said Ebba as she sat down again and then waited for Erica to take a seat too.

'What do you mean?'

'Well, I assume that you want to write about my family disappearing. So you've come on the right day.'

'I heard that you found something in the house,' said Erica.

'Yes, we discovered it when we broke up the floor in

113

the dining room,' said Tobias. 'We weren't sure what it was, but it looked like blood. The police came and had a look, and they decided to investigate closer. That's why all these people are here.'

Erica began to understand why Patrik had been so evasive when she asked him what had happened. She wondered what he thought about all this, whether he suspected that the family had been killed in the dining room and then their bodies taken away. She wanted to ask the couple whether they'd found anything other than blood, but she restrained herself.

'It must be terribly upsetting for you. I can't deny that the case has interested me, but for you, Ebba, it's so personal.'

Ebba shook her head. 'I was so young at the time, I don't remember my family. I can't grieve for people that I don't remember. It's not like . . .' She stopped and looked away.

'I think my husband, Patrik Hedström, was one of the police officers who was out here. And he came to see you on Saturday too. I heard that you were the victims of a nasty incident.'

'That's one way to describe it. And it was definitely nasty. I can't understand why anyone would want to harm us.' Tobias threw out his hands.

'Patrik thinks it might have something to do with what happened here in 1974,' said Erica before she could stop herself. She swore under her breath, knowing how furious Patrik would be if it turned out her revelation could have an impact on the investigation.

'How could it be related? That happened so long ago.' Ebba turned to gaze at the house. From where they were sitting, they couldn't see what was going on, but they could hear the sound of wood splitting as the floor was broken apart.

'If it's okay with you, I'd like to ask a few questions about the disappearance,' said Erica.

Ebba nodded. 'Sure. As I said to your husband, I don't think I have much to contribute, but go ahead and ask.'

'Would it be all right if I record our conversation?' Erica said as she removed a tape recorder from her handbag.

Tobias cast an enquiring glance at Ebba, who shrugged. 'I don't mind.'

As the tape began rolling, Erica felt her stomach tingle with anticipation. She hadn't sought out Ebba when she lived in Göteborg, even though she'd often thought about it. But now she was right here, and maybe Erica could find out some detail that would move her research forward.

'Do you have anything left that belonged to your parents? Any items you took with you from here?'

'No, nothing. My adoptive parents told me that I had only a little suitcase filled with clothes when I came to them. And I don't think I brought it from here. According to Mamma, some nice people sewed the clothes for me and embroidered my initials on them. I still have those clothes. Mamma saved them for me in case I ever had a daughter of my own.'

'No letters? No photographs?' asked Erica.

'No. I've never seen any.'

'Did your parents have any relatives who might have kept things like that?'

'No one. I told that to your husband too. From what I understand, my grandparents on both sides were dead, and apparently my parents had no siblings. If there are any distant relatives, they've never tried to contact me. And no one wanted to take me in.'

That sounded terribly sad, and Erica gave her a sympathetic look, but Ebba smiled.

'There's no need to feel sorry for me. I have a mother

115

and a father who love me, and two wonderful siblings. I've never wanted for anything.'

Erica returned her smile. 'Not many people can say that.'

She could feel herself warming to this petite woman sitting across from her.

'Do you know much about your biological parents?'

'No. I suppose I've never really been interested in finding out. Of course I've always wondered what happened, but I suppose I didn't want to let any of that into my own life. Maybe I worried that if I showed an interest in my biological parents it might make Mamma and Pappa feel as if they weren't good enough.'

'Do you think you'd be more interested in tracking down your roots if the two of you had children of your own?' asked Erica cautiously. She didn't know much about Ebba and Tobias, and this might be a sensitive issue.

'We had a son,' said Ebba.

Erica flinched as if she'd been slapped. That was not the answer she was expecting. She wanted to ask more, but Ebba's body language clearly showed that she had no intention of discussing this topic.

'You might say that moving here was one way for Ebba to seek out her roots,' said Tobias.

He nervously shifted position on the bench, and Erica noticed that the couple had unconsciously moved away from each other, as if they couldn't bear to be too close. The mood was suddenly tense, and she felt like an intruder, witnessing something very private.

'I've been doing some research about your family history, and I've found out quite a lot. Just let me know if you're interested in seeing what I discovered. I have all my notes at home,' she said.

'That's nice of you,' said Ebba without enthusiasm, as if what energy she'd possessed had drained out of her.

Realizing there was no use continuing the conversation, Erica stood up.

'Thank you for taking the time to talk to me. I'll get back to you again, or you can always call me.' She took out her notebook to write down her phone number and email address. Then she tore off the page and handed it to them. She turned off the tape recorder and put it back in her handbag.

'You know where to find us. All we do is work on the house twenty-four seven,' said Tobias.

'That's what I heard. Can you do all the work yourselves?'

'That's what we planned. At least as much as possible.'

'If you know anyone around with an eye for interior design, let us know,' Ebba interjected. 'Tobias and I are hopeless at that sort of thing.'

Erica was about to say she didn't know of anyone when an idea came to her.

'I know a great person who I'm sure could help out. Let me get back to you about it.'

She said goodbye and walked around to the front of the house. Torbjörn was standing outside, giving instructions to two members of his team.

'How's it going?' called Erica, trying to be heard over the whine of a chainsaw.

'None of your business,' yelled Torbjörn. 'But I'll ring your husband and give him my report later on. So you can ask him about it tonight.'

Erica laughed and waved. As she walked down to the dock, her expression turned serious. What had happened to the Elvander family's belongings? Why did Ebba and Tobias behave so oddly towards each other? What happened to their son? And most important of all: Were they telling the truth when they said they had no idea who had tried to burn down the house? The conversation with Ebba may not have been as productive as she'd hoped, but her mind was a whirl of activity as she started up the boat and headed for home.

Gösta was muttering to himself. Mellberg's criticism didn't really bother him, but it seemed so unnecessary to complain about the fact that he'd taken home investigative material. Wasn't it more important that he'd saved everybody a lot of time? It was difficult to find information that had been gathered in the days before computers were in common use, and he'd spared them the job of wading through the archives in search of the files.

He set pen and paper next to him and opened the first folder. How many hours of his life had he spent studying these photographs, going through the interview transcripts and the reports from the crime scene inspection? Yet if they were to do this properly, he had to be as methodical as possible. Patrik had assigned him the task of making a list and prioritizing who they should re-interview from the original investigation. They couldn't talk to everybody at once, so it was important that they started with the key witnesses.

Gösta slumped on his chair as he ploughed through the interviews, which said so little. Since he had read them countless times before, he knew there was nothing concrete to be gleaned from them. It was a matter of focusing on the nuances and reading between the lines. But he was having a hard time concentrating. His thoughts kept shifting to the little lass who had grown into a woman. It had been very odd to see her again and to have a flesh-and-blood image to add to the one he had conjured up in his imagination.

He shifted on his chair impatiently. It had been years since he'd shown any interest in his work, and for all that he was keen to do this task right, his brain didn't want to obey the new instructions he was trying to send. He put the reports aside and instead went slowly through the photographs, which included a picture of the boys who had stayed at the school over the holiday. Gösta closed his eyes and thought back to that sunny but chilly day before Easter Sunday in 1974. He and his now deceased colleague, Henry Ljung, had walked up towards the big white house. Everything was so quiet, almost eerily quiet, or maybe that was just something he imagined after the fact. But he definitely remembered shivering as they made their way along the path. He and Henry had exchanged glances, uncertain what they would encounter after the strange phone call to the station. The police chief at the time had assigned the two of them to check it out. 'It's probably some kids playing a joke on us,' he said and then sent them off – mostly so his back would be covered if, against all odds, it turned out to be something more than a childish prank by some bored rich kids. They'd had a lot of problems at the start of the autumn term when the school opened, but after the police chief gave Rune Elvander a call, the trouble had stopped. Gösta had no idea how the headmaster had managed it, but whatever he'd done, it had worked. Until now.

He and Henry had come to a halt outside the front door. Not a sound could be heard from inside. Then the loud, shrill cries of a child pierced the silence and roused them from the temporary inertia that seemed to have settled over them. They knocked once and then went in. 'Hello?' called Gösta. And now, as he sat here at his desk in the station so many years later, he wondered how he was able to remember everything in such detail. Nobody had replied, but the child's cries got louder. They hurried towards the sound and then stopped abruptly as they entered the dining room. A little girl was tottering about

119

all alone, crying her heart out. Instinctively Gösta rushed over and picked her up.

'Where's the rest of the family?' said Henry, peering around. 'Hello?' he shouted and then went back to the hall.

No answer.

'I'll check upstairs,' he said, and Gösta nodded, fully occupied with trying to soothe the little girl.

He'd never held a child before, so he was uncertain what to do to make her stop crying. Awkwardly he rocked her in his arms, stroking her back and humming a tune. To his surprise, it worked. The little girl's cries subsided to a few sobs, and he could feel her chest rise and fall as she leaned her head on his shoulder. Gösta continued to rock her as he hummed, filled with emotions that he couldn't put into words.

Henry came back into the dining room shaking his head. 'There's nobody up there either.'

'Where could they have gone? How could they leave such a little girl all alone? Something terrible could have happened to her.'

'Yes, and who the hell made that phone call?' Henry took off his cap and scratched his head.

'Do you think they've gone out for a walk around the island?' Gösta cast a sceptical glance at the table with the half-eaten Easter food. 'But in the middle of lunch? They must be pretty odd to do something like that.'

'That's for sure.' Henry put his cap back on. 'And what's this sweet little girl doing here all alone?' he cooed, moving towards the child in Gösta's arms.

She immediately started to cry, clinging so tightly to Gösta's neck that he could hardly breathe.

'Leave her alone,' he said, taking a step back.

A sense of warm contentment filled his chest, and he wondered if this was what it would have been like if their boy had lived – the son that he and Maj-Britt had had. He quickly dismissed the thought. He had made up his mind not to think about what might have been.

'Was their boat down there?' he asked after a moment when the child had stopped crying.

Henry frowned. 'There was a boat tied up at the dock, but don't they have two? I think they bought Sten-Ivar's boat last fall, and all I saw was the Fiberglas boat. But would they really set off in the boat and leave the little girl behind? Surely they can't be that crazy, even if they are city folk.'

'Inez is from here,' Gösta automatically corrected him. 'Her family is from Fjällbacka and goes back generations.'

Henry sighed. 'Well, it's definitely strange. I suppose we'll have to take the child to the mainland with us and then wait for somebody to show up.' He turned to leave.

'The table is set for six,' said Gösta.

'Yes, but it's the Easter holiday, so presumably only the family are here.'

'Should we leave things like this?' The situation was odd, to say the least, and the departure from routine made Gösta uneasy. He paused to think. 'Okay, we'll do as you suggest and take the girl with us. If we don't hear from anyone, we'll come out here tomorrow. If they're not back by that time, we'll have to assume that something has happened to them. And in that case, this is a crime scene.'

Still not sure that they were doing the right thing, they went outside, closing the front door behind them. They walked down towards the dock, and when they were only a short distance away, they saw a boat approaching on the water.

'Look, there's Sten-Ivar's boat,' said Henry, pointing.

'I can see several people in the boat. Maybe that's the rest of the family.'

'If it is, I'm going to give them a piece of my mind. How could they leave this little girl here like this? They deserve a good thrashing.'

Henry strode down to the dock. Gösta had to jog to keep up, but he didn't dare go any faster for fear of stumbling and dropping the child. The boat pulled up to the dock, and a boy who looked about fifteen jumped out. He had raven-black hair and he was glaring at them angrily.

'What are you doing with Ebba?' he snarled.

'And who might you be?' asked Henry when the boy took up position in front of him, his hands on his hips.

Four more boys climbed out of the boat and came over to Henry and Gösta, who had now joined his colleague.

'Where are Inez and Rune?' asked the boy with the black hair. The others stood behind him, silently waiting. It was clear that he was the leader of the group.

'That's what we'd like to know too,' said Gösta. 'Somebody rang the police station to say that something had happened here, and when we arrived, we found the girl all alone in the house.'

The boy stared at him in surprise. 'Ebba was all alone?'

So her name is Ebba, thought Gösta. This little girl whose heart was beating fast against his own.

'Are you Rune's students?' Henry now wanted to know, speaking with the voice of authority, but the boy didn't seem intimidated. He calmly stared at the officer and replied politely:

'We're pupils at the school. We're staying here over the holiday.'

'Where have you been?' Gösta gave them a stern glare.

'We went out in the boat early this morning. The family was going to have Easter lunch, but we weren't invited. So we went out fishing instead, to "build character".'

'Catch anything?' Henry's tone of voice showed that he didn't believe the boy's story.

'We caught a whole shitload of fish,' replied the boy, pointing at the boat.

Gösta looked in that direction and saw the towline tied firmly to the stern.

'You'll need to come with us to the station until we work out what's going on,' said Henry, leading the way to his own boat.

'Can't we wash up first? We're filthy, and we stink of fish,' said one of the boys, sounding alarmed.

'Do as the officer said,' snapped the boy who seemed to be in charge. 'Of course we'll go along. I apologize if we've been rude. It made us nervous to see strangers with Ebba. My name is Leon Kreutz.' He reached out to shake hands with Gösta.

Henry had already gone on board the boat and was waiting for them. Holding Ebba in his arms, Gösta followed the boys. He cast one last glance up at the house. Where on earth was the family? What had happened here?

Gösta returned to the present. His memories were so vivid that he could almost feel the warmth of the little girl in his arms. He sat up straight and pulled a photo from the stack. The picture was taken at the station on that Easter eve. It showed the five boys: Leon Kreutz, Sebastian Månsson, John Holm, Percy von Bahrn, and Josef Meyer. Their hair was dishevelled, their clothes dirty, their expressions sombre. All except Leon. He was smiling cheerfully at the camera, and he looked older than his sixteen years. He was a handsome boy, almost beautiful, Gösta realized as he stared at the old photo. He hadn't really given it much thought back then. He leafed through the investigative material. Leon Kreutz. I wonder what he's done with his life? Gösta jotted down a note. Of the five boys, it was Leon who had left the strongest impression on his memory. He'd be a good person to start with.

FJÄLLBACKA 1920

The girl cried constantly, day and night, and even if Dagmar put her hands over her ears and roared, she couldn't drown out the sound. All she heard was the child screaming and the neighbours pounding on the wall.

This was not how it was supposed to be. She could still feel his hands on her body, see his eyes as she lay naked in bed beside him. She was convinced that her feelings had been returned, so something must have happened to him. Otherwise he would not have left her to this life of poverty and degradation. Maybe he'd been forced to return to Germany. No doubt they needed him there. He was a hero who had dutifully responded when summoned by his homeland, regardless of the heartbreak he must endure at leaving her behind.

Before she realized that she was with child, she had searched for him, using every means possible. She'd written letters to the German legation in Stockholm and asked everyone she met whether they knew of the war hero Hermann Göring and what had happened to him. When he found out that she had given birth to his child, he was bound to return. No matter how important his work in Germany, he would drop everything to rescue her and Laura. He would never allow her to live in such misery, among these loathsome people who looked down on her and refused to believe her story when she told them who Laura's father was. They would be surprised when Hermann stood outside her door, so handsome in his pilot's uniform, holding his arms open wide and with a fancy automobile waiting.

The child cried louder and louder in her cradle, and Dagmar felt anger surge inside of her. She had no peace, not even for a few minutes. The baby was wilfully doing this, that was clear from the expression on her face. As tiny as she was, she displayed the same scorn for Dagmar as everyone else did. Dagmar hated them all. Let them burn in hell, every single gossip-monger and every lecherous bastard who, in spite of their jeers, came to her in the night, paying her a pittance to stick it inside her. They would lie on top of her, groaning and rooting around – she seemed to be good enough for that.

Dagmar threw off the blanket and went into the cramped kitchen. Every surface was covered with dirty dishes, and a fetid odour rose up from the rotting scraps of leftover food. She opened the door to the pantry. It was empty except for a bottle of rubbing alcohol that a chemist had given her. She picked it up and took it back to bed with her. The child was still crying, and the neighbours were again pounding on the wall, but Dagmar didn't care. She coaxed the cork out, used the sleeve of her nightgown to wipe off the mouth of the bottle, and then took a good swig. If she drank enough, all the persistent sounds around her would disappear.

With a sense of anticipation, Josef opened the door to Sebastian's work room. On the desk lay the drawings for the site where he hoped the museum would stand in the not too distant future.

'Congratulations!' said Sebastian, coming forward to greet him. 'The local council has agreed to support the project.' He slapped Josef on the back.

'Good,' said Josef. He really hadn't expected anything else. How could they say no to such an amazing opportunity? 'When can we make a start?'

'Take it easy. I don't think you realize how much work we've got ahead of us. We have to begin producing the peace symbols, plan the construction, draw up a budget. Above all, we have to raise plenty of cash.'

'But the widow Grünewald is giving us the land, and we've had lots of donations. And since you're the contractor, aren't you the one who decides when work gets under way?'

Sebastian laughed. 'Just because it's my company, it doesn't mean we can build it for free. I have to pay the workers' wages, and we need to buy materials. This is going to be an expensive project.' He tapped his finger on the drawings. 'I'll have to bring in subcontractors, and they won't work for nothing. Not like me.'

Josef sighed and sat down on a chair. To say he was sceptical about Sebastian's motives would be putting it mildly.

'We'll start with the granite,' said Sebastian, propping his feet on the desk. 'I've drawn up a few cool sketches of how the peace symbols could look. Then we need to produce some clever marketing materials and put together a good package, and then we can start selling the whole damn thing.' He grinned when he saw Josef's expression.

'Go ahead and laugh. For you, it's all about money. Don't you understand the symbolic value of this? The granite was supposed to have been a part of the Third Reich, but instead it's going to be a testimony to the Nazis' defeat and the fact that the forces of good were victorious. We can make something out of that, and by extension create this—' Josef pointed at the drawings. He was so angry that he was practically shaking.

Sebastian's grin stretched even wider. He threw out his hands.

'Nobody's forcing you to work with me. We can tear up our agreement right here and now, and you're free to go to anybody you like.'

The thought was tempting, and for a moment Josef considered doing just that. Then he slumped on his chair. He needed to complete this project. Up until now he'd wasted his life. He had nothing to show to the world, nothing that would honour the memory of his parents.

'You know very well that you're the only one I can turn to,' he said at last.

'And we're going to stick together.' Sebastian took his feet down from the desk and leaned forward. 'We've known each other for a long time. We're brothers, and you understand how I am. I always want to help out a brother.'

'Sure, we're going to stick together,' said Josef. He gave Sebastian a searching look. 'Did you hear that Leon is back?'

'I heard a vague rumour. Imagine seeing him here again. And Ia. I never thought that would happen.'

'Apparently they've bought a house that was for sale above Brandparken.'

'They've got the cash, so why not? By the way, maybe Leon would like to invest. Have you asked him?'

Josef shook his head. He'd do anything to push forward the work on the museum. Anything except approaching Leon.

'I saw Percy yesterday,' said Sebastian laconically.

'How's he doing?' Josef was happy to change the subject. 'Does he still own the manor?'

'Yes, he's lucky that Fygelsta is an entailed estate. If he had to share the inheritance with his siblings, he'd have been broke long ago. But it sounds as though his funds have run out for good, and that's why he contacted me. To ask for a little temporary help, as he put it.' Sebastian sketched quote marks in the air. 'Evidently the tax authorities are after him, and they're not the sort that you can charm with noble ancestors and a fancy name.'

'Are you going to help him out?'

'Don't look so worried. I haven't decided yet. But as I said, I always like to help a brother, and Percy is my brother just as much as you are. Right?'

'Of course,' said Josef, gazing out of the window at the water. They were brothers for all eternity, united by darkness. His eyes returned to the drawings. The dark would be driven away by light. He would do it for his father's sake, and his own.

*   *   *

'What's going on with Martin?' Patrik was standing in the doorway to Annika's office. He didn't like to pry, but it was obvious something was wrong. It was making him uneasy.

Annika turned to face him, clasping her hands in her lap.

'I can't say anything. When Martin is ready, he'll tell you.'

Patrik sighed, and all sorts of thoughts whirled through his head as he sat down on the visitor's chair next to the door.

'So what do you think about this case?'

'I think you're right.' Annika was clearly relieved that Patrik had chosen to change the subject. 'The fire and the disappearance are connected in some way. And considering what was discovered under the floor, it seems likely that somebody was afraid Ebba and her husband would find it as they were renovating the house.'

'My dear wife has been fascinated by the story of the missing family for a long time.'

'And now you're worried that she's going to stick her sweet nose in the investigation,' Annika added.

'You could put it that way, but I'm hoping Erica's smart enough not to interfere this time.'

Annika smiled, and Patrik realized that he didn't believe his own words.

'She probably has a lot of interesting background information, since she's so good at doing research. Provided she can manage to keep a low profile when it comes to the actual investigation, she might actually be able to help us out,' said Annika.

'Except that she's not very good at keeping a low profile.'

'But she *is* good at taking care of herself. So where are you planning to start?'

'I'm not sure.' Patrik crossed his legs and absentmindedly fidgeted with the toe of his shoe. 'We need to interview everybody who was involved when it happened. Gösta is getting us contact information for all the teachers and students. The most important thing is to have a talk with those five boys who were on the island that day. I've asked Gösta to prioritize the list of individuals and decide who he thinks we should interview first. Then I was thinking that you could do background checks, based on what Gösta finds out. I don't have the greatest faith in his organizational abilities, so I really should have asked you to work with him on this assignment. But he's the one who knows most about the case.'

'At least he seems very keen to pursue the investigation. For a change,' said Annika. 'And I think I know why. I've heard that he and his wife took in the little Elvander girl for a while.'

'Ebba lived with Gösta?'

'That's what I've heard.'

'That explains why he was acting so strange out there on the island.' Patrik recalled the way Gösta had looked at Ebba. How he had behaved, touching her arm.

'That's probably why he hasn't ever been able to forget about the case. Apparently they got very attached to the little girl.' Annika's gaze fell on the large framed photo of Leia that she kept on her desk.

'That makes sense,' said Patrik. There was so much that he didn't know, so much he needed to find out about what happened back then on Valö. Suddenly the task ahead of him seemed daunting. Was it really possible to solve this old case after all these years? And how urgent was it?

'Do you think the person who tried to burn down the house will try again?' asked Annika, as if she had read his thoughts.

Patrik pondered the question. Then he nodded.

'It's possible. We can't afford to take any risks. We'll

have to work fast to find out what really happened on that Easter Eve. Whoever it was that tried to hurt Ebba and Tobias must be stopped before they strike again.'

Anna stood naked in front of the mirror, tears welling up in her eyes. She didn't recognize herself. Slowly she raised her hand to touch her hair. When it grew out again after the accident, her hair was darker and more wiry than before, and it was still much shorter. A visit to the hairdresser might fix things, but the idea didn't appeal to her. A new hairstyle wasn't going to change her body.

With a trembling hand she traced the scars that ran across her skin, forming a criss-crossing map. The lines had faded a bit, but they would never disappear completely. Listlessly she pinched the roll of fat at her waist. She'd always managed to stay thin with minimum effort, and she'd been so proud of her figure. Now she gazed with disgust at her plump flesh. Because of her injuries, she hadn't been able to move around much, and she hadn't cared what she stuffed in her mouth. Anna raised her head to study her face, hardly daring to meet her own eyes. Thanks to the children and to Dan, she'd fought her way back to life, out of a darkness that had been worse than anything she'd ever experienced, worse even than those years with Lucas. The question now was whether it had been worth it. She didn't yet know the answer.

The sound of the doorbell startled her. She was home alone, so she would have to go and see who it was. Taking one last look at her body, she threw on her comfy clothes, which lay in a heap on the floor, and rushed downstairs. When she saw Erica standing outside the door, she was filled with relief.

'Hi, what's going on?' said Erica.

'Nothing much. Come in. Where are the kids?'

'At home. Kristina is babysitting. I had a few things

that I needed to get done. So I thought I'd drop by before I head back there.'

'Good idea,' said Anna and led the way to the kitchen to make coffee. Again she pictured her plump white flesh in the mirror, but then she pushed the image aside and took some chocolate macaroons out of the fridge.

'Oh, no, I daren't eat any of those,' said Erica with a frown. 'I put on a bikini over the weekend, and it was not a pleasant sight.'

'How can you say that? You look great,' said Anna, unable to hide a hint of bitterness. Erica followed her outside to the small patio at the back of the house.

'Nice lawn furniture. Is it new?' She ran her hand over the white-painted wood.

'Yes, we found them at Paulssons, near the old Evas Livs supermarket, you know.'

'You're really good at finding nice things,' said Erica, positive that Anna was going to like the idea she'd come up with.

'Thanks. So where have you been today?'

'Out at the summer camp,' said Erica. And she told her sister about the visit.

'How exciting. So they've found blood but no bodies? Something must have happened there, at any rate.'

'It certainly seems that way.' Erica reached for a macaroon. She picked up a knife to divide it in half, but changed her mind and set the knife down. She took a bite of the pastry.

'Big smile,' said Anna, for a moment feeling a warm surge of childish glee.

Erica understood exactly what she was thinking and smiled broadly, showing her teeth covered with chocolate.

'Check this out,' she then said, taking two straws from the tray. She stuck one in each nostril and crossed her eyes, smiling again to reveal her brown teeth.

Anna couldn't help giggling. She remembered how she'd loved it whenever her big sister acted silly when they were kids. Erica had always been so grown up and serious, more like a mother than an older sister.

'I bet you can't drink through your nose like you used to,' said Erica.

'Of course I can,' replied Anna, insulted. She stuck a straw in each nostril, then leaned forward and put the straws in the glass. She breathed in through her nose. When the juice reached her nostrils, she started coughing and sneezing uncontrollably, and Erica burst out laughing.

'What on earth are the two of you doing?'

Dan had arrived without them hearing, and when they saw his expression, the sisters collapsed with laughter. They pointed at each other and tried to explain, but they were laughing so much they couldn't manage a single word.

'I can see that I should never come home un-announced.' Dan shook his head and left.

Finally they calmed down, and Anna noticed that the lump in the pit of her stomach had eased a bit. She and Erica had had their differences over the years, but nobody could affect her as deeply as her sister. No one could make her as angry as Erica did, but no one could make her so happy either. They were for ever linked by an invisible bond, and Anna realized how much she needed her sister as she sat across from Erica and wiped the tears of laughter from her eyes.

'After he's seen you like this, you better not count on any hugs and kisses tonight,' said Erica.

Anna snorted. 'I doubt it'll make the slightest differ-ence. But let's change the subject. It seems a little inces-tuous to talk about my sex life when my fiancé used to sleep with my sister . . .'

'Good Lord, that was a hundred years ago. To be honest, I can't remember what he looks like naked.'

Anna made a show of sticking her fingers in her ears, and Erica shook her head, laughing.

'Okay, I promise. Let's talk about something totally different.'

Anna took her fingers from her ears. 'So tell me more about Valö. What's the daughter like? What's her name? Ebba?'

'Yes, Ebba,' said Erica. 'She's living there with her husband, Tobias. They're planning to renovate the place and open a bed and breakfast.'

'Do you think they can make a go of it? The tourist season is short here.'

'I haven't a clue, but I suspect they're not doing it for the money. The project seems to have a different purpose.'

'Well, it might work. The place does have potential.'

'I know. And that's where you come in.' Erica pointed at her sister, a hint of excitement in her voice.

'Me?' said Anna. 'How did I get mixed up in this?'

'You're not. At least, not yet. But you could be. I've had the most amazing idea.'

'So modest, as always,' giggled Anna, but her curiosity was aroused.

'Ebba and Tobias were actually the ones who brought up the subject. They're good at doing the renovation and manual labour, but they need help with the finishing touches, creating the right sort of ambience. And you're exactly who they need: you have a flair for interior design, you know antiques, and you have good taste. So you're the perfect person for the job!' Erica caught her breath and then took a sip of juice.

Anna could hardly believe her ears. This might be a way to find out if she could work as a freelance interior designer. This could be her first consulting job. She could feel the smile forming on her face.

'What did you tell them? Do you think they want to hire

somebody? Can they afford it? What sort of style do you think they have in mind? It doesn't have to cost a lot of money. In fact, it would be more fun to go around to country auctions and source good furniture and odds and ends at knockdown prices. I'd think that out there on the island a rather old-fashioned, romantic style would work best, and I know where to get hold of some beautiful fabrics, and . . .'

Erica raised her hand.

'Hey, calm down! The answer is no – I didn't tell them about you. All I said was that I might know someone who could help. I have no idea what their budget is, but why don't you give them a call? Then we could head out there together and have a meeting with them, if they're interested.'

Anna narrowed her eyes and looked at Erica.

'You just want an excuse to go out there again and snoop around.'

'Maybe . . . But I also think it's a brilliant idea for you to meet them. You'd be terrific at this kind of project.'

'It's true that I've been thinking about starting some sort of business of my own.'

'So let's go! I'll give you their number, and you can call them yourself.'

Anna sensed a spark of something new ignite inside of her. Enthusiasm. That was probably the word that best described it. For the first time in ages she felt truly enthusiastic.

'Okay, give me the number before I change my mind,' she said, picking up her mobile.

The interview continued to bother him. It was so frustrating to have to watch what he said and not speak his mind. The journalist he'd talked to this morning was an idiot. Most people were idiots. They refused to see things as they really were, which made his responsibility even greater.

'Do you think the party will suffer any damage?' John Holm twirled his wine glass in his hands.

His wife shrugged. 'Probably not. It's not one of the major newspapers.' She tucked her hair behind her ear and put on her glasses to start reading through the stack of documents in front of her.

'It doesn't take much for an interview to get picked up by other papers. They're after us like hawks, always alert for the smallest reason to attack.'

Liv peered at him over the top of her reading glasses. 'Don't tell me that you're surprised. You know who has the power over the media in this country.'

Holm nodded. 'No need to preach to the choir.'

'But after the next election, things are going to be different. People will finally wake up to what's happening in our society.' She gave him a triumphant smile and went back to leafing through the documents.

'I wish I had your faith. Sometimes I wonder whether the public will ever understand. Have Swedes grown too lazy and stupid, too multicultural and degenerate to comprehend that the monster is spreading? They might have too little pure blood flowing in their veins for us to have anything worth working for.'

Liv stopped reading. Her eyes glinted as she sized up her husband.

'Now listen here, John. Ever since we met, you've had a very clear goal. You've always known what you have to do, what you're destined to do. If no one listens – well, then you need to speak louder. If someone questions your views – well, then you need to present a better argument. We finally have a seat in parliament, and it's the people, the very people that you're now doubting, who have seen fit to put us there. Forget about some minor journalist quibbling over our budget figures. We know that we're right, and that's the only thing that matters.'

Holm smiled at her. 'You sound exactly the same as when I met you at the youth association. Although I have to say that you look better with hair than without.' He went over and kissed the top of her head.

Aside from her quick temper and fierce rhetoric, there was nothing about his aloof, fashionably dressed wife to remind him of the skinhead in military garb that he'd fallen in love with. But he loved her more than ever now.

'It's an article in a local paper, that's all.' Liv squeezed his hand, which he'd placed on her shoulder.

'I suppose you're right,' said Holm, but he couldn't rid himself of an uneasy feeling. He had to carry out the plan he'd set for himself. The monster had to be rooted out, and it was his job to do that. He only wished he had more time.

The bathroom tiles felt wonderful against her forehead. Ebba closed her eyes and let the cool sensation wash over her.

'Aren't you coming to bed soon?'

She heard Tobias's voice from the bedroom but didn't answer. She didn't want to go to bed. Every time she lay down next to Tobias, she felt as if she were betraying Vincent. The first month she couldn't bear to be in the same house with him. She couldn't even look at Tobias, and if she happened to catch his eye in the mirror, she would turn her face away. She felt nothing but guilt.

Her parents had taken care of her around the clock, watching over her as if she were a baby. They had talked to her, pleaded with her, telling her that she and Tobias needed each other. Finally she had started to believe them, and then she decided to relent because it was easier.

Slowly and reluctantly she had drawn closer to him. She moved home. They had spent those first weeks in silence, afraid of what would happen if they began talking to each other and said something that could never be taken back. Then they'd started to say ordinary things.

'Please pass the butter.'

'Have you done the laundry?'

Harmless, innocent subjects that couldn't provoke any accusations. Over time their sentences got longer, and they found more safe topics for conversation. They had started talking about Valö. Tobias was the one who'd suggested that they should move there. But she too had viewed it as an opportunity to leave behind everything that would remind them of a different life. A life that may not have been perfect, but at least it was happy.

As she sat there with her eyes closed and her forehead pressed against the bathroom tiles, for the first time she began to question whether they'd done the right thing. The house was sold, the house where Vincent had lived his whole, brief life. The place where they had changed his nappies; spent nights walking about, holding him in their arms; where he had learned to crawl, walk, and talk. The house was no longer theirs, and she wondered whether they'd actually made a decision or had simply moved away.

And now they were here. In a house where they might not even be safe, and where the entire dining-room floor had been broken apart because her family had been obliterated in there. It was affecting her more than she was willing to admit. When she was growing up she hadn't devoted much time to speculating about her roots. But she couldn't go on pushing her past aside. Seeing that dark stain that had been hidden under the floorboards, she had experienced a terrible clarity. This was not some vague enigma, it was all too real. Her mother and father had presumably died on that very spot, and for some strange reason, that seemed more real than the discovery that someone may have been trying to kill her and Tobias. She didn't know how she was going to handle this reality, living right in the midst of it, but there was nowhere else to go.

'Ebba?'

She could hear in his voice that if she didn't answer he would come looking for her. So she lifted her head and called towards the door:

'I'm almost done!'

She took her time brushing her teeth as she studied herself in the mirror. Tonight she didn't look away. She stared at this woman with the dead expression, at the mother who had no child. Then she spat into the sink and wiped her mouth on a towel.

'That took you long enough.' Tobias was holding a book open, but she noticed that he was on the same page as last night.

She didn't reply, just lifted the covers and crawled into bed. Tobias put his book down on the bedside table and turned off the lamp. The blinds that they'd put up when they moved in made the room pitch-black, even though it never got completely dark outside.

Ebba lay there motionless, staring up at the ceiling. She felt Tobias's hand fumbling for hers. She pretended not to notice, but he didn't withdraw his hand, as he usually did. Instead, it inched towards her thigh, gently moved under her T-shirt to stroke her stomach. She felt the nausea rise in her throat as his hand purposefully continued upward, grazing her breast. The same breast that had given Vincent milk, the same nipples that his tiny mouth had so hungrily suckled.

Bile filled her mouth, and she leaped out of bed, rushing for the bathroom. She barely managed to lift the lid of the toilet before her stomach turned inside out. When she was done, she collapsed weakly on the floor. From the bedroom she could hear that Tobias was crying.

FJÄLLBACKA 1925

Dagmar stared at the newspaper lying on the ground. Laura was tugging at her sleeve, saying over and over 'Mamma, Mamma,' but Dagmar paid her no mind. She was so tired of hearing that demanding, whining voice, and the word was repeated so often that she thought it would drive her mad. Slowly she leaned down and picked up the paper. It was late in the afternoon, and she was having trouble seeing clearly, but there was absolutely no doubt. In black type it said: 'German ace pilot Göring returns to Sweden.'

'Mamma, Mamma!' Laura was pulling at her even harder, and Dagmar gave her such a swat that the girl tumbled off the bench and started to cry.

'Stop your whining!' snapped Dagmar. She hated that phoney sobbing. The child lacked for nothing. She had a roof over her head, clothes to wear, and she wasn't starving, although they had little enough at times.

Dagmar returned to the article, haltingly spelling her way through it. Her heart started pounding very fast. He'd come back, he was in Sweden, and now he would be coming to fetch her. Then her eyes fell on a sentence further down: 'Göring is moving to Sweden with his Swedish wife Carin.' Dagmar felt her mouth go dry. He'd married somebody else. He'd betrayed her! Fury rushed through her, made worse by Laura's shrill cries that were causing passers-by to turn and look at them.

'Shut up!' She slapped Laura with such force it made her hand sting.

The child fell silent, clutching her fiery red cheek and gazing at her mother, wide-eyed. Then she started sobbing again, louder than ever, as Dagmar felt despair slicing right through her. She fixed her eyes on the newspaper, re-reading the article until the name Carin Göring echoed over and over in her mind. The article didn't say how long they'd been married, but since she was Swedish, they must have met here in Sweden. Somehow this woman must have tricked Hermann into marrying her. It must be Carin's fault that Hermann hadn't come back to get Dagmar, that he couldn't be with her and their daughter, with his family.

She nodded as she crumpled up the paper and reached for the bottle on the bench beside her. Only a few dregs remained, which surprised her, since the bottle had been full that morning. But she didn't think anything more about it. She drank what was left, savouring the lovely burning sensation in her throat from the blessed liquor.

The child had stopped howling. She was sitting on the ground, sniffling, with her legs drawn up and her arms wrapped around her knees. No doubt feeling sorry for herself, as usual. Only five years old and already the girl was cunning as a fox. But Dagmar knew what had to be done. It was still possible to put everything right. Once Hermann was reunited with them, he'd soon teach Laura to behave. A father who could rule with a firm hand was exactly what that child needed, because nothing seemed to work, no matter how much Dagmar tried to beat some sense into her.

Dagmar smiled as she sat there on the bench in Brandparken. She'd worked out what was at the root of all their troubles, and now she was going to fix things for herself and for Laura.

✣

Gösta's car pulled into the driveway, and Erica sighed with relief. There had been a risk that Patrik might see him as he left for work.

She opened the door before Gösta could ring the bell. Behind her the children were making so much noise that he probably felt like he was stepping into a wall of sound.

'Sorry about all the commotion. This place is going to be condemned as a workplace any day now.' She turned around to stop Noel from chasing a sobbing Anton.

'Don't worry. I'm used to Mellberg shouting at us,' said Gösta, squatting down. 'Hi, you guys. You certainly look like a couple of rascals.'

Anton and Noel stopped in their tracks, suddenly turning shy, but Maja stepped forward boldly.

'Hi, old man. My name is Maja.'

'Maja! We don't say things like that,' Erica told her daughter, giving her a stern look.

'It's okay.' Gösta laughed loudly and stood up. 'Out of the mouths of babes and idiots – that's how we hear the truth. And I'm definitely an old man. What do you think, Maja?'

She nodded, then glared at her mother triumphantly before heading off. The twins still didn't dare come forward. Instead, they slowly backed away towards the living room without taking their eyes off Gösta.

'Those two don't exactly warm to strangers, do they?' he said as he followed Erica into the kitchen.

'Anton has always been shy. Noel, on the other hand, is usually quite outgoing, but he seems to be in a phase where he's scared of anyone he doesn't know.'

'Not a bad attitude to have, in my opinion,' said Gösta as he sat down on a kitchen chair, glancing around nervously. 'Are you certain Patrik won't be coming back for anything?'

'He left for work half an hour ago, so he's probably already over at the station.'

'I'm not sure this is such a good idea.' He traced his finger over the pattern on the tablecloth.

'I think it's a great idea,' said Erica. 'There's no need to get Patrik involved. He doesn't always appreciate my help.'

'And with good reason. Sometimes you have a tendency to get yourself mixed up in things.'

'But everything turns out well in the end.'

Erica refused to be deterred. She thought the idea she'd had last night was a stroke of genius, and she'd quickly slipped away to ring Gösta. And now here he was, although it had taken some persuasion to get him to come over without mentioning it to Patrik.

'We share a common interest, you and I,' she said, sitting down across from him. 'We're both desperate to find out what happened out on Valö during that Easter holiday.'

'Yes, but now the police are working on the case.'

'And that's good. But you know how investigations can get bogged down by all the rules and procedures police officers have to follow. I, on the other hand, am at liberty to pursue alternative methods.'

143

Gösta was still sceptical. 'That's as may be, but Patrik won't be pleased if he finds out about this, and I'm not sure that I want to—'

'That's precisely why Patrik is not going to find out,' Erica interrupted him. 'All you have to do is see to it that I get to study the case files in secret, and I'll let you in on anything that I manage to dig up. As soon as I find something, I'll pass it on to you. You present it to Patrik, and you'll be the hero of the day. After the case is closed, I use the information in one of my books. Everybody wins, especially Patrik. He wants to solve this case and catch the arsonist. He's not going to ask awkward questions. He'll just be grateful for whatever information is offered. Besides, you're short-staffed at the station, what with Martin out sick and Paula on holiday. So it won't hurt if you have an extra person working on the case.'

'I suppose.' Gösta's expression relaxed, and Erica surmised that he liked the idea of being the hero of the day. 'And you really don't think that Patrik will get suspicious?'

'Not at all. He knows how involved you are in this case; trust me, he won't suspect a thing.'

It sounded as if a riot had started up in the living room, so Erica got up and dashed out to see what was going on. After directing a few words of warning to Noel to leave Anton alone, and then switching on a Pippi Longstocking movie, things calmed down and Erica was able to return to the kitchen.

'So now the question is: Where do we start? Have you heard any more about the blood?'

Gösta shook his head. 'No, not yet. But Torbjörn and his team are still out there working, trying to see if they can find anything else. And sometime later today he's hoping to receive a report that will tell us whether we're dealing with human blood. All we have at the moment

144

is a preliminary report about the fire, which Patrik received before I left the office yesterday.'

'Have you started interviewing people?' Erica was so eager that she could hardly sit still. She didn't intend to give up until she'd done everything she could to help solve the mystery. The fact that it might provide material for an amazing book was an added bonus.

'Yesterday I compiled a list, prioritizing which individuals I think we should talk to first, and then I started trying to find contact information for them. But it's not exactly an easy task, given the amount of time that's passed. It can be difficult to track people down, and what they remember could be pretty vague by now. We can only wait to see what emerges from the interviews.'

'Do you think the boys might have been involved?'

He understood at once which boys she was referring to. 'Naturally, the thought has occurred to me, but I just don't know. We interviewed them on a number of occasions, and their stories always matched up. And we didn't find any physical evidence to indicate that—'

'Did you find any physical evidence at all?' asked Erica.

'No, there wasn't much to go on. After my colleague Henry and I found Ebba alone in the house, we went back down to the dock. That's where we met the boys, as they arrived in the other boat, and it did look as though they'd been out fishing.'

'Did you search the boat? It's conceivable that the bodies could have been dumped at sea.'

'The boat was searched very carefully, but there were no traces of blood or anything like that, which there would have been if they'd loaded five bodies into the boat. And I wonder whether they would have been capable of lugging the bodies that far. They were quite slender lads. And besides, bodies usually float to the surface. Some of the family members should have washed up sooner or

145

later, unless the boys made sure to weigh down the corpses – and that would require heavy objects that might not be so easy to come by on the spur of the moment.'

'Did you talk to other pupils at the school?'

'Yes, but some of the parents were reluctant to allow us access to their sons. I suppose they regarded themselves as too upper-class, and they didn't want to risk a scandal.'

'So did you find out anything interesting?'

Gösta snorted. 'No, just a bunch of nonsense about how awful the parents thought it was. They told us their sons had nothing to say about life at the school. Everything was excellent. Rune was excellent, the teachers were excellent, and there were no conflicts or quarrels. And the pupils simply repeated what their parents had told us.'

'What about the teachers?'

'Of course we interviewed both of them. And at first we had our suspicions about Ove Linder. But later it turned out that he did have an alibi.' Gösta fell silent for a moment. 'We had no suspects. We couldn't even prove that a crime had been committed. But . . .'

Erica placed her arms on the table and leaned forward. 'But what?'

He hesitated. 'I don't know. Your husband is always talking about his gut feelings, and we usually tease him, but I have to admit that back then my gut feeling was that we were missing something. We did our best, but it got us nowhere.'

'So we're going to try again. A lot has changed since 1974.'

'My experience is that some things never change. Those upper-crust types will always look out for themselves.'

'We'll try again,' said Erica patiently. 'Finish making the list of names of all the pupils and teachers. Then let me have a copy, so we can work on two fronts at once.'

'Just don't tell—'

'Patrik is not going to know about this. And I'll keep you up to date on everything I find out. That was our agreement, right?'

'Yes.' A worried expression appeared on Gösta's lean face.

'By the way, I went out to have a talk with Ebba and her husband yesterday.'

Gösta stared at her. 'How's she doing? Is she upset about what happened? How . . .?'

Erica laughed. 'Take it easy. One question at a time.' Then she turned serious. 'I'd say she was subdued but composed. They claim that they don't know anything more about who might have set the fire, but I can't tell whether they're lying or not.'

'I think they should stay somewhere else.' It was obvious that Gösta was extremely concerned. 'At least until we work everything out. It's not a safe place for them, and it was pure luck that they got out of the house in time.'

'They don't seem like the kind of people to give up easily.'

'She's a stubborn sort,' said Gösta with obvious pride.

Erica looked at him in surprise but didn't ask any questions. She knew from experience how personally involved she could get in the lives of the people that she wrote about. It was probably the same for police officers. Over the course of their careers they became entangled in the fates of so many individuals.

'When I met Ebba there was one thing that I wondered about and thought a bit strange.'

'What's that?' said Gösta, but a scream made Erica jump up to rush into the living room to see who was hurt. It took a few minutes before she returned to the kitchen to take up the thread of their conversation.

'Where were we? Oh, right. I thought it was strange

that Ebba didn't have any of the belongings that her family left behind. The house wasn't just a boarding school, it was their home, so there ought to have been loads of personal possessions. I took it for granted that they'd been given to Ebba, but she had no idea what had happened to all those things.'

'Good point.' Gösta rubbed his chin. 'I need to check whether an inventory was carried out. I can't remember seeing any lists.'

'I thought it might be worth it to take a look at their things with fresh eyes.'

'Not a bad idea. I'll see what I can find.' He glanced at his watch and then jumped to his feet. 'Jesus, the time has flown by. Hedström must be wondering where I am.'

Erica put her hand on his arm to reassure him.

'You'll think up a good excuse. Say you overslept or something like that. He won't suspect a thing, I swear.'

'Easy for you to say,' replied Gösta, heading out to the hall to put on his shoes.

'Don't forget what we've agreed. I need contact details for everyone involved, and you're going to find out where the Elvanders' belongings got to.'

Erica leaned forward and impulsively gave Gösta a hug. He awkwardly hugged her back.

'Okay, let me go. I promise to get to work on everything as soon as I can.'

'You're a rock,' said Erica, winking.

'Right. Well, best see to your kids now. I'll be in touch when I have something.'

Erica closed the door after him and did exactly as he'd said. She sat down on the sofa and as all three children climbed up to claim the best place on her lap, she absent-mindedly watched the adventures of Pippi Longstocking unfolding on the TV.

*   *   *

It was nice and quiet at the station. For a change, Mellberg had come out of his office to sit in the kitchen. Ernst, who was never more than a metre away from his master, had settled under the table, hoping that sooner or later it would be time for a snack.

'What a bloody idiot!' snarled Mellberg, pointing to the latest issue of *Bohusläningen* on the table in front of him. The newspaper had printed the interview with John Holm as its feature article.

'I don't understand how people can elect guys like him to the Riksdag. That's the flip-side of democracy, if you ask me.' Patrik sat down across from Mellberg. 'By the way, we need to have a talk with him. Holm was apparently one of the boys who was out on Valö that Easter.'

'In that case we'd better hurry. It says he's only staying here a week before heading back to Stockholm.'

'Yes, I saw that. I'm planning on seeing him this morning. I was thinking of taking Gösta with me.' He turned to peer over his shoulder at the hallway. 'But where is he? Annika – have you heard anything from Gösta?'

'Not a word. Maybe he overslept,' replied Annika from the reception area.

'I could go with you instead,' said Mellberg, closing the newspaper.

'Oh, that's not necessary. I'll wait for Gösta. He should be here any minute. I'm sure you have more important things to do.' Patrik could feel panic rising. Taking Mellberg along to an interview always spelled disaster.

Mellberg snapped his fingers a few times, and Patrik tried feverishly to come up with an argument to dissuade him from going.

'Maybe we should phone ahead to make an appointment.'

Mellberg snorted. 'It pays to catch a guy like that . . .

what's the expression? . . .' He snapped his fingers again. 'En garde.'

'Off guard,' Patrik corrected him. 'You mean off guard.'

A few minutes later they were in the car heading for Fjällbacka. Mellberg was whistling to himself. At first he had insisted on driving, but that was where Patrik drew the line.

'People like that are so narrow-minded and petty. They have no respect for other cultures or human diversity.' Mellberg nodded at his own statements.

Patrik was itching to remind his boss how narrow-minded he used to be, throwing out comments that the Friends of Sweden would undoubtedly have approved of. But in Mellberg's defence, it had to be said that he'd rid himself of his prejudices the moment he fell in love with Rita.

'That's the boathouse, right?' Patrik turned into the small gravel area in front of one of the red boathouses on Hamngatan. They'd agreed to take a chance that Holm would be there, rather than the house in Mörhult.

'It looks like somebody is sitting on the dock, at any rate.' Mellberg craned his neck to peer over the fence.

The gravel crunched under their shoes as they approached. Patrik wasn't sure whether he should knock, but that seemed silly, so he simply pushed open the gate.

He immediately recognized John Holm. The photographer for *Bohusläningen* had captured his almost stereotypical Swedish features while at the same time managing to make the photos of the broadly smiling man seem disturbingly menacing. He was smiling now, but there was confusion in his blue eyes as he came to greet them.

'Hi. We're from the Tanum police,' said Patrik, introducing himself and Mellberg.

'Oh?' Holm's expression turned wary. 'Has something happened?'

'That depends on how you look at it. We're here to talk to you about something that happened a long time ago, but unfortunately it's in the spotlight once again.'

'Valö,' said Holm. It was no longer possible to decipher his expression.

'Yes, that's right,' said Mellberg, taking an aggressive tone. 'It's about Valö.'

Patrik took a couple of deep breaths in order to stay calm.

'Could we sit down and talk?' he asked, and Holm nodded.

'Of course. Have a seat. The sun is quite fierce out here. I enjoy it, but if you think it's too hot, I can put up the umbrella.'

'No, it's fine.' Patrik waved his hand dismissively. He wanted to get this over with as fast as possible, before Mellberg made a mess of things.

'I see you've been reading *Bohusläningen*.' Mellberg gestured towards the newspaper, which lay open on the table.

Holm shrugged. 'Shoddy journalism is always so tiresome. I was misquoted and misinterpreted. The whole article is filled with insinuations.'

Mellberg tugged at his shirt collar. He had already started turning red in the face. 'I think it's well written.'

'The newspaper has clearly taken sides, but you have to put up with these sorts of attacks when you get into this business.'

'All the things he's questioning have featured in propaganda put out by you and your group. For instance, the nonsense about how an immigrant who commits a crime should be deported regardless of whether he has a residence permit. How is that going to work? Should somebody who has lived in Sweden for years and put down roots be sent back to his native country just because he or she stole a bicycle?' Mellberg had raised his voice, and spittle was spraying from his mouth as he talked.

Patrik sat there as if paralysed. It was like witnessing a car accident that was about to happen. Even though he agreed with what Bertil was saying, this was not the proper occasion to discuss politics.

Unperturbed, Holm told Mellberg, 'That's an issue our opponents have chosen to misinterpret completely. I could give you a detailed explanation, but I assume that's not why you're here.'

'No, as I said, we're here to talk about the events that occurred on Valö in 1974. Right, Bertil?' Patrik quickly jumped in. He fixed his eyes on Mellberg, who paused for a few seconds before nodding reluctantly.

'I've heard rumours that something happened out there,' said Holm. 'Have you found the family?'

'Not exactly,' said Patrik evasively. 'But someone tried to burn down the house. And if they'd succeeded, then the daughter and her husband might have been burned alive.'

Holm sat up straighter in his chair.

'The daughter?'

'Yes, Ebba Elvander,' said Patrik. 'Or Ebba Stark, as she is called now. She and her husband have taken over the place and are in the process of renovating it.'

'I'm sure it needs it. From what I've heard, it's practically derelict.' Holm turned to gaze towards Valö, which was right across the gleaming water from where they were sitting.

'But you haven't been out there in a long time?'

'Not since the boarding school was closed down.'

'Why not?'

Holm threw out his hands. 'There simply wasn't any reason for me to go out there.'

'What's your view of what happened to the family?'

'I suppose my guess is as good as anyone's, but I really have no idea.'

'But you do have a little more insight than most people,' Patrik persisted. 'You lived with the family, and you were there when they disappeared.'

'That's not strictly true. Some of the other pupils and I were out fishing. We were shocked when we came ashore and found two police officers there. Leon was furious. He thought that strangers were abducting Ebba.'

'So you don't have any theories? You must have thought about it over the years.' Mellberg sounded sceptical.

John Holm paid no attention to him. Instead he turned to Patrik and said, 'Just to clarify: we didn't actually live with the family. We went to school there, but there were strict boundaries between the pupils and the Elvander family. For instance, we were not invited to their Easter lunch. Rune was very careful to keep us at a distance, and he ran that school like a military operation. That was why our parents loved him as much as we hated him.'

'Did the students stick together, or were there conflicts among you?'

'There were plenty of arguments. It would have been strange if there weren't, in a school full of teenage boys. But nothing serious.'

'What about the teachers? What did they think of the headmaster?'

'Those wimps were so scared of him that they probably didn't dare have an opinion. At least we never heard them say anything about him.'

'Rune's children were roughly the same age as you back then. Did you spend any time with them?'

Holm shook his head. 'Rune wouldn't have stood for that. Although we did see quite a lot of his oldest son because he was a kind of assistant at the school. A real shithead.'

'It sounds as if you had rather strong feelings about some of the family members.'

'I detested them. All the boys at the school did. But not enough to kill them, if that's what you're thinking. It's part of being a teenager to rebel against authority.'

'What about the other Elvander children?'

'They mostly kept to themselves, else they'd have been in trouble. Same for Inez. She was in charge of all the cleaning, laundry, and cooking. Rune's daughter, Annelie, also helped out a lot. But as I said, we weren't allowed to interact with them, and there may have been a reason for that. Lots of the boys were real jerks, pampered and spoiled all their lives. I assume that's why they ended up at that school. Their parents finally realized that they'd raised lazy, useless individuals, so they tried to rectify the situation by sending their sons to Rune.'

'Your own parents weren't exactly destitute.'

'They had money,' said Holm, with emphasis on the word 'had'. Then he fell silent to show that he had no intention of discussing this subject. Patrik let it go, but he made a note to follow up with a check on Holm's family background.

'How is she?' Holm asked suddenly.

It took a second for Patrik to understand who he meant. 'Ebba? She seems fine. As I said, she's fixing up the house.'

Again Holm gazed out at Valö. Patrik wished he could read the man's thoughts.

'Well, thank you for your time,' Patrik said, standing up. Clearly Holm had told them all he was going to for the time being, but that had been enough to make Patrik more curious than ever about what had gone on at the boarding school.

'Yes, thanks. I realize that you're a very busy man,'

said Mellberg. 'And by the way, I wanted to say hello on behalf of the woman I live with. She's from Chile. Emigrated here in the seventies.'

Patrik tugged at Mellberg's arm to get him to leave. With a strained smile, Holm closed the gate after them.

Gösta was planning to slip unnoticed into the station, but he didn't get far.

'Did you oversleep? That's not like you,' said Annika.

'The alarm didn't go off,' he said, not daring to meet her eye. Annika could see right through lies, and he wasn't comfortable keeping secrets from her. 'Where is everybody?'

Not a sound could be heard from the corridor, and Annika seemed to be all alone at the station. Only Ernst emerged from the hall when he heard Gösta's voice.

'Patrik and Mellberg went out to have a talk with John Holm, so Ernst and I are holding down the fort. Aren't we, old fellow?' she said, scratching the big dog behind the ear. 'Patrik was wondering where you were. So you'd better practise that story about the alarm clock a little more before he gets back.'

She gave him a long look. 'Maybe if you tell me what you've been up to, I can help so you won't get caught.'

'I haven't a clue what you're talking about,' said Gösta, but he knew he was defeated. 'Well, okay, but first I need a cup of coffee.'

He headed for the kitchen, and Annika followed.

'All right, tell me,' said Annika once they were both sitting down.

Reluctantly Gösta told her about his agreement with Erica. Annika laughed.

'You've certainly got yourself into a mess this time. You know what Erica's like – give her an inch and she'll take a mile! Patrik is going to be furious when he finds out.'

'I know,' said Gösta, squirming. He knew she was right, but at the same time, this was important to him. And he was smart enough to understand why. It was for her sake that he was doing it – the girl that he and Maj-Britt had failed.

Annika had stopped laughing and was studying him with a serious expression.

'This means a lot to you, doesn't it?'

'Yes, it does. And Erica can help. She has a mind like a steel trap. I know that Patrik won't approve of me getting her mixed up in the case, but it's her job to dig out facts from the past, and that's exactly the skill that we need right now.'

Annika didn't say anything for a moment. Then she took a deep breath.

'Okay. I won't tell Patrik. On one condition.'

'What's that?'

'You keep me informed about what the two of you come up with, and I get to help where I can. I'm not bad at digging for facts myself.'

Gösta looked at her in surprise. This was not at all what he'd expected.

'Agreed. But as you said, there'll be hell to pay if Patrik finds out.'

'We'll cross that bridge when we come to it. So how far have you got? What can I do?'

Relieved, Gösta told her about his conversation with Erica that morning.

'We need contact details for all of the pupils and teachers at the school. I've got an old list, but by now a lot of it is out of date. We can use it as a starting point though. And some of the individuals had unusual surnames, so it's possible somebody at their old address will know where to find them.'

Annika raised her eyebrows.

'You mean you don't have their state identity numbers?'

He stared at her, feeling like a complete idiot for not having thought of it himself.

'Am I to understand from your expression that you do have their ID numbers? All right then. I can have an updated list ready for you by this afternoon, or tomorrow morning at the latest. Is that soon enough?'

She smiled, and Gösta said, 'That would be great. For my part, I was thinking of going with Patrik to have a talk with Leon Kreutz.'

'Why start with him?'

'No particular reason, but he was one of the boys I remember best. I had the impression that he was the leader of the group. Besides, I've heard that he and his wife just bought that big house up on the hill. In Fjällbacka, you know.'

'The white mansion? The asking price was ten million kronor!' said Annika.

The prices of houses with a sea view was a source of constant fascination to the locals, who kept a keen eye on asking prices and what the properties actually sold for. But ten million was enough to make the most blasé observer sit up and take notice.

'From what I understand, they can afford it.' Gösta thought of the boy with the dark eyes and handsome face. Even back then he had radiated wealth and something else that Gösta couldn't define. A sort of innate self-confidence was the closest he could come to describing it.

'All right, let's get to work,' said Annika. She put her coffee cup in the dishwasher and after giving Gösta a look, he followed suit. 'By the way, I forgot that you had an appointment with the dentist this morning.'

'A dental appointment? But I didn't . . .' Gösta stopped abruptly and smiled. 'Oh, right. I told you yesterday that

157

I had to go to the dentist. See: no cavities.' He pointed to his mouth and winked.

'Don't complicate a good lie by adding too many details,' said Annika, wagging her finger reproachfully before heading for her computer.

STOCKHOLM 1925

They had nearly been thrown off the train. The conductor took the bottle away from her and shouted that she was too drunk to travel. Of course she wasn't. She just needed a little pick-me-up now and then to be able to go on with life, which anyone should be able to understand. She was constantly forced to beg for money and perform the most degrading tasks that were tossed her way, out of charity and 'for the girl's sake', and usually she ended up having to put up with those panting, hypocritical whoremongers paying visits to her room.

It was for the girl's sake that the conductor had taken pity on her and allowed them to stay on the train all the way to Stockholm. And that was lucky, because if he'd thrown them off halfway there, Dagmar had no idea how they would have made it back home. It had taken her two months to save up for a one-way ticket to Stockholm, and now she hadn't so much as an öre to her name. But that didn't matter, because once they got there and had a chance to talk to Hermann, they would never need to worry about money again. He would take care of them. When they met and he realized what she'd been through, he would immediately leave that deceitful woman he'd married.

Dagmar stopped at a shop window to study her reflection in the glass. It was true that she'd aged a bit since they last saw each other. Her hair was not as thick, and now that she came to think about it, she hadn't washed it in a while. Her dress, which she'd stolen from a clothesline before they left, hung like a sack on her thin frame. Whenever she had money she chose booze over food, but that wouldn't happen any more. Soon she would look as she once had. Hermann would feel such tenderness for her when he heard how hard her life had been after he left her.

She took Laura's hand and started walking again. The girl resisted so much that Dagmar had to drag her along.

'Get moving!' she snarled. Why did the child always have to be so slow?

They had to keep stopping to ask the way, but eventually they found the right door. Tracing his address had turned out to be easy, because it was listed in the phone book: Odengatan 23. The building was as big and impressive as she had imagined. She tugged on the handle, but the door was locked. As she stood frowning, a gentleman came towards them, took out a key, and unlocked the door.

'Who did you want to see?'

She pulled herself up and announced proudly, 'The Görings.'

'Ah, well, I can see why you might need some help,' he said and let them into the building.

For a moment Dagmar wondered what he meant by that, but then she reminded herself that it didn't matter. They were here now. She studied the names listed on the board in the lobby, took note of which floor the Görings lived on, and began dragging Laura up the stairs. With a trembling hand Dagmar rang the bell. Soon they would be together again. She and Hermann. And Laura. His daughter.

Hard to believe it was so easy, thought Anna as she stood at the tiller of the boat that she and Dan owned. When she'd phoned Tobias, he had suggested that she come out to Valö as soon as she had time, and ever since she'd thought of nothing else. The whole family had noticed how her mood had changed for the better, and last night the house had been filled with an air of hope.

But in reality it wasn't that easy. This was her first step towards a new independence. All her life she'd been dependent on others. When she was little, Erica had been the one that she leaned on. After that she was dependent on Lucas, which had led to the disaster that she and the children still carried with them. And then Dan. Warm, safe Dan, who had taken both her and her wounded children under his wing. It had felt so wonderful to be allowed once again to be like a child and trust that someone else would take care of everything.

But the accident had taught her that not even Dan could handle everything. To be honest, that was probably what had affected her most. The loss of their baby had been an unfathomable sorrow, but her feeling of loneliness and vulnerability had almost been worse.

If she and Dan were going to continue to live together,

she needed to learn to stand on her own two feet. Despite the fact she was a late developer in this regard, deep down she knew that she had the necessary strength. Landing this interior design commission would mark a new beginning for her. It remained to be seen whether she had the necessary talent; the first hurdle would be to promote herself well enough to land the job.

With a pounding heart she knocked on the front door. She heard footsteps approaching, and the door opened. A man of about her own age stood there, dressed like a carpenter, with protective glasses pushed up on his fore-head. His friendly face took on an enquiring expression, but for a moment Anna could only stand there, lost for words.

'Hi,' she said at last. 'I'm Anna. We spoke on the phone yesterday.'

'Anna! Of course! Sorry, I didn't mean to be rude. I get so involved in the work that I forget about everything else. Please come in. Welcome to our chaos.'

He moved aside to allow her to enter. He wasn't wrong about the chaos within, but Anna could immediately see the potential. She'd always been gifted that way; it was as if she had a pair of magic glasses that allowed her to foresee the finished result.

Tobias followed her gaze. 'As you can tell, we've got some work ahead of us.'

She was about to reply when a thin, blonde woman came down the stairs. 'Hi. I'm Ebba,' she said, wiping her fingers on a rag. Splotches of white paint covered her hands and her clothes, and she had tiny specks of paint on her face and hair. The strong smell of turpentine brought tears to Anna's eyes.

'Sorry, I'm in a terrible mess,' Ebba added, holding up her hands. 'We'd better skip the handshake.'

'Don't worry. I know you're in the middle of renovating.

I'm more concerned about . . . well, about everything else you're having to deal with right now.'

'So Erica told you what happened?' asked Ebba, although it was more of a statement than a question.

'I heard about the fire. And the other thing,' said Anna. Finding blood under the floor of your house seemed such an absurd discovery that she couldn't bring herself to say the words out loud.

'We're trying to keep working as best we can,' said Tobias. 'We can't afford not to.'

From inside the house came the sound of voices and splintering floorboards.

'The tech team is still here,' Ebba explained. 'They're breaking up the entire dining-room floor.'

'Arc you sure it's safe for you to stay?' Anna realized it was none of her business, but there was something about this couple that aroused her maternal instincts.

'We're fine,' said Tobias, his voice strangely flat. He reached out to embrace Ebba, but as if anticipating the move she stepped away and his arm dropped to his side.

'So you're in need of a little help, is that right?' said Anna, wanting to change the subject. The mood was so oppressive that she was finding it hard to breathe.

Tobias seemed grateful of the distraction. 'As I said on the phone, we're at a loss how to proceed once the basic remodelling's finished. Interior design isn't our thing.'

'I really admire what you're doing. This is quite a job you've taken on. But I think it's going to be wonderful. I can picture a slightly old-fashioned, shabby country style, with rustic white furniture, pastel colours, romantic roses, lovely linen fabrics, pewter, and interesting little knick-knacks that will catch the eye.' The images whirled through her head as she talked. 'I don't think expensive antiques would be right here – better to go for a mixture of flea-market finds and reproduction furniture that we

163

can rough up to look old. All you need is some steel-wool and chains and . . .'

Tobias laughed, and his face lit up. Anna found herself thinking that he was quite attractive.

'You certainly know what you want. But keep talking. I think it sounds good to both of us.'

Ebba nodded. 'That's exactly the way I envisioned things too. I just hadn't a clue how to go about it, from a practical point of view.' She frowned. 'Our budget is almost non-existent. And I suppose you're used to being able to spend a lot and command a high salary—'

Anna interrupted her. 'I understand your situation – Tobias already explained. But you would be my first clients, so if you're pleased with my work, I could use you as a reference. I'm sure we can agree on a price that's within your budget. As for the furnishings, the idea is to make everything look as if it's inherited or bought in a flea market. I'd view it as a challenge to get by as cheaply as we can.'

Her sales pitch delivered, Anna held her breath and waited for their response. She wanted this commission so badly, and what she'd just told Ebba and Tobias was true. To be given a free hand in turning the old summer camp into the gem of the archipelago would be the perfect way to launch her new enterprise.

'I have my own business too, so I know exactly what you mean. Word of mouth is the best form of advertizing.' Ebba seemed almost shy about mentioning this.

'What kind of business do you have?' asked Anna.

'Jewellery. I make silver necklaces, with angel motifs.'

'Sounds wonderful. How did you come to start doing that?'

It was as if the shutters had come down: Ebba lowered her eyes and turned her face. Embarrassed, Tobias dived in to break the silence.

'We can't say when we'll be done with the renovation work. The police investigation and the damage in the front hall from the fire have thrown off our schedule, so it's hard to judge how long it will be before you can start.'

'That doesn't matter, I can fit in with whatever suits you,' said Anna, still puzzling over Ebba's reaction to her question. 'Perhaps for the time being we could just discuss colour choices for the walls, things like that. And then I could do some sketches for you and start checking out local auctions to see if I can find anything.'

'That sounds perfect,' said Tobias. 'We're hoping to be open on a small scale by Easter of next year, and then get into full swing by summer.'

'So we have plenty of time. Is it okay if I walk around and jot down some notes before I leave?'

'Of course. Make yourself at home,' said Tobias. Then he thought of something. 'But you'd better stay out of the dining room.'

'No problem. I can come back another time to see that.'

Ebba and Tobias went off to resume what they'd been doing when she arrived and left her to wander about in peace. She took copious notes, feeling enthusiasm bubbling up inside of her. This place could be so amazing. It could be the start of her new life.

Percy's hand shook as he prepared to sign the documents. He took a deep breath to calm himself. Buhrman, his attorney, frowned.

'Are you absolutely sure about this, Percy? Your father would not have approved.'

'Father is dead!' he snapped, but quickly murmured an apology and then went on. 'It may seem drastic, but it's either this or sell the manor.'

'What about a bank loan?' said Buhrman. He had been Percy's father's attorney as well. Percy wondered how old he actually was. Thanks to all the hours he spent on the golf course near his home in Mallorca he resembled a mummy; his body was in such a state he could have been put on display in a museum.

'What do you take me for? Of course I've spoken to the bank.' Again Percy had to force himself to lower his voice and speak calmly. Burhman had a tendency to speak to him as if he were still a boy. He seemed to forget that Percy was now Count von Bahrn. 'They made it very clear that they no longer wish to offer me help.'

Buhrman raised a startled eyebrow. 'But we've always had such a good relationship with Svenska Banken. Your father and the old director both attended Lundsberg Gymnasium. Are you sure you spoke to the right person? Shall I try to arrange a meeting? They ought to—'

'The old director left the bank a long time ago,' Percy cut in. He was on the verge of losing all patience with Burhman. 'In fact, he left this world so long ago that bones are probably all that's left of him. We live in a different world now. The bank is staffed by bean-counters and young whippersnappers from the School of Economics. They have no idea how to behave. We're talking about the kind of people who take off their shoes indoors!' Angrily he signed the final document and shoved it across to the attorney, who was shaking his head, utterly perplexed.

'Well, I do think it's strange,' he said. 'Next thing you know they'll be trying to abolish the laws governing entailed estates so that properties can be divided up willy-nilly. Speaking of which – couldn't you speak to your siblings about this? Mary has married into wealth, and Charles is making a fortune on his restaurants, from what I understand. Maybe they would be willing to help out. You're family, after all.'

Percy stared at him. The old man was out of his mind. Had he forgotten the heated arguments and lawsuits that followed his father's death fifteen years ago? Percy's siblings had been foolish enough to challenge the law which entitled him, as the eldest son, to inherit the estate in its entirety. Fortunately, the law was very clear. Fygelsta Manor was his birthright and his alone. It might have been considered proper to share some of the estate with his siblings, but after their wilful attempt to take from him what was legally his, he hadn't felt particularly generous. So they'd been left empty-handed; and to add insult to injury they'd had to pay his legal expenses. As Buhrman said, neither of them was hurting financially, and that was something Percy consoled himself with whenever he felt a pang of guilt. But there was no way he would ever approach them, cap in hand.

'This is my only option,' he said, nodding at the documents. 'I'm lucky to have good friends who are willing to step up, and I'll pay them back as soon as I've straightened out this unfortunate situation with the tax authorities.'

'Well, do as you please, but you're putting a great deal at risk.'

'I trust Sebastian,' said Percy. He only wished he was as confident as he sounded.

Kjell slammed down the phone on the desk so hard that the force reverberated up his arm. The pain merely increased his fury, and he swore as he massaged his elbow, clenching his hands into fists to stop himself from hurling something at the wall.

'What's going on?' Rolf, his best friend and colleague, stuck his head in the door.

'What do you think?' Kjell ran his hand through his dark hair, which had begun acquiring the odd strand of silver a few years back.

'Beata?' said Rolf, coming into the room.

'Who else? I'm sure you heard that at the last minute

she stopped me from having the kids over the weekend, even though it was my turn. Now she's on the phone, screaming and yelling that she won't let them go with me to Mallorca. Apparently a week is too long for them to be away.'

'But didn't they have two weeks with her in the Canary Islands in June? And didn't she book that trip without consulting you? Why shouldn't they spend a week with their father?'

'Because they're "her" kids. That's what she's always saying. "My" children. Evidently I'm only allowed to borrow them.'

Kjell tried to force himself to breathe slower. He hated the fact that she still had the power to upset him. And that she didn't care about what was best for the children. All she wanted was to make his life as miserable as possible.

'But I thought the two of you were granted joint custody,' said Rolf. 'You should be allowed to have the kids more often than you do now, if that's what you want.'

'Yes, I know. At the same time I want them to have a stable life. I shouldn't have to do battle every time it's my turn to have the kids. One week's holiday – is that too much to ask? I'm their father, and I have every bit as much right to be with them as Beata.'

'They're getting older, Kjell. Eventually they'll understand. Try to be a better person, a better parent. They need peace and quiet. Make sure they have that when they're with you, and things will work out. But don't ever stop fighting to see them.'

'I refuse to give up,' said Kjell grimly.

'Good,' said Rolf. Then he waved the daily newspaper, which he was holding in his hand. 'That was a great piece you wrote, by the way. You really pushed him hard. I think it's the first article I've ever read where somebody actually dared to put John Holm and his party on the spot.' He sat down in the visitor's chair.

'I can't understand what's wrong with the other journalists.' Kjell shook his head. 'There are such obvious holes in the rhetoric spouted by the Friends of Sweden. It shouldn't be so hard.'

'We can only hope more will follow your lead,' said Rolf, pointing to the paper, which was open to Kjell's article. 'We need to show our readers what these people are like.'

'The worst part is that some voters buy into their cheap propaganda. They put on those fancy suits, publicly kick out a few members who've attracted negative press, and try to talk about budget cuts and economizing. Behind the facade, they're still the same old fascists. Only these days, if they give the Nazi salute and wave swastika flags, they make sure they do it under cover of darkness. Then they sit there on TV and moan that they've been vilified and unfairly attacked.'

'You don't need to preach to me. We're on the same side,' laughed Rolf, holding up his hands.

'I'm convinced he's hiding something else,' said Kjell, massaging the bridge of his nose.

'Who?'

'John Holm. He's too smooth, too polished. Everything's too perfect. He hasn't even bothered to cover up his past as a member of the skinhead movement. Instead he brazens it out, sitting on the studio sofa on morning TV shows, apologizing and lamenting. So none of that stuff is news to the voters. No, I need to dig deeper. He can't have purged himself of all his sins.'

'I agree. But his secrets aren't going to be easy to uncover. Holm has put too much effort into the whitewash.' Rolf tossed the newspaper aside.

'At least I've got to—' Kjell was interrupted by the

169

phone ringing. 'If that's Beata again . . .' He hesitated for a second and grabbed the phone. 'Yes?'

When he heard who it was, his tone of voice changed at once. He noticed that Rolf was watching him with amusement.

'Hi, Erica . . . No, no problem . . . Sure, of course . . . What did you say? You're kidding, right?'

He cast a glance at Rolf and smiled broadly. A couple of minutes later he ended the conversation. He'd made a few hasty notes, and now he tossed down the pen, leaned back, and clasped his hands behind his head.

'Looks as though things are starting to move.'

'What is it? Who was that on the phone?'

'That was Erica Falck. Apparently I'm not the only one interested in John Holm. She complimented me on the article and wondered whether I had any background material she could see.'

'Why is she interested in him?' asked Rolf. Then he opened his eyes wide. 'Is it because he was on Valö? Is Erica writing about the family that disappeared?'

Kjell nodded. 'Yes, that's what it sounds like. But that's not the best part. You won't believe this.'

'Come on, Kjell. Don't keep me in suspense.'

Kjell grinned. He knew that Rolf was going to love what he had to say.

STOCKHOLM 1925

The woman who opened the door was not at all the way Dagmar had pictured her. She was neither beautiful nor seductive, but tired and haggard. She also appeared to be older than Hermann, and everything about her exuded an unexpected ordinariness.

Dagmar gawped at her in silence. Had she come to the wrong place? But it said 'Göring' on the doorplate, so she decided this woman must be the couple's housekeeper. She took a firm grip on Laura's hand.

'I've come to see Hermann.'

'Hermann isn't here.' The woman looked her up and down.

'Then I'll wait until he comes home.'

Laura was trying to hide behind Dagmar, and the woman gave the child a kind smile before she said:

'I'm Mrs Göring. Is there something I can help you with?'

So this really was the woman that Dagmar hated. The woman who had been in her thoughts ever since she'd read her name in the newspaper. Dagmar regarded Carin Göring with surprise: the sturdy, practical shoes, the well-tailored ankle-length skirt, the blouse that was primly buttoned up to her throat, and her hair pulled back in a bun. Tiny lines were visible around her eyes, and her complexion had a sickly pallor. Suddenly everything fell into place. Of course, this was the woman who had duped

171

her Hermann. An old spinster like her could never get a man like Hermann without some wicked trickery.

'Well, we have a few things to talk about, you and I.' Dagmar yanked on Laura's hand and stepped inside.

Carin moved away, doing nothing to stop her. She merely nodded at the child. 'Shall I take your coat?'

Dagmar eyed her suspiciously. Then without waiting to be invited she barged into the room closest to the front hall, stopping abruptly on the threshold of the large parlour. The flat was as beautiful as she'd expected Hermann's home to be – spacious, with tall windows, a high ceiling, and a gleaming parquet floor – but it was almost empty.

'Why don't they have any furniture, Mamma?' asked Laura, her eyes big as she surveyed her surroundings.

Dagmar turned to Carin. 'Yes, why don't you have any furniture? Why would Hermann live like this?'

Carin frowned for a moment, indicating that she found the question impertinent, but then she replied in a friendly enough tone:

'Things have been a bit difficult lately. But now you must tell me who you are.'

Dagmar pretended not to hear the request, merely giving Mrs Göring a disdainful glance. 'Difficult? But Hermann is rich. He can't possibly be living like this.'

'Did you hear what I said? If you don't tell me who you are and what you're doing here, I'll be forced to ring the police. For the child's sake, I'd prefer not to do that.' Carin nodded at Laura, who was once again hiding behind her mother.

Dagmar grabbed her arm and pushed her towards Carin.

'This is my daughter. And Hermann's. From now on, he's going to live with us. You've had him long enough, and he doesn't want you. Don't you understand that?'

Carin Göring flinched but maintained a calm demeanour as she studied Dagmar and Laura in silence for a full minute.

'I have no idea what you're talking about. Hermann is my husband. I'm Mrs Göring.'

'I'm the one he loves. I'm the great love of his life,' said Dagmar, stomping her foot. 'Laura is his daughter, but you took him away before I could tell him that. If he knew about Laura, he would never have married you, no matter what you did to force him into marriage.' She was beside herself with rage. Laura had crept behind her again.

'I think you should leave before I call the police.' Carin's voice remained calm, but Dagmar could see the fear in her eyes.

'Where is Hermann?' she insisted.

Carin pointed at the front door. 'Get out!' Still pointing, she moved resolutely towards the telephone. The clack of her heels echoed in the empty flat.

Dagmar seemed to calm down as she paused to think. She realized that Mrs Göring was not going to say where her husband was, but at least the woman knew the truth now, and that gave Dagmar a sense of satisfaction. Now she just had to find Hermann. Even if it meant sleeping in the doorway, she would wait here until he came home. Then they would be together for all eternity. Keeping a tight hold on Laura's collar, Dagmar dragged the child towards the door. With a final triumphant glare at Carin Göring, she closed the door behind her.

✤

'Thank you, dear Anna.' Erica kissed her sister on the cheek and then rushed out to the car after waving a quick goodbye to the children. She felt a pang of guilt at leaving them again, but judging by the happy shouts when their aunt Anna came in, there was really no need for her to feel bad.

She drove towards Hamburgsund, her mind filled with questions. She was annoyed that she hadn't got any further in her search to find out what had happened to the Elvander family. She kept coming up against dead ends, and she was no closer than the police to solving their disappearance. But she wasn't about to give up. The family's history was fascinating, and the more she dug into the archives, the more interesting it got. It was as if the women in Ebba's family had some sort of curse hanging over them.

But for the time being, Erica pushed aside all thoughts of the past. Thanks to Gösta, she finally had a lead worth following. He had mentioned a name, and after doing a bit of further research she was now sitting in her car, on her way to see a source she hoped would have valuable information. Researching old cases was often like putting together a gigantic puzzle which was missing a number of vital pieces. Experience had taught her that it was best to ignore those missing pieces and concentrate on slotting everything else into place; sooner or later the image would manifest itself. This case was a long way from becoming clear, but she was hoping that the puzzle would soon acquire more pieces so that she'd be able to form an idea of what the picture was meant to portray. Otherwise, all her efforts would be in vain.

When she came to Hansson's petrol station, she pulled in to ask for directions. She had a vague idea where she was going, but there was no point driving around aimlessly. Behind the counter stood Magnus, who owned the station along with his wife. Aside from his brother Frank and his sister-in-law Anette, who ran the sausage stand on the square, no one knew more about the people of Hamburgsund than Magnus.

He gave Erica a rather strange look but didn't say a word as he drew her a detailed map on a piece of scrap paper. She drove off, keeping one eye on the road and the other on the map, until she finally came to what had to be the right building. Only then did she realize that it was possible there'd be no one at home on such a nice day. Most people who had the day off would be at the beach or out on some island in the archipelago. But now that she was here, she might as well ring the bell. When she got out of the car and heard music, she was more hopeful.

As she waited for someone to come to the door, she hummed the melody: '*Non, je ne regrette rien,*' sung by Édith Piaf. She knew only the words of the refrain, in her faulty French, but she was drawn in by the music and barely registered the door opening.

'Ah, I sense a Piaf admirer!' said a short man in a dark purple silk gown with gold trim. He was wearing stage make-up.

Erica couldn't hide her surprise.

The man smiled. 'All right, sweetheart. Are you selling

175

something, or are you here for some other reason? If you're selling, I already have everything I want, but otherwise you're welcome to come in and keep me company on the veranda. Walter doesn't like the sun, so I'm sitting there all by my lonesome. And there's nothing sadder than drinking a good rosé wine all alone.'

'Oh, yes, well . . . There *is* a reason why I'm here,' Erica managed to say.

'Excellent!' The man clapped his hands with pleasure and backed up to allow her to come in.

Erica looked around the front hall. Everywhere she saw gold and tassels and velvet. To say the decor was 'ostentatious' didn't begin to do it justice.

'I furnished this floor, while Walter was allowed to do whatever he liked with the upstairs. If you want a marriage to last as long as ours has, you have to be willing to compromise. We're about to celebrate our fifteenth anniversary, and we lived in sin for ten years before that.' He turned to the stairs and shouted: 'Darling, we have a visitor! Come down and have a drink with us in the sunshine instead of sitting up there sulking!'

He moved on through the hall, gesturing upstairs.

'You should see what it's like up there. It reminds me of a hospital. Totally sterile. Walter says it's stylistically pure. He's so enamoured of the so-called Nordic design, and there's nothing cosy about that. And it's not exactly hard to accomplish either. All you have to do is paint everything white, bring in a few of those disgusting IKEA pieces of furniture made out of birch, and *voilà* – you've created a Swedish home.'

He walked around a huge armchair upholstered in red brocade and headed for the open French doors leading on to the balcony. A bottle of rosé was sitting in an ice bucket on the table, with a half-empty wine glass next to it.

'May I offer you a glass?' He was already reaching for the bottle. His silk gown fluttered around his thin, pale legs.

'That would be lovely, but I'm driving,' said Erica, thinking how good it would be to have a glass of wine on this sunny veranda with its view of the sound and Hamburg Island.

'Oh, but that sounds so boring. You sure I can't tempt you to have even a teeny drop?' He waved the bottle enticingly as he lifted it out of the ice bucket.

Erica couldn't help laughing. 'My husband is a police officer, so I'm afraid I daren't, no matter how much I'd like to.'

'I'll bet he's terribly handsome! I've always loved men in uniform.'

'Me too,' said Erica, sitting down on one of the patio chairs.

The man moved away to turn down the volume on the CD player. He poured Erica a glass of water and handed it to her with a smile.

'So, why is a lovely girl like you paying me a visit?'

'My name is Erica Falck, and I'm a writer. At the moment I'm doing research for my next book. You're Ove Linder, right? And you were a teacher at Rune Elvander's boarding school for boys in the early seventies.'

His smile faded. 'Ove. That was a long time ago . . .'

'Have I come to the wrong place?' said Erica, realizing that she might have misread Magnus's convoluted directions.

'No, no, but it's been a while since I was Ove Linder.' Pensively he twirled the glass in his hands. 'I haven't officially changed my name. If I had, you wouldn't have been able to find me, but nowadays I'm called Liza. No one says Ove, except Walter, and that's only if he's cross with me. I chose the name Liza after Liza Minelli, of course, although I'm only a pale imitation.' He cocked his head, apparently waiting for Erica to protest.

'Stop fishing for compliments, Liza.'

Erica turned her head. She assumed that the person in the doorway had to be Walter, the husband.

'There you are. Come here and say hello to Erica,' said Liza.

Walter came outside, standing behind Liza and tenderly placing his hands on her shoulders. Liza put her free hand over her husband's and squeezed it. Erica found herself hoping that she and Patrik would be as loving towards each other after they'd been together for twenty-five years.

'What's this all about?' asked Walter as he sat down. Unlike his partner, he would have passed unnoticed in a crowd: average height and build, with a receding hairline and discreet attire. The kind of person witnesses would find it impossible to remember if asked to identify him in a criminal case, Erica thought. But he had intelligent eyes, and he seemed nice. In a strange way, she had the feeling that this odd pair was perfectly matched.

She cleared her throat. 'As I said, I'm trying to find out more about the boarding school on Valö. You were one of the teachers, right?'

'Yes, unfortunately,' said Liza with a sigh. 'That was an awful time. I hadn't yet come out, and back then it wasn't as acceptable to be gay as it is today. Plus Rune Elvander was a terrible bigot, and he wasn't afraid to air his prejudices. Before I decided to accept my true self, I tried desperately to fit in with everyone else. I've never been the lumberjack type, of course, but I made an effort to appear to be heterosexual and so-called normal. I got plenty of practice while I was growing up.'

He gazed down at the table, and Walter stroked his arm sympathetically.

'I think I managed to fool Rune. But I had to put up

178

with a lot of taunting from the students. That school was full of nonentities who got a kick out of finding other people's weak spots. I was only there six months, and I probably wouldn't have lasted much longer. In fact, I wasn't planning to go back after the Easter holiday, but I was saved the trouble of handing in my resignation.'

'What was your reaction to the disappearance? Do you have any theories?' asked Erica.

'Of course it was dreadful, no matter what I thought of the family. I assume that something horrible happened to them.'

'But do you have any clue what that might be?'

'No, it's as much a mystery to me as it is to everybody else,' said Liza.

'What was the atmosphere like at the school? Were there people who didn't get along?'

'That's putting it mildly. That place was an absolute pressure cooker.'

'How do you mean?' Erica felt her pulse quicken. For the first time she had the chance to find out what had gone on behind the scenes. Why hadn't she thought of this earlier?

'According to the teacher whose place I took, the pupils were at each other's throats right from the start. They were accustomed to having their own way, but they were also under a lot of pressure from home to succeed. Which inevitably resulted in cock-fights. By the time I started at the school, Rune had cracked the whip and the boys were toeing the line, but I could sense the tension simmering below the surface.'

'What was the boys' relationship with Rune?'

'They hated him. He was a sadistic psychopath.' Liza's voice was coldly matter-of-fact.

'You don't paint a very nice picture of Rune Elvander.' Erica regretted not bringing along her tape recorder. She was going to have to try to remember as much as possible from this conversation.

Liza shuddered. 'Rune Elvander was one of the most despicable people I've ever met. And believe me . . .' Liza cast a glance at Walter, 'if you live a life like ours, you run into plenty of unpleasant types.'

'What about his relationship with his family?'

'That depends on which family members you're talking about. I wouldn't have said Inez was happy. It's hard to see why she married Rune. She was young and sweet. I suspected that it was her mother who forced her into the marriage. But the old crone died shortly after I started at the school – which probably came as a relief for Inez, because that woman was a nasty piece of work.

'What about Rune's children?' Erica went on. 'How did they view their father and stepmother? It can't have been easy for Inez to become part of the family. Wasn't she only a few years older than her oldest stepchild?'

'Yes. An awful boy, much like his father.'

'What was his name, the oldest son?'

'Claes.'

A long pause followed. Erica waited patiently.

'He's the one I remember most. I get shivers just thinking about him. I can't say why that should be. He was always polite to me, but there was something about Claes that made me unwilling to turn my back whenever he was present.'

'Did he and Rune get along?'

'It's hard to say. They circled around each other like two planets, without ever crossing paths.' Liza laughed with embarrassment. 'I sound like some New Age woman or a bad poet . . .'

'Not at all. Please go on,' said Erica, leaning forward. 'I get what you mean. So there were never any conflicts between Rune and Claes?'

'No, they pretty much kept to their own turf. Claes seemed to obey Rune's slightest command, but how he felt about his father is anyone's guess. Yet there was at least one thing that they had in common. They both worshipped Carla – Rune's deceased wife and Claes's mother – and they both seemed to despise Inez. In Claes's case, that might be understandable, since she was supposed to take his mother's place, but Rune was the one who'd married her.'

'So Rune treated Inez badly?'

'Yes. Or at least, it was not a loving relationship. He was always ordering her around, as if she was his subordinate instead of his wife. Claes, on the other hand, was openly mean and shameless in the way he treated his stepmother. And he didn't seem to have any affection for Ebba either. It wasn't much better when it came to his sister Annelie.'

'What did Rune make of his children's behaviour? Did he encourage them?' Erica took a sip of water. It was hot out on the veranda, even in the shade of the big umbrella.

'In Rune's eyes, they could do no wrong. He used his military tone of voice with them too, but he was the only one who was ever allowed to reprimand his children. If anyone else complained about them he would fly into a rage. I know that Inez tried it once, but never again. No, the one member of that family who was nice to her was Rune's youngest, Johan. He was considerate and sweet and very attached to Inez.' Liza's expression turned sad. 'I wonder what happened to little Ebba.'

'She's back on Valö. She and her husband are renovating the house. And the day before yesterday . . .'

Erica bit her lip. She didn't know how much she dared reveal, but at the same time, Liza had been so open with her. She took a deep breath.

'The day before yesterday they found blood when they pulled up the floor in the dining room.'

Liza and Walter stared at her. Off in the distance they could hear the sound of boats and people talking, but on the veranda it was utterly silent. Finally Walter spoke:

'You've always said that they must be dead.'

Liza nodded. 'Yes, that seemed most likely. Besides . . .'

'Besides what?' said Erica.

'Oh, it's too silly.' He waved his hand, making the sleeve of his silk gown flutter. 'I never mentioned it to anyone back then.'

'Nothing is too insignificant or too silly. Tell me.'

'It wasn't anything in particular, but I had the feeling that things were about to take a turn for the worse. And I heard . . .' He shook his head. 'No, it's too stupid.'

'Go on,' said Erica, resisting the impulse to lean across the table and shake the words out of him.

Liza took a big gulp of wine and then looked her in the eye.

'There were noises in the night.'

'Noises?'

'Yes. Footsteps, doors opening, a distant voice. But when I got up to investigate, there was no one there.'

'As if they were ghosts?' said Erica.

'I don't believe in ghosts,' said Liza sombrely. 'The only thing I can say is that I heard noises, and I had a feeling that something terrible was going to happen. So I wasn't surprised when I heard about the family disappearing.'

Walter nodded. 'You've always had a sixth sense.'

'Oh, what rubbish I'm jabbering,' said Liza. 'Things are getting much too sad around this table. Erica will think we're a couple of real doomsayers.' Suddenly the gleam was back in his eyes, and he smiled broadly.

'Not at all. I want to thank you for allowing me to come here and talk to you. You've given me a lot to think about, but I'd better head home now,' said Erica, getting to her feet.

'Give my greetings to little Ebba,' said Liza.

'I'll do that.'

They made a move to accompany her to the door, but she motioned for them to stay where they were.

'Don't get up. I can find my way out.'

As she passed the sea of gold and tassels and velvet cushions, she heard behind her Édith Piaf singing about her broken heart.

'Where the hell were you this morning?' said Patrik, going into Gösta's office. 'I wanted you to go with me to interview John Holm.'

Gösta glanced up. 'Didn't Annika tell you? I had a dental appointment.'

'Dental appointment?' Patrik sat down and gave him a searching look. 'No cavities, I hope?'

'Nope. No cavities.'

'How's it going with the list?' Patrik indicated the stack of documents on the desk in front of Gösta.

'Well, I've compiled most of the current addresses for the former pupils.'

'That was fast.'

'State ID numbers,' said Gösta, pointing at the old roster of students. 'All you have to do is use your brain.' He handed a paper to Patrik. 'How'd it go with the Nazi leader?'

'I don't think he'd particularly care for that description,' said Patrik as he began scanning the list.

'Well, that's what he is. They've stopped shaving their heads, but they haven't changed. Did Mellberg behave himself?'

'What do you think?' said Patrik, putting the list on his lap. 'You might say that the Tanum police didn't exactly show their best side during the interview.'

'Did you at least find out something new?'

Patrik shook his head. 'Not much. John Holm doesn't know anything about the disappearance. And nothing had happened at the school that might explain it. There was nothing to report, other than the tensions one would expect between a bunch of teenagers and a strict headmaster. Etcetera.'

'Have you heard anything from Torbjörn yet?' asked Gösta.

'No. He promised to put a rush on it, but since we don't have any fresh corpses to present, the case is probably not a high priority. Besides, the statute of limitations has expired, even if it should turn out that the family was murdered.'

'But the report on the blood analysis could give us some leads that are relevant for our arson investigation. Have you forgotten that somebody tried to burn down the house the other night, with Ebba and Tobias inside? You're the one who was so adamant that the fire and the disappearance were connected. And what about Ebba? Doesn't she have a right to hear what happened to her family?'

Patrik held up his hands. 'I know, I know. But as yet I haven't found anything of interest in the old investigative materials, and it's starting to feel a bit hopeless.'

'Is there anything at all to go on in Torbjörn's report about the fire?'

'No. It was ordinary petrol, ignited by an ordinary match. Nothing else concrete.'

'Then we need to start at the other end of the puzzle.' Gösta turned and nodded at a photograph hanging on the wall. 'I think we need to put some pressure on those boys. They know more than they told us back then.'

Patrik got up and went over to study the picture of the five boys.

'You're probably right. I saw from the list that you

184

think we should start by interviewing Leon Kreutz. Why don't we go and have a talk with him now?'

'Unfortunately, I don't know where he is. His mobile is switched off, and at the hotel they said that he and his wife had moved out. Presumably they're getting settled in their new house. Shall we wait until tomorrow, after they've had time to unpack? Then we can talk to them in peace and quiet.'

'Okay. In that case, why don't we go see Sebastian Månsson and Josef Meyer instead? They both live nearby.'

'Sure. First I need to clean up in here a bit.'

'And we mustn't forget to check up on this mysterious "G".'

'G?'

'Yes, the person who's been sending a birthday card to Ebba every year.'

'Do you really think that's necessary?' Gösta began fidgeting with the papers on his desk.

'You never know. As you just said: we need to find a thread and then follow it.'

'If you pull on too many threads at once, you might get everything all tangled up,' muttered Gösta. 'It doesn't sound relevant.'

'I disagree,' said Patrik, patting him on the shoulder. 'I suggest that . . .'

His mobile buzzed and he glanced at the display.

'I need to take this call,' he said, and left the room.

A few minutes later Patrik came back into the office with a triumphant expression on his face.

'We might finally have the lead we've been hoping for. That was Torbjörn on the phone. There wasn't any more blood under the dining-room floor, but they found something else even better.'

'What's that?'

'Wedged under the floorboards was a bullet. So it looks

185

as though a shot was fired in the very room where the family was gathered before they disappeared.'

Patrik and Gösta exchanged sombre glances. A moment earlier they had been feeling discouraged, but in an instant the investigation had come to life again.

Erica had planned to drive straight home to relieve Anna, but her curiosity got the better of her, and she continued on to Fjällbacka, heading for Mörhult. After hesitating about whether to turn left at the mini-golf course and go down to the boathouses, she decided to take the chance that they would be at home. By now it was late afternoon.

The door was propped open by a wooden clog decorated with flowers, and she stuck her head into the front hall. 'Hello?' she called.

She heard sounds from inside and a moment later John Holm appeared, holding a tea towel.

'I'm sorry, am I interrupting your dinner?' said Erica.

He glanced down at the towel. 'No, not at all. I was washing my hands. Can I help you?'

'My name is Erica Falck, and right now I'm working on a book . . .'

'Aha, so you're Fjällbacka's famous author? Come join me in the kitchen. Would you like a cup of coffee?' he said, giving her a warm smile. 'So what brings you here?'

They sat down at the kitchen table.

'I'm planning to write a book about what happened out on Valö.' She thought she caught a hint of uneasiness in his blue eyes, but it vanished so swiftly that she might have just imagined it.

'It's strange how everybody seems to be so interested in Valö all of a sudden. If I've understood the local gossip correctly, then it was your husband that I talked to earlier today.'

'Yes, I'm married to a police officer. Patrik Hedström.'

'He had somebody else with him who was quite . . . interesting.'

It didn't take much for Erica to realize who he was talking about.

'I see you've had the honour of meeting Bertil Mellberg – the man, the myth, the legend!'

Holm laughed and Erica could feel herself falling under the spell of his charm. And that annoyed her. She detested everything that he and his party stood for, but at the moment he seemed harmless. Quite engaging, actually.

'I've met his type before. Your husband, on the other hand, seems very good at his job.'

'I'm partial, of course, but he's a good policeman. He keeps digging until he finds out what he wants to know. Just like I do.'

'You must make a dangerous team.' Holm smiled again, showing two perfect dimples.

'I suppose so. But sometimes it's possible to get stuck. I've been researching the disappearance off and on for a few years, and now I've decided to take up the story again.'

'And you're going to write a book about it?' This was accompanied by another glimmer of anxiety in Holm's eyes.

'That's the plan. Would you mind if I asked you a few questions?' She took out a pen and paper.

For a moment John Holm seemed to hesitate. 'That's fine,' he said eventually. 'But as I explained to your husband and his colleague, I don't really have much to contribute.'

'As I understand it, there were certain conflicts among members of the Elvander family.'

'Conflicts?'

'Yes. Apparently Rune's children weren't very fond of their stepmother.'

'As pupils, we didn't get involved in their family dynamics.'

'But it was such a small school. You must have noticed what went on within the family.'

'It didn't interest us. We didn't want anything to do with them. It was bad enough having to deal with Rune.' Holm appeared to regret having agreed to answer her questions. He hunched his shoulders and fidgeted, which only increased Erica's determination to press on. Apparently there was something about this line of enquiry that made John Holm uncomfortable.

'What about Annelie? A sixteen-year-old girl and a bunch of teenage boys – how did that work?'

Holm snorted. 'Annelie was totally boy-crazy, but none of us ever encouraged her. There are certain girls that you learn to stay away from, and Annelie was one of them. Besides, Rune would have murdered us if we so much as touched his daughter.'

'What do you mean when you say that she was the kind of girl you learned to stay away from?'

'She kept running after us and acting strange, and I think she would have loved getting us in trouble. One time she stretched out right outside our window to sunbathe topless, but Leon was the only one who dared look at her. He was a death-defying kind of guy, even back then.'

'What happened? Did her father catch her?' Erica felt herself being drawn into a whole different world.

'Her brother Claes used to protect her. On that occasion he saw her and dragged her away. He was so rough that I thought he was going to tear her arm off.'

'Did she have a crush on any of you boys?'

'Naturally. Who do you think?' said Holm, but then he realized that Erica had no idea what he meant. 'Leon, of course. He was the perfect boy. His family was filthy rich, he was handsome, and he possessed a self-confidence that none of the rest of us could even approach.'

'But he wasn't interested in her?'

'As I said, Annelie was the kind of girl who caused trouble, and Leon was too smart to get involved with her.' A mobile began ringing in the living room, and he jumped up. 'Sorry, but do you mind if I answer that?'

Without waiting for her reply, he left the kitchen, and Erica heard him speaking in a low voice. No one else seemed to be at home. She gazed around the room while she waited. A pile of documents stacked up on a kitchen chair caught her interest. Casting a quick glance over her shoulder, she began leafing through the pages. They seemed for the most part to be records of parliamentary proceedings and meetings, but then she gave a start. Between two printouts she found a piece of paper covered with scribbles that she couldn't decipher. From the living room she heard Holm saying goodbye, so she quickly pulled the page out of the pile of documents and slipped it into her handbag. When he returned to the kitchen, she gave him an innocent smile.

'Everything okay?'

He nodded and sat down again.

'That's the disadvantage of my job. I'm never off duty, not even while on holiday.'

Erica murmured her sympathy. She didn't want to get into a discussion of Holm's political activities. Her own views would become all too obvious, and there was a risk that they would end up at loggerheads. Then she wouldn't find out anything more about Valö.

She picked up her pen. 'So how was Inez with the pupils?'

'Inez?' Holm looked away. 'We didn't see much of her. She was busy taking care of the house and her little daughter.'

'But surely you had some sort of relationship with her?

I'm familiar with the house, and it's not especially big, so you must have run into each other fairly often.'

'Of course we saw Inez. But she was a silent and brow-beaten woman. She didn't care for us, and we didn't care for her.'

'Apparently her husband wasn't overly fond of her either.'

'No. It was incomprehensible that a man like him had managed to sire four children. We speculated that they had to be the result of immaculate conception.' Holm gave her a crooked smile.

'What did you think of the two teachers at the school?'

'They were both real characters. Excellent teachers, but Per-Arne was an old military man, and even more rigid than Rune, if that was possible.'

'What about the other teacher?'

'Ove? Hmm . . . There was something fishy about him. A closet homosexual. That was the predominant theory. I wonder if he ever came out.'

Erica had to stop herself from laughing. She pictured Liza, with the false eyelashes and beautiful silk gown.

'Maybe he did,' she said with a smile.

Holm gave her a puzzled look, but she didn't explain any further. It was not up to her to inform Holm about Liza's life, and besides, she was well aware of the Friends of Sweden stance on homosexuals.

'You don't recall anything in particular about the teachers?'

'No, nothing. There were clear boundaries between the students, the teachers, and the family. Everyone was expected to know his place. Each group kept to itself.'

Rather like your policies, thought Erica, and she had to bite her tongue to keep from commenting. She could sense that Holm was starting to get impatient, so she asked her last question:

190

'According to one person that I've talked to, there were some strange noises in the house at night. Do you remember anything like that?'

He gave a start. 'Who said that?'

'It's not important.'

'Rubbish,' said Holm and stood up.

'So you don't know about these noises?'

'Absolutely not. And now I'm afraid I must make a few phone calls.'

Erica realized that she wasn't going to find out anything else, at least not now.

'Thanks for taking the time to talk to me,' she said, gathering up her things.

'My pleasure.' He'd turned on the charm again, but he rushed her out the door so fast her feet barely touched the ground.

Ia pulled up Leon's underpants and trousers and helped him over to the wheelchair from the toilet.

'All right, you can stop grimacing,' she said.

'I don't understand why we can't hire a nurse to do this sort of thing,' said Leon.

'I want to take care of you myself.'

'Your heart is overflowing with kindness,' Leon snorted. 'You're going to strain your back if you keep on this way. We need to have someone come in to help you.'

'It's nice of you to worry about my back, but I'm very strong, and I don't want somebody else coming in and . . . getting in the way. It's you and me. Until death do us part.' Ia tried to caress the uninjured side of his face, but he shrank from her touch, and she drew her hand back.

He wheeled himself away from her as she sat down on the sofa. They had bought the house fully furnished, and today they had finally been allowed to move in after the bank in Monaco had approved their withdrawal. They had paid the entire sum in cash. From the window they could see all of Fjällbacka, and she was enjoying the amazing view more than she thought she would. She heard Leon swearing out in the kitchen. Nothing had been adapted for wheelchair access, so he was having a hard time reaching things, and he kept on running into corners and cabinets.

'I'm coming,' she shouted but didn't jump up immediately. Sometimes it was good to make him wait for a bit. So he wouldn't take her help for granted. The same way he had taken her love for granted.

Ia looked down at her hands. They were just as scarred as Leon's. When she went out she always wore gloves to hide the scars from prying eyes, but here at home she wanted him to see the injuries she had sustained when she pulled him out of the burning car. Gratitude – that was what she demanded. She'd given up all hope of love. She was no longer sure whether Leon was capable of loving another person. Once upon a time she had thought so. Back then his love was the only thing that mattered. When had that love turned to hatred? She didn't know. For so many years she had tried to discover her flaws, tried so hard to correct whatever he criticized, done her utmost to give him what he seemed to want. But he had continued to torment her as if deliberately trying to hurt her. The mountains, the sea, the deserts, the women. None of it was important. They were all his mistresses. And the long periods of waiting for him to come home had been unbearable.

She touched her face. It was smooth, without expression. She suddenly remembered the pain of the operations. He was never there to hold her hand when she woke up from the anaesthesia. He was never there when she came home. The healing seemed to take forever. Now she didn't recognize herself when she looked in the mirror. But she didn't have to try hard any more. There were no mountains that Leon could climb, no deserts that he could drive through, no women for whom he could leave her. He was hers. All hers.

Tobias frowned as he stretched. His body ached from the endless manual labour, and he'd almost forgotten what it was like not to be in pain. He knew that it was the same for Ebba. When she thought he wasn't looking, she would often massage her shoulders and joints, grimacing the same way he did.

But the ache in their hearts was worse. They lived with it day and night, and the loss was so great that it was impossible to see where it started or ended. But Vincent was not the only one he missed; he missed Ebba too. And things had got worse when the loss was combined with the anger and guilt that they couldn't escape.

He sat on the steps with a mug of tea in his hand, gazing across the water at Fjällbacka. The view was most beautiful in the golden light of the evening sun. Somehow he'd always known that they would come back here. Even though he believed Ebba when she said that she'd had a good childhood, he'd sometimes sensed that she carried with her a question that would not go away until she at least tried to find the answer. He was certain that if he had broached the subject before everything fell apart, she would have denied it. But all the same Tobias had remained convinced that one day they would come here, to the place where it all began.

When circumstances finally forced them to flee – to something that was both familiar and unfamiliar, to a life in which Vincent had never existed – Tobias had harboured such hope. He hoped that they'd find their way back to each other and be able to leave the anger and guilt behind. But Ebba had shut him out and rejected all his attempts at intimacy. Did she have the right to do that? The pain and grief were not hers alone; they were his too. Surely he deserved to see that she was at least willing to try?

Tobias gripped the mug harder as he gazed out at the horizon. He pictured Vincent in his mind. His son had been so much like him. They had laughed about that even in the maternity ward. Newborn and swaddled in a blanket, Vincent had lain in his pram like a little caricature of Tobias. The resemblance had grown stronger, and Vincent had worshipped his father. At the age of three he would follow Tobias around like a puppy, and it was always his pappa that he called for first. Occasionally Ebba had complained, saying that it was ungrateful of Vincent, after she'd carried him for nine months and endured a painful birth. But she didn't mean it. It made her happy to see Vincent and Tobias grow so close, and she was content to take the number two spot.

Tears filled Tobias's eyes, and he swiped them away with his hand. He couldn't bear to cry any more, and besides, it served no purpose. The only thing he wanted was for Ebba to come back to him. He would never give up. He would keep on trying until she realized that they needed each other.

Tobias got up and went inside. He continued on upstairs, straining to hear where she was, although he already knew. Whenever they weren't working on the house, she would be sitting at her work table, engrossed in making a new necklace that some customer had ordered. He went into the room and stood behind her.

'Did you get a new order?'

She gave a start. 'Yes,' she said and continued shaping the silver.

'Who's the customer?' Anger at her indifference surged inside him, and he had to stop himself from losing his temper.

'Her name is Linda. Her son died when he was only four months old. Sudden infant death syndrome. He was her first child.'

'I see,' he said, turning away. He couldn't understand how she could bear to hear such stories, all that grief from unknown parents. Wasn't her own sorrow enough? He didn't need to look to know that she was wearing her necklace. It was the first one she'd made, and she always had it on. Vincent's name was engraved on the back. There were moments when he wanted to tear that necklace off of her, when he didn't think she was worthy to bear her son's name around her neck. But there were also moments when he wanted nothing more than for her to have Vincent close to her heart. Why did it have to be so hard? What would happen if he let it all go, accepted what had happened and acknowledged that they were both to blame?

Tobias set his mug on a shelf and took a step towards Ebba. He hesitated for a moment but then placed his hands on her shoulders. He felt her body stiffen. Gently he began massaging her muscles, sensing that she was as tense as he was. She didn't say a word, merely stared straight ahead. Her hands, which had been working on the silver angel, sank to the table, and the only sound was his breathing and hers. He felt hope stirring. He was touching her, feeling her body under his hands. Maybe there was a way forward.

Abruptly Ebba got to her feet. Without saying anything, she left the room, and he stood there with his hands in midair. For a moment he stared at her work table, which was covered with clutter. Then, as if of their own volition, his arms moved in a great arc and sent the whole lot crashing to the floor. In the silence that followed, he realized that there was only one path to take. He was going to have to risk everything.

STOCKHOLM 1925

'I'm cold, Mamma.' Laura was whining unhappily, but Dagmar paid no attention. They were going to wait here until Hermann came home. Sooner or later he'd have to return, and he would be so happy to see her. She longed to see his eyes light up, to see the desire and love that would be so much stronger after all these years of waiting.

'Mamma . . .' Laura was shaking so hard that her teeth chattered.

'Hush!' snapped Dagmar. The child was always ruining everything. Didn't she want them to be happy? Dagmar could no longer contain the rage inside of her, and she raised her hand to strike.

'I wouldn't do that if I were you.' A strong hand grabbed her wrist, and Dagmar turned around in fright. Behind her stood an elegant gentleman wearing a dark overcoat, dark trousers, and a hat.

She tossed her head. 'Sir, you have no right to interfere with how I raise my child.'

'If you hit her, I will hit you just as hard. Then you'll see how it feels,' he said calmly, and his voice indicated that he would not stand for any backchat.

Dagmar considered telling this man what she thought of people who stuck their noses in matters that were none of their business, but she could see it would do her no good.

'Please forgive me,' she said. 'The girl has been impossible all day. It's not easy to be a mother, and sometimes . . .' She shrugged apologetically, gazing down at the ground so that he wouldn't see the fury in her eyes.

Slowly the man released his hold on her wrist and took a step back.

'What are you doing here, outside my front door?'

'We're waiting for my pappa,' said Laura, giving the stranger a pleading look. She was not shamed by the fact that someone had dared to defy her mother.

'And your pappa lives here?' The man scrutinized Dagmar.

'We're waiting for Captain Göring,' she said, drawing Laura close.

'Well then, you're going to have a long wait,' he said, still studying them with interest.

Dagmar felt her heart start to pound in her chest. Had something happened to Hermann? Why hadn't that miserable woman upstairs said anything?

'What do you mean?' she demanded.

The man crossed his arms. 'An ambulance came to get him. They took him away in a straitjacket.'

'I don't understand.'

'He's in Långbro Hospital.' The man wearing the elegant coat stepped over to the door, apparently in a hurry now to put an end to this conversation with Dagmar. She tried to take his arm, but he pulled away with a grimace.

'Please, sir, can you tell me how to find that hospital? I must see Hermann!'

His whole face radiated displeasure, and he opened the door and stepped inside without replying. When the heavy door closed behind him, Dagmar sank down to the ground. What was she going to do now?

Head resting on her knees, she sobbed as if her heart were breaking. Laura tugged at her mother, trying to get her back on her feet. Dagmar shook her off. Why couldn't the child leave her alone and go away? What was she going to do with the girl if she couldn't find Hermann? Laura was not simply her *child. She was theirs.*

Patrik rushed into the station, coming to an abrupt halt in the reception area. Annika was deeply immersed in something and didn't look up for a moment. When she noticed Patrik standing there, she smiled and then looked down again.

'Is Martin still sick?' asked Patrik.

'Yes,' said Annika, her eyes fixed on the computer screen.

Patrik gave her a puzzled glance and then turned on his heel. There was only one thing to do.

'I've got an errand to run,' he said and went back outside. He saw Annika open her mouth, but he didn't hear what she said.

Patrik glanced at his watch. It was just before nine in the morning. A little too early to appear on somebody's doorstep, but by now he was so worried that he didn't care if he woke them.

It took him only a few minutes to drive to the block of flats where Martin lived with his family. Standing in front of their door, Patrik hesitated. Maybe nothing was wrong, maybe Martin really was sick and in bed, and he was going to wake him up for no good reason. He might even be insulted, thinking that Patrik had come over to check up on him. But his gut feeling told him otherwise. Martin should have phoned him by now, regardless how ill he was. Patrik pressed the doorbell.

He waited a long time and considered ringing it again, but he knew that the flat wasn't very big, so they must have heard the bell. Finally he heard footsteps approaching.

When the door opened, Patrik had a shock. There was no doubt that Martin looked ill. He was unshaven, his hair was dishevelled, and he smelled faintly of sweat, but worst of all was the vacant expression in his eyes. Patrik almost didn't recognize him.

'What are you doing here?' Martin asked.

'Can I come in?'

Martin shrugged, turned, and shuffled into the flat.

'Is Pia at work?' asked Patrik, looking around.

'No.' Martin paused near the balcony door in the living room to stare out of the window.

Patrik frowned. 'Are you sick?'

'I called the office to say I wasn't coming in. Didn't Annika tell you?' He sounded cross as he turned around. 'Maybe you want a doctor's certificate or something? Are you here to make sure that I'm telling the truth and not out sunbathing?'

Normally Martin was the most easy-going and good-natured person. Patrik had never known his colleague to succumb to this sort of outburst before, and he felt even more worried. Something was very wrong.

'Why don't we sit down,' he said, motioning towards the kitchen.

Martin's anger subsided as swiftly as it had flared up, and the dead look returned to his eyes. He nodded listlessly and followed his colleague. They sat down at the kitchen table, and Patrik studied Martin with real concern.

'What's going on here?'

For a moment Martin didn't speak.

'Pia is dying,' he said then, fixing his eyes on the table.

His words made no sense, and Patrik refused to believe what he'd just heard.

'What do you mean?'

'She went in for treatment the day before yesterday. She was lucky they could get her in so quickly.'

'Treatment for what?' Patrik shook his head. He'd bumped into Pia and Martin over the weekend, and at that time everything seemed fine.

'Unless there's some sort of miracle, the doctors say she might have only six months left.'

'Six months of treatment?'

Slowly Martin raised his head and looked his colleague in the eye. The naked pain in his expression almost made Patrik recoil.

'Six months until she dies. Then Tuva won't have a mother any more.'

'What . . . How . . . When did you . . .?' Patrik heard himself stammering, but he simply couldn't find anything sensible to say.

And Martin didn't reply. Instead, he laid his head on the table and began sobbing so hard that his whole body shook. Patrik got up and went over to put his arms around him. He had no idea how much time passed, but finally Martin stopped crying, and his body relaxed.

'Where's Tuva?' asked Patrik, still holding Martin.

'With Pia's mother. I can't . . . not right now.' He started to cry again, the tears running silently down his cheeks.

Patrik stroked his back. 'It's okay, just let it all out.'

What a cliché that was, and he felt a bit foolish, but what else was there to say in a situation like this? Was there any right or wrong thing to say? His words really didn't matter, and it was unclear whether Martin was even listening.

'Have you eaten?'

Martin sniffled, wiped his nose on the sleeve of his bathrobe, and then shook his head. 'I'm not hungry.'

'That doesn't matter. You have to eat.' Patrik went over to the fridge to see what he could find. There was plenty of food, but he could tell it wasn't the right time to cook a proper meal, so he merely took out some butter and cheese. Then he toasted a few slices of French bread that he found in the freezer and made two open-face sandwiches. He thought that was about all Martin could handle at the moment. Then he made another sandwich for himself. He figured it would be easier for Martin to eat if he had company.

'Now tell me all about it,' he said after Martin had finished the first sandwich and a little colour had returned to his face.

Haltingly Martin told Patrik all that he knew about Pia's cancer and the shock they'd had. One day everything was fine, and then only a few days later they found out that she had to be admitted to the hospital and undergo a rigorous course of treatments that might not help her.

'When does she get to come home?'

'Next week, I think. I'm not really sure. I haven't . . .' Martin's hand shook as he lifted his sandwich. He looked ashamed.

'You haven't talked to them? Have you gone to see Pia since she was admitted?' Patrik was doing his best not to sound reproachful. That was the last thing Martin needed right now, and in a strange way he could understand his colleague's reaction. He'd seen enough people in shock to recognize that vacant stare and the wooden movements.

'I'm going to make some tea,' he said before Martin could reply. 'Or would you rather have coffee?'

'Coffee,' said Martin. He was chewing and chewing, and it seemed he was having a hard time swallowing.

Patrik filled a glass with water. 'Here. Drink some water to wash it down. The coffee will be ready in a few minutes.'

'I haven't gone to see her,' said Martin, as he finished chewing.

'That's not so strange. You're in shock,' said Patrik as he measured coffee grounds into the filter.

'I've failed her. She needs me so much right now, but I've failed her. And Tuva. I couldn't take her over to Pia's mother fast enough. As if this isn't hard for her too. Pia is her daughter, after all.' He seemed on the verge of tears again, but he took a deep breath and then made an effort to calm his breathing. 'I've no idea where Pia gets her strength. She's phoned me several times, and she's worried about me. How crazy is that? She's getting radiation and chemotherapy and who knows what the hell else. She must be scared to death and feeling really sick. But she's worried about me!'

'That's not so strange either,' said Patrik. 'Now here's what we'll do. You go take a shower and shave, and when you're done with that, the coffee will be ready.'

'No, I . . .' Martin began, but Patrik held up his hand.

'Either you take a shower this minute, or I'm going to drag you in there and scrub you myself. That's not something I'd particularly like to do, so I'm hoping you'll take care of it on your own.'

Martin couldn't help laughing. 'You're not getting anywhere near me with a towel. I'll do it myself.'

'Good,' said Patrik and turned around to hunt for coffee mugs in the cupboards. He heard Martin get up and go off to the bathroom.

Ten minutes later he was a new man when he came back into the kitchen.

'Now you're starting to look like yourself,' said Patrik, pouring steaming hot coffee into his mug.

'I feel better. Thanks,' said Martin, sitting down. His

203

face was still haggard and pale, but there was more life in his green eyes. His damp red hair was sticking straight up. He resembled an older version of Kalle Blomkvist from Astrid Lindgren's stories.

'I have a suggestion,' said Patrik, who'd been thinking about things while Martin was in the shower. 'You need to spend as much time as you can supporting Pia. And you also need to take over responsibility for Tuva. So why don't you take a holiday, starting now, and then we'll see how things go and how much more time you might require.'

'I only have three weeks of holiday left.'

'We'll work it out,' said Patrik. 'Never mind about the practical details right now.'

Martin gave him a dazed look and nodded. Patrik was suddenly reminded of Erica and the car accident she'd been involved in. It could have been him sitting here. He had come so close to losing everything.

She'd been lying in bed thinking all night long. After Patrik left for work, she had sat on the veranda, gathering her thoughts in peace and quiet. For once the children were playing on their own. She loved the view of the Fjällbacka archipelago, and she was so grateful that she'd managed to save this house where she and Anna had grown up. Now her own children could grow up here too. It was not an easy house to take care of. The wind and salt water took their toll on the wooden siding, and the place needed constant repairs and upkeep.

At the moment they didn't have any major financial problems. It had taken years of hard work, but these days she brought in a good income from her books. She hadn't particularly changed her routine, but it was nice to know that she didn't have to worry about breaking the household budget if she needed a new saucepan or they had to renovate the house.

She was well aware that there were many who did not enjoy the same sort of security. When there was never enough money or redundancy took its toll, it was easy to look for a scapegoat. That accounted, at least in part, for the success of the Friends of Sweden. Ever since her meeting with John Holm, Erica couldn't stop thinking about him and what he stood for. She had hoped he would be an unpleasant man who was a blatant manifestation of his offensive views. Instead she'd found something much more dangerous. An articulate person who invited trust and was able to provide simple answers. Someone who could help the voters identify a scapegoat and then promise to make it disappear.

Erica shivered. She was convinced that Holm was hiding something. It remained to be seen whether there was any connection to what happened on Valö, but she knew who she would talk to next.

'Kids, we're going for a ride!' she yelled, turning towards the living room. Her words prompted cheers from her children, who loved car rides.

'Mamma just has to make one phone call. Maja, put on your shoes, and then I'll come and help Anton and Noel.'

'I can help them,' said Maja, taking her brothers by the hand and pulling them out to the front hall. Erica smiled. Maja was becoming more and more like a little mother with each day that passed.

Fifteen minutes later they were all in the car, heading to Uddevalla. She'd called to make sure that Kjell would be in. She didn't want to take her kids out there for nothing. At first she'd considered explaining everything on the phone, but then she realized that Kjell should see the note with his own eyes.

They sang kids' songs all the way to Uddevalla, so Erica's voice was hoarse by the time she announced their arrival to the receptionist. After a moment Kjell came out to greet them.

'Whoa, did you bring the whole gang?' he said, eyeing the three children who were shyly peering at him.

Kjell gave Erica a hug, his beard scratching her cheek. She smiled. She was glad to see him. They'd met a few years back when a murder investigation had revealed that her deceased mother, Elsy, and Kjell's father had been friends during the Second World War. She and Patrik both liked Kjell, and she had a great deal of respect for the work he did as a journalist.

'No babysitter today,' she explained.

'That's okay. It's good to see all of you,' said Kjell, giving the children a friendly smile. 'I think I've got some toys in a basket that you can play with while I have a talk with your mother.'

'Toys?' Their shyness evaporated, and Maja hurried after Kjell, eager to see the promised basket.

'Here it is. Paper and crayons mostly,' said Kjell, dumping the contents on to the floor.

'I should warn you, you're liable to end up with spots on the rug,' said Erica. 'They're not very good about staying on the page.'

'Do you honestly think a few spots will make any difference on this rug?' said Kjell, sitting down at his desk.

Seeing the state of the rug, Erica realized he had a point.

'I met John Holm yesterday,' she said, sitting down in the visitor's chair.

Kjell gave her a searching look.

'What was your impression?'

'Charming. But very dangerous.'

'That pretty much sums him up. In his youth Holm belonged to one of the worst groups in the skinhead movement. That's also where he met his wife.'

'It's a little hard picturing him with a shaved head.' Erica turned to see what the kids were up to, but so far they were behaving perfectly.

'Well, he's certainly worked on his image. But in my opinion, those guys don't change. They just get smarter with the years and learn how they ought to behave.'

'Does he have a police record?'

'No. He's never been charged with anything, although he had a few close calls when he was younger. At the same time, I don't believe for a minute that Holm's views have changed one iota since those years when he participated in the skinhead demonstrations in Lund every November thirtieth. On the other hand, I can say with one hundred per cent confidence that it's because of him that his party now has a seat in the Riksdag.'

'Why is that?'

'His first brilliant idea was to exploit the division that arose among various national socialist groups after the school fire in Uppsala.'

'You mean when those three Nazis were convicted of the crime?' said Erica, recalling the headlines in the papers from years ago.

'Exactly. In addition to the splits within and between the various groups, there was suddenly huge interest from the media, and the police were keeping an eye on right-wing extremists. That's when John Holm stepped in. He gathered the best brains from the different groups and suggested a collaboration, which resulted in the Friends of Sweden becoming the leading party. Since then he's spent years cleaning up the party faithful, at least on the surface, and drumming in the message that their politics are a grass-roots phenomenon. They've positioned themselves as the workers' party, the voice of the common man.'

'But isn't it hard to keep a party like that together? There must be a lot of extremists among the members.'

Kjell nodded. 'True. Some people have deserted because they found Holm's views too lightweight, and he's been accused of betraying the old ideals. Apparently there's an unspoken rule that prohibits open discussion of immigration policies. There are too many different opinions and that means there's a risk of breaking up the party. Some are of the opinion that all immigrants should be put on the first available plane and sent back to their native countries, while at the other end of the spectrum there are those who argue that more stringent requirements should be levied against everyone who comes here.'

'Which category does John Holm belong to?' asked Erica, turning around to hush the twins, who were getting noisy.

'Officially, the latter group, but unofficially . . .? Personally I wouldn't be surprised if he kept a Nazi uniform hanging in his wardrobe.'

'How did he end up in these circles?'

'I did some more checking on his background after you phoned yesterday. I knew that Holm's family were extremely wealthy; his father started an export company during the 1940s, and after the war he continued to expand. Business was booming – until 1976 . . .' Kjell paused for effect, and Erica sat up straighter.

'Yes?' she said.

'There was a scandal that rocked Stockholm's upper echelons. John's mother, Greta, left his father, Otto, for a Lebanese executive that Otto had done business with. It also emerged that Ibrahim Jaber – that was his name – had duped Otto out of most of his fortune. In late July 1976, deserted and destitute, Otto shot himself while sitting at his desk.'

'What happened to Greta and John?'

'Otto's death was not the end of the tragedy. It turned out that Jaber already had a wife and children, and he'd never had any intention of marrying Greta. He simply took her money and abandoned her. Several months later, John Holm's name appeared for the first time in connection with the National Socialists.

'And his hatred hasn't diminished,' said Erica, reaching for her handbag. She took out the note and handed it to Kjell. 'I found this in Holm's house yesterday. I can't read what it says, but maybe it's important.'

He laughed. 'Define what you mean by *found*.'

'You sound exactly like Patrik,' said Erica, smiling. 'It was just lying there. I'm sure it's only a scribbled note that nobody will ever miss.'

'Let me see.' Kjell put on his reading glasses, which he'd pushed up on his forehead. 'Gimle,' he read aloud, frowning.

'Yes. What does that mean? I've never come across the word before. Is it an abbreviation of some sort?'

Kjell shook his head. 'Gimle is what comes after Ragnarök, the end of the world in Nordic mythology. A sort of heaven or paradise. It's a well-known concept and frequently used in neo-Nazi circles. It's also the name of a cultural association. They claim not to be affiliated with any political party, but I have my doubts on that score. They're certainly popular with both the Friends of Sweden and the Danish People's Party.'

'And what do they do?'

'According to their literature, their aim is to revive nationalistic feelings and a shared identity through reviving old Swedish traditions, folk dancing, ancient Swedish poetry, relics of antiquity, and so on. All of which fits in with the purported goal of the Friends of Sweden to promote Swedish traditions.'

'So Gimle might also be a reference to that association?' She pointed at the paper.

'It's impossible to tell. It could mean anything. And

209

it's hard to know what these numbers signify: 19202118516121114. And then it says: 5 08 1400.'

Erica shrugged. 'I haven't a clue. I thought they might have been scribbled down in a hurry, the way you do when you're on the phone.'

'Could be,' said Kjell. He waved the paper in the air. 'Can I keep this?'

'Sure, go ahead. I'll just use my mobile to take a picture, in case I suddenly get a flash of inspiration and crack the code.'

'Good idea.' He pushed the paper across to her, and she took a picture. Then she knelt down on the rug and began tidying up after the children.

'Do you have any idea what you're going to do with that?'

'No, not really. I might start by exploring a few archives, see if I can come up with more information.'

'So you think it's more than a phone doodle?' she said.

'It could be. In any case, it's worth checking out.'

'Keep me posted, and I'll let you know if I find anything new.' She began ushering the kids towards the hall.

'Of course. We'll keep in touch,' Kjell said, reaching for the phone.

It was so typical. If Gösta arrived late, there was hell to pay, while Patrik could be gone half the morning and nobody raised an eyebrow. Erica had phoned last night and told Gösta about her visits to Ove Linder and John Holm. Now he was impatiently awaiting Patrik's arrival so they could go see Leon. Sighing at the unfairness of life, he returned to studying the list on his desk.

A second later the phone rang and he grabbed the receiver.

'Hello. Flygare here.'

'Gösta,' said Annika. 'Torbjörn's on the phone. The

results of the blood analysis have come in. He's asking for Patrik, but would you mind taking the call?'

'Of course.'

Gösta listened carefully as he made detailed notes, even though he knew that Torbjörn would fax over a copy of his report. But the official reports were usually written in such convoluted language, and it was easier to understand the information when Torbjörn explained it.

The moment Gösta put down the phone there was a knock on the open door to his office.

'Annika said that Torbjörn rang. What did he say?' Patrik sounded eager to hear the news, although his expression was glum.

'Is something wrong?' asked Gösta without answering the question.

Patrik dropped heavily on to a chair. 'I went to check up on Martin.'

'How's he doing?'

'He'll be taking a leave of absence for a while. Three weeks, to start with. Then we'll see.'

'Why?' Gösta felt his concern rise. Though he sometimes gave his young colleague a hard time, he liked Martin Molin. Everyone liked Martin.

When Patrik told him what he knew about Pia's condition, Gösta swallowed hard. The poor guy. And their little girl was only a couple of years old, and now she was going to lose her mother. He swallowed again and turned away, blinking frantically. He couldn't sit here in his office blubbering.

'The best thing we can do is to keep working,' Patrik concluded. 'What did Torbjörn say?'

Gösta discreetly wiped his eyes and cleared his throat before turning to the notes he'd written down.

'The crime lab confirmed that it's human blood. But it's so old that they were unable to get any DNA results that

211

could be compared with Ebba's. And it's not clear whether the blood came from more than one individual.'

'Okay. That's pretty much as I expected. What about the bullet?'

'Torbjörn sent it to a weapons specialist yesterday. They ran a quick analysis, but unfortunately it's not a match for any bullets used in other crimes.'

'Well, it was worth a try,' said Patrik.

'Sure. Apart from that they could only confirm that it's a nine millimetre bullet.'

'Nine millimetres? That doesn't exactly tell us much about the type of gun that was used.' Patrik slumped on his chair.

'No, but Torbjörn said there were clear grooves on the bullet, so his expert is going to examine it more closely to see if he can determine the type of gun used. And if we find the gun, then the bullet can be matched up with it.'

'But first there's that small detail of finding the gun.' He looked at Gösta. 'How thoroughly did you search the house and surroundings?'

'You mean in 1974?'

Patrik nodded.

'We did the best we could,' said Gösta. 'We were short-staffed, but we went over the island with a fine-tooth comb. If someone had tossed a gun somewhere, we would have found it.'

'Most likely it's at the bottom of the sea,' said Patrik.

'You're probably right. By the way, I've started phoning the former pupils from the school, but no results yet. Quite a few didn't answer the phone, but that's not too surprising, since it's the summer holiday.'

'It's good that you've made a start, at least,' said Patrik, running a hand through his hair. 'Make a note if there's anyone who might warrant further attention, and maybe we can go see them in person.'

'They're scattered all over Sweden,' said Gösta. 'It's going to require a hell of a lot of driving if we try to speak to them one on one.'

'Let's discuss it again once we know how many people we're talking about.' Patrik got up and headed for the door. 'How about we drop by Leon Kreutz's house after lunch? We're lucky that he lives so close.'

'Sure. Hopefully we'll learn more than we did from the interview yesterday. Josef was as taciturn as he was back in 1974.'

'It was like getting blood from a stone. And that Sebastian was a slippery character,' said Patrik as he left the room.

Gösta's hand hovered over the phone, preparing to tap in another number. He hated talking on the phone, and if it hadn't been for Ebba, he would have tried to get out of it. At least he wouldn't have to do the whole list, since Erica had promised to do some of it.

'Gösta? Come here a minute.' Patrick's voice interrupted him.

Out in the corridor stood Tobias Stark. He had a grim expression on his face, and he was holding a plastic bag containing what appeared to be a postcard.

'Tobias has something to show us,' said Patrik.

'I put it in a bag as soon as I could,' said Tobias. 'But I did touch it, so I might have ruined any prints.'

'You did the right thing,' Patrik said, wanting to reassure him.

Gösta peered through the plastic at the card. It was a typical card showing a yellow kitten on the front. He opened it and read the brief message.

'What the hell?' he exclaimed.

'Apparently "G" is starting to show his true colours,' said Patrik. 'This can only be interpreted as a threat.'

LÅNGBRO HOSPITAL 1925

There must have been some sort of misunderstanding, or else it was the fault of that awful woman. But Dagmar could help him. No matter what had happened, it would all work out as soon as they were together again.

She had left the girl in a pastry shop in town. She'd be fine there. If anyone asked her why she was all alone, she was to say that her mother had gone to the toilet.

Dagmar studied the building. It hadn't been hard to find. After stopping a few people to ask for directions, she'd finally met a woman who was able to tell her how to get to Långbro Hospital. Now her biggest worry was working out how to slip inside. There were too many staff on duty at the main entrance for her to slip by unnoticed. She had considered introducing herself as Mrs Göring, but if Carin had already been here to visit, they'd see through her ploy, and she wouldn't get another chance.

Cautiously, so as not to be seen by anyone looking out of the windows, Dagmar crept around to the back of the building. There she found what seemed to be an employee entrance. She watched for a while as women of various ages went in and out, all of them wearing starched uniforms. Some of them stopped by a cart to the right of the door and dropped in dirty laundry. That gave Dagmar an idea. Surreptitiously she approached the laundry cart, keeping one eye on the door in case anyone came out. But the door remained closed, and swiftly she rummaged through the contents of the cart. It was mostly sheets and tablecloths, but at the very bottom was a uniform identical to the ones the nurses had on. She pulled it out and slipped around the corner to put it on.

When she was ready, she straightened her back and tucked her hair under the cap. The hem of the uniform was a bit soiled, but otherwise it looked presentable. With luck the hospital was big enough that the nurses wouldn't notice that a stranger had suddenly appeared among them.

Dagmar opened the door and peeked inside what appeared to be a changing room for employees. It was empty, and she hurried along the corridor, constantly scanning for a clue to Hermann's whereabouts. She walked close to the wall, passing a long row of closed doors. There were no nameplates, and she began to realize that she might never find him. Despair rose up inside her, and she put a hand to her mouth to prevent a whimper escaping. She wasn't ready to give up yet.

Two young nurses came walking towards her. They were talking in low voices, but as they drew closer, Dagmar pricked up her ears. Did they just say the name Göring? She walked slower, trying to eavesdrop. One of the nurses carried a tray, and it sounded as if she was complaining to her colleague.

'The last time he threw the food at me,' she said, shaking her head.

'That's why matron said that from now on there must be two of us when we go to Göring's room,' said the other nurse. She too sounded a bit scared.

They stopped outside a door, both of them hesitating. Realizing that she needed to seize this opportunity, Dagmar cleared her throat and put on an authoritative voice.

'I've been ordered to see to Göring, so you girls won't have to do it,' she said, reaching for the tray.

'You have?' said the nurse. She sounded surprised, but the relief on her face was obvious.

'I know how to handle patients like Göring. All right then, off you go, both of you. Leave me to take care of this. But first open the door for me.'

'Thank you,' said the girls, curtseying. One of them took out a big key ring and inserted one of the keys in the lock. She pulled open the door, and as soon as Dagmar stepped inside, the two nurses hurried off, happy to have been relieved of such an unpleasant task.

Dagmar felt her heart pounding. There he lay, her Hermann, curled up on a cot with his back to her.

'Everything's going to be fine, Hermann,' she said, setting the tray on the floor. 'I'm here now.'

He didn't move. She studied his back, shivering with pleasure at being so close to him at last.

'Hermann,' she said, laying her hand on his shoulder.

He shrugged it off, and in one swift movement he turned over and sat up on the edge of the bed. 'What do you want?' he bellowed.

Dagmar recoiled. Was this Hermann? The dapper pilot who had made her whole body tremble? That straight-backed, broad-shouldered man whose hair had gleamed like gold in the sun? This couldn't possibly be him.

'Give me my medicine, you fucking bitch. I need it! Don't you know who I am? I'm Hermann Göring, and I need my medicine.' He spoke Swedish with a strong German accent, and he paused between each word, as if translating in his head.

Her throat seemed to close up. This man who was hollering like a madman was fat and his skin had a sickly pallor. His thin hair was plastered to his scalp. Sweat ran down his face.

Dagmar took a deep breath and forced herself to speak. 'Hermann. It's me. Dagmar.' She kept her distance, afraid that at any moment he might lunge at her.

The blood vessels in his forehead bulged, and his pale skin took on a bright red flush that spread from his neck upwards.

'Dagmar? I don't give a shit what you whores are called. I

want my medicine. It's the Jews who have locked me up in here, and I have to get out. Hitler needs me. Where's my medicine?'

He was so agitated that spittle sprayed Dagmar's face. Terrified, she tried again.

'Don't you remember me? We met at a party given by Doctor Sjölin. In Fjällbacka.'

He abruptly stopped shouting and frowned as he stared at her in astonishment.

'In Fjällbacka?'

'Yes, at Doctor Sjölin's party,' she repeated. 'We spent the night together.'

His eyes lit up, and she realized that he did remember her. At last. Now everything was going to be fine. She would work it all out and Hermann would again become her handsome captain.

'You're the waitress,' he said, wiping the sweat from his forehead.

'My name is Dagmar,' she said, an uneasy feeling settling in her stomach. Why hadn't he jumped up and taken her in his arms, the way she'd always pictured it in her dreams?

Then he began to laugh, making his fat paunch jiggle.

'Dagmar. Exactly.' He laughed again, and Dagmar clenched her hands into fists.

'We have a daughter. Laura.'

'A daughter?' He narrowed his eyes. 'You're not the first to try that one! It can never be proved. Especially with a waitress.'

He uttered the last words with such contempt that Dagmar again felt her fury rise. In this sterile white room, where not even a sliver of daylight could penetrate the window, all her dreams and hopes had finally been shattered. Everything she thought she'd known about her life had turned out to be a lie – the years she'd spent longing and pining and putting up with a screaming child, his daughter, who constantly made demands – it had all been in vain.

Determined to hurt him as much as he had hurt her, she threw herself at him, her fingers curled into claws. Guttural sounds came from her throat as her fingers dug in, scratching at his face. As if from far away, she heard him screaming in German. The door opened, and she felt them pulling at her, dragging her off the man she had loved for so long.

Then everything went black.

❧

It was his father who had taught him how to negotiate a good business deal. Lars-Åke 'Lovart' Månsson was a legend, and while he was growing up, Sebastian had worshipped him. His father's nickname, which meant 'windward' in Swedish, had been given to him because he invariably managed to pull through, even in the most impossible straits. It was said that Lars-Åke led such a charmed existence he could spit into the wind and not a drop of saliva would land on his face.

Lovart had discovered that it was actually quite simple to get people to do what he wanted. The basic principle was the same as in boxing: identify your opponent's weak spot and then attack it over and over until it was time to raise your arms in victory. Or, as in his own case, bring home the loot. His way of doing business won him neither popularity nor respect, but as he often said: 'Respect never fed a hungry man.'

That had become Sebastian's motto too. He was aware that he was despised by many and feared by most, but as he sat next to the pool with a cold beer in his hand, he knew that none of that really mattered. He wasn't interested in making friends. Having friends would mean compromise and surrendering some of his power.

'Pappa? The guys and I are thinking of going over to Strömstad, but I haven't got any money.' Wearing swimming trunks and a pleading expression, Jon came sauntering over to his father.

Sebastian shaded his eyes as he studied his twenty-year-old son. Sometimes Elisabeth grumbled that he spoiled Jon and his sister Jossan, who was two years younger, but he paid no heed. A difficult childhood with rules and regulations was not for his children. A life of privilege would teach them what the world had to offer and how to take whatever they could get. There would be plenty of time to bring Jon into the firm and teach him the things Lovart had taught Sebastian. Until then, the boy should be allowed to play.

'Take my gold card. It's in my wallet in the front hall.'

'Cool. Thanks, Dad!' Jon dashed into the house as if afraid that Sebastian might change his mind.

When he'd borrowed his father's gold card for tennis week in Båstad, the bill had come to seventy thousand kronor. But that was nothing in the grand scheme of things. And most importantly, it had helped Jon to maintain his position among the friends he'd made at Lundsberg. There the rumours of his father's wealth had quickly attracted boys who in the future would be influential men.

Naturally Lovart had taught Sebastian the importance of cultivating the right contacts. They were much more valuable than friends. That was why Lovart had selected the school on Valö for his son. The other boys who had enrolled came from the best families – with one exception. The Jewish boy, as Lovart called him, had neither money nor the appropriate background, and his presence detracted from the school's status. But when Sebastian thought back to that strange and distant time, he realized that Josef had been the student he'd liked best. Josef had the same drive and obsessive motivation that he recognized in himself.

Now that they'd been reunited because of Josef's lunatic plans, Sebastian had to admit that he admired Josef's determination to do whatever it took to achieve his goal. It wasn't relevant that their goals were not the same. Inevitably the wake-up call, when it came, would be brutal. But he sensed that Josef, in his heart, had understood from the start that this would not end happily for him. Still, hope is always the last thing to die. And Josef was aware that he had to do Sebastian's bidding, the same as everyone else.

The recent developments were certainly interesting. Rumours that a discovery had been made on the island had spread rapidly. Of course, the gossip had started up the moment Ebba came back. The fact that the police were now poking around had only added grist to the rumour mill.

Sebastian pensively twirled his beer glass and then pressed it to his chest to cool off. He wondered what the others made of it all, and whether they too had been visited by the police. From the driveway he heard the sound of the Porsche starting up. So the little bastard had swiped his car keys, which were lying next to his wallet. Sebastian smiled. Good tactics. If he were still alive, Lovart would have been proud.

Ever since Anna had returned from Valö yesterday, she'd been thinking about decorating ideas. This morning she'd practically leaped out of bed. Dan had laughed at her eagerness, but she could tell that he was happy for her sake.

It would be a long wait before she could actually get going on the project, but Anna could hardly contain herself. She felt drawn to the place. Maybe it was because Tobias had been so openly enthusiastic about her

221

suggestions. He had looked at her with something that resembled admiration, and for the first time in ages she had felt like an interesting and capable person. When she rang to find out if it would be okay for her to come back to take measurements and photographs, he had said that she was more than welcome.

Anna found herself missing his presence as she measured the distance between the windows in the master bedroom. The mood in the house was different when Tobias wasn't there. She cast a glance at Ebba, who was painting the doorframe.

'Don't you get lonely out here?'

'Not really. I think it's nice to have some peace and quiet.'

She seemed reluctant to talk, and the silence in the room was so oppressive that Anna felt compelled to carry on the conversation.

'Are you in touch with any of your relatives? Your biological relatives, I mean?' She could have bitten her tongue. The question sounded intrusive, and would no doubt make Ebba even less inclined to chat.

'There's no one left.'

'Have you researched your family history? You must be curious to know who your parents were.'

'I never was before.' Ebba stopped painting and held the paintbrush in the air. 'But ever since I came back here, I've started to wonder about them.'

'Erica has quite a lot of material.'

'Yes, that's what she said. I was thinking of going into town some day and having a look at it. I just haven't got around to it yet. It's so nice out here. I suppose I'm beginning to feel attached to the island.'

'I saw Tobias when I arrived. He was on his way to town.'

Ebba nodded. 'He took the shuttle in to do some grocery

222

shopping, pick up the post, and take care of all the other errands. I'm trying to get a bit of work done, but . . .'

Anna almost asked about the child that she'd heard Ebba and Tobias had lost. But she didn't quite dare. Her own grief was still too great for her to talk to someone else who had suffered a similar loss. At the same time she was puzzled. From what she could see, there was no trace of a child in the house. No photos, no items that might indicate that they had once been parents. But there was a look in Ebba's eyes that she recognized. She saw that same look in the mirror every day.

'Erica said she was going to try to find out what happened to your family's belongings. There might be some personal possessions still around,' she said as she began measuring the floor.

'I know. I agree with her that it seems odd that everything vanished. They lived in this house, so there must have been all sorts of stuff here. I'd love to find some of the clothes and toys from when I was a child. Like the things that I saved from . . .' She stopped talking abruptly and went back to painting, filling the room with the swishing sound of her brush. Every once in a while she would lean down and dip the brush in a can of white paint that was almost gone.

When she heard Tobias's voice from downstairs, she froze.

'Ebba?'

'I'm upstairs!'

'Do you need anything from the cellar?'

Ebba went out to the landing to answer him. 'A can of white paint. Thanks. Anna is here.'

'I know. I saw her boat,' Tobias replied. 'I'll go and get the paint. How about making some coffee for us?'

'Okay.' Ebba went back in the room and said to Anna, 'Would you like to take a break?'

'Sure,' Anna replied, folding up the measuring tape.

'You can keep working for a while. I'll give you a shout when the coffee is ready.'

'Okay, I'll do that. Thanks.' Anna unfolded the measuring tape again and continued jotting down the measurements on a sketch that she'd made. This would make the task of choosing the decor much easier.

She focused on the job, vaguely conscious of Ebba pottering about in the kitchen downstairs. A cup of coffee would be welcome about now, preferably sitting in the shade. The heat upstairs was starting to get unbearable, and her shirt was sticking to her back.

Suddenly she heard a loud bang followed by a shrill scream. The unexpected sounds made Anna jump, and she dropped the measuring tape. Then there was another bang, and without thinking she ran downstairs, moving so fast that she almost slipped on the worn steps.

'Ebba?' she yelled, racing for the kitchen.

In the doorway she stopped in her tracks. The window overlooking the back of the house had shattered, and shards of broken glass were strewn all over the room. Ebba was huddled on the floor in front of the stove, arms wrapped around her head. She had stopped screaming, but her breathing was ragged.

Anna dashed into the kitchen, glass crunching under her feet. She put her arms around Ebba, trying to see whether she was injured, but there didn't seem to be any blood. Next she scanned the room to see what could have broken the window. When her gaze fell on the far wall of the kitchen, she gasped. Two bullet holes were clearly visible in the wall.

'Ebba? What the hell was that?' Tobias came rushing up the cellar steps and into the kitchen. 'What happened?'

His eyes went from Ebba to the window, and then he was at his wife's side.

224

'Are you hurt? She's not hurt, is she?' He reached for Ebba and knelt cradling her in his arms.

'I don't think so,' said Anna. 'But it looks as though someone tried to shoot her.'

Anna's heart was racing, and she suddenly realized that they could all be in danger. Was the shooter still outside?

'We have to get away from here,' she said, motioning towards the broken window.

Tobias immediately understood what she was getting at.

'Don't stand up, Ebba. We need to stay away from the window.' He spoke slowly, as if addressing a child.

Ebba nodded and did as he said. Crouching low, they dashed for the front hall. Anna cast a terrified glance at the door. What if the shooter came in, stepped across the threshold and shot them all? Tobias saw her expression and threw himself at the door, turning the lock.

'Is there any other way for someone to get in?' she asked him, her heart still hammering.

'The cellar door, but it's locked.'

'What about the kitchen window? The glass is completely gone now.'

'It's too high up,' he said, sounding calmer than he looked.

'I'm calling the police.' Anna reached for her handbag, which lay on a shelf in the hall. Her hands shook as she got out her mobile. As she listened to the phone ringing, she watched Tobias and Ebba. They were sitting on the stairs. Tobias had his arm around his wife, and Ebba was leaning her head on his chest.

'Hi there. Where did you get to?'

Erica jumped with fright when she heard a voice coming from inside the house.

'Kristina?' She stared at her mother-in-law, who had come out of the kitchen with a dishrag in her hand.

225

'I let myself in. It was lucky that I still had a key from when I watered your flowers while you were on Mallorca, otherwise I would have driven all the way out here from Tanumshede for nothing,' she said cheerfully and then headed back to the kitchen.

You could have phoned ahead to ask if it was convenient for you to visit, thought Erica. She pulled off the children's shoes, took a deep breath, and went into the kitchen.

'I thought I'd drop by and help out for a couple of hours. It's obvious you could use a hand. In my day, the house would never have got in this state. There's no telling who might come over for a visit, and you wouldn't want them to see your house like this,' said Kristina, energetically wiping the sink.

'It's true. You never know when the king might drop by for a cup of coffee,' snapped Erica.

Kristina turned, eyebrows raised in astonishment. 'The king? Why would the king come here?'

Erica clenched her teeth so hard that her jaw hurt, but she didn't say a word. Silence was often the best response.

'Well, where have you been?' Kristina asked again as she ran the dishrag over the kitchen table.

'In Uddevalla.'

'You put the kids in the car and drove all the way to Uddevalla and back? My poor sweet darlings. Why didn't you ring me? I would have come over and stayed with them. Of course I'd have had to cancel my morning coffee with Görel, but I'd do anything for my children and grandchildren. That's my lot in life. You'll understand it better when you get older and your children are bigger.'

She paused for effect before going back to rubbing at a spot of marmalade that had congealed on the oilcloth covering the table.

'There'll come a day I won't be able to help out any more,' Kristina went on. 'It could happen at any time.

226

I'm over seventy now, and I don't know how long my energy will last.'

Erica nodded and forced a grateful smile.

'Have the children had anything to eat?' asked Kristina, and Erica gave a start. She'd forgotten to feed the kids. They were probably starving, but no way was she going to admit this to her mother-in-law.

'We stopped for sausages on the way there. But I'm sure they're ready for lunch by now.'

She strode resolutely over to the fridge to see what she could make. The fastest would be cornflakes and yogurt, so she set the yogurt on the table and took a box of Frosties out of the cupboard.

Kristina let out a sigh of dismay. 'In my day, we would never have dreamed of giving children anything but a properly cooked lunch. Patrik and Lotta never ate processed foods, and look how healthy they are. The basis for good health is proper food – that's what I've always said, but nobody seems to listen to conventional wisdom these days. You young people think you know best, and everything has to be done fast.' She had to pause to draw breath, and at that moment Maja appeared.

'Mamma, I'm starving and Noel and Anton are too. My tummy is empty.' She ran her hand over her stomach, still pudgy with baby fat.

'But you had a sausage when you were out driving in the car,' said Kristina, patting Maja's cheek.

'No, we didn't. We only had breakfast, and now I'm hungry. Really hungry!'

Erica glared at her little traitor. She could feel Kristina's disapproving gaze on the back of her neck.

'I could make them pancakes,' said Kristina, and Maja started jumping up and down with joy.

'Grandma's pancakes! I want Grandma's pancakes!'

'Thank you,' said Erica, putting the yogurt back in the

fridge. 'I'll just go upstairs to change and check on something for my work.'

Kristina had turned away and was getting out the ingredients for her pancake batter. The pan was already on the stove, heating up.

'You go ahead. I'll see to it that these poor children get something to eat.'

Erica slowly counted to ten as she climbed the stairs. There wasn't actually anything that she needed to check on, but she could use a little time to herself. Patrik's mother meant well, but she knew exactly which buttons to press that would drive Erica crazy. Strangely enough, Patrik was not affected in the same way, and that irked Erica even more. Every time she tried to talk to him about Kristina, about some insensitive thing she had said or done, he would simply reply: 'Oh, don't let her get to you. Mamma can be a bit of a busy-body at times, but her intentions are good.'

Maybe that was how things always were between mothers and sons, and maybe some day she would be just as vexing a mother-in-law to the wives of Noel and Anton. But in her heart she didn't think so. She was going to be the world's best mother-in-law. Her sons' wives would think of her as a friend, someone in whom they could confide. They would ask her and Patrik to go along on all of their trips, and she would help out with the kids, and if they had a lot to do at work, she would go over to their house and help with the cleaning and cooking. Most likely she'd have her own key and . . . Erica came to an abrupt halt. Perhaps, in spite of everything, it wasn't so easy to be the perfect mother-in-law.

In the bedroom she changed into a pair of denim shorts and a T-shirt. The white shirt was her favourite. She imagined that it made her look thinner. Her weight had fluctuated over the years, but she'd always been able to wear size 12. But for several years now, ever since Maja was born, she'd been forced to buy size 16. How had that happened? Patrik wasn't any better. To say he was buff when they met would be an exaggeration, but his stomach had been flat. Now it bulged out quite a bit, and unfortunately she had to admit that she thought beer-bellies were not very attractive. It made her wonder whether he thought the same about her. She was a far cry from the slim young woman she'd been when they'd met.

She cast one last glance at herself in the full-length mirror, and then abruptly turned around. Something was different in here. She surveyed the room, trying to remember how everything had looked earlier that morning. It was hard to conjure up an image of that particular morning, but she could swear that something had changed. Had Kristina been up here? No, because she would have felt compelled to tidy up and make the bed, and that hadn't happened. The bedclothes and pillows were all jumbled together, and the coverlet in a heap at the foot of the bed, as usual. Erica took another look around but then shrugged. It was probably just her imagination.

She went into her work room, turned on the computer, and pulled up the log-in screen. She stared at it in surprise. Somebody had tried to log in on her computer. After three failed attempts, it was now asking for an answer to one of her security questions: 'What was the name of your first pet?'

With an eerie feeling she inspected her work room. Someone had definitely been in here. It might seem that there was no particular order to things in the apparent chaos, but she knew exactly where everything was, and now she could tell that stuff had been moved. But why? Were they searching for something? If so, what? She spent a while trying to work out whether anything was missing, but drew a blank.

229

'Erica?'

Kristina was calling her from downstairs, and with the eerie feeling still in her body, she got up to find out what her mother-in-law wanted.

'Yes?' She leaned over the railing.

Kristina was standing in the front hall glaring at her reproachfully.

'You need to remember to close the veranda door properly. It could have had disastrous consequences if I hadn't happened to see Noel through the kitchen window. He was already outside and heading for the street. I managed to catch him, but you really can't go leaving doors open when you have young children in the house. They take off faster than you can blink an eye!'

Erica was stunned. She had a clear recollection of closing the veranda door before they set off. After hesitating for a moment, she picked up the phone to ring Patrik. A second later she heard the ringtone of his mobile coming from the kitchen. He'd left his phone on the bench. So she ended the call.

Paula got up from the sofa with a groan. Lunch was ready, and even though the thought of food made her feel sick, she knew she needed to eat. Usually she loved her mother's cooking, but she'd lost her appetite since the pregnancy. Given the choice, she would have subsisted on salty crackers and ice cream.

'Here comes the hippo!' said Mellberg, pulling out a chair for her.

She wasn't in the mood to argue, and besides, she'd heard his joke countless times before. 'What's for lunch?'

'Stew, cooked in an iron pot. It's important for you to get enough iron,' said Rita, dishing up an enormous portion and setting the plate in front of Paula.

'Thanks for letting me have lunch with you. I just don't

feel like cooking lately. Especially when Johanna's away at work.'

'We're glad to have you here, sweetie,' said Rita, giving her daughter a smile.

Paula took a deep breath and then forced herself to take a bite. It seemed to swell in her mouth, but she stubbornly kept chewing. The baby needed nourishment.

'How's it going at work?' she asked Mellberg. 'Are you making any progress on the Valö case?'

Mellberg finished off his portion of stew before answering.

'It's moving along. I have to keep cracking the whip, of course, but that's what gets results.'

'What have you found out so far?' asked Paula, knowing that in spite of being the police chief, Bertil probably wouldn't have the answer.

'Hmm . . .' He looked confused. 'Well, we haven't quite pieced together the results yet.'

His mobile rang. Grateful for the interruption, he got up and took the call.

'Mellberg here . . . Hi, Annika . . . So where the hell is Hedström? What about Gösta? Why can't you get hold of them? . . . Valö? All right, I can . . . I said, I'd take care of it!' He ended the call and muttered to himself as he headed for the front hall.

'Where are you going? You haven't cleared away the dishes,' Rita called after him.

'Important police business – a shooting out on Valö. I haven't time for household chores.'

Paula was suddenly alert. She scrambled to her feet as quickly as she could manage.

'Wait, Bertil! What did you say? Somebody got shot on Valö?'

'I don't know the details, but as I said to Annika, I'm heading out there to take care of it personally.'

231

'I'm coming with you,' said Paula. Breathing hard, she sat down on a stool to put on her shoes.

'Out of the question,' said Bertil. 'Besides, you're on holiday.'

Rita came rushing out of the kitchen to back him up.

'Are you crazy!' she cried, so loudly that it was a miracle she didn't wake Leo, who was taking a nap on the spare bed in Rita and Bertil's bedroom. 'You can't go, not in your condition.'

'Right. Talk some sense into your daughter.' Mellberg reached for the door handle, trying to slip away.

'You're not going anywhere without me. If you do, I'll hitchhike to Fjällbacka and make my way out to the island alone.'

Paula had made up her mind. She was tired of having to sit still, tired of doing nothing. Her mother kept on yelling, but she waved away all objections.

'Damnit, I'm surrounded by crazy women,' said Mellberg.

Defeated, he went out to his car. By the time Paula had made her way downstairs, he had started up the engine and turned on the air conditioning.

'Promise me you'll take it easy and keep out of the way if there's trouble.'

'I promise,' said Paula, climbing into the passenger seat. For the first time in months she felt like herself instead of a walking incubator. As Mellberg rang Victor Bogesjö at the Coast Guard to tell him they needed transport, Paula wondered what they would encounter out on the island.

FJÄLLBACKA 1929

School was a torment. Each morning Laura tried to put off leaving for school until the very last second. In the playground the ugly words and names would rain down on her, and of course it was all her mother's fault. Everyone in Fjällbacka knew who Dagmar was: a crazy woman, the town drunk. Sometimes on her way to school Laura would see her mother wandering around the marketplace, howling at people and raving about Göring. Laura just kept walking. Pretending not to see her, she would hurry past.

Her mother was seldom home. She stayed out late at night and was usually asleep when Laura left for school. Then she'd be gone when her daughter came home. The first thing Laura would do was tidy up the flat. Only after she'd removed all traces of her mother's presence would she feel any sense of calm. She gathered up the clothes that had been tossed on the floor, she put away the butter that had been left out, and she examined the bread to see if it was still edible after her mother had neglected to put it in the bread bin. Then Laura would dust and clear up. When everything was in its proper place and all the surfaces gleamed, she finally allowed herself to play with her dollhouse. It was her dearest possession. One day when her mother wasn't home a nice neighbour had knocked on the door and given her the dollhouse.

Sometimes people were kind and brought her things: food, clothing, toys. But most of them just stared and pointed. Ever since the time when her mother had left her alone in Stockholm, Laura had learned not to ask for help. On that occasion, the police had come to fetch her, and for two days it had felt as if she'd ended up in heaven. A family had taken her in, and both the mother and father had such kind eyes. She may have been only five at the time, but she could still remember every detail of those two days. The mother had made the biggest stack of pancakes that Laura had ever seen and urged her to eat more until her stomach was so full that she thought she'd never be hungry again. From a chest of drawers they had taken out lovely floral dresses for her to wear – dresses that were not ragged or dirty. She'd felt like a princess in her finery. For two nights she was tucked into a beautiful bed and given a kiss on the forehead. She had slept so soundly between those clean sheets. The mother with the kind eyes had smelled wonderful, not boozy and musty like her own mother. And they had the nicest house, with porcelain figurines and tapestries hanging on the wall. On the very first day Laura had begged to be allowed to stay. The mother didn't say a word as she hugged the little girl close in her soft arms.

But all too soon Laura and her mother were back home together. It was as if nothing had happened except that her mother was angrier than ever. Laura received thrashing after thrashing, till she could hardly sit down. That was when she made a decision: She would no longer dream about the mother who had been kind to her. No one was going to rescue her, and there was no use struggling. Regardless what happened, she would only end up back with her mother in the dark, cramped flat. But when she grew up, she would have a beautiful home with little porcelain cats sitting on crocheted doilies and embroidered tapestries in every room.

She knelt down in front of the dollhouse. The flat was clean and tidy, and she had folded and put away the laundry. Then she'd eaten a sandwich, and now she could allow herself to enter a different and better world. In her hand she held the mamma doll, who was so light and beautiful. Her dress was white, with lace and a high collar, and her hair was gathered in a knot. Laura loved the mamma doll. With her finger she stroked the doll's cheek. She was lovely, just like the mother who had smelled so good.

Gently Laura set the doll on the sofa in the parlour. That was the room she liked best. Everything was perfect. There was even a little crystal chandelier hanging from the ceiling. Laura could spend hours staring at those tiny prisms, amazed that anyone could make something so perfect and small. She squinted her eyes to inspect the room. Was it really perfect, or was there anything she could improve? She tried moving the dining table a bit to the left. Then one by one she moved the chairs, and it took a while to get them to line up properly at the table. Finally everything met with her approval – until she noticed there was an empty spot in the middle of the parlour. She couldn't have that. Picking up the mamma doll with one hand, she moved the sofa with the other. Satisfied, she put the sofa back down and then searched the dollhouse for the two children. They could come in too, as long as they behaved themselves. There was to be no running around or creating a mess in the parlour. They had to be polite and sit still. She was very firm about that.

She set the children on either side of the mamma doll. When Laura tilted her head at an angle, it was almost as if the mamma doll was smiling. She was so lovely and perfect. When Laura grew up, she was going to be exactly like her.

✤

Patrik was breathing hard by the time they reached the front door. The house was beautifully situated on a hill near the sea, and he had parked the car on Brandparken so they could walk up the path. It bothered him that he sounded like a bellows after climbing the winding path, while Gösta seemed completely unaffected.

'Hello?' said Patrik, poking his head in the open door. It was not unusual to do that in the summertime. Everybody left their doors and windows open, and instead of knocking or ringing the bell, visitors would simply yell a greeting.

A woman appeared wearing a sunhat, sunglasses, and some sort of fluttery, colourful tunic. In spite of the heat she had on thin gloves.

'Yes?' Her tone of voice suggested that she would have preferred not to speak to them.

'We're from the Tanum police. We're looking for Leon Kreutz.'

'That's my husband. I'm Ia Kreutz.' She shook hands without taking off her gloves. 'We're just having lunch.'

She clearly wasn't happy about them showing up. Patrik and Gösta exchanged glances. If Leon was as standoffish as his wife, this was going to be hard work. They followed her out to the balcony where a man was sitting in a wheelchair at the table.

'We have visitors. The police.'

The man nodded. He didn't seem at all surprised to see them.

'Have a seat. We're just having a light salad. My wife likes this kind of food.' Leon gave them a wry smile.

'My husband would prefer to skip lunch and smoke a cigarette instead,' said Ia. She sat down and spread a napkin on her lap. 'Do you mind if I finish eating?'

Patrik motioned for her to continue with her salad while they talked to Leon.

'I assume you're here to talk about Valö?' Leon had stopped eating and placed his hands in his lap. A wasp landed on a piece of chicken on his plate and was allowed to feast in peace.

'Yes, that's right.'

'What's going on out there anyway? We've been hearing wild rumours.'

'We've made certain discoveries,' replied Patrik, not wanting to say too much. 'I understand that you've recently returned to Fjällbacka.'

He studied Leon's face. One side was smooth with no trace of injury, while the other side was scarred and the corner of his mouth was permanently pulled upward, revealing his teeth.

'Yes. We bought the house a few days ago, and we moved in yesterday,' said Leon.

'What made you come back here after so many years?' asked Gösta.

'I suppose the yearning to return grows stronger as the years pass.' Leon turned his head to gaze out over the water. Patrik now saw only the good side of his face, and it was painfully obvious how handsome Leon must have once been.

'I would have preferred to stay in our house on the Riviera,' said Ia. She and her husband exchanged an inscrutable glance.

'Normally she gets what she wants.' Again Leon gave them that odd smile of his. 'But in this case, I insisted. I've been longing to come back.'

'Your family had a summer place here, didn't they?' said Gösta.

'Yes. A house on the island of Kalvö. Unfortunately, my father sold it. Don't ask me why. He had his whims, and he was a bit eccentric in his old age.'

'I heard that you were involved in a car accident,' said Patrik.

'If Ia hadn't saved me, I wouldn't be here today. Right, darling?'

Her fork and knife clattered so loudly that Patrik gave a start. She stared at Leon in silence. Then her expression softened.

'That's true, darling. Without me, you wouldn't be alive today.'

'And you never let me forget it.'

'How long have you been married?' asked Patrik.

'Almost thirty years.' Leon turned to face them. 'I met Ia at a party in Monaco. She was the most beautiful girl there. And she played hard to get. I had to really work at it.'

'It's not so strange that I was sceptical, considering your reputation.'

Their bickering reminded Patrik of a well-rehearsed dance, but it seemed to calm them both down. For a moment he thought he glimpsed a hint of a smile on Ia's lips. He wondered what she looked like without the huge sunglasses. Her skin was stretched tight over her jaw, and her lips were so unnaturally full that he suspected her eyes would merely confirm the impression that here was

238

someone who had paid a fortune to enhance her appearance.

Patrik again turned to Leon. 'We've come here to talk to you because, as I mentioned, certain discoveries have been made out on Valö. They indicate that the Elvander family was murdered.'

'That doesn't surprise me,' said Leon after a pause. 'I've never understood how a whole family could simply disappear.'

Ia started coughing. Her face had turned pale.

'You'll have to excuse me. There's really nothing I can contribute, so I think I'll go inside to finish my lunch in peace and let you carry on your discussion without me.'

'That's fine. Leon is the one we came to talk to.' Patrik moved his feet to allow Ia to pass. Carrying her plate, she swept past in a cloud of perfume.

Leon squinted at Gösta. 'I have the impression I know you from somewhere. Weren't you the officer who came out to Valö? The one who took us to the police station?'

Gösta nodded. 'Yes, that's right.'

'I remember how nice you were. Your colleague, on the other hand, was quite gruff. Is he still on the force?'

'Henry transferred to Göteborg in the early eighties. I lost contact with him, but I heard that he passed away a few years ago,' replied Gösta. Then he leaned forward. 'From what I recall, you were the kind of kid who took charge.'

'I don't know about that. But it's true that I've always been able to get people to listen to me.'

'The other boys seemed to look up to you.'

Leon nodded. 'You're probably right about that. What a group that was!' He laughed. 'Only at a boarding school for boys would you ever find such an odd bunch.'

'But didn't you have a lot in common? You all came from well-to-do families,' said Gösta.

'Not Josef. He was there only because of the grand ambitions of his parents. It was as if they'd brainwashed him to believe his Jewish heritage involved certain obligations. They seemed to expect some kind of major achievement from him, to make up for everything they'd lost during the war.'

'No small task for a young boy,' said Patrik.

'He took it very seriously. To this day, he's still trying to meet their expectations. Have you heard about the Jewish museum?'

'I believe I read something about it in the newspaper,' Gösta said.

'Why does he want to build that sort of museum here?' asked Patrik.

'This area has numerous associations with the war. In addition to presenting the history of the Jews, the museum will also highlight Sweden's role during the Second World War.'

Patrik thought about an investigation they'd carried out a few years earlier, and he realized that Leon was right. Bohuslän was close to the Norwegian border, and the white buses had brought former prisoners from the concentration camps to Uddevalla. There were mixed feelings among the people here. Neutrality was a later invention.

'You seem well informed about Josef's plans,' said Patrik.

'We met him at Café Bryggan the other day.' Leon reached for his glass of water.

'Have the five of you who were on the island that day kept in touch?'

Leon put his glass down after taking a long drink. A little water dribbled down his chin, and he wiped it away with the back of his hand.

'No. Why would we do that? We split up after the

Elvanders disappeared. My father sent me to a school in France. He was rather over-protective. I assume that the other boys were also sent to different schools. As I said, we didn't have much in common, and we haven't kept in contact over the years. Although I can only speak for myself, of course. According to Josef, Sebastian has done business both with him and with Percy.'

'But not with you?'

'Good Lord, no! I'd rather go diving with white sharks. Which I've done, by the way.'

'Why wouldn't you want to do business with Sebastian?' asked Patrik, even though he thought he knew the answer to the question. Sebastian Månsson was notorious in the area, and Patrik's visit yesterday hadn't altered his own opinion about the man.

'If he hasn't changed, then he'd sell his own mother if it suited him.'

'Aren't the others aware of that? Why would they agree to do business with him?'

'I really can't say. You'll have to ask them.'

'Do you have any theories as to what happened to the Elvander family?' asked Gösta.

Patrik cast a glance towards the living room. Ia had finished her lunch and the plate was still on the table, but she was nowhere in sight.

'No.' Leon shook his head. 'Naturally I've given it a lot of thought, but I can't for the life of me understand who would have wanted to murder them. It must have been burglars or some crazy person. Like Charles Manson and his gang.'

'If so, they were awfully lucky to arrive just when you boys happened to be out fishing,' said Gösta drily.

Patrik tried to catch his attention. This was a preliminary conversation, not an interrogation. It would serve no purpose to antagonize Leon.

241

'I can't think of any other explanation.' Leon threw out his hands. 'Maybe something in Rune's past finally caught up with him. Maybe somebody had been watching the house and saw us leave. Because it was the Easter holiday, there were only five of us to worry about. During the school term there would have been considerably more students present, so it was an opportune moment if somebody intended to get at the family.'

'And there was no one at the school who might have wished to harm them? Did you notice anything suspicious before they disappeared? Strange noises in the night, for instance?' said Gösta, and Patrik gave him a puzzled look.

'Not that I recall.' Leon frowned. 'Everything was perfectly normal.'

'Could you tell us a bit about the family?' Patrik swatted away a wasp that was stubbornly buzzing in front of his face.

'Rune ruled them with an iron fist, or at least that was his intention. He was strangely blind to the shortcomings of his own children. Especially the two older ones: Claes and Annelie.'

'What sort of things did Rune fail to see when it came to those two? It sounds as though you have something specific in mind.'

Leon's expression went blank. 'Not really. They were both insufferable – as most teenagers are. Claes liked to bully the weaker students behind Rune's back. As for Annelie . . .' He seemed to be considering how best to phrase it. 'If she'd been a little older, you probably would have called her man-crazy.'

'What about Rune's wife, Inez? How were things for her?'

'I don't think she had an easy time of it. She was expected to manage the entire household and take care of Ebba. She also had to put up with all sorts of mischief from Claes and Annclie. Inez would spend the day slaving over the laundry, only to find it scattered on the ground. She would spend hours making stew, then find it burned because someone had turned up the heat on the stove. That sort of thing was forever going on, but Inez never complained. She knew that it would do no good to raise the matter with Rune.'

'Couldn't you boys have helped her?' asked Gösta.

'Unfortunately, none of us ever saw who did those things. It was easy enough to guess who was to blame, but there was no proof to take to Rune.' He gave the two police officers an enquiring look. 'How does it help the investigation to know about relationships between the family members?'

Patrik paused before answering. The truth was he had a gut feeling that the key to what had happened lay in the relationships between the people living on the island. He had no faith in the notion of a bloodthirsty gang of burglars. What was there to steal?

'Why did the five of you stay at the school during the Easter holiday?' he asked, opting to ignore Leon's question.

'Percy, John and I were there because our parents were travelling. In Sebastian's case, he was not there by choice. He'd been caught doing something or other, and was forced to stay. Poor Josef was there to get some extra tutoring. His parents didn't see why he should have a holiday, so they paid Rune to give their son private instruction during the break.'

'It sounds as if there were ample reasons for the five of you to quarrel.'

'Why's that?' Leon looked Patrik in the eye.

But it was Gösta who answered.

'Four of you were the sons of wealthy fathers. You were used to getting whatever you wanted. I can imagine that would have led to a good deal of competition. Josef, for his part, came from an entirely different background, plus he was a Jew.' Gösta paused. 'And we all know what John's views are.'

'John wasn't like that back then,' said Leon. 'It's true his father wasn't best pleased that John was attending school with a Jewish boy, but ironically those two boys were close friends.'

Patrik nodded. For a moment he wondered what had made John change. Had he been infected by his father's opinions as he grew older? Or was there some other explanation?

'What about the others? How would you describe them?'

Leon didn't respond immediately. As if in need of time to consider, he stretched his muscles and turned to call towards the living room, 'Ia? Are you there? Could you make us some coffee?' Then he settled back into his wheelchair.

'Percy is a Swedish aristocrat, through and through. He was pampered and spoiled, but he didn't have a mean bone in his body. He'd had it drummed into him that he was superior to other people, and he liked to talk about battles that his ancestors had fought, but Percy was scared of his own shadow. And Sebastian, as I said, was always on the lookout for a good business deal. He actually carried on quite a lucrative trade out there on the island. No one knew how he managed it, but I think he paid local fishermen to deliver goods, which he then sold for exorbitant prices. Chocolate, cigarettes, soft drinks, and porn magazines. On a few occasions he even sold booze, but he stopped after Rune almost caught him at it.'

Ia came out carrying a tray and set the coffee cups on the table. She didn't seem comfortable in the role of attentive wife.

244

'I hope the coffee is all right. I don't really know how to work those machines.'

'I'm sure it's fine,' said Leon. 'Ia isn't used to living such a spartan existence. Back home in Monaco we have staff to make us coffee, so this is a bit of an adjustment for her.'

Patrik didn't know whether he imagined it, but he thought there was a hint of animosity in Leon's voice. Then it was gone, and Leon was again the amiable host.

'I learned to live very simply during my summers on Kalvö. In the city we had every imaginable comfort. But out there,' he gazed across the water, 'Pappa would hang up his suit and put on shorts and a T-shirt. We would go fishing and pick wild strawberries and swim. Simple pleasures.'

He stopped talking as Ia reappeared to serve the coffee.

'But you haven't exactly lived a simple life since then,' said Gösta, sipping his coffee.

'Touché,' said Leon. 'No, there hasn't been much of that sort of thing. I was more attracted to adventures than to quiet places.'

'Is it the kick you get out of it that's so appealing?' asked Patrik.

'That's a rather simplistic way of describing it, but I suppose you could call it a kick. I suppose it must be a little like narcotics, though I've never polluted my body with drugs. Certainly, it's addictive. Once you start, you don't want to stop. You lie awake at night wondering: Can I climb higher? How deep can I dive? How fast can I drive? Those are questions that eventually require an answer.'

'But now that's all over,' Gösta said.

Patrik wondered why he'd never ordered Gösta and Mellberg to attend an intensive course in interrogation techniques, but Leon didn't seem offended.

'Yes, now it's over.'

'How did the accident happen?'

'It was a perfectly ordinary car accident. Ia was driving, and as I'm sure you're aware, the roads in Monaco are narrow and winding, and in places very steep. There was an oncoming vehicle, Ia swerved too hard, and we ran off the road. The car caught fire.' His tone was no longer so nonchalant, and he was staring straight ahead, as if he was seeing it all happen again. 'Do you have any idea how rare it is for a car to catch fire? It's not like in the movies, where cars explode as soon as they crash. We were unlucky. Ia was more or less okay, but my legs were wedged tight, and I couldn't get out. I could feel my hands and legs and clothes burning. Then my face. After that I lost consciousness, but Ia pulled me out of the car. That was how her hands got injured. Aside from that, she miraculously suffered only a few cuts and two broken ribs. She saved my life.'

'When did this happen?' asked Patrik.

'Nine years ago.'

'There's no possibility that you might . . .' Gösta nodded at the wheelchair.

'No. I'm paralysed from the waist down. I'm grateful that I can even breathe unaided.' He sighed. 'One side effect is that I tire easily, and I usually rest for a while at this time of day. Is there anything else I can help you with? If not, I hope you won't think me rude if I ask you to leave.'

Patrik and Gösta exchanged glances. Then Patrik stood up.

'That's all we have for the moment, but we may have occasion to come back to see you again.'

'You're welcome to do so.' Propelling his wheelchair ahead of them, Leon went into the house.

Ia came downstairs and in an elegant farewell gesture, offered her hand to shake.

As they were stepping outside, Gösta turned to speak to Ia, who seemed eager to close the door after them.

'It'd be good to have the address and phone number for your house on the Riviera.'

'You mean in case we decide to leave town?' She gave them a weak smile.

Gösta merely shrugged in reply. Ia went to the hall table and wrote down the address and phone number on a notepad. Then she tore off the page and handed it to Gösta, who stuffed it in his pocket without comment.

When they were sitting in the car, Gösta tried to discuss their meeting with Leon, but Patrik was barely paying attention. He was too busy searching for his phone.

'I must have left my mobile at home,' he said at last. 'Can I borrow yours?'

'Sorry. You always have your phone with you, so I didn't bother to bring mine.'

Patrik considered delivering a lecture on why it was important for police officers always to carry a phone, but he realized now wasn't exactly the best time. He turned the key in the ignition.

'We'll drive past my house on the way back. I need to pick up my mobile.'

They were both silent for the few minutes that it took them to reach Sälvik. Patrik couldn't shake off the feeling that they'd overlooked some important detail during their talk with Leon. He wasn't sure whether it had been provoked by anything specific, but he had a strong sense that something wasn't right.

Kjell was looking forward to lunch. Carina had to work in the evening, so she'd phoned to ask whether they could have lunch together at home. It was hard to find time to see each other when one person worked shifts and the other kept normal office hours. If she had several late shifts in a row, days might pass before they saw one another. But Kjell was proud of her. She worked so hard. During the years they were separated, she had supported herself and their son without complaint. Afterwards he discovered that she'd had problems with alcohol, but she'd managed to pull herself out of it all on her own. Oddly enough, it was his father Frans who had persuaded her to do that. One of the few good things he ever did, thought Kjell with a mixture of bitterness and reluctant affection.

Beata, on the other hand . . . She preferred not to do any work if she could help it. When they were living together, they'd had constant arguments about money. She grumbled about the fact that he wasn't getting promotions so that he could earn a manager's salary, while she did little to contribute to their finances. 'I take care of the household,' she would always say.

He parked in the driveway, trying to bring his breathing under control. He was still filled with revulsion every time he thought about his ex-wife Beata. It was made worse by the contempt he felt for himself. How could he have wasted so many years on her? Of course he didn't regret having the children, but he did regret allowing himself to be duped. She had been sweet and young, while he had been much older and easily flattered.

He got out of the car, shaking off all thought of Beata. He refused to allow anything to ruin his lunch with Carina.

'Hi, sweetheart,' she said when he came in. 'Sit down. The food is ready. I've made potato pancakes.'

She set a plate on the table in front of him, and he leaned over to breathe in the aroma. He loved potato pancakes.

'How's it going at work?' she asked as she sat down across from him.

Carina had aged well. The delicate laugh lines around her eyes suited her, and she had a nice suntan from the hours she devoted to her favourite pastime: pottering about in the garden.

'It's a bit slow. I'm researching a lead I've been given on John Holm, but I'm not sure how to proceed.'

He took a bite of pancake. It tasted as good as it looked.

'Is there no one you can ask for help?'

Kjell was on the verge of dismissing the suggestion when it struck him that she had a point. This was important enough that he needed to put his pride aside. Everything he'd learned about Holm told him that there was some major secret that needed to be exposed. He actually didn't care whether he was the one who got the story or not. For the first time in his career as a journalist, he found himself in a situation that he'd previously only heard about. He was in possession of the kernel of a story that was bigger than him.

He leapt to his feet. 'I'm sorry, but there's something that I have to do.'

'Right now?' said Carina, glancing at his half-eaten pancakes.

'Yes, I'm really sorry. I know you cooked this special lunch, and I was looking forward to having some time together, but I . . .'

When he saw the disappointment on her face, he almost sat down. He had disappointed her so many times in the past, and he didn't want to do it again. But then her face lit up and she smiled.

'Go and do what you have to. I know you wouldn't run away from a half-eaten potato pancake unless it was a matter of national security.'

Kjell laughed. 'Right. It's something like that.' He leaned down and kissed her on the lips.

Back at the newspaper office, he wondered how to pitch his proposal. It was probably going to take more than a gut feeling and phone doodles to attract the interest

249

of one of Sweden's foremost political reporters. He scratched his beard and then realized what he'd say. Erica had told him about the blood, but no newspaper had published anything about the discovery out on Valö. He was almost done writing his article and was planning to offer it to *Bohusläningen* first. The rumours were probably already flying through the region, and it would be only a matter of time before the other papers caught wind of the story, so he convinced himself that it would be okay if he revealed the news. Besides, even if *Bohusläningen* lost out on the scoop, the paper was so familiar with the local area that it would do a much better job with follow-up articles than any of the major papers.

For several seconds he simply stared at the phone, gathering his thoughts and jotting down notes. He needed to be well prepared when he rang Sven Niklasson, the political reporter for *Expressen*, to enlist his help in finding out more about John Holm. And about Gimle.

Paula gingerly climbed out of the car. Mellberg had been scolding her all the way to Valö, first in the car and then on board *MinLouis*, one of the Coast Guard boats. But his grumbling had not sounded very convincing. By now he knew her well enough to realize that he wouldn't be able to change her mind.

'Watch your step. Your mother would kill me if you fell.' He held her hand as Victor took the other to help her out of the boat.

'Give me a call if you need a ride back,' said Victor, and Mellberg nodded.

'I can't understand why you insisted on coming along,' Mellberg said as they walked towards the house. 'Maybe the boat hasn't set off yet. This could be dangerous, and it's silly to put your life at risk.'

'It's been almost an hour since Annika rang. I'm sure

the boat has already left. And I'm guessing that Annika will try to get hold of Patrik and Gösta, so they'll be on their way here too.'

'Yes, but . . .' Mellberg began, but then stopped as they reached the front door and called out: 'Hello! The police are here!'

A blond man wearing a distraught expression came towards them, and Paula surmised he must be Tobias Stark. During the boat ride, she'd managed to get Mellberg to fill her in on the case.

'We were waiting upstairs in our bedroom. We thought that might be . . . safest.' He glanced over his shoulder at the stairs where two other people now appeared.

Paula gave a start when she recognized one of the women. 'Anna? What are you doing here?'

'I'm here to take some measurements for the remodelling.' She was a bit pale, but otherwise composed.

'Is everyone all right?'

'Yes, thank goodness,' said Anna, and the other two nodded.

'Has anything else happened since you rang the police?' asked Paula, looking around. Even though she thought the shooter must be long gone, she wasn't about to risk taking it for granted. She was listening alertly to every sound.

'No, we haven't heard a thing. Do you want to see where the shots were fired?' Anna seemed to have taken charge. Tobias and Ebba stood behind her, silently waiting. Tobias had his arm around Ebba, who was staring straight ahead, hugging herself.

'Of course,' said Mellberg.

'It's in here, in the kitchen.' Anna led the way, stopping in the doorway to point. 'As you can see, the shot came through that window.'

Paula surveyed the damage. There were glass splinters

all over the floor, but most of the glass was immediately below the shattered window.

'Was anyone in here when the shots were fired? And are you sure there were several shots and not just one?'

'Ebba was in the kitchen,' said Anna, giving Ebba a nudge. Slowly she raised her eyes to look around the kitchen, as if seeing it for the first time.

'There was a huge bang,' she said. 'The sound was so loud. I didn't know what it was. Then there was another bang.'

'So two shots,' said Mellberg, entering the kitchen.

'I don't think we should be walking around in here, Bertil,' said Paula. She wished that Patrik had come with them. She wasn't sure she'd be able to stop Mellberg on her own.

'Don't worry. I've been to more crime scenes than you'll ever see in your career, and I know what to do and what not to do.' He stepped on a big piece of glass, crushing it under his weight.

Paula took a deep breath. 'I still think we should let Torbjörn and his boys examine the scene before we go disturbing anything.'

Mellberg pretended not to hear her. He went over to inspect the bullet holes in the kitchen wall.

'Aha! I see those little rascals! Have you got any plastic bags?'

'In the third drawer,' said Ebba absentmindedly.

Mellberg pulled open the drawer and took out a roll of freezer bags. He tore off one and put on a pair of rubber gloves that were draped over the tap. Then he returned to the wall.

'Let's see, they're not in very deep, so it should be easy enough to pluck them out. This is going to be a simple job for Torbjörn,' he announced, prising the two bullets out of the wall.

'But they need to take photos first,' Paula objected.

Mellberg wasn't listening to a word she said. Triumphantly he held out the bag to show them before stuffing it into his shirt pocket. Then he peeled off the gloves and tossed them in the sink.

'We can't forget about fingerprints,' he said. 'That's very important in terms of collecting evidence. After so many years on the force, it's something that just comes naturally.'

Paula bit her lip so hard that she tasted blood. Hurry up, Hedström, said the voice in her head. But her plea went unheeded, and all she could do was watch as Mellberg, unconcerned, stomped around on the broken glass.

FJÄLLBACKA 1931

Dagmar could feel everyone's eyes watching her. People thought she was oblivious to what was going on, but she wasn't about to be fooled, especially not by Laura. Her daughter was good at garnering sympathy. They'd praise her for being a little house-wife, and feel sorry for her because she had a mother like Dagmar. None of them knew what Laura was really like, but Dagmar saw through the hypocrisy. She knew what was under that pretty surface. Laura bore the same curse she did. The mark might be under her skin and hidden from view, but she was branded all the same. Laura's fate would be no different to her mother's, and she shouldn't think otherwise.

Dagmar was shaking slightly as she sat at the kitchen table. Along with her morning dram she'd eaten a piece of plain crispbread, scattering as many crumbs as she could. Laura hated it when there were crumbs on the floor and never had any peace until she'd swept up every last one. A few crumbs had landed on the table, and Dagmar brushed them on to the floor as well. Now the girl would have something to keep her busy when she came home from school.

Restlessly Dagmar drummed her fingers on the flowery table-cloth. She was always filled with a nervous energy that demanded some sort of release; she had long since lost the ability to sit still. Twelve years had passed since Hermann had left her, yet even now she could feel his hands on her body, which had changed so much that she no longer bore any resemblance to the young woman she once was.

The anger that she'd felt towards him inside that small, sterile room in the hospital had evaporated. She loved him and he loved her. Nothing had turned out as she'd imagined, but it was good to know who was to blame. Every waking hour and even in her dreams, she would picture Carin Göring's face, always with a superior, scornful expression. It was clear that Carin had enjoyed seeing the humiliation that she and Laura had suffered. Dagmar drummed her fingers harder on the table-cloth. Thoughts of Carin filled her head. It was thanks to those thoughts and to alcohol that she was able to keep herself going day after day.

She reached for the newspaper lying on the table. Since she couldn't afford to buy a paper, she stole old editions from the bundles that were tossed behind the store, waiting to be picked up. She always read every page with great care, because sometimes she would find articles about Hermann. He had returned to Germany, and the name Hitler, which he'd shouted in the hospital, was frequently mentioned in the papers. She had read the articles, feeling her excitement rise. The man in the newspapers was her Hermann. Not that fat, shrieking person wearing hospital garb. He was in uniform once more, and although he wasn't as handsome or stylish as he'd been when they first met, he was again a man who wielded power.

Her hands were still shaking as she opened the newspaper. It seemed to take longer and longer each morning for her first drink to take effect. She might as well have another. Dagmar got up and poured herself a sizeable shot. She downed it in one gulp, feeling the warmth immediately spread throughout her body, easing the shaking. Then she sat down again and started leafing through the paper.

She had almost come to the last page when she discovered the article. The letters began blurring together, and she had to force *herself to focus on the headline: 'Göring's wife buried. Wreath from Hitler.'*

Dagmar studied the two photographs. Then a smile spread across her lips. Carin Göring was dead. It was true, and it made her laugh with joy. Now there was nothing to stop Hermann. Now he would finally come back to her. She stamped her feet on the floor.

This time he'd gone out to the granite quarry alone. If Josef was being honest, he didn't particularly care for the company of other people. What he was seeking was to be found only if he looked inward. It was not something anyone else could give him. Sometimes he wished that he had been different – or rather, more like other people. He wished he was able to feel a sense of belonging, that he was part of something, but he refused to let even his own family get close to him. The knot in his chest was too hard, and he felt like a child pressing his nose against a toy-shop window, staring at all the marvels inside without daring to open the door. Something stopped him from going inside, from reaching out his hand.

He sat down on a block of granite, and his thoughts turned again to his mother and father. Ten years had passed since their death, but he still felt lost without them. And he was ashamed that he'd kept his secret from them. His father had always emphasized the importance of trust, of being honest and speaking the truth, and he had let Josef know that he realized his son was keeping something from him. But how could he have told them? Certain secrets were too big, and his parents had sacrificed so much for his sake.

During the war they had lost everything: relatives, friends, possessions, security, their homeland. Everything except their faith and their hopes for a better life. While they suffered, Albert Speer had walked around here, pointing and shouting and ordering stone to build the foremost city in the empire that was built on blood. Josef didn't know whether Speer had actually been here in person, but no doubt one of his henchmen had strutted about the quarry outside of Fjällbacka.

The war did not seem like an event from the distant past. Every day of his childhood Josef had heard stories about how the Jews had been hunted down and humiliated, what the smoke smelled like as it poured from the chimneys in the camps, and how the horrified expressions of the liberating soldiers reflected their degradation. Sweden had welcomed them with open arms but at the same time stubbornly refused to acknowledge its own role in the war. Every day his father had talked about this, about how his new country needed to acknowledge the crimes it had committed, until it was imprinted on Josef's mind as indelibly as the numbers tattooed on his parents' arms.

Clasping his hands in prayer, he gazed up at the sky. He prayed for the strength to carry on his heritage, to be able to cope with Sebastian and the past that now threatened to destroy what he was planning to accomplish. The years had passed so swiftly, and he'd been good at forgetting. A man could create his own past. He had wanted to erase that particular part of his life, and he wished that Sebastian had done the same.

Josef got up, brushing off the granite dust from his trousers. He hoped that God had heard his prayers, in this place that symbolized both what might have been and what was now about to be built. From this stone he would create knowledge, and from that knowledge would come understanding and peace. He would pay off the debt to his ancestors, to the Jews who had been tormented and oppressed. Later, when his mission was complete, the shame would be erased for good.

Erica's mobile rang, but she didn't pick up. It was her publisher, and no matter what the reason for the call, it would require more time than she had at the moment.

For the hundredth time she looked around her work room. She hated the feeling that someone had been in here, snooping amongst things that she considered strictly private. Who could it have been? And what was he or she looking for? She was so lost in her own thoughts that she flinched when she heard the front door open and close.

Quickly she ran out of the room and down the stairs. Patrik and Gösta were standing in the front hall.

'Hi! What are you doing here?'

Gösta evaded her eye and looked very uncomfortable. Their secret agreement did not seem to be something he could accept with equanimity, and she couldn't resist teasing him a bit.

'I haven't seen you in a while, Gösta. How are things?' She could hardly conceal her smile as she watched him turn bright red. Even his earlobes were pink.

'Hmm . . . fine,' he muttered, staring at his shoes.

'Everything okay here?' asked Patrik.

Erica's expression instantly turned serious. For a moment she'd managed to forget that someone had probably been inside their house. She realized that she ought to inform Patrik of her suspicions, but so far she had no proof. It was lucky he hadn't answered his phone when she rang earlier. She knew how upset he got whenever anything affected his family. It was possible that he might send her and the children to stay somewhere else if he thought that some-body had broken into their home. So she decided not to say anything for the time being, despite the sense of unease that was nagging at her. It was all she could do to keep from glancing at the veranda door, as if at any moment someone might step inside again.

She still hadn't answered Patrik's question when Kristina came up from the laundry room with the children in tow.

'What are you doing home, Patrik? Do you know what happened earlier? I practically had a heart attack. I was standing in the kitchen, making pancakes for the children, when I caught sight of Noel tottering towards the street as fast as his little legs could carry him, and I have to tell you that I caught him in the nick of time. He could have come to serious harm if I hadn't been on hand. You must remember to shut all of the doors properly, because those little ones are fast. Something terrible might happen, and then you'd regret it for the rest of your life . . .'

Erica was staring at her mother-in-law, waiting to see if she was ever going to pause to draw breath.

'I forgot to close the veranda door,' she told Patrik without meeting his eye.

'Okay, good advice, Mamma. We'll have to be extra careful now that the twins are starting to get around on their own.' He gathered up the boys, who had come rushing towards their father, throwing themselves into his arms.

'Hi, Uncle Gösta,' said Maja.

Gösta turned beet red again and gave Erica a desperate look. But Patrik seemed not to notice anything because he was busy playing with his sons.

After a moment he glanced up at Erica.

'We actually dropped by to pick up my mobile. Have you seen it?'

Erica pointed towards the kitchen. 'You left it on the bench this morning.'

260

Patrik went to get the phone. 'I see you tried to call me. Was it anything special?'

'No, I just wanted to say that I love you,' she said, hoping he wouldn't see through her white lie.

'I love you too, sweetie,' said Patrik distractedly as he studied the display. 'I've got five missed calls from Annika. I'd better ring her and find out what's up.'

Erica tried to eavesdrop on his conversation, but Kristina was chattering non-stop with Gösta so she caught only a few words. When Patrik was done with the call his expression told her it was bad news.

'A shooting on Valö. Someone fired into the house. Anna is out there too. Annika said she was the one who rang the station.'

Erica's hand flew to her mouth. 'Anna? Is she okay? Was she hurt? Who . . .?' She could hear how incoherent she sounded, but the only thing she could think of was that something might have happened to Anna.

'From what I understand, no one was hurt. That's the good news.' He turned to Gösta. 'The bad news is that Annika was forced to ring Mellberg when she couldn't reach us.'

'Mellberg?' said Gösta, his expression dubious.

'Yes. So we'd better get out there as fast as we can.'

'Don't tell me you're going out there if somebody's shooting,' said Kristina, putting her hands on her hips.

'Of course we are. That's my job,' said Patrik, annoyed.

Kristina gave an offended snort, tossed her head, and went into the living room.

'I'm coming with you,' said Erica.

'Not on your life.'

'If Anna is there, I'm coming.'

Patrik shook his head. 'There's some lunatic shooting at people out there. No way I'm letting you come!'

'The place will be crawling with police, so what could

261

possibly happen? I'll be perfectly safe.' She began tying the laces on her white trainers.

'And who'll take care of the kids?'

'I'm sure Kristina can stay here and mind them.' She stood up and gave him a look that said it would do no good to protest.

On their way down to the boat, Erica felt her concern for her sister growing with every heartbeat. Patrik could sulk as much as he liked: Anna was her responsibility.

'Pyttan? Where are you?' Percy said in surprise as he walked through the flat. She hadn't told him that she was going anywhere.

They'd come to Stockholm for a few days to attend a friend's sixtieth birthday celebration, an event they didn't think they could miss. Countless members of the Swedish aristocracy were bound to turn up for the occasion, along with some VIPs from the business world – although they weren't necessarily considered VIPs at such gatherings. The hierarchy was firmly established, and being the CEO of one of the biggest corporations in Sweden counted for nothing if the individual in question didn't have the proper background, the proper surname, and hadn't attended the proper schools.

Percy met all of the above criteria. Until recently, he'd never given it a second thought. His social standing had been part of his life, something he took for granted. The problem was that he now risked becoming a count without a manor, and that would have dire consquences. He wouldn't land as far down the social ladder as the nouveau riche, but he would definitely find himself demoted.

In the living room he stopped in front of the drinks cart to pour himself a tumbler of Mackmyra Preludium, which cost almost 5,000 kronor a bottle. If he had to resort to drinking Jim Beam whisky, he might as well take his father's old Luger and shoot himself in the head.

What weighed on him most was the knowledge that he had failed his father. He was the eldest son and had always received preferential treatment. And the old man had never made any bones about it. In a matter-of-fact tone, without any show of emotion, he had told his two younger children, 'Percy is special. He's the one who will take over one day.' Secretly Percy had felt a certain glee whenever the old man put his siblings in their place. It made up for the knowledge that his father considered him weak, timid, and spoiled rotten. Perhaps it was true that his mother had been overly protective towards him, but he had been born two months premature, so small and frail that he was not expected to survive. For the first and last time in his life, Percy had shown great resilience. Against all odds, he had lived, though his health remained fragile.

He gazed out across Karlaplan. The flat had a beautiful bay window facing the open square with the fountain. Holding his whisky glass, Percy watched the swarms of people below. In the winter, the square was deserted, but now the benches were fully occupied, and scores of children were playing, eating ice cream, and enjoying the sunshine.

He heard footsteps on the stairs and listened intently. Was that Pyttan? She'd probably nipped out to do some shopping; he only hoped that the bank hadn't put a hold on their credit cards. What sort of society was he living in, anyway? Demanding an entire fortune in taxes. Those bloody communists. Percy tightened his grip on the whisky glass. Mary and Charles would relish his situation if they knew the extent of his financial problems. They were still spreading their lies about how he had evicted them from their home and robbed them of what was rightfully theirs.

Suddenly he found himself thinking about Valö. If only he'd never ended up there. Then none of it would have happened – the things he had decided not to think about, although he couldn't stop the ghastly images from seeping into his thoughts on occasion.

At first he'd thought it an excellent idea to change schools. The atmosphere at Lundsberg had become unbearable after he'd been singled out as one of the boys who had watched as a couple of bullies forced the school's scapegoat to drink a big glass of laxative right before the closing ceremonies in the auditorium. The boy's white summer clothes had been stained brown all the way up his back.

After that incident the headmaster had summoned Percy's father to Lundsberg. Anxious to avoid a scandal, he hadn't gone so far as to expel Percy, but he'd made it clear that the boy would have to continue his studies elsewhere. The old man tried to argue that Percy had merely been a spectator, and surely that couldn't be considered a crime? But in the end he'd admitted defeat, and after discreet enquiries he had decided that Rune Elvander's boarding school on Valö would be the best option. In truth, Percy's father would have preferred to send him abroad, but for once his mother had put her foot down. So Percy had been enrolled in Rune's school, and that was how he'd ended up haunted by dark memories that he struggled to suppress.

Percy took a big swig of the whisky, hoping it would dilute the humiliation that threatened to overwhelm him, and surveyed his surroundings. Pyttan had been given free rein to handle the interior decorating. This sort of rustic, white-painted furniture might not be his taste, but as long as she didn't touch the rooms in the manor, she could do whatever she liked with the flat. The manor had to remain exactly as it had been during his father's and grandfather's and great-grandfather's time. It was a matter of family honour.

The vague sense of uneasiness grew stronger as he went into the bedroom. Pyttan ought to be home by now. They were due to attend a cocktail party that evening, and she usually started getting ready for social events early in the afternoon.

He set his glass on Pyttan's night table and then opened the doors to her wardrobe. A few coathangers swayed in the sudden draught; other than that, the wardrobe was empty.

No one would believe that only an hour ago someone was shooting at people out here, thought Patrik as he pulled into dock. The whole place seemed unnaturally quiet and calm.

Before he had even managed to tie the mooring line, Erica jumped out of the boat and began running towards the house. With Gösta following close behind, Patrik took off after her. But she was moving so fast that he couldn't keep up, and when he entered the house, he found her with her arms around Anna. Tobias and Ebba were huddled together on the sofa, and next to them stood Mellberg and Paula.

Patrik had no idea why she was there, but he was grateful. At least now he could expect to hear a sensible account of what had happened.

'Is everyone okay?' he asked, going over to Paula.

'Everybody's fine. They're all a little upset, especially Ebba. Someone fired shots through the kitchen window when she was in there alone. We haven't seen anything to indicate that the shooter is still in the vicinity.'

'Have you phoned Torbjörn?'

'Yes, his team is on the way. But you might say that Mellberg has already begun the forensic examination.'

'That's right. I found the bullets,' said Mellberg, taking out a plastic bag containing two bullets. 'They weren't embedded very deep in the wall, and it was easy to prise them out. Whoever did the shooting must have been a good distance away because the bullets had lost so much speed by the time they entered the wall.'

Patrik felt anger surge inside of him, but the last thing he wanted was to create a scene. There would be plenty of time later to have a serious talk with Mellberg about the rules that needed to be followed when investigating a crime scene.

He turned to Anna, who was wriggling out of Erica's arms. 'Where were you when this happened?'

'I was upstairs,' she replied, pointing. 'Ebba had gone down to the kitchen to make coffee.'

'What about you?' Patrik asked Tobias.

'I was in the cellar. I'd come back from the mainland and was fetching some more paint. I'd only got as far as the bottom of the cellar stairs when I heard a bang.' His face was pale under the suntan.

'When you arrived, did you see an unfamiliar boat at the dock?' asked Gösta.

Tobias shook his head. 'No, just Anna's.'

'And you haven't spotted any strangers around?'

'No, none.' Ebba was staring straight ahead, as if dazed.

'Who would do something like this?' Tobias asked Patrick. 'Who is after us? Do you think it has anything to do with the card that I gave you?'

'I'm afraid we don't know.'

'What card?' asked Erica.

Patrik ignored her question, but the piercing look that Erica directed at him made it clear that eventually he would have to tell her.

'From now on, nobody goes into the kitchen. Consider it off limits.' He turned to Ebba and Tobias. 'We'll need to search the island, so it would be best if you two found somewhere to stay on the mainland until we're finished.'

'But we don't want to do that,' said Tobias.

'Yes, we do.' Ebba suddenly sounded quite determined.

'And where are we going to find a room at the height of the tourist season?'

'You can stay with us. We have a guestroom,' said Erica.

Patrik gave a start. Was she out of her mind? Inviting Ebba and Tobias to be their guests in the middle of an investigation?

'Really? Are you sure?' said Ebba, looking up at Erica.

'Of course. While you're with us, you can read everything I've collected about your family history. I was going through it again yesterday, and it's really quite fascinating.'

'I don't think that . . .' Tobias began. Then his shoulders slumped. 'Here's what we'll do: you go to the mainland, and I'll stay here.'

'I'd prefer not to have anyone remain here,' said Patrik.

'I'm not leaving.' Tobias cast a glance at Ebba, who offered no objection.

'Okay, then I suggest that Ebba, Erica and Anna leave now so that we can get started on our work while we wait for Torbjörn. Gösta, you check the path down to the beach to see if anyone could have come that way. Paula, could you take care of the area closest to the house? I'll search a wide circle around the house. It'll be easier when we get a metal detector out here, but for the time being we'll have to make do without it. If we're lucky, the shooter may have tossed the gun into a shrub somewhere.'

'And if we're unlucky, this gun will be at the bottom of the sea, same as the last one,' said Gösta.

'That's possible, but the priority is to carry out a search and see what we can find.' Patrik turned to Tobias. 'You need to keep out of our way as best you can. As I said, it's not a good idea for you to stay here, especially not at night when you'll be here all by yourself after we leave.'

'I can work upstairs. I won't get in your way,' he said in a flat voice.

Patrik studied him for a moment but decided not to force the issue. If Tobias refused to leave the island, there was nothing anyone could do about it. He went over to Erica, who was standing in the doorway, ready to leave.

'I'll see you later,' he said, giving her a kiss on the cheek.

'Okay. Anna, can we go back in your boat?' she said. Like a sheepdog she herded together the little group that she was going to escort home.

Patrik couldn't help smiling. He gave them a wave and then turned to the motley group of police officers. It would be a miracle if they managed to find anything at all.

The door opened quietly. John Holm took off his reading glasses and put down his book.

'What are you reading?' asked Liv, sitting down on the edge of the bed.

He held up the book so she could see the cover. '*Race, Evolution and Behaviour* by Philippe Ruston.'

'That's a good book. I read it a few years ago.'

He took her hand and smiled. 'It's too bad that the holiday is almost over.'

'Yes, if you can call this past week a holiday, considering how many hours we've worked each day.'

'I know.' He frowned.

'Are you still worrying about the article in *Bohusläningen*?'

'No. You're right, it doesn't matter. By next week it'll be forgotten.'

'Is it Gimle?'

John gave her a stern look. She knew better than to mention that word out loud. Only those who belonged to the inner circle knew about the project, and he bitterly regretted the fact that he hadn't immediately burned the piece of paper that he'd scribbled on. It was an unforgivable mistake, even though he wasn't sure that Erica Falck had taken it. It might have blown away or been lost somewhere in the house, but in his heart he knew the explanation couldn't be that simple. The note was in the stack of papers before Erica arrived, and when he searched for it after she left, it was gone.

'It'll all work out.' Liv stroked his cheek. 'I believe in it. We've come so far, but there's a risk that we won't get any further unless we do something drastic. We need to create more space to manoeuvre. It's best for everyone.'

'I love you.' He could honestly say that to her. Nobody understood him the way Liv did. They had shared ideas and experiences, successes and setbacks, and she was the only one he had ever confided in, the only one who knew what had happened to his family. Of course plenty of people knew about his past, since it had been the subject of gossip for years, but he had never told anyone but Liv about the thoughts he'd had during that time.

'Can I sleep here tonight?' Liv asked suddenly.

Seeing the uncertainty in her face, John was filled with conflicting emotions. In his heart he wanted nothing more than to have her warm body near, to fall asleep with his arm around her, breathing in the scent of her hair. At the same time, he knew that it wouldn't work. Intimacy entailed so many expectations and caused all the disappointments and unfulfilled promises to rise to the surface.

'Couldn't we try again?' she said, caressing his hand. 'It's been a while now, and maybe things have . . . changed.'

Abruptly he turned from her, snatching his hand away.

The memory of his impotence nearly suffocated him. He couldn't bear to go through that again. Doctors' appointments, little blue pills, artificial pumps, the look in Liv's eyes every time he couldn't get it up. It was no good.

'Leave, please.' He picked up his book and held it like a shield in front of him.

He stared at the page without seeing a single word as he listened to her feet moving across the floor, and then she gently closed the door behind her. His reading glasses were still lying on the bedside table.

It was late by the time Patrik got home. Erica was sitting alone on the sofa, watching TV. After the children went to bed, she hadn't felt like tidying up, so Patrik had to pick his way through the toys scattered over the floor.

'Is Ebba asleep?' he asked, sitting down next to his wife.

'Yes. She went to bed around eight. She seemed totally exhausted.'

'I'm not surprised.' Patrik propped his feet on the coffee table. 'What are you watching?'

'*Letterman.*'

'Who's the guest?'

'Megan Fox.'

'Ah . . .' said Patrik, sinking deeper into the sofa cushions.

'Are you planning to sit there and get all excited having fantasies about Megan Fox, which you later try to act out with your poor wife?'

'You got it,' he said, nuzzling his face against her neck.

Erica pushed him away. 'How did it go out on Valö?'

Patrik sighed. 'Not too well. Reinforcements arrived in the shape of Torbjörn and his boys about half an hour after you left, and we searched as much of the island as we could before it got dark. But we didn't find anything.'

'Nothing?' Erica picked up the remote to turn down the volume.

'No. No traces whatsoever of the shooter. And it seems most likely that he or she threw the gun into the sea. But maybe the bullets will tell us something. Torbjörn sent them off to the lab for analysis.'

'What was that card that Tobias mentioned?'

Patrik hesitated. It was always a balancing act. He couldn't reveal too much to his wife about an ongoing investigation, but at the same time, there had been several instances when the police had benefited from Erica's ability to dig up information. Having come to a decision, he replied.

'All her life Ebba has received birthday cards from someone who signed them with the initial "G". The messages have never been threatening. Until now. Tobias came to the station today to show us one that had just arrived in the post. The message was very different from all the previous cards.'

'So you suspect that whoever is sending these cards is also behind the events on Valö?'

'We don't have any specific theories at the moment, but of course it's something that we need to consider. I'm thinking of taking Paula with me to Göteborg tomorrow to have a word with Ebba's adoptive parents. As you know, Gösta isn't very good at interviewing people. And Paula begged me to let her get back to work. Apparently she's climbing the walls at home.'

'Just make sure she doesn't overdo it. It's easy for a person to overestimate her own strength.'

'You're such a mother hen,' said Patrik with a smile. 'I've been through two pregnancies now. So I'm not completely ignorant in that regard.'

'Let's clarify that. You're not the one who's been through two pregnancies. As I recall, you've never

271

experienced swollen ankles, leg cramps and heartburn, or gone through twenty-two hours of labour pains and a Caesarean section.'

'Okay, I get it.' Patrik held up his hands. 'And I promise to keep an eye on Paula. Mellberg would never forgive me if anything happened to her. Say what you like about him, but he'd go through hell and high water for the sake of his family.'

The credits for *Letterman* had started rolling on the screen, and Erica began channel surfing. 'So what's Tobias doing out there? Why would he insist on staying?'

'I don't know. I didn't want to leave him out there. If you ask me, he's on the verge of falling apart. He seems calm enough, and he's handling it all with extraordinary composure, but he reminds me of a duck smoothly gliding over the surface of the water, but all the while its feet are paddling frantically underneath. Do you know what I mean? Or am I babbling?'

'No, I know exactly what you mean.'

Erica continued pressing the remote. Finally she settled on *Deadliest Catch* on the Discovery Channel. She gazed absently at the flickering images of a Gore-Tex-clad man in the midst of a horrendous storm, hauling in trap after trap of massive spiderlike king crabs.

'Are you planning to take Ebba with you tomorrow?'

'No, I think it's better if we talk to her parents alone. Paula will be here at nine, so we'll take the Volvo to Göteborg.'

'Good. Then I can show Ebba the background material that I've collected.'

'You know, I haven't seen this research of yours. Is there anything that might be relevant to the investigation?'

Erica thought for a moment but then shook her head. 'No, I've told you the few details that might be useful. What I've uncovered about Ebba's family history goes back further, and I think she's the only one who would find it interesting.'

'I'd still like to see it. But not tonight. Right now I'm too comfortable.' He moved closer to Erica, put his arm around her, and leaned his head on her shoulder. 'Christ, what a job those guys have. It looks super dangerous. Good thing I'm not a crab fisherman.'

'You're right, sweetheart. That's something that I'm grateful for every day. Thank God you're not a crab fisherman.' She laughed and kissed the top of his head.

Since the accident, Leon had occasionally been plagued by a feeling that his joints were pulsating. An aching sensation, mixed with shooting pains, like a premonition that something was about to happen. He felt it now.

Ia was accustomed to reading his moods. Usually she would scold him for brooding, but not this time. Instead they were carefully avoiding one another, each of them moving about the house separately.

He found that a bit annoying. Boredom had always been his worst enemy. When he was a kid, his father would laugh at his inability to sit still and the fact that he was forever searching for new challenges and pushing the limits. His mother had fussed over all the broken bones and scrapes that resulted, but his father had been proud.

After that Easter holiday, he never saw his father again. Leon went abroad without saying goodbye. Then the years passed, and he was busy with his own life. Yet his father had been very generous, sending more funds whenever his bank account was empty. There was no reproaching his son or trying to rein him in. He had allowed Leon to fly free.

In the end, Leon had flown too close to the sun, just as he'd always known he would. His parents had died

273

before that happened. Pappa was spared having to witness how the accident on that winding mountain road had robbed him of his body and his adventurous spirit, how it had left him fettered.

He and Ia had travelled a long road together, but now it was approaching the decisive moment. The only thing required was a little spark to ignite it all. And he didn't plan on ever allowing someone else to light that spark. That was his job.

Leon listened to the house. Everything was quiet inside. Ia had probably gone to bed. He picked up his mobile from the table and placed it on his lap. Then he rolled his wheelchair out to the balcony and without hesitation began ringing them, one after the other.

When he was done talking, he let his hands rest on his thighs and gazed out over Fjällbacka. In the evening darkness the town was lit by scores of lamps, like a gigantic glittering tavern. Then he turned his gaze towards the water and Valö. In the old summer camp all the lights were out.

LOVÖ CEMETERY 1933

Two years had passed since Carin's death, but Hermann hadn't come to fetch her. As faithful as a dog, Dagmar had waited as the days became weeks, the months became years.

She still scoured the newspapers for word of him. Hermann had become a government official in Germany. In the photographs he looked so handsome in his uniform. A powerful and important associate for that man called Hitler. As long as Hermann was in Germany and involved in his career, Dagmar could understand why he had to let her wait, but when the papers reported that he was once again in Sweden, she had decided to make things easy for him. He was a busy man, and if he couldn't come to her, then she would go to him. As the wife of a prominent politician, she would be forced to adapt to his needs, and most likely she would also have to move to Germany. She realized that the girl could not come with her. It wouldn't do for a man in Hermann's position to have a daughter born out of wedlock. But Laura was thirteen now; she could fend for herself.

The papers didn't mention where Hermann was staying, leaving Dagmar unsure how to find him. She went to his old address on Odengatan in Stockholm, but a stranger opened the door and told her that the Görings hadn't lived there for years. She was standing outside the building, pondering her next move, when she suddenly remembered reading about the place where

275

Carin was buried. Maybe Hermann would go there to visit his wife's grave. It turned out that Lovö cemetery was located somewhere outside the city. Eventually she managed to find a bus that would take her almost all the way there.

Now she was squatting down in front of the headstone, staring at Carin's name and the swastika that had been etched underneath. Golden autumn leaves whirled around her in the cold October wind, but she hardly noticed. She'd thought that her hatred would fade when Carin died, but as she sat in her worn coat, filled with thoughts of all the years of hardship she'd endured, she felt her old fury awaken once more.

She sprang to her feet and took a few steps back from the grave. Then she launched herself at the headstone with all her might. An intense pain radiated from her shoulder to her fingertips, but the stone hadn't budged. Frustrated, she attacked the flowers that adorned the grave, yanking them up by the roots. Then she again backed up and rushed forward in an attempt to dislodge the green swastika made of iron that stood next to the headstone. It gave way and fell flat on the grass. She dragged it as far from the grave as she could. With glee she surveyed the destruction she had wrought until a hand grabbed her by the arm.

'What on earth are you doing?' A big, hefty man was standing next to her.

She smiled happily. 'I'm the future Mrs Göring. I know that Hermann doesn't think Carin deserved to have such a fine grave, so I've taken care of the matter, and now I must go to him.'

Dagmar kept on smiling, but the man's face was grim. He muttered something to himself as he shook his head. Then with a firm grip on her arm, he dragged her towards the church.

When the police arrived an hour later, Dagmar was still smiling.

The terraced house in Falkeliden sometimes seemed much too small. Dan was taking the children to spend the weekend in Göteborg with his sister, and during the packing frenzy that morning, Anna had felt she was in the way, no matter where she stood. She'd also been forced to run down to the petrol station several times to buy sweets, soft drinks, fruit, and comic books for the trip.

'Do you have everything now?' Anna surveyed the mountain of bags and other odds and ends piled up in the front hall.

Dan was going back and forth to the car, stowing the luggage. She could already see that there wouldn't be enough room, but that was his problem. He was the one who had told the children to do their own packing, and he'd promised they could take anything they liked.

'Are you sure you don't want to come with us? I don't like leaving you alone after what you went through yesterday.'

'Thanks, but I'm fine. It will actually be nice to have the house to myself for a couple of days.' She gave Dan a pleading look, hoping he would understand and not be hurt.

He nodded and put his arms around her.

'I know exactly what you mean, sweetheart. You don't have to explain. Have a wonderful time, and don't think about anyone but yourself. Treat yourself to a good meal, go for one of those long swims that you love, and do some shopping. Do whatever you want, so long as the house is still standing when I get back.' He gave her one last hug, then resumed the task of carrying suitcases to the car.

Anna felt her throat tighten. She came close to telling him that she'd changed her mind, but she bit back the words. Right now she needed time to think, and the scare yesterday wasn't the only thing that she had to work through. Life stretched out in front of her, and yet she couldn't keep from staring in the rear-view mirror. It was time she figured out a way to shake off the past and turn her gaze forward.

'Why aren't you coming with us, Mamma?' Emma was tugging at her sleeve.

Anna squatted down, struck by how tall her daughter had grown. She'd really shot up during the spring and summer. She was a big girl now.

'I told you: I have a lot of things to do here at home.'

'Yes, but we're going to Liseberg!' Emma stared at her mother as if Anna had taken leave of her senses. And in the world of an eight-year-old, that was undoubtedly the case, since she was voluntarily missing out on a visit to the amusement park.

'I'll go with you next time. Besides, you know what a scaredy-cat I am. I probably wouldn't dare to go on any of the rides. You're much braver than me.'

'Yes, I am!' Emma proudly straightened her shoulders. 'I'm going on the roller-coaster, and even Pappa won't ride it.'

It didn't matter how many times Anna heard Emma and Adrian call Dan 'Pappa', she was touched every time. And that was yet another reason why she needed these two days of solitude. She had to find a way to become whole again. For the family's sake.

She kissed Emma on the cheek. 'I'll see you Sunday evening.'

Emma ran out to the car, and Anna leaned on the door frame with her arms wrapped around her, enjoying the commotion in the driveway. Dan was starting to sweat, and it appeared he was finally beginning to realize it would be impossible to take everything along.

'Good Lord, I can't believe they've packed so much stuff,' he said, wiping his forehead.

The boot of the car was already full to the brim, and there was still a big pile of stuff in the front hall.

'Don't say anything!' He waved his finger at Anna.

She threw out her hands. 'I won't say a word.'

'Adrian! Do you have to take Dino along?' He picked up Adrian's favourite stuffed animal, a metre-tall dinosaur that Erica and Patrik had given the boy as a Christmas present.

'If Dino can't come, then I'm staying home,' shouted Adrian, snatching the dinosaur out of Dan's hands.

'Lisen?' Dan then yelled. 'Do you really need to take all of your Barbie dolls? Can't you just choose two of them?'

Lisen promptly began to cry, and Anna shook her head. She blew Dan a kiss.

'I don't think I should get involved in any of this. One of us has to be left standing. Have fun.'

Then she went inside and climbed the stairs to their bedroom. She lay down on top of the quilt and used the remote to turn on the portable TV. After much consideration, she decided on Oprah on channel three.

Annoyed, Sebastian threw down his pen on top of the notepad. His usual good humour refused to return even though everything had gone as planned.

279

He loved the feeling of being able to control Percy and Josef, and his joint business ventures with them were about to become very lucrative. Sometimes he didn't understand other people. He would never consider getting involved with somebody like himself, but they were both desperate, each in his own way. Percy was terrified of losing his ancestral inheritance, while Josef was searching for redress and his parents' approval. Sebastian understood Percy better than Josef. Percy was about to lose something important: money and status. But Josef's motive was a mystery. What did it matter what Josef did now? The idea of opening a Holocaust museum made no sense. The project was never going to get off the ground, and if Josef wasn't such an idiot, he'd be able to see that for himself.

Sebastian got up and went to the window. The entire harbour was filled with boats flying Norwegian flags, and out on the street, everyone was speaking Norwegian. Not that he had anything against that. He'd made some excellent estate sales to Norwegians. The wealth they'd acquired from the North Sea oil had made them willing to spend money, and they'd paid way too much for their houses with views of the sea along the Swedish west coast.

Slowly he turned his gaze towards Valö. Why did Leon have to come back here and start stirring things up again? For a moment Sebastian thought about Leon and John. Although he had them both in his power, he'd always been careful not to exploit the situation. Instead, like a born predator, he'd identified the weaker elements in the herd and separated them from the rest. Now Leon was trying to gather the herd back together, and Sebastian had a feeling that it would not be to his advantage. But events had already been set in motion, and there was nothing he could do about it. He wasn't about to start worrying about things that were beyond his control.

*   *   *

Erica watched from the window until she saw Patrik's car disappear. Then she quickly got the children dressed and put them in the car. She left a note for Ebba, who was still asleep, saying that she'd gone out to run an errand and had taken the children with her. There were breakfast items in the fridge. Erica had sent a text message to Gösta the moment she awoke, so she knew that he would be waiting for them.

'Where are we going?' Maja was sitting in the back seat, holding her doll on her lap.

'To visit Uncle Gösta,' said Erica, instantly realizing that Maja was bound to tell Patrik. Oh well, sooner or later he'd find out about the agreement that she'd made with Gösta. She was more worried that she hadn't told Patrik about the break-in at their house.

She took the turn-off towards Anrås, refusing to contemplate who might have been rummaging about in her work room. In truth, she knew who it must be. Or rather: there were only two possibilities. It was either someone who believed that she'd dug up some sensitive information concerning the summer camp, or it was because of her visit to John Holm and the note that she'd taken. Considering the timing of the break-in, she was inclined to think it was the latter.

'I see you brought your entire brood,' said Gösta when he opened the door. But the gleam in his eye made up for the cross tone of his voice.

'If you've got any family heirlooms, you'd better move them out of reach right now,' Erica said as she took off the children's shoes.

The twins were shy and clung to her legs, but Maja stretched out her arms and cried: 'Uncle Gösta!'

He seemed startled, unsure how to handle this overwhelming gesture of affection. Then his expression softened, and he picked Maja up.

'What a good little girl you are.' He carried her into the house and announced without turning around: 'I've set the table out in the garden.'

Erica gathered up the twins, balancing one on each hip, and followed. Overcome with curiosity, she peered at everything in Gösta's small house, which was conveniently situated near the golf course. She didn't know what she'd expected, but this was not a dreary bachelor's home. It was pleasant and comfortable, with potted plants on the windowsills. The garden behind the house was also surprisingly well-kept, even though it was so small that it probably didn't require much work to keep it tidy.

'Are they allowed to have juice and buns, or are you one of those parents who insists that everything should be organic and healthy?' Gösta set Maja down on a chair.

Erica couldn't help laughing and wondered if he spent his spare time secretly reading *Mama* magazine.

'Buns and juice would be wonderful,' she said, putting the twins down. Slowly they began moving away from her.

Maja caught sight of some raspberry bushes, and with a shout of joy she jumped off her chair and ran over to them.

'Is it all right for her to pick raspberries?' Erica knew her daughter well enough to predict that in a very short time there wouldn't be a single berry left.

'Sure, let her eat them,' said Gösta, pouring coffee for Erica and himself. 'Otherwise the birds will get them all. Maj-Britt used to pick the berries to make jam and juice, but it's not the sort of thing I enjoy. Ebba . . .' He stopped himself and pressed his lips tight as he stirred a lump of sugar in his cup.

'What about Ebba?' said Erica. She recalled Ebba's expression during the boat trip back from Valö. A mixture of relief and concern. She seemed to be torn between a desire to stay there and a wish to leave.

282

'Ebba also liked to pick raspberries, and she'd eat every single one of them,' said Gösta reluctantly. 'There weren't any left to make jam or juice during that summer she lived with us. But Maj-Britt didn't care. It was so much fun to see the little lass standing there in her nappy, stuffing handfuls of raspberries into her mouth, with the juice running down her tummy.'

'Ebba lived here with you?'

'Yes, but only for the summer. Then she moved to a family in Göteborg.'

Erica sat in silence, trying to take in what Gösta had just told her. How odd. When she'd done her research on the case, she'd found no mention of Ebba living with Gösta and Maj-Britt. Suddenly she understood why he was so involved in this investigation.

'Did you ever think about keeping her?' she asked.

Gösta stared at his coffee cup as he stirred the spoon round and round. For a moment Erica regretted asking the question. Although his face was turned away from her, she sensed that tears had welled up in his eyes. Then he cleared his throat and swallowed hard.

'Of course we did. We talked about it many times. But Maj-Britt didn't think we were the right people to take care of her. And I let her persuade me to give Ebba up. I suppose we convinced ourselves that we didn't have much to offer her.'

'Did you have any contact with her after she moved to Göteborg?'

Gösta hesitated. Then he shook his head. 'No, we decided it would be best to make a clean break. The day that she left . . .' His voice broke, and he couldn't finish the sentence, but it wasn't necessary. Erica understood.

'How does it feel to see her again?'

'It's a bit strange. She's a grown woman now, a stranger. At the same time, I can still see the little lass in her, the

283

girl who stood here picking raspberries and laughing at us.'

'She's not doing much laughing these days.'

'No, she's not.' He frowned. 'Do you know what happened to their son?'

'I haven't wanted to ask. But Patrik and Paula are on their way to Göteborg to talk to Ebba's adoptive parents. I'm sure they'll find out.'

'I don't like her husband,' said Gösta, reaching for a bun.

'Tobias? I don't think there's anything wrong with him. They just seem to be having some problems in their marriage. They have to work through the loss of their child, and I know from my sister's experience how that can take its toll on a relationship. A shared sorrow doesn't always bring people closer together.'

'You're right about that.' Gösta nodded, and Erica realized that he knew all too well. He and Maj-Britt had lost their first and only child days after he was born. And then they lost Ebba too.

'Look, Uncle Gösta! There's tons of raspberries!' shouted Maja from the bushes.

'Eat as many as you want,' he told her, his eyes sparkling again.

'Maybe you'd like to babysit sometime,' said Erica, only half joking.

'I'm not sure I could handle three of them, but I'd be happy to look after the little girl if you ever need help.'

'I'll keep that in mind.' Erica decided to see to it that Gösta had a chance to babysit for her daughter someday soon. Maja was never shy with strangers, but she seemed to have taken a special liking to Patrik's morose colleague. And it was obvious that Gösta had an empty space in his heart that Maja might help fill.

'So what do you think about the shooting yesterday?'

Gösta shook his head. 'I can't make head or tail of it. The family disappeared in 1974, most likely murdered. Since then, nothing's happened. Not until Ebba returned to Valö. Then all hell breaks loose. But why?'

'It can't be because she witnessed anything. Ebba was so young that she can't possibly remember.'

'I know. I'm more inclined to think that someone wanted to prevent Ebba and Tobias from finding the blood. But the shots fired yesterday don't fit with that theory. By that time, the damage had already been done.'

'The card Tobias brought in is proof that somebody means to harm her. And since the cards began arriving in 1974, we can conclude that everything that has happened to Ebba during the past week is somehow connected to her family's disappearance. On the other hand, this is the first time the message on the card has seemed threatening.'

'Well, I . . .'

'Maja! Don't push Noel!' Erica jumped up and ran over to the children, who were in the midst of a loud quarrel next to the raspberry bush.

'But Noel took the raspberry. It was mine. And he ate it!' cried Maja, trying to give Noel a kick.

Erica took her daughter by the arm and warned her, 'Stop it! You're not allowed to kick your little brother. And there are still plenty of raspberries left.' She pointed at the bush, which was loaded with ripe red berries.

'But I wanted that one!' Maja's face made it clear that she felt herself unfairly treated, and when Erica let go of her arm to pick up Noel and comfort him, she rushed off.

'Uncle Gösta! Noel took my raspberry,' she sniffled.

He looked down at the little girl, covered in raspberry juice. With a smile he picked her up and set her on his lap. She promptly curled herself in a pitiful little ball.

'It's okay, sweetie,' said Gösta, stroking her hair as if

he had long experience soothing unhappy three-year-olds. 'You know what? That raspberry wasn't the best one.'

'It wasn't?' Maja abruptly stopped crying and gazed up at Gösta.

'No. I happen to know where the very best berries are. But it's a secret. You can't tell your brothers or even your mother.'

'I promise.'

'All right then. I trust you,' said Gösta. And he bent down and whispered something in her ear.

Maja listened carefully, then slid off his lap and headed back to the bush. By now Noel had calmed down, and Erica returned to the table and sat down.

'What did you say to her? Where are the best raspberries?'

'I could tell you, but then I'd have to kill you,' said Gösta with a smile.

Erica turned to see Maja, standing on tiptoe, reaching for the raspberries that were too high up for the twins to pick.

'That was clever of you,' she said, laughing. 'So where were we? Oh, yes, the attempt on Ebba's life yesterday. We need to work out how to proceed. Have you found out what happened to the family's belongings? It could be so helpful to have a chance to go through them. Was everything thrown away? Did someone come in afterwards to clean up the house? Did they employ a cleaner and gardener, or did the family do it all themselves?'

Gösta suddenly sat up straight. 'Good Lord, how could I be so stupid? Sometimes I think I must be going senile.'

'What do you mean?'

'I should have thought of this before . . . He was like part of the scenery out there, but that's all the more reason why it should have occurred to me.'

Erica glared at him. 'What are you talking about?'

'Junk-Olle.'

'Junk-Olle? You mean the old guy who has a junkyard out in Bräcke? What does he have to do with Valö?'

'He came and went as he pleased, doing odd jobs whenever he was needed.'

'And you think that Junk-Olle might have taken possession of the family's belongings?'

Gösta threw out his hands. 'That might be one explanation. The old guy collects stuff, and if no one claimed the belongings, I wouldn't be surprised if he carted it all away.'

'The question is whether he still has it.'

'You mean Junk-Olle might have done a bit of spring-cleaning and actually got rid of something?'

Erica laughed. 'No, if he took the family's things, we can be pretty sure that he still has them. Maybe we should go out there now and have a chat with him.' She was already halfway out of her chair, but Gösta motioned for her to sit down.

'Relax. If those items are in the junk heap, they've been lying there for over thirty years. They're not about to disappear overnight. And that's no place to take the kids. I'll ring him later, and if he has the stuff out there, we can drive over when you have a babysitter.'

Erica knew he was right, but she couldn't shake off the sense there was something she ought to be doing.

'How is she?' asked Gösta, and it took a second for Erica to realize who he was talking about.

'Ebba? She seems completely worn out. I had the feeling that, in spite of everything, she was relieved to get away from the island for a while.'

'And away from Tobias.'

'I think you've misjudged him, but you're probably right. It's just the two of them out there, and they seem to be getting on each other's nerves. She's interested in learning more about her family's history, so when I get home and put the twins down for their nap, I thought I'd show her what I've found.'

'I'm sure she would appreciate that. She has quite a colourful past.'

'You can say that again.' Erica drank the rest of her coffee. It had gone cold, and she grimaced. 'By the way, I had a talk with Kjell at *Bohusläningen*. He gave me some background information on John Holm.' She briefed Gösta on the family tragedy that had set Holm on such a hateful path. She also told him about the note that she'd found. She hadn't dared mention it to Gösta before.

'Gimle? I have no idea what it means. There's nothing to suggest that it's connected with Valö.'

'I know, but it might have made him nervous enough to get someone to break into our home,' she said before she could stop herself.

'Someone broke in? What does Patrik say about that?'

Erica didn't reply, and Gösta stared at her.

'You haven't told him?' His voice rose to a falsetto. 'How certain are you that Holm and his followers are behind it?'

'I'm only guessing, and it's really no big deal. Someone got in through the veranda door and snooped around in my work room. They tried to log in to my computer, without success. Thankfully they didn't steal my hard drive.'

'Patrik will go berserk when he finds out. And if he hears that I knew about it and didn't tell him, he's going to be furious with me too.'

Erica sighed. 'I'll tell him. But the interesting part is that I appear to have something in my work room that's valuable enough to risk breaking in. And I reckon it's that note.'

'Would John Holm really go to such lengths? The

Friends of Sweden have a lot to lose if it got out that he'd broken into a policeman's home.'

'It might be important enough. But I've given the note to Kjell, so it's up to him to work out what it means.'

'Good,' said Gösta. 'Now promise me you'll tell Patrik about it when he gets home tonight. Otherwise I'll be in trouble too.'

'Okay, okay,' she said wearily. She wasn't looking forward to that conversation, but it had to be done.

Gösta shook his head. 'I wonder whether Patrik and Paula will find out anything in Göteborg. I'm beginning to feel a little discouraged.'

'We can always hope that Junk-Olle will have something to tell us,' said Erica, happy to change the subject.

'We can always hope,' agreed Gösta.

ST JÖRGEN HOSPITAL 1936

'We consider it unlikely that your mother will be released anytime soon,' said Dr Jansson. He was a white-haired man in late middle-age with a beard that made him resemble Santa Claus.

Laura sighed with relief. She had achieved a sense of order in her life now, with a good job and a new place to live. As one of Mrs Bergström's lodgers on Galärbacken, she had only a small room, but it was all hers, and it was as nice as the dollhouse that had pride of place on the tall chest of drawers next to her bed. Life was much better without Dagmar. For three years her mother had been a patient at St Jörgen Hospital in Göteborg, and it was a relief not to have to worry about what trouble she might be getting into.

'What exactly is wrong with my mother?' she asked, trying to sound as if she cared.

She was nicely dressed, as always. She sat with her legs turned primly to one side, her handbag resting on her lap. Although she was only sixteen, she felt much older.

'We haven't been able to arrive at a specific diagnosis, but most likely she suffers from what we call delicate nerves. Unfortunately, the treatment has been unsuccessful. She still clings to her delusions about Hermann Göring. It's not unusual for people with delicate nerves to develop fantasies about famous people.'

'My mother has talked about him for as long as I can remember,' said Laura.

The doctor gave her a sympathetic look.

'From what I understand, you haven't had an easy childhood. But you seem to be doing well. Not only do you have a pretty face, but you appear to be a very sensible young girl.'

'I do what I can,' she said shyly, but the bile rose up in her throat as images from her childhood came flooding in.

She hated not being able to control those thoughts. Normally she could suppress the memories of her mother and that dark, cramped flat with its stench of alcohol, which she'd never been able to erase, no matter how hard she scrubbed and cleaned. She had also buried the jeers of her classmates. No ugly words were hurled at her now. No one brought up the subject of her mother. Laura was respected for what she was: conscientious, proper, and meticulous in everything she undertook.

But still the fear remained. Fear that her mother would get out and ruin everything.

'Would you like to see your mother? I can't advise you to do so, but . . .' Dr Jansson threw out his hands.

'Oh, no, I think it's best that I don't. My mother always gets so . . . upset.' Laura remembered every word that Dagmar had flung at her during that first visit. She had called her daughter such vile names that Laura couldn't bear to repeat them. Dr Jansson obviously hadn't forgotten either.

'I think that's a wise decision. We try to keep Dagmar calm.'

'I hope you're not letting my mother read the newspapers.'

'No, after what happened, she does not have access to any papers.' He shook his head emphatically.

Laura nodded. Two years ago the hospital had phoned her to say that Dagmar had read a newspaper report that Göring had moved the earthly remains of his wife Carin to Karinhall, his estate in Germany. He had also erected a memorial in her honour. Dagmar had flown into a rage, completely destroying her room and injuring one of the nurses so badly that he required stitches.

291

'You'll keep me informed if anything changes, won't you?' Laura said, standing up. She held her gloves in her left hand as she held out her right to bid the doctor goodbye.

As she turned and left the doctor's office, a smile played over her lips. For now, at least, she was free.

They were approaching Torp, just north of Uddevalla, when they got caught in a traffic jam. Patrik had to slow down, and Paula kept shifting position, trying to get comfortable in the passenger seat.

He glanced at his colleague with concern. 'Do you really feel like driving to Göteborg and back?'

'Of course. And don't you start worrying too. There are enough people worrying about me at the moment.'

'Well, let's hope it's worth the trouble. The traffic is terrible today.'

'There's nothing we can do about it,' said Paula. 'How's Ebba, by the way?'

'I don't know. She was asleep when I came home yesterday, and she was still sleeping when I left. Erica said she was totally exhausted.'

'I'm not surprised. This whole thing must be a nightmare for her.'

'Hey, step on it!' Patrik pressed his hand on the horn as the driver in the car ahead of them failed to react when a gap appeared in the queue of vehicles.

Paula shook her head but refrained from commenting. She'd driven with Patrik often enough to know that he was a different person the minute he got behind the wheel.

It took them almost an hour longer to reach Göteborg in the summertime traffic, and Patrik was fit to explode as they climbed out of the car on the quiet residential street in Partille. He tugged on his shirt to fan himself.

'God, it's hot today. Aren't you dying in this heat?'

Paula cast a smug glance at his forehead, which was shiny with sweat.

'I'm a foreigner. I don't sweat,' she said, raising her arms to emphasize her point.

'Then I reckon I'm sweating enough for the both of us. I should have brought along an extra shirt. What will they make of us? I'm completely soaked, and you look like a beached whale. This'll have them wondering about the Tanum police force,' said Patrik, pressing the doorbell.

'I am not a beached whale, I'm pregnant. So what's your excuse?' Paula gave Patrik a poke in the stomach.

'This is just a slight paunch. It'll disappear in a flash, as soon as I start working out again.'

'I heard the gym had put out an APB on you.'

The door opened before Patrik had a chance to offer a retort.

'Hello. Welcome. You must be the police officers from Tanumshede,' said a man in his sixties, giving them a friendly smile.

'That's right,' said Patrik, introducing himself and Paula.

A woman about the same age joined them and said hello.

'Come in! I'm Berit. Sture and I were thinking we could sit in the retiree incubator to have a talk.'

'Retiree incubator?' Paula whispered to Patrik with a bewildered look.

'The glass veranda,' he whispered back, and she grinned.

In the small sunny veranda Berit pulled a big wicker

chair over to the table and motioned to Paula. 'Have a seat here. It's the most comfortable.'

'Thanks! You'll probably have to get a crane to haul me out of it,' said Paula, sinking gratefully on to the thick cushion.

'And prop your feet up on this stool. It can't be easy to be so late in your pregnancy in this heat wave.'

'It's getting a bit difficult,' Paula agreed. After the long ride in the car, her calves were like footballs.

'I remember so well the summer when Ebba was expecting Vincent. It was hot then too, and she . . .' Berit stopped in mid-sentence and her smile faded. Sture put his arm around his wife and tenderly patted her shoulder.

'All right then. Let's sit down and offer our guests some coffee and cake. This is Berit's tiger cake. The recipe is top secret – even I don't know how she makes it.' He kept his tone light in an attempt to lift the mood, but his eyes were as sorrowful as his wife's.

Patrik sat down, but he realized that sooner or later he would have to broach the subject that was clearly so painful for Ebba's parents.

'Help yourselves.' Berit pushed the cake platter towards the police officers. 'Do you and your husband know whether it's a boy or a girl?'

Paula paused with a piece of cake halfway to her mouth. Then she looked directly at the woman sitting across from her and said:

'No, my partner Johanna and I decided that we didn't want to know ahead of time. But we have a son, so of course it would be nice to have a girl this time. But as everyone says, the most important thing is for the baby to be healthy.' She stroked her stomach, steeling herself for the couple's reaction.

Berit's face lit up. 'How nice that your son is going to be a big brother! He must be so proud.'

'With such a beautiful mother, I'm sure the baby will be lovely, whether it's a boy or a girl,' said Sture with a warm smile.

Paula smiled happily. They didn't seem in the least bothered that the child was going to have two mothers.

'Now you must tell us what's going on,' said Sture, leaning forward. 'We can't get much out of Ebba and Tobias when they phone, and they don't want us to visit.'

'No, it's best if you don't do that,' said Patrik, thinking that the last thing they needed was to have more people on Valö.

'Why's that?' Berit's eyes shifted anxiously from Patrik to Paula. 'Ebba mentioned that they found blood when they broke up the floor. Is it from . . .'

'Yes, that seems most likely,' replied Patrik. 'But the blood is so old that we can't be sure whether it came from Ebba's family, or how many different people we might be talking about.'

'How dreadful,' said Berit. 'We've never talked much to Ebba about what happened. We only knew what social services told us, and what we read in the newspapers. So we were surprised that she and Tobias wanted to take over the house.'

'I don't think they particularly wanted to go there,' said Sture. 'It was more a case of wanting to get away from here.'

'Would you be willing to tell us what happened to their son?' said Paula cautiously.

Berit and Sture exchanged glances, and then Sture told them the story. Slowly he described the day when Vincent died, and Patrik felt a lump settle in his throat as he listened. Sometimes life seemed so cruel and meaningless.

'How soon afterwards did Ebba and Tobias move?' he asked when Sture fell silent.

'It was about six months later,' said Berit.

Sture nodded. 'Yes, that's right. They sold the house. It wasn't far from here.' He pointed vaguely down the street. 'And Tobias gave up his job as a carpenter. Ebba has been on sick leave ever since it happened. She worked as an economist for the Internal Revenue Department, but she never went back. We're a bit worried about how they're going to manage financially, but they do have money in the bank from the sale of their house.'

'We're trying to help them as best we can,' Berit said. 'We have two other children, who are our own, so to speak, although we consider Ebba to be our daughter too. Ebba has always been the apple of their eye, and they'd like to help her if they can, so I'm sure everything will work out.'

Patrik nodded. 'That place is going to be quite something. Tobias seems to be a very skilled carpenter.'

'He's incredibly talented,' said Sture. 'When they lived here, he always had work. Maybe too much work at times, but that's always better than having a son-in-law who's lazy.'

'More coffee?' asked Berit. Without waiting for an answer she got up and headed for the kitchen to fetch the coffee pot.

Sture watched her go and then said, 'This has taken its toll on my wife, but she doesn't want to show it. Ebba came to our family like a little angel. Our older children were six and eight at the time, and we'd talked about having another. It was Berit's idea to see if there might be a child we could help by taking her in.'

'Had you taken in other foster children before Ebba?' asked Paula.

'No. Ebba was our first and only one. She ended up staying with us, and later we decided to adopt her. Berit could hardly sleep at night, waiting for the adoption to be finalized. She was terrified that someone would come and take her away from us.'

'What was she like as a child?' asked Patrik, mostly out of curiosity. Something told him that the Ebba he'd met was merely a pale copy of her true self.

'Oh, she was a proper little whirlwind, let me tell you.'

'Ebba? Yes, she was.' Berit came in, carrying the coffee pot. 'That child was always getting into mischief. But she was so cheerful, and you could never stay cross with her for long.'

'That's what has made the whole thing so much harder to bear,' said Sture. 'We didn't only lose Vincent, we lost Ebba too. It feels as though a big part of her died with Vincent. And the same is true of Tobias. He's always had a rather mercurial temperament and suffered bouts of depression, but until Vincent died, things were good between them. Now . . . now I don't know. At first they could hardly stand to be in the same room, and now they're out on an island in the archipelago. As I said, we can't help but worry about them.'

'Do you have any theory as to who might have set the fire, or who could have fired shots at Ebba yesterday?' asked Patrik.

Berit and Sture stared at him in horror.

'Didn't Ebba tell you?' he said, glancing at Paula. It hadn't occurred to him that Ebba's parents knew nothing of the shooting, otherwise he would have been more careful about how he phrased the question.

'No, the only thing she told us about was the blood they found,' said Sture.

Patrik was searching for the right words when Paula came to his aid. In a calm and matter-of-fact voice she told them about the fire and the shooting.

Berit gripped the edge of the table so hard that her

knuckles turned white. 'I can't understand why she didn't tell us.'

'She probably didn't want to worry us,' said Sture, but he seemed just as upset as his wife.

'But why are they staying out there? That's madness! They need to leave the island at once. Let's go out there and talk to them, Sture.'

'They seem determined to stay,' Patrik told them. 'But for the moment Ebba is at our house. My wife brought her home yesterday and she spent the night in our guest-room. Tobias refused to leave the island, so he's still there.'

'He's out of his mind,' said Berit. 'We're going over there. Now.' She was about to get up, but Sture gently pressed her back down on her chair.

'Let's not do anything hasty. We'll phone Ebba and hear what she has to say. You know how stubborn they both are. There's no sense in making a fuss.'

Berit shook her head but made no further move to get up.

'Can you think of any reason why someone would try to harm them?' Paula was restlessly shifting about. Even sitting in this comfortable armchair, her joints had started to ache.

'No, none at all,' said Berit firmly. 'They live a completely ordinary life. And why would anyone want to cause them more pain? They've already had enough grief and sorrow.'

'It must have something to do with what happened to the Elvander family,' said Sture. 'Perhaps someone is afraid that they'll find out something.'

'That's our theory too, but so far we don't have much to go on,' Patrik told them. 'There's one thing that puzzles us. We heard that Ebba has been receiving cards signed with the initial "G".'

'Yes,' said Sture. 'Those cards have arrived for every birthday. We thought it odd, but assumed that some distant relative was sending them. It seemed harmless so we never bothered to investigate.'

'Ebba received a new card yesterday that was definitely not harmless.'

Ebba's parents stared at Patrik in surprise.

'What did it say?' Sunlight was reflecting off the table into their eyes. Sture got up to draw the curtains.

'Let's just say that it sounded threatening.'

'If so, that would be the first time. Do you think it was sent by the same person who's been trying to harm Ebba and Tobias?'

'We don't know. But it would be helpful if we could see some of the other cards. Do you have any?'

Sture shook his head apologetically. 'I'm afraid we never kept them. We showed them to Ebba and then threw them out. There were no personal messages. They just said "Happy Birthday" and were signed "G". Nothing else. It didn't occur to us to save them.'

'I understand,' said Patrik. 'And there was nothing else about the cards that might reveal who sent them? Could you tell where they were postmarked?'

'They came from here in Göteborg, so that wasn't much of a clue.' Sture fell silent. Then he gave a start and looked at his wife. 'The money,' he said.

Berit's eyes opened wide. 'Why didn't we think of that?' She turned to Patrik and Paula. 'From the time Ebba first came to us up until her eighteenth birthday, money was deposited anonymously in the bank for her every month. We received a letter saying that a bank account had been opened in Ebba's name. We saved up the money and gave it to her when she and Tobias decided to buy a house.'

'And you have no idea who deposited the money? Have you ever tried to find out?'

Sture nodded. 'We were curious, of course. But the bank told us that the person wanted to remain anonymous, so we had to give up. We thought it must be the same person who sent the birthday cards. Probably a distant relative.'

'Which bank sent the initial letter about the account?'

'Handelsbanken. The branch on Norrmalmstorg in Stockholm.'

'We'll check it out.'

Patrik raised an enquiring eyebrow at Paula. She nodded, so he stood up and shook hands with Sture.

'Thank you so much for taking the time to see us. Let us know if anything else occurs to you.'

'We will. Naturally we want to help in any way we can.' Sture gave him a wan smile, and Patrik knew that he and Berit would phone their daughter the moment they were alone.

The trip to Göteborg had turned out to be more productive than he'd dared to hope. 'Follow the money,' as they said in American movies. If they could track down where the money had come from, they might get the lead they needed to move forward.

When they were back in the car, he checked his mobile. Twenty-five missed calls. Patrik sighed and turned to Paula.

'Something tells me that the media are on to the story.' He started up the car and headed towards Tanumshede. It was going to be a rough day.

Expressen had published the news about Valö, and when Kjell's boss heard via the grapevine that *Bohusläningen* could have been first out with the story, he was not happy – and that was putting it mildly. When he finished bellowing, he sent Kjell off with orders to outdo the big-city paper. 'Just because we're smaller and provincial doesn't mean that we have to be worse,' he said.

Kjell leafed through his notes. Naturally it had gone

against all his journalistic principles to give up the story, but his fight against the anti-immigrant organizations was more important. If he had to sacrifice a scoop in order to root out the truth about the Friends of Sweden and John Holm, he was prepared to do it.

It was all he could do to stop himself phoning Sven Niklasson to find out how it had gone. Most likely he wouldn't find out much until he read about it in the newspaper, but he still couldn't help brooding over the possible meaning of 'Gimle'. He was convinced that Sven's voice had changed when he heard about the note that Erica had found at Holm's house. It sounded as if Sven had heard of Gimle before and already knew something about it.

Kjell opened his copy of *Expressen* and read what they'd written about the discovery on Valö. The paper had devoted four pages to the story, and it would probably be followed up with more articles over the next few days. The police in Tanum had called a press conference for the afternoon, and Kjell was hoping to hear something that would serve as a basis for his article. But there were still several hours to go, and the challenge was not to make use of the same information that the other reporters would have, but to come up with a fresh lead. Kjell leaned back in his chair to think. Locals had always been fascinated by the mysterious events on Valö, and in particular the role of the boys who had been staying at the school that Easter holiday. Over the years there had been a lot of speculation about what the boys knew or didn't know, and whether they'd had anything to do with the family's disappearance. If he dug up as much information as he could find about the five boys, he might be able to write an article that none of the other newspapers could match.

He turned to his computer and began entering data into a search engine. It should be possible to find out a lot about the men that the boys had become by combing

302

through public records. He'd already interviewed Holm; the next step would be to contact the other four. It was going to require a lot of work in a short period of time, but if he managed to find out anything new, it would be worth it.

Something else occurred to him, and he quickly jotted a memo to himself. He needed to talk to Gösta Flygare, who had been involved in the original investigation. If he was lucky, Gösta might be prepared to share his thoughts on the boys, maybe recall his first impressions after interviewing them. That would add some weight to the article.

The word 'Gimle' kept popping up in his mind, but Kjell resolutely pushed it aside. That was no longer his responsibility, and maybe it didn't mean anything. He picked up his mobile to start making calls. He had no time to sit around brooding.

Slowly Percy packed his suitcase. He would not be attending the sixtieth birthday party of their friend. After a few phone calls he'd found out that not only had Pyttan left him, but she'd moved in with the man whose birthday was being celebrated.

Early in the morning Percy would get into the Jaguar and drive to Fjällbacka. He wasn't sure it was a good idea, but his conversation with Leon had served to confirm that his whole life was on the verge of collapse. So what did he have to lose?

As always, when Leon commanded, he obeyed. Even back then Leon had been in charge, and it was both strange and rather frightening to realize that he'd had the same authority at the age of sixteen as he had today. Perhaps his life would have turned out different if Percy hadn't followed Leon's orders, but he wasn't going to think about that now. He'd spent years suppressing what

303

happened on Valö, and he'd never returned to the island. As they sat in the boat on that Easter eve, he hadn't given it so much as a backward glance.

Now he was going to be forced to remember. He knew that he ought to stay in Stockholm, get thoroughly drunk, and then sit and watch life pass by on Karlavägen as he waited for the creditors to knock on the door. But Leon's voice on the phone had stripped him of all willpower, just as it had back then.

He gave a start when the doorbell rang. He wasn't expecting visitors, and Pyttan had already taken everything of value. He had no illusions that she might regret her actions and come back to him. She wasn't that stupid. She knew he was about to lose everything, so she'd made her escape. And when it came right down to it, he understood. He had grown up in a world where people married spouses who had something to offer – a form of aristocratic barter.

He opened the door. There stood Attorney Buhrman.

'Do we have an appointment?' asked Percy, trying to remember.

'No, we don't.' The attorney took a step forward, forcing Percy to back up and allow him in. 'I had a number of errands here in town, and I was supposed to head home this afternoon. But this can't wait.'

Buhrman was avoiding meeting his eye, and Percy felt his knees begin to tremble. This was not good.

'Come in,' he said, fighting to keep his voice under control.

In his mind he heard his father saying: 'No matter what happens, never show any sign of weakness.' Memories flooded over him from the time when he failed to follow this advice and had fallen to the floor in tears, begging and pleading. He swallowed hard and closed his eyes for a moment. This was not the time to allow the past to intrude. He'd have to endure enough of that tomorrow. Right now he had to deal with Buhrman.

'Would you like a whisky?' he asked, going over to the drinks cart and pouring one for himself.

With an effort the attorney slowly sank to the sofa. 'No, thank you.'

'Coffee?'

'No, thank you. Now sit down.' Buhrman thumped his cane on the floor, and Percy did as he was told. He sat in silence as the attorney talked, merely nodding occasionally to show that he understood. His expression gave no clue to what he was thinking. He father's voice echoed louder in his head: 'Never show any sign of weakness.'

After Buhrman had left, Percy resumed packing. There was only one thing he could do. He'd been weak then, so long ago. He had allowed evil to triumph. Percy zipped up the suitcase and sat on the bed, staring straight ahead. His life was in ruins. There was no meaning to anything. But he would never again show that he was weak.

FJÄLLBACKA 1939

Laura studied her husband as he sat at the breakfast table. They'd been married a year. The day that Laura turned eighteen she had accepted Sigvard's proposal, and a month later they were married in a quiet ceremony in the garden. Sigvard was fifty-three, old enough to be her father. But he was rich, and she knew that she would never again have to worry about her future. She had sat down to make a list of arguments, for and against the marriage, and the positive side had won out. Love was for fools. It was a luxury that a woman in her situation could not afford.

'The Germans have invaded Poland,' said Sigvard, sounding agitated. 'Mark my words, this is only the beginning.'

'I can't be bothered with politics.'

Laura made herself half a sandwich. She didn't dare eat more than that. Constant hunger was the price she had to pay for being perfect, and at times she struggled with how absurd this was. She had married Sigvard for security, for the knowledge that she'd always have food on the table. And yet she went hungry as often as she had when she was a child and Dagmar was spending her money on booze instead of food.

Sigvard laughed. 'Your father is mentioned here too.'

She gave him a frosty look. She was willing to put up with a lot, but she had repeatedly asked him not to speak of anything having to do with her lunatic mother. She needed no reminders of what her life had once been. Dagmar was safely locked up in St Jörgen Hospital, and if Laura was lucky, she would stay there for the rest of her miserable life.

'Must you talk about that?' she said.

'Forgive me, darling. But there's no need to be ashamed. On the contrary. Göring is Hitler's favourite, and he's head of the Luftwaffe. Not bad.' He nodded pensively and then went back to his newspaper.

Laura sighed. She wasn't interested. For years she'd had to put up with her mother's demented fantasies, and now she was forced to hear about that man all the time, simply because he was one of Hitler's closest associates. Good Lord, what did it matter to them in Sweden if the Germans invaded Poland?

'I was thinking of redecorating the drawing room. May I?' she asked, using her softest tone of voice. It hadn't been long since she'd had the entire room redone. It had turned out lovely, but it still wasn't perfect. Not like the drawing room in the dollhouse. The fancy sofa that she'd bought didn't quite fit, and the prisms in the crystal chandelier were not as shiny and spar-kling as she'd expected.

'You're going to drive me to rack and ruin,' said Sigvard, but he gave her an adoring look. 'Do whatever you like, sweetheart. As long as it makes you happy.'

'Anna is coming over, if that's okay.' Erica cast a hesitant glance at Ebba. The moment she'd invited her sister, she realized it might not be such a good idea, but Anna had sounded as if she needed company.

'That's fine.' Ebba smiled but she still seemed exhausted.

'What did your parents say? Patrik felt terrible that they had to hear about the fire and the shooting in that way, but he assumed you'd already told them.'

'I should have done, but I was putting it off. I know how worried they get. They would have wanted us to give up and move back.'

'Have you considered doing that?' said Erica as she put in the *Lotta on Bråkmakargatan* DVD. The twins were asleep, worn out from the expedition to Gösta's house, but Maja was sitting on the sofa, waiting for the movie to begin.

Ebba paused to think before answering. Then she shook her head. 'No, we can't go back home. If this doesn't work out, I don't know what we'll do. I know it's idiotic to stay here, and I *am* scared, but at the same time . . . the worst thing that could happen to us has already happened.'

'What . . .' Erica began. She had finally gathered her

courage to ask about their son, but at that moment the front door opened and Anna walked in.

'Hello!' she called.

'Come on in. I'm just putting in the Lotta DVD for the thousandth time.'

'Hi,' said Anna, nodding to Ebba. She gave a cautious smile, as if not sure how to act after what they'd been through the previous day.

'Hi, Anna,' said Ebba, equally hesitant. But in her case, the wariness seemed part of her personality, and Erica wondered whether she'd been a more open sort of person before her son died.

The movie started playing, so Erica stood up. 'Head on into the kitchen, and I'll be right there.'

Anna and Ebba went into the kitchen and sat down at the table.

'Did you get some sleep?' asked Anna.

'Yes, I slept more than twelve hours, but I feel as if I could sleep for another twelve.'

'It's probably the shock.'

Erica came in to join them, carrying a stack of papers.

'What I've collected isn't comprehensive, by any means, and you've probably already seen some of it,' she said, setting the papers on the table.

'I haven't seen anything,' said Ebba, shaking her head. 'This may sound odd, but I never thought much about my background until I took over the house and we moved here. I had a good life, and it all seemed a little . . . absurd.' Her eyes fell on the pile of papers as if she might absorb the information merely by staring at it.

'Right then.' Erica opened a notebook and cleared her throat. 'Your mother, Inez, was born in 1951 and was only twenty-three when she disappeared. I haven't been able to find out much about her before she married Rune. She was born and raised in Fjällbacka, got average grades in school, but that's all I could find in the archives. She married your father, Rune Elvander, in 1970, and you were born in January 1973.'

'January third,' Ebba added with a nod.

'Rune was significantly older than Inez, as I'm sure you know. He was born in 1919 and had three children from a previous marriage: Johan, who was nine; Annelie, who was sixteen; and Claes, who was nineteen when they disappeared. Their mother, Carla, who was Rune's first wife, died one year before Rune and Inez got married. And according to the people I've talked to, it wasn't exactly easy for your mother to become part of that family.'

'I wonder why she married a man who was so much older,' said Ebba. 'Pappa must have been . . .' she silently did the calculation in her head, 'fifty-one when they were married.'

'Your maternal grandmother seems to have had a lot to do with it. She was clearly – how should I put this . . .'

'I have no relationship with my grandmother, so I won't mind if you speak bluntly. My family is in Göteborg. This part of my life is purely of academic interest so far as I'm concerned.'

'Then you won't be offended if I say that your grand-mother was considered a real bitch.'

'Erica!' said Anna reproachfully.

For the first time since they'd met Ebba, she laughed heartily.

'Don't worry.' She turned to Anna. 'It doesn't upset me. I want to hear the truth, or at least as much of it as we can find out.'

'Okay,' said Anna, but she sounded sceptical.

Erica went on: 'Your maternal grandmother was named Laura, and she was born in 1920.'

'So my grandmother was about the same age as my

father,' said Ebba. 'That makes me wonder even more about what went on.'

'As I said, Laura seems to have played a major role. Apparently she was the one who got your mother to marry Rune. But it's not something that I can prove, so you should take it with a grain of salt.'

Erica began rummaging through the stack of papers and pulled out a copy of a photo, which she placed in front of Ebba.

'This is a picture of your grandparents, Laura and Sigvard.'

Ebba leaned forward. 'She's not exactly cheerful,' she said, staring at the stern-faced woman. The man next to her didn't seem any happier.

'Sigvard died in 1954, shortly after this photo was taken.'

'They look wealthy,' said Anna as she too leaned forward to study the picture.

'They were,' said Erica, nodding. 'At least up until Sigvard's death. Then it turned out that he'd made a number of bad business investments. There wasn't much money left, and since Laura didn't have a job, the funds slowly ran out. Presumably Laura would have ended up destitute if Inez hadn't married Rune.'

'Was my father rich?' asked Ebba. She had picked up the photo and was holding it close to her eyes, examining it in minute detail.

'I wouldn't call him rich, but he was well-to-do. He had enough to pay for a respectable widow's flat for Laura over on the mainland.'

'But she was dead by the time my parents disappeared, wasn't she?'

Erica paged through the notebook on the table in front of her.

'Yes. Laura died of a heart attack in 1973. Out on Valö,

311

as a matter of fact. Rune's eldest son, Claes, found her behind the house. She was already dead.'

Erica licked her thumb and then began going through the stack until she found a photocopy of a newspaper article. 'Here's what it said in *Bohusläningen*.'

'My grandmother seems to have been something of a celebrity around here,' said Ebba when she'd finished reading.

'Yes, everyone knew who Laura Blitz was. Sigvard had made his fortune from the shipping trade, and it was rumoured that he'd made deals with the Germans during the Second World War.'

'Were they Nazis?' said Ebba, horrified.

'I don't know how involved they were,' Erica replied hesitantly. 'But it was generally known that your grand-parents harboured certain sympathies with the Germans.'

'Mamma too?' said Ebba, her eyes wide. Anna glared at Erica.

'I've never heard anyone say that,' replied Erica, shaking her head. 'Nice but a bit naive. That was how most people described Inez. And terribly dominated by her mother.'

'That would explain why she married my father.' Ebba bit her lip. 'Wasn't he also a very authoritarian kind of person? Or is that something I've imagined because he was the headmaster of a boarding school?'

'No, that seems to be right. He was said to be a very stern and harsh man.'

'Was my grandmother originally from Fjällbacka?' Ebba again picked up the picture of the woman with the forbid-ding expression.

'Yes, her family had lived in Fjällbacka for several generations. Her mother was named Dagmar, and she was born in Fjällbacka in 1900.'

'So she was . . . twenty when she had my grandmother?

312

But I suppose it was quite common at the time to be so young. Who was Laura's father?'

'It says "father unknown" in the birth registry. And Dagmar was apparently quite a character.' Erica again licked her thumb and then continued her search until she found a paper almost at the bottom of the stack. 'This is an excerpt from the judicial registry.'

'Convicted of loose living? Was my great-grandmother a prostitute?' Ebba gave Erica a surprised look.

'She was a single woman with an illegitimate child, so she probably did whatever she had to do, in order to survive. I'm sure it wasn't an easy life. She was also convicted several times of theft. Dagmar was generally thought to be a bit crazy, and she drank too much. There are documents showing that she spent a long time in an insane asylum.'

'What a terrible childhood my grandmother must have had,' said Ebba. 'It's not so strange that she would turn out to be mean.'

'Growing up with Dagmar must have been very difficult. Today it would probably be considered scandalous that Dagmar was allowed to keep Laura. But those were different times, and there was an enormous contempt for unmarried mothers.' Erica could vividly picture the mother and daughter. She had devoted so many hours to delving into the history of these women that they now seemed very real to her. She didn't fully understand why she'd gone so far back in time when she was supposed to be unravelling the mystery of the disappearance of the Elvander family. But the fate of those two women had captured her interest, and she had kept on researching their stories.

'What happened to Dagmar?' asked Ebba.

Erica took out another sheet of paper. It was a copy of a black-and-white photo that appeared to have been taken in a court of law.

'Good Lord, is that her?'

'Let me see,' said Anna, and Ebba held up the paper.

'When was this picture taken? She looks so old and worn out.'

Erica referred to her notes. 'It's from 1945, which means Dagmar would have been forty-five. It was taken when she was committed to St Jörgen Hospital in Göteborg.'

Erica paused for effect.

'And by the way, it was taken four years before Dagmar disappeared.'

'Disappeared?' said Ebba.

'Yes, it seems to be a family trait. The last report that mentions Dagmar is dated 1949. After that she seems to have vanished in a puff of smoke.'

'Didn't Laura know anything?'

'I've been told that Laura had ceased all contact with Dagmar long before that. By then she was married to Sigvard, and she was living an entirely different sort of life to the one she'd had with Dagmar.'

'Are there any theories as to what happened to her?' asked Anna.

'Yes. The most convincing was that she got drunk and drowned in the sea. But her body was never found.'

'Yikes,' said Ebba, picking up the picture of Dagmar again. 'A great-grandmother who was a thief and a whore and who later disappeared. I'm not sure how to handle this.'

'It gets worse.' Erica was enjoying the fact that she had the full attention of her audience. 'Dagmar's mother . . .'

'Yes?' said Anna impatiently.

'Er, I think we should have lunch first. We can talk about it later,' said Erica, although she had no intention of waiting that long to reveal the rest of the story.

'Tell us!' shouted Anna and Ebba in unison.

'Do either of you know the name Helga Svensson?'

Ebba paused to consider but then shook her head. Anna frowned, then her eyes widened in recognition.

'The Angelmaker!' she said.

'What do you mean?' said Ebba.

'Fjällbacka is famous for more than the King's Cleft and Ingrid Bergman,' Anna explained. 'We also have the dubious honour of being the hometown of the Angelmaker, Helga Svensson, who was beheaded. In 1909, I think.'

'No, 1908,' Erica corrected her.

'Beheaded for what?' Ebba was still confused.

'She murdered children who had been left in her care. Drowned them in a basin. It wasn't discovered until one of the mothers regretted her decision and returned to fetch her child. When she didn't find her son there, after Helga had sent her letters about him for a whole year, the mother got suspicious and went to the police. They believed her story, and early one morning they stormed into Helga's house. She was there with her husband and the children – both her own daughter and the ones that Helga was caring for. It seems they were lucky to be still alive.'

'When the police dug up the cellar floor, they found the bodies of eight children,' Anna interjected.

'How awful,' said Ebba, the colour draining from her face. 'But I don't understand what this has to do with my family.' She gestured towards the stack of papers on the table.

'Helga was Dagmar's mother,' said Erica. 'The Angelmaker, Helga Svensson, was Dagmar's mother, and your great-great-grandmother.'

'You're not serious?' Ebba stared at Erica in disbelief.

'It's true. So you can see why I thought it was a strange coincidence when Anna told me that you make jewellery with little angels.'

'I wonder if I should have left this stone unturned,' said Ebba, but she didn't sound as if she meant it.

'But it's so exciting that . . .' Regretting her choice of words, Anna stopped herself. 'I'm sorry, I didn't mean . . .'

'I think it's exciting too,' said Ebba. 'And I do see how ironic it is that I make this sort of jewellery. How strange. It makes me wonder about fate.'

A shadow passed over her face, and Erica suspected that she was thinking about her son.

'Eight children,' she said. 'Eight little children, buried in a cellar.'

'What would make a person do something like that?' wondered Anna.

'What happened to Dagmar when they executed Helga?' Ebba wrapped her arms around herself. She seemed more vulnerable than ever.

'Helga's husband – Dagmar's father – was also beheaded,' said Erica. 'He was the one who had buried the bodies, so he was considered an accomplice to the murders, even though it was Helga who had drowned the children. So Dagmar was orphaned and ended up living with a farmer's family outside of Fjällbacka for a number of years. I don't know what her life was like with them. But I can imagine that things must have been difficult for her, as the daughter of a woman who had killed eight children. People around here wouldn't forgive a sin like that.'

Ebba nodded. She looked completely exhausted, and Erica decided that they'd heard enough for one day. It was time for lunch. Besides, she wanted to check her mobile to see if Gösta had called. She crossed her fingers that he'd heard from Junk-Olle. She was hoping that they would finally have some luck.

A fly was buzzing at the window, throwing itself repeatedly against the pane in a hopeless battle. It was probably puzzled. There was no visible obstruction and yet it kept slamming into something. Tobias understood how the fly must feel. He watched it for a while before slowly reaching out his hand and catching it between his thumb and forefinger. He watched in fascination as he pressed his fingers together, squeezing the fly until it was flattened. Then he wiped his fingers on the windowsill.

Now that the buzzing had stopped, the room was utterly silent. He was sitting in Ebba's desk chair, with the things she used for her jewellery-making spread out in front of him. A half-finished silver angel lay on the desk, and he wondered whose sorrow it was meant to ease. Although it didn't necessarily have to be for someone who was grieving. Not all the necklaces were commissioned to commemorate a death. Many people bought them simply because they were beautiful. But he sensed that this particular one had been ordered by someone in mourning. Ever since Vincent had died, Tobias had been able to sense other people's sorrow even if they weren't present. He picked up the half-finished angel and knew that it was for someone who felt the same emptiness, the same point-lessness that he felt.

He clutched the necklace harder. Ebba didn't under-stand that together they could fill part of that emptiness. All she needed to do was allow him to come near again. And she had to acknowledge her guilt. For a long time he had been blinded by his own guilt, but now he under-stood much more clearly that it was Ebba's fault. If only she would admit it, then he would forgive her and offer her another chance. But she said nothing, merely watching him with that accusatory expression, searching for guilt in his eyes.

Ebba had rejected him, and he couldn't understand it. After everything that had happened, she should have allowed him to take care of her, she should have leaned on him. In the past she had been the one who made all the decisions. Where they should live, where they should

317

go on holiday, when they should have a child. Even on that morning, she was the one who had decided what they should do. People were always fooled by Ebba's blue eyes and slight figure. They saw her as shy and compliant, which wasn't true. She'd been the one who made the decision on that morning. But from now on, it was his turn to decide.

He got up, tossing the angel aside. Covered with something red and sticky, it landed on the cluttered desk. Astonished, he looked down at the palm of his hand to see dozens of tiny cuts. Slowly he wiped his hand on his trousers. Ebba needed to come back home. There were things he had to explain to her.

Liv was feverishly wiping off the patio furniture. It had to be done every day if she wanted to keep the chairs clean, so she kept on scrubbing until the plastic gleamed. Beads of sweat ran down her back in the strong sunlight. After all the hours they'd spent at the boathouse, her skin had turned a beautiful golden brown, but dark circles were visible under her eyes.

'I don't think you should go,' she said. 'Why do you need to meet again now? You know how fragile the situation is for the party. We need to lie low until . . .' She broke off abruptly.

'I know, but there are certain things that are beyond our control,' said John, pushing his reading glasses up on to his forehead.

He was sitting at the table, ploughing his way through the newspapers. Every day he read the national papers as well as a few local ones. So far he'd never made it through the stack of newspapers without being repulsed by the stupidity that filled the pages. All those liberal journalists, columnists, and so-called experts who thought they understood how the world worked. Thanks to their combined efforts, the Swedish people were slowly but surely being corrupted. It was his responsibility to make them open their eyes. A high price would have to be paid, but it was impossible to wage a war without casualties. And this was war.

'Is that Jew coming too?' Liv started wiping off the table, having decided that the chairs were now clean enough.

John nodded. 'I assume Josef will be there.'

'What if somebody were to see you and take your picture with him? What do you think would happen if that got into the papers? Imagine what your supporters would say. You would be compromised – maybe even forced to resign. We can't let that happen, not when we're so close.'

John gazed out across the harbour, trying to avoid meeting Liv's eye. She knew nothing. How could he tell her about the darkness, the cold fear that erased all racial boundaries? Back then, at that time and place, it had been a matter of survival. Whether he liked it or not, he and Josef were linked for all eternity. There was no way he could explain that to Liv.

'I have to go,' he said, using a tone of voice that made it clear the discussion was over. Liv knew better than to argue, but she kept on muttering to herself. John smiled and looked at his wife, at her lovely face and her expression, which revealed an iron will. He loved her, and they had shared so much, but the darkness was something he could share only with those who had been there too.

For the first time in all these years they would meet again. It would be the last time. The task he had before him was too important, and he would have to put a stop to the past. What happened in 1974 may have risen to the surface, but it could just as easily vanish again, if only they could all agree. It was best to keep old secrets in the darkness where they were created.

The only person he was concerned about was Sebastian. Even back then Sebastian had enjoyed his superior position, and he might present a problem. But if reasoning with him didn't work, there were always other methods at his disposal.

Patrik took a deep breath. Annika was doing her best to make the final preparations for the press conference, which had even drawn a few journalists from Göteborg. Some of them would file reports with the national newspapers, so tomorrow the story would appear in all the major publications. Patrik knew from experience that from now on the investigation would be a circus, and in the midst of it all would be Mellberg, playing the ringmaster. That was something else Patrik had witnessed before. Mellberg hadn't been able to hide his glee when he heard that they'd been forced to call a press conference. Right now he was probably in the bathroom, tending to his comb-over.

In addition to the usual nerves about fielding questions without giving away too much, Patrik was wondering how to limit the damage that Mellberg was likely to do. At the same time, he was grateful that this story hadn't exploded in the media a couple of days earlier. Nothing that happened in Fjällbacka escaped the attention of the locals, so it was pure luck that no one had tipped off the media about the goings on in Valö prior to this. But their luck had now run out, and it would be impossible for the police to keep a lid on the story.

A cautious knock on the door roused him from his gloomy reveries. The door opened, and Gösta came in. Without waiting for an invitation, he sat down on the visitor's chair in front of Patrik's desk.

'So, the hyenas are all here,' said Gösta mournfully. He was staring down at his hands as he twiddled his thumbs nervously.

'They're only doing their job,' said Patrik, despite the fact he'd been having similar thoughts. There was no point viewing the reporters as adversaries. Occasionally the media could even prove useful.

'How'd it go in Göteborg?' asked Gösta, still without meeting Patrik's eye.

'Okay. It turned out Ebba hadn't told her parents about the arson or the shooting.'

Gösta looked up. 'Why not?'

'I think she didn't want to worry them. I suspect that they threw themselves at the phone as soon as we left. Her mother was all for heading straight out to Valö.'

'Maybe that's not a bad idea. It would be better if someone could persuade Ebba and Tobias to stay away until we've solved the case.'

Patrik nodded. 'I wouldn't have hung on a minute longer than necessary if someone had tried to kill me out there – not just once but twice.'

'People are strange.'

'Yes. Well, at least Ebba has nice parents.'

'So they seemed pleasant?'

'Yes, I think she's had a good life with them. She also seems to have an excellent relationship with her siblings. And it's a decent neighbourhood. Older houses with lots of rose bushes.'

'That does sound like a good place to grow up.'

'But we didn't come up with any sort of lead as to who might have sent those cards.'

'So they didn't keep any of them?'

'No, they threw them all out. But they were only birthday greetings, nothing threatening, not like the card that just arrived. And they were clearly postmarked Göteborg.'

'Odd.' Gösta was again studying his thumbs.

'What's even more odd is that someone deposited money

in a bank account for Ebba every month until she turned eighteen.'

'What? Anonymously?'

'Exactly. So if we can track down where the money came from, maybe we'll get somewhere. At least, I hope so. It's conceivable that the same person sent the cards. But I've got to go now.' Patrik got up. 'Was there anything particular you wanted?'

After a moment's silence Gösta cleared his throat and looked up at Patrik.

'No, nothing else. Nothing at all.'

'Okay.' Patrik opened the door and had just stepped into the hallway when Gösta called him back.

'Patrik?'

'Yes, what is it? The press conference starts in one minute.'

Another moment of silence.

'Nothing. Forget it,' said Gösta.

'Okay.'

Patrik headed for the meeting room at the end of the corridor with a nagging feeling that he should have stopped and tried to coax Gösta into telling him what he'd wanted to say.

Then he stepped into the room and quickly forgot about everything except the task in hand. All eyes turned to him. Mellberg was already standing at the front of the room, smiling broadly. At least one person in the station was ready to meet the press.

Josef ended the call. His legs gave way and he slowly sat down with his back against the wall. He stared at the floral wallpaper that had decorated the hallway ever since they'd bought the house. Rebecka had wanted to change it, but Josef could never understand why they should spend the money when the wallpaper was still in good

322

condition. Why change something that didn't need changing? They should be grateful to have a roof over their heads and food on the table. There were far more important things in life than wallpaper.

Now Josef had lost the most important thing of all, and to his surprise, he found himself unable to stop staring at the wallpaper. It was hideous, and he wondered whether he should have listened to Rebecka and allowed her to have it replaced. Should he have listened to her more in general?

It was as if for the first time he was seeing himself from the outside. A small and arrogant man. A man who had believed that dreams could come true, and that he was meant to achieve greatness. Instead, here he sat, revealed as the naive fool that he was, and he had only himself to blame. Ever since he had become cloaked in darkness, ever since the humiliation had hardened his heart, he had succeeded in convincing himself that he would someday obtain redress. Of course that would never happen. Evil was more powerful. It had been part of his parents' life, and although they had never spoken of it, he knew that it had forced them to commit ungodly acts. He too was infected with evil, but in his hubris, he had believed that God had presented him with an opportunity to be cleansed.

Josef began pounding the back of his head against the wall. At first lightly, then harder and harder. It felt wonderful, and all of a sudden he was reminded that there and then he had found a way to get past the pain. For his parents there had been no solace in the fact that they shared their suffering with others; the same was true for him. It had merely made the shame greater. He too had stubbornly believed that he could free himself if only the penance was sufficiently great.

He wondered what Rebecka and the children would

say if they knew, if everything were revealed. Leon wanted all of them to meet; he wanted to revive the suffering that ought to have remained forgotten. When he phoned last night, fear had nearly paralysed Josef. Now the threat was about to become real, and there was nothing he could do to prevent it. Today it no longer seemed important. It was all too late. he was as powerless now as he'd been back then, and he had no strength left to fight. Nor would it serve any purpose. From the very beginning, the dream had existed only in his own mind. Above all else, he reproached himself for not having realized that.

THE KARINHALL ESTATE 1949

Dagmar wept, but her sorrow was mixed with joy. Finally she had reached Hermann. For a while she had despaired. The money that she got from Laura had been enough to bring her only part of the way, and far too much had disappeared when thirst overcame her. She hardly remembered some of those days, but each time she'd climbed back on her feet and carried on. Her Hermann was waiting.

She knew quite well that he was not buried at the estate of Karinhall. An unpleasant individual had gleefully told her as much on one of the many train journeys when she explained where she was headed. But it made no difference where his body was buried. She had read the articles and seen the pictures. It was here he belonged. It was here that his soul would be found.

Carin Göring was also here. Even after her death, that odious bitch had retained her hold on Hermann. Dagmar clenched her fists in her coat pockets, breathing hard as she gazed out across the fields. This had been his domain, but now it was all destroyed. She felt the tears well up in her eyes again. How could this have happened? The estate lay in ruins, and the garden, which at one time must have been so beautiful, was now overgrown and abandoned. The leafy woods that surrounded the fields were encroaching with each passing day.

She had walked for several hours to get here. From Berlin

she'd hitched a ride and then proceeded on foot to the wooded area north of the city, which she'd read was the location of Karinhall. It had been difficult to persuade anyone to offer her a ride. People had stared with suspicion at her tattered appearance, and she didn't speak a word of German, but she had simply repeated 'Karinhall' until an elderly man had reluctantly allowed her to get into his car. When the road divided, he had waved his hand to indicate that he was headed in one direction while she should go in the other. So she got out of his car and walked the rest of the way. Her feet began to hurt, but she kept on going. The only thing she wanted was to be close to Hermann.

Then she had wandered through the ruins. The two sentry boxes at the entrance bore witness to how grand the buildings must once have been. Here and there Dagmar saw the remnants of walls and decorative stones, making it easy for her to imagine the past magnificence of the estate. If it hadn't been for Carin, this place would have been named for Dagmar.

Hatred and grief overwhelmed her, and she fell sobbing to her knees. She recalled that lovely summer night when she had felt Hermann's breath on her skin, when he had covered her body with kisses. That was the night when she had both received and lost everything at the same time. Hermann's life would have been so much better if he had chosen her. She would have taken care of him and not, like Carin, allowed him to become the human wreckage that she'd seen in the hospital. She would have been strong enough for both of them.

Dagmar picked up a fistful of soil and let it slowly trickle out between her fingers. The sun was hot on the back of her neck, and in the distance she heard the howling of the wild dogs. Nearby a broken statue lay toppled on the ground. The nose and one arm were missing, and the eyes of stone gazed unseeing up at the sky. Suddenly she realized how tired she was. Her skin felt hot under the sun, and she wanted to find some shade where she could rest. It had been a long journey, filled with intense yearning, and she needed to lie down and close her eyes for a short time. She looked around for some shade. Next to a staircase which now led nowhere, a thick pillar had fallen so that it was leaning against the top step, and beneath was a patch of blessed shadow.

She was too tired to stand up, so she crawled across the uneven ground to the staircase, curled up as much as she could, and lay down in the cramped space with a sigh of relief, closing her eyes. Ever since that night in June, she had been on her way to him. To Hermann. Now she needed to rest.

The press conference had been over for a couple of hours, and they were now gathered in the kitchen. Ernst, who had quietly stayed in Mellberg's office, had now been released and was stretched out, as usual, at his master's feet.

'So that went well, didn't it?' said Mellberg with a satisfied smile. 'Shouldn't you be going home to rest, Paula?' He spoke so loudly that Patrik jumped in his chair.

Paula glared at him. 'If you don't mind, I'll decide for myself when I need to rest.'

'You come running over here even though you're on leave, and then you ride all the way out to Göteborg and back. If anything goes wrong, just remember that I . . .'

'I think we have the situation under control,' said Patrik, trying to avert the quarrel that was brewing. 'Right now those boys are going to be feeling the heat.'

It was absurd to use the term 'boys' for men who were now well over fifty. But when Patrik thought about them, he always pictured the five boys in the photograph, wearing seventies clothing and with slightly wary expressions on their faces.

'You're right about that. Especially John Holm,' said Mellberg, scratching Ernst behind the ear.

'Patrik?' Annika stuck her head in the kitchen and motioned for him to come with her. He got up and followed her out to the hall, where she handed him a cordless phone. 'It's Torbjörn. They've found something.'

Patrik felt his pulse quicken. He took the phone and went into his office, closing the door behind him. For almost fifteen minutes he listened to Torbjörn, asking him several follow-up questions. When he ended the call, he hurried back to the kitchen where Paula, Mellberg, Gösta, and Annika were all waiting. Even though it was late, no one showed any sign of wanting to go home.

'What did he say?' asked Annika.

'Hold your horses. First I need some coffee.' Moving with exaggerated slowness, Patrik went over to the coffee maker and reached for the pot, but before he could get to it, Annika stood up. She grabbed the pot, filled a cup so abruptly that the coffee sloshed over the side, and then set it down on the table in front of Patrik's empty chair.

'All right. Now sit down and tell us what Torbjörn said.'

Patrik grinned but did as he was told. He cleared his throat.

'Torbjörn found a clear fingerprint on the back of the stamp on the card from "G". So now we have a chance to match the print with a potential suspect.'

'That's great,' said Paula, propping her swollen legs on a chair. 'But you look like the proverbial cat that swallowed a canary, so there must be even bigger news.'

'You're right.' Patrik took a sip of the scalding coffee. 'It has to do with the bullet.'

'Which one?' asked Gösta, leaning forward.

'That's the thing. The bullet that was found under the floorboards and the bullets that were, contrary to regulations, prised out of the kitchen wall after the attempt on Ebba's life . . .'

'Okay, okay,' said Mellberg, waving his hand. 'I get the message.'

'Well, they were probably fired from the same gun.'

Four pairs of eyes stared at him. Patrik nodded.

'It sounds incredible, but it's true. An unknown number of members of the Elvander family were murdered in 1974, and they were most likely shot with the same gun that was used yesterday in an attempt to kill Ebba Stark.'

'Could it really be the same perpetrator after so many years?' Paula shook her head. 'That's hard to believe.'

'I've always thought that the attacks on Ebba and her husband had something to do with the family's disappearance. And this proves it.'

Patrik threw out his hands. In his head he heard the echo of similar questions from the press conference. He hadn't been able to provide any answers, other than to acknowledge that it was one of their theories. Only now did the police have some proof to go on.

'Based on the bullet's grooves, Forensics have also been able to ascertain the type of gun used,' he went on. 'So we need to find out whether anyone in the area owns or has owned a Smith & Wesson .38.'

'If we look at the bright side, this means that the gun used to murder the Elvander family isn't lying at the bottom of the sea,' said Mellberg.

'At least not yesterday when the shots were fired at Ebba. Of course, it might have ended up there afterwards,' Patrik pointed out.

'I don't think so,' said Paula. 'If someone has been saving that gun all this time, it's hard to imagine them getting rid of it now.'

'You could be right. Maybe this person regards the gun as some sort of trophy and is keeping it as a souvenir. Whatever the case, we need to focus our efforts on establishing what happened in 1974. We'll have to re-interview

330

the four men we've already talked to, see if we can't clarify the precise sequence of events on the day in question. And we need to locate Percy von Bahrn ASAP. We should have done so already, and I'll take full responsibility for failing to interview him. We also need to talk to that teacher, the one who's still alive. What's his name? You know, the one who was on holiday during Easter . . .' Patrik snapped his fingers.

'Ove Linder,' said Gösta. His voice had taken on an anxious note.

'Exactly. Ove Linder. Doesn't he live in Hamburgsund now? We'll go out there and have a talk with him tomorrow morning. He might have valuable information about what went on in that school. You and I will go out there together.' He reached for pen and paper, which were always at hand on the table, and began making a list of the most urgent tasks.

'Well, er . . .' said Gösta, rubbing his chin.

Patrik went on writing.

'Tomorrow we need to meet with all five of the boys. We'll divide them up among us. Paula, do you think you could do some more digging into where the money came from that was deposited in the bank for Ebba?'

Paula's face lit up. 'Absolutely. I've already contacted the bank to ask for their help.'

'Er, Patrik?' Gösta ventured again, but his colleague was too busy doling out assignments to hear. 'Patrik!'

All eyes turned to Gösta. It wasn't like him to raise his voice.

'Yes, what is it? What did you want to say?' Patrik studied Gösta's face, and realized all at once that he wasn't going to like what he was about to hear.

'Well, the thing is, that teacher named Ove Linder . . .'

'Yes?'

'Somebody has already talked to him.'

'Somebody?' Patrik repeated, and then waited to hear more.

'I thought it might be smart to have more people working the case. And you can't deny that she's good at digging up information, and we have such limited resources. So I thought it wouldn't hurt to get some help. And as you just said, it's something that we ought to have done by now, which in a sense we already have. So it's actually all fine.' Gösta paused to catch his breath.

Patrik stared at him. Was the man out of his mind? Was he trying to make excuses for having gone behind the backs of his colleagues? Was he attempting to put a positive spin on his actions? Then Patrik was seized with a suspicion that he hoped would not be confirmed.

'When you say "she" – are you referring to my dear wife? Did Erica go out to talk to that teacher?'

'Er . . . yes,' said Gösta, eyes downcast.

'Oh, Gösta,' Paula said reproachfully, sounding as if she were talking to a child who had been caught stealing a biscuit.

'Is there anything else I should know?' asked Patrik. 'You might as well tell me. What has Erica been up to? And you too, for that matter.'

With a heavy sigh Gösta began recounting what Erica had told him about her visits with 'Liza' and John Holm, about what Kjell had said about John's background, and about the note that she'd found. Then he seemed to hesitate for a moment before he finally told everyone about the break-in at Erica and Patrik's house.

Patrik's expression turned icy cold. 'What the hell are you saying?'

Gösta stared down at the floor in shame.

'Never mind, I've heard enough!' Patrik leaped to his feet, dashed out of the station, and jumped into his car. He could feel his blood boiling. As he turned the key in the ignition and the engine started up, he forced himself to take several deep breaths. Then he floored the accelerator.

Ebba couldn't stop looking at the pictures. She had asked for some time alone and had taken all the material about her family up to Erica's work room. After casting a glance at the cluttered desk she had simply sat down on the floor and spread out the copies of the photos in a fan-shape in front of her. These were her family members, her roots. Even though she'd had a good life with her adoptive family, she had sometimes been envious that they had blood relatives to whom they were connected. The only thing she was connected to was a mystery. She thought about all the times she'd studied the framed photos on top of the large bureau in the living room: maternal grandparents, paternal grandparents, aunts and cousins – all of them related, so that their descendants felt that they were links in a long chain. Now she was studying pictures of her own relatives, and she was filled with a feeling both wondrous and strange.

Ebba picked up the photo of the Angelmaker. What a beautiful name for something so ghastly. She held the picture closer, trying to see if there was anything in Helga's eyes that would reveal the evil she had done. Ebba didn't know whether the photo had been taken before or during the period when all the children were murdered, but the little girl in the picture, who had to be Dagmar, was so young that it must have been taken around 1902. Dagmar was wearing a light-coloured dress with flounces, and she had no idea of the fate that awaited her. What had happened to her? Had she drowned in the sea, as so many apparently believed? Had her disappearance been a natural end to a life that was already shattered when the crime that her parents had committed was discovered? Had Helga felt remorse? Did she understand the effect it would have

333

on her daughter when her crime was discovered? Or was she convinced that no one would ever miss those unwanted children? The questions began to pile up inside Ebba's head, but she knew that she would never learn the answers. Yet she felt such a connection to these women.

She examined the other picture of Dagmar. Her face bore clear traces of a hard life, but it was obvious that she had once been beautiful. What had happened to her daughter Laura on those occasions when the police had arrested Dagmar, or when she was taken to the hospital? From what Ebba understood, Laura had no other relatives. Had friends taken care of her, or had she ended up in an orphanage or foster home?

Suddenly Ebba remembered that she had found herself wondering about her roots when she was pregnant with Vincent. It was his past too, after all. Strangely enough, those speculations had ceased as soon as he was born. Partly because she hadn't had time to spare for any sort of pondering, and partly because he had taken her over so completely – she was consumed by his scent, the fine down on the nape of his neck, and the dimples on his little knuckles. Everything else seemed utterly unimportant. She herself had become unimportant. She and Tobias had been reduced, or perhaps elevated, to mere extras in the film about Vincent. She had loved her new role, but it had made the void even greater when he was gone. Now she was a mother without a child, a meaningless extra in a film that suddenly lacked its star. But the pictures spread out in front of her gave her a renewed sense of continuity.

She could hear Erica moving around in the kitchen downstairs, with the children playing and shouting, while here she sat, surrounded by her relatives. All of them were dead, but she still felt an enormous solace in the knowledge that they had once existed.

Ebba drew her knees up to her chin and wrapped her

arms around her legs. She wondered how Tobias was doing. She had barely given him a thought since she'd come here, and if she was perfectly honest, she hadn't really cared much for him after Vincent died. How could she, when she was immersed in her own grief? But somehow this new sense of family connection was now making her realize for the first time in a while that Tobias was a part of her. Who could she share her memories with other than Tobias? He had been at her side, caressed her stomach as her pregnancy progressed, and watched Vincent's heartbeat on the ultrasound monitor. He had wiped the sweat from her brow, massaged her back, and brought her water during the birth – that long, terrible and yet amazing twenty-four hours when she had fought to bring Vincent into the world. The baby had resisted, but when he finally opened his eyes to the light and peered at them cross-eyed, Tobias had grabbed her hand and squeezed it tight. He'd made no effort to hide his tears, merely wiped his cheeks on his shirtsleeve. And later they had shared all those wakeful nights when Vincent cried, and his first smile, and the appearance of his first teeth. They had cheered him on as he wobbled back and forth when he was learning to crawl, and Tobias had filmed the first faltering steps he took. Their son's first word, first sentence, and his first day at the day-care centre; laughter and tears; good days and bad. Tobias was the only person who truly understood when she talked about any of these things. There was no one else.

As she sat there on the floor, Ebba felt her heart growing warmer. That tiny piece that had been so cold and hard was starting to thaw. She would stay here one more night, but then she would go back home. To Tobias. It was time to let go of the guilt and start living again.

Anna steered the boat out of the harbour and lifted her face to the sun. To be without her husband and children filled her with an unexpected sense of freedom. She had borrowed Erica and Patrik's boat since there was no more petrol in the Finnish Buster motorboat, and she was enjoying driving the familiar *snipa*. The evening light made the cliffs surrounding Fjällbacka harbour shimmer like gold. She heard laughter coming from the Café Bryggan, and music playing. No one seemed to have ventured out on the dance floor yet, but after a few beers, it would undoubtedly get quite crowded.

She cast a glance at her bag holding the fabric samples. It was on the floor in the middle of the boat, and she checked to see that the zipper was securely closed.

Ebba had already seen the samples and immediately selected several favourites that she wanted Tobias to approve. Her comments had prompted Anna to consider going out to Valö that very same evening. At first she had hesitated. The island was not a safe place, as she had so dramatically discovered the day before, and an impulsive trip out there seemed more like something she would have done in her old life, when she seldom thought about consequences. But for once she decided to follow up on her initial inclination. What could possibly happen? She would go out there, show Tobias the samples, and then return home. It was just a way of passing the time, she told herself. And maybe Tobias would be happy for some company. Ebba had decided to spend another night at Erica's house in order to take a closer look at the materials about her family, although Anna suspected that was just a pretext. Ebba seemed reluctant to return to the island, and understandably so.

As Anna neared the dock, she saw Tobias waiting there for her. She had phoned ahead to tell him of her visit, and he must have been keeping an eye out for her arrival.

'So you dare to come back out here to the wild west?' he said with a laugh as he reached for the bow.

'I've always liked defying fate.' Anna tossed the line to Tobias, who moored the boat with a practised hand. 'You look like you're already an old salt,' she said, pointing to the half-hitch he'd tied around one of the bollards on the dock.

'You've got to be if you live in the archipelago.' He held out his hand to help her ashore. His other hand was wrapped in a bandage.

'Thanks. What did you do to your hand?'

Tobias examined the bandage as if he'd never noticed it before. 'Oh, that's just the sort of thing that happens when you're doing renovation work. All part of the job.'

'How very macho of you,' said Anna and found herself smiling foolishly. She felt a pang of guilt because she was more or less flirting with Ebba's husband, but it was all in fun and totally harmless, although she couldn't deny that she found him incredibly attractive.

'Let me take that.' Tobias lifted the heavy bag of samples from her shoulder, and Anna gratefully followed him up to the house.

'Normally I would say that we should sit in the kitchen, but there's a bit of a draught in there right now,' said Tobias when they came inside.

Anna laughed. She felt light-hearted. It was a relief to talk to someone who wasn't always thinking about the troubles she'd endured.

'And it would be difficult to use the dining room, since there's no floor,' he went on, giving her a wink.

The gloomy Tobias that she'd encountered before seemed to have vanished, but maybe that wasn't so odd. Ebba had also seemed less downhearted when Anna had seen her at Erica's house.

'If you don't mind sitting on the floor, I think it'd be best if we went upstairs to the bedroom.' He headed up the stairs without waiting for an answer.

'It seems a little odd to be bothering with fabric samples right now, after what happened yesterday,' she said apologetically as she followed.

'Don't worry about it. Life goes on. In that regard, Ebba and I are very much alike. We're both extremely practical.'

'But I'm surprised that the two of you dare stay here.'

Tobias shrugged. 'Sometimes there are things you just have to do,' he said, setting the bag on the floor in the middle of the room.

Anna knelt down next to it and began pulling out fabric swatches, spreading them on the floor. With great enthusiasm she talked about what could be used for furniture, curtains, and cushions, and which types would go well together. After a while she fell silent and turned to Tobias. He wasn't looking at the fabric but instead had his eyes fixed on her.

'You certainly seem very interested,' she said sarcastically, but she felt her cheeks flush. Nervously she tucked a strand of hair behind her ear. Tobias was still staring at her.

'Are you hungry?' he asked.

She nodded hesitantly. 'Actually, I am.'

'Good.' Tobias quickly got to his feet. 'Stay here and put away the samples. I'll be right back.'

He set off downstairs to the kitchen while Anna remained where she was, surrounded by the swatches of fabric laid out on the beautiful, newly polished hardwood floor. The sun was slanting in through the windows, and she realized that it was later than she'd imagined. For a moment she thought she needed to get back to take care of the kids, until she remembered that no one was home. The house was empty. All she had to look forward to was a lonely supper in front of the TV, so she might as well stay. Tobias was alone too, and it would be much nicer to eat dinner together. Besides, he was already in the process of making something for them, and it would be rude of her to leave after she'd accepted his invitation.

Nervously Anna began gathering up the fabric. When she'd finished piling all the swatches on top of the chest of drawers that stood against the wall, she heard footsteps on the stairs, along with the clinking of glasses. A moment later Tobias came into the room carrying a tray.

'It's going to be a supper à la Cajsa Warg: some cold cuts and cheese, and I've toasted a few slices of bread. But maybe it'll be all right if we have a good red wine.'

'Absolutely. But I'll have to make do with only one glass. It would be a real scandal around here if I was arrested on my way home for drinking while driving a boat.'

'Well, I certainly don't want to be the cause of any scandal.' Tobias set down the tray.

Anna felt her heart beating faster. She really shouldn't stay here, eating cheese and drinking wine with a man who made the palms of her hands sweat. At the same time, that was precisely what she wanted to do. She reached for a piece of toast.

Two hours later she knew that she was going to stay even longer. It was not a conscious decision, and they hadn't discussed it, but that wasn't necessary. As dusk fell, Tobias lit some candles, and in the glow from the flickering flames, Anna decided to live for the moment. For just a brief time she would forget about everything that had happened to her. Tobias made her feel alive again.

She loved the evening light. It was so much more flattering and forgiving than the merciless light of the sun. Ia studied her face in the mirror and slowly ran her hand over her smooth features. When had she started caring so much about how she looked? Back when she was young, other matters had been considerably more important. Then love had become the only thing that mattered, and Leon was accustomed to being surrounded by beauty. Ever since their fates had become intertwined, Leon had sought out bigger and more dangerous challenges, while her love for him had grown stronger and more devoted. She had allowed Leon's wishes to govern her life, until there was no turning back.

Ia leaned closer to the mirror but could see no regret in her eyes. As long as Leon had remained as bound to her as she was to him, she had been willing to sacrifice everything, but then he had begun to withdraw, forgetting about the fate that united them. The accident had made him understand that only death could separate them. The pain she had felt when she pulled him from the car was nothing compared to what she would have experienced if he had left her. That was something she could not have survived – not after all she had given up for his sake.

But she could no longer stay here. She couldn't understand why Leon had wanted to come back. She shouldn't have allowed him to do it. Why visit the past when it held so much sorrow? Even so, she had complied with his wishes. But now she had reached her limit. She couldn't stand by and watch as he brought about his own destruction. The only thing she could do was to go home and wait for him to follow so that they could continue to live the life that they'd created together. He couldn't get by on his own, and this way he would be forced to realize that.

Ia stretched and cast a lingering glance at Leon, who was sitting on the balcony with his back turned. Then she started packing her bags.

Erica was in the kitchen when she heard the front door open. A moment later Patrik came rushing into the room.

'What the hell have you been doing!' he shouted. 'Why the devil didn't you tell me that we'd had a break-in?'

'Well, I wasn't really sure . . .' she ventured, though she knew it was pointless. Patrik was as angry as Gösta had predicted he would be.

'Gösta said that you suspected John Holm was behind it, and yet you never said a word to me. Those people are dangerous!'

'Lower your voice. I've just put the kids to bed.' Actually, she made the request as much for her own sake. She hated conflict, and her whole body shut down whenever anybody yelled at her – especially Patrik, maybe because he so seldom raised his voice to her. And the situation felt worse this time, because she had to admit that he was partially right.

'Sit down and let's talk about this. Ebba is upstairs in my work room, going through my research.'

She saw that Patrik was struggling to control his temper. He took a couple of deep breaths, exhaling through his nose. It looked as if he'd succeeded, more or less, but he was still slightly pale when he nodded and sat down at the kitchen table.

'I hope you have a very good explanation, including for why you and Gösta have been going behind my back.'

Erica sat down across from Patrik and stared at the tabletop for a few moments. She was trying to work out how to formulate her words so that she would be completely honest with Patrik but at the same time present herself in the most advantageous light. She started off by telling Patrik how she had contacted Gösta after learning that he had been personally involved in the case when the Elvander family disappeared. She admitted that she hadn't wanted to tell Patrik since she knew that he wouldn't approve. Instead, she had persuaded Gösta to collaborate with her for a while. Patrik didn't look happy,

341

but at least he was listening to what she had to say. When she told him about her visit to John Holm's house and how she had discovered that someone had tried to get into her computer, Patrik again turned pale.

'You should be glad they didn't swipe your computer. I assume that it's too late to bring someone in to dust for fingerprints?'

'Yes, I don't think it would do any good. I've been typing on the keyboard, and the kids are always running around with sticky fingers.'

Patrik shook his head in resignation.

'And I don't really know whether Holm is behind it,' said Erica. 'That was an assumption I made because the break-in occurred after I happened to take that note.'

'*Happened* to take it?' said Patrik, snorting.

'But now I've turned it over to Kjell, so there's no longer any danger.'

'The people who are looking for it don't know what you've done with it.' Patrik stared at her as if she were an idiot.

'I realize that. But nothing else bad has happened.'

'Still, it would have been nice to find out about this a little earlier. Gösta has at least told me some of what the two of you have managed to find out.'

'And tomorrow we're going to see Junk-Olle and get back the family's possessions.'

'Junk-Olle?'

'Didn't Gösta tell you? We found out what happened to everything that belonged to the Elvander family. Junk-Olle was apparently a sort of handyman out at the summer camp when it was a boarding school, and when Gösta phoned him to ask about the family's belongings, he said: "It's amazing how long it's taken the police to come asking about those things!"' Erica laughed.

'So Junk-Olle has been keeping them all these years?'

'Yes, and at ten o'clock tomorrow morning I'm going over there with Gösta to go through it all.'

'No, you're not,' said Patrik. 'I'm going out there with Gösta.'

'But I . . .' Erica began, but then realized that it would be better to give in. 'Okay.'

'From now on, you're to keep out of this investigation,' he warned her, but she saw to her relief that he was no longer angry.

They heard footsteps on the stairs. Ebba was about to join them.

Erica got up to finish washing the dishes.

'Friends?' she said.

'Friends,' said Patrik.

He sat in the dark, watching her. It was her fault. Anna had exploited his vulnerable state and tricked him into breaking his vows to Ebba. He had promised to love Ebba in sickness and in health, until death did them part. That fact didn't change just because he now realized that she was the one to blame for what had happened. He loved her and would forgive her. He had stood before her, dressed in his best suit, and vowed to be faithful. She had been so beautiful in her simple white dress, and she had looked him in the eye, listened to his words, and then locked them in her heart. Now Anna had ruined everything.

She gave a faint grunt and burrowed her head in the pillow. Ebba's pillow. Tobias wanted to tear the pillow away to keep Anna's scent from sullying it. Ebba had always used the same shampoo and the pillowcase was usually fragrant from her hair. He clenched his fists as he sat there in bed. Ebba should have been the one lying next to him with the moonlight illuminating her lovely face, casting shadows around her nose and eyes. It should have been Ebba's chest rising and falling, naked above the edge of the blanket. He stared at Anna's breasts. They were so different from Ebba's, which were like tiny buds, and below he could see the scars winding their way towards Anna's stomach. Earlier in the night they had felt rough under his hands, and now he was disgusted by the sight of them. Cautiously he reached out, grabbed the blanket, and pulled it up to cover her body. Her repulsive body that had pressed against him and erased the memory of Ebba's skin.

The thought made him nauseated. He had to undo this so that Ebba could come back. For a moment he sat perfectly still. Then he picked up his own pillow and slowly lowered it over Anna's face.

FJÄLLBACKA 1951

It was most unexpected. She wasn't ill-disposed towards children, but as the years passed and nothing happened, she had calmly come to the conclusion that she would never have any of her own. Sigvard already had two grown sons, so he didn't seem concerned about the fact that she was barren.

But then a year ago she suddenly began to feel terribly and inexplicably tired. Sigvard presumed the worst and sent her to their family doctor for a thorough examination. She too thought it might be cancer or something equally fatal, but it turned out that at the age of thirty she had suddenly become pregnant. The doctor could offer no explanation, and it took Laura several weeks to assimilate the news. These days her life was largely uneventful, and that suited her just fine. She preferred to stay at home, in the house where she was the mistress and everything had been deliberately chosen and arranged. Now something was going to erase the perfect order that she had so meticulously established.

Along with the pregnancy came peculiar symptoms and unwelcome physical changes. The realization that there was something inside of her body that she could not control brought her to the verge of panic. The actual birth was horrible, and she decided that never again would she allow herself to be subjected to such an experience. She refused to undergo the pain, powerlessness, and bestial condition of giving birth to another child, so Sigvard had to move into the guestroom for good. He didn't seem to mind, satisfied as he was with his life.

She had spent the first days with Inez in a state of shock. Then she found Nanna, blessed and wonderful Nanna, who lifted from her shoulders all responsibility for the baby and allowed her to go on with her own life. Nanna immediately moved into the house, and her room was next door to the nursery, so she could quickly tend to Inez in the night or whenever she needed attention. Nanna took over her care completely, and Laura was then free to come and go as she pleased. Usually she would stop by the nursery for a short visit, and on those occasions she was able to enjoy being with her daughter. By the time Inez was eighteen months old, she could be charming and sweet, as long as she wasn't crying because she was hungry or needed to be changed. But such matters were Nanna's concern, and Laura thought that everything had been arranged so well, in spite of the unexpected turn that her life had taken. She wasn't fond of changes, so the less the birth of the baby altered her life, the easier it was for her to accept her daughter.

Laura straightened the framed photos on the bureau. There were pictures of her and Sigvard and of Sigvard's two sons with their families. They still hadn't managed to frame any photographs of Inez, and she would never dream of displaying a picture of her mother. She preferred to forget all about her mother and grandmother.

To Laura's relief, her mother now seemed to have disappeared for good. It had been two years since she'd last communicated, and no one in the area had seen hide nor hair of her. Yet their last meeting was still fresh in Laura's mind. Dagmar had been released from the mental hospital a year earlier, but she hadn't dared turn up at the house where Laura and Sigvard lived. People said that she was often seen staggering around town, exactly as she'd done when Laura was a child. When Dagmar finally stood on their doorstep – toothless, filthy, her clothes in rags – she was as crazy as always, and Laura couldn't understand why the

346

doctors had discharged her. At least in the hospital Dagmar had been given medicine, and they hadn't let her touch any booze. Much as Laura would have liked to tell her mother to get lost, she let her into the house, moving quickly so that the neighbours wouldn't see.

'What a fancy lady you've become,' said Dagmar. 'Looks like you've come up in the world.'

Laura clenched her fists behind her back. Everything that she'd chased away, everything that now appeared only in her dreams, had suddenly caught up with her.

'What do you want?'

'I need help.' Dagmar sounded on the verge of tears. She moved in a strange, lurching fashion, and her face twitched.

'Do you need money?' Laura reached for her purse.

'Not for me personally,' said Dagmar, fixing her eyes on the purse. 'But I need money so I can go to Germany.'

Laura stared at her. 'Germany? What are you going to do there?'

'I never had a chance to say goodbye to your father. I never said goodbye to my Hermann.'

Dagmar started to cry, and Laura glanced around nervously. She didn't want Sigvard to hear something and come out to the hall to find out what was going on. He mustn't see her mother here.

'Shh! I'll give you the money. But calm down, for God's sake!' Laura held out a bundle of bills. 'Here! This should be enough for a ticket to Germany.'

'Oh, thank you!' Dagmar flung herself forward and seized the money. Then she grabbed her daughter's hands and kissed them. Disgusted, Laura yanked her hands out of Dagmar's grasp and wiped them on her skirt.

'Go now,' she said. The only thing she wanted was to get her mother out of the house, out of her life, so that perfection would reign once again. After Dagmar left, she sank with relief on to a chair in the hall.

Now a couple of years had passed, and it seemed likely that her mother was dead. Laura doubted that the money would have taken her very far, especially in the chaos after the war. And if Dagmar had raved about saying goodbye to her Hermann Göring, she probably would have been seen as the crazy woman that she was and been stopped somewhere along the way. It was not a good idea to speak of knowing a man like Göring. The brutality of his crimes was not diminished simply because he had killed himself in prison a year after the war ended. Laura shuddered at the thought that her mother had continued to tell people in the area that he was the father of her child. It wasn't a matter for boasting. Laura had only a vague memory of visiting his wife in Stockholm, but she did remember the shame, and the look that Carin Göring had given her. Carin's eyes had been filled with sympathy and warmth, and it was undoubtedly because of Laura that she hadn't called for help, even though she must have been terrified.

Well, that was all in the past now. Her mother was gone, and no one talked any more about Dagmar's deranged fantasies. And Nanna saw to it that Laura could live her own life, as she was used to doing. Order had once again been restored and everything was perfect. Exactly as it should be.

Gösta looked at Patrik, who was drumming his fingers on the steering wheel, his eyes resolutely fixed on the cars in front of them. The traffic was practically gridlocked, and the narrow country roads weren't made for such a crush, so he had to stay close to the verge.

'You weren't too hard on her, were you?' Gösta turned his head to gaze out the window on his side of the car.

'I think both of you have behaved stupidly, and I'm not about to change my mind about that,' said Patrik, but he sounded significantly calmer than he had the day before.

Gösta didn't reply. He was too tired to argue. He'd been up most of the night, going through the files. But that wasn't something he wanted to tell Patrik, who probably wouldn't appreciate anyone doing anything on his own initiative at the moment. He put up his hand to hide a yawn. He was still feeling disappointed at the lack of results from his night's work. He hadn't discovered anything new, and nothing had stirred his interest. At the same time, he couldn't shake off the feeling that the answer was there, right in front of his nose, hidden somewhere in that pile of documents. Initially it had been curiosity, possibly combined with professional pride, that had motivated him to keep going. But now it was a sense of unease that was driving him. Ebba was no longer safe, and her life depended on the police finding out who was responsible for these attempts on her life.

'Take that exit on the left.' He pointed to a side road a short distance ahead.

'I see it,' said Patrik, making a death-defying swerve to the left.

'Apparently you never passed the driver's test,' muttered Gösta as he gripped the handle above the passenger door.

'I'm an excellent driver,' said Patrik.

Gösta snorted. He motioned with a nod of his head at Junk-Olle's place.

'His kids are going to have a lot of trouble cleaning up when he dies.'

It was more like a junkyard than a home. Everyone who lived in the area knew to call Olle if they wanted to get rid of something. Happy to be of service, he would come to fetch whatever it was, which meant that now there were cars, refrigerators, trailers, washing machines, and everything else imaginable piled up around a couple of outbuildings and warehouses. Gösta even spotted a hairdryer from a beauty salon as Patrik parked between a discarded freezer and an old Volvo Amazon.

A skinny old man wearing bib overalls came out to greet them.

'It would have been better if you could have come earlier. Half the day is already gone.'

Gösta glanced at his watch. It was 10.05 in the morning.

'Hi, Olle. I hear you've got some things for us.'

'You sure took your sweet time about it. I don't understand what you do over there at the police station. Nobody ever asked about these things, so I just held on to them. They're over there with the stuff belonging to the crazy duke.'

They followed Junk-Olle into a dark barn.

'The crazy duke?' queried Patrik.

'I don't know whether he's really a duke, but he had some sort of noble name.'

'Do you mean von Schlesinger?'

'That's right. He was notorious around here because he sympathized with Hitler, and his son went off to fight on the side of the Germans. The kid no sooner arrived down there than he took a bullet in the head.' Olle started rummaging through all the rubbish. 'And if the old man wasn't crazy before, that did him in. He thought the Allies were going to come out to the island and attack him. You'd never believe me if I told you all the weird things he was doing out there. Finally he had a stroke and died.' Junk-Olle paused and peered at them in the dim light as he scratched his head. 'That was in 1953, if I remember right. After that there was a series of owners until Elvander bought the place. Good Lord, what a thing to do! Opening a boarding school out there and attracting all those toffee-nosed boys. Anybody could see that it was bound to end badly.'

He went back to rummaging around as he muttered to himself. A cloud of dust rose into the air, and both Gösta and Patrik started coughing.

'Here we are. Four boxes of stuff. The furniture stayed in the house when it was rented out, but I was able to pick up a lot of loose items. You shouldn't just throw things out and besides, nobody knew whether they might come back. Although most people, me included, thought they were probably dead.'

'And it never occurred to you to contact the police to say that you had the family's belongings?' asked Patrik.

Junk-Olle straightened up and folded his arms. 'I told Officer Henry about it.'

'What? You mean Henry knew that these things were here?' said Gösta. In fact, it wasn't the first time that

Henry had neglected to pass on vital information, but there was no use getting angry with someone who was no longer alive to defend himself.

Patrik examined the boxes. 'There should be enough room in the car for them, don't you think?'

Gösta nodded. 'If necessary, we can fold down the back seats.'

'All I can say is, it's about time,' laughed Olle. 'It's taken over thirty years for you to come and fetch this stuff.'

Gösta and Patrik glared at him but refrained from replying.

'What are you going to do with all these things you've got here, Olle?' Gösta couldn't help asking. Personally, he felt almost panic-stricken at the sight of so much stuff. His small house might not be particularly modern, but he was proud of keeping it neat and clean. He was not about to turn into one of those old hoarders who wade around through a lot of rubbish.

'You never know what might come in handy one day. If everybody was as thrifty as me, the world would be a different place. You can count on that.'

Patrik leaned down and tried to lift one of the boxes but gave up with a groan.

'We're going to have to carry it together, Gösta. It's too heavy.'

Gösta gave him an alarmed look. A pulled muscle could ruin his entire golf season.

'I'm not supposed to lift anything heavy. Because of my back.'

'Come on, give me a hand.'

Realizing that further excuses would be pointless, Gösta reluctantly bent his knees and picked up one side of the box. Dust tickled his nose and he sneezed several times.

'Bless you,' said Junk-Olle, smiling broadly and revealing that three of his upper teeth were missing.

'Thanks,' said Gösta. Muttering complaints, he helped Patrik place the boxes in the boot of the car. At the same time he was filled with anticipation. Maybe there was something in the boxes that would give them a much-needed lead. Even better was the thought of telling Ebba that they'd found her family's belongings. If he hurt his back, it would be worth it.

For a change he and Carina had decided to sleep in. He'd worked late the night before, and he felt he deserved a few extra hours in bed.

'My God,' said Carina, putting her hand on his shoulder. 'I'm still sleepy.'

'Me too, but who said we had to get up?' Kjell snuggled closer, pulling her towards him.

'Mmm . . . I'm too tired.'

'I just want a hug.'

'Oh right. And you think I'd believe that?' she said, but she began sensually stroking his neck.

Kjell's mobile rang shrilly from the pocket of his trousers, which were hanging at the foot of the bed.

'Don't answer that.' Carina pressed closer to him.

But the mobile kept on ringing, and finally he couldn't stand it any longer. He sat up, grabbed his trousers, and took out the phone. The display said 'Sven Niklasson' and he fumbled with the buttons to take the call.

'Hello? Sven? No, not at all, I wasn't asleep.' Kjell glanced at the clock. It was past ten. He cleared his throat. 'Did you find out anything?'

Sven talked for a long time, and Kjell listened with growing astonishment. His only comment was an occasional mumbled 'uh-huh'. He could see Carina studying his face as he lay down on his side, resting his head on one arm.

'I can meet you at Malöga,' he finally told Sven. 'I

appreciate the fact that you're letting me in on this. Not every colleague would be so accommodating. Have the Tanum police been informed? Göteborg? Well, that's probably better, considering the situation. Yeah, they held a press conference yesterday, and they've got their hands full with that investigation. I assume you've heard most of the details from your reporter who was there. We'll talk more when I pick you up. See you soon.'

Kjell was practically out of breath as he ended the call. Carina smiled at him.

'I'm guessing something big is going on if Sven Niklasson is coming here.'

'You won't believe it.' Kjell got out of bed and began to get dressed. He was no longer the least bit tired. 'You won't believe it,' he repeated, although mostly to himself this time.

Quickly Erica stripped the bed in the guest room. Ebba had left. She wanted to take the research about her relatives with her, but Erica had asked if she could make copies for her instead. She should have thought of doing that before.

'Noel! Stop hitting Anton!' she shouted towards the living room without bothering to check who was the cause of all the ruckus. No one seemed to listen to her as the crying escalated.

'Mamma! Maaammaaa! Noel's hitting Anton,' yelled Maja.

With a sigh Erica put down the bed linens. She felt an almost physical need to be allowed to finish a task without being interrupted by shrieking children demanding her attention. She needed time to herself. She needed to be allowed to be an adult. Nothing was more important in her life than the children, but sometimes it felt as if she had to sacrifice everything that she personally wanted to do. Even though Patrik had taken a few months of paternity leave, she'd been the one who was in charge, making sure that everything functioned smoothly. Patrik helped out a lot, but that was the key phrase: he helped out. And when one of the kids was sick, she was the one who had to push back her deadline or cancel an interview so that Patrik could go to work. She did her best to fight it, but she was beginning to feel bitter about the fact that her needs and work always came last.

'Stop it, Noel!' she said, pulling him away from his twin brother, who lay on the floor, sobbing. Noel immediately began crying too, and Erica felt guilty because she'd grabbed his arm so hard.

'Stupid Mamma,' said Maja, glaring at Erica.

'Yes, your mother is stupid.' Erica sat down on the floor and took the sobbing twins into her arms.

'Hello?' said a voice from the front hall.

Erica gave a start but then realized who it was. There was only one person who would come into the house without bothering to ring the bell.

'Hi, Kristina,' she said, getting to her feet with an effort. The twins abruptly stopped crying and ran to their grandmother.

'Orders from the boss. I'm supposed to take over here,' said Kristina, wiping the tears from the boys' cheeks.

'Take over?'

'You have to go over to the station,' said Kristina, looking as if this were obvious. 'That's all I know. I'm merely a retiree who's expected to show up at a moment's notice. Patrik phoned and asked me to come over here right away. It was lucky he found me at home. I might have had something important to do, who knows, or I might even have had a date or whatever it's called these days, and I told Patrik that I'd do it this time, but otherwise I expect to be given more advance warning. I actually

355

do have a life of my own, although you may think I'm too old for that.' She stopped to catch her breath and glared at Erica. 'What are you waiting for? Patrik said you needed to go over to the station.'

Erica still didn't understand what was going on, but she decided not to ask any more questions. No matter what this was about, it would at least give her a brief respite, and that was exactly what she needed right now.

'As I said to Patrik, I can only stay for the day because tonight *Sommarkrysset* is on, and I wouldn't miss that show for the world. And before then I need to do the laundry and grocery shopping, so I can't stay past five o'clock, because otherwise I won't have time to get everything done, and I need to do a few things around the house too. I can't constantly be at your beck-and-call, although Lord knows there's plenty to do here.'

Erica slammed the door behind her and smiled. Freedom.

As she got into the car, she grew pensive. What could be so urgent? The only thing she could think of was that it must have something to do with the visit to Junk-Olle's place. Presumably Patrik and Gösta had found the family's belongings. Whistling, she began driving towards Tanumshede. Suddenly she regretted her complaints about Patrik, at least to some extent. If he allowed her to help comb through everything, she would gladly do all the household chores single-handed for a whole month.

She pulled into the car park at the station and dashed inside the ugly, low building. The reception area was empty.

'Patrik?' she called as she walked down the corridor.

'We're in here. In the conference room.'

She stopped in the doorway. The entire table and floor were covered with all sort of items.

'This wasn't my idea,' said Patrik with his back turned. 'Gösta thought that you deserved to be present.'

She threw a kiss to Gösta, who blushed and turned away.

'Have you found anything interesting yet?' she asked.

'No. We're still unpacking, and we haven't got very far.' Patrik blew the dust off of several photo albums, which he set on the table.

'Shall I help unpack, or should I start examining what's here?'

'The boxes are almost empty, so go ahead and start.' He turned around to face her. 'Did Mamma come over to the house?'

'No, the kids are old enough so I thought I could leave them on their own for a while.' She laughed. 'Of course Kristina came over. Otherwise I wouldn't have known that I was supposed to come here.'

'I tried to get hold of Anna first, but she didn't answer the landline or her mobile.'

'She didn't? That's strange.' Erica frowned. Anna was seldom more than a few metres away from her mobile.

'Dan and the children are away, so I'll bet she's dozing outside in a deck chair, having a wonderful time.'

'You're probably right.' She shook off the uneasy feeling and began going through all the things spread out in the room.

They worked in silence for a long time. The boxes had contained mostly ordinary things that anyone would have: books, pens, hairbrushes, shoes, and clothes that now smelled musty and mildewy.

'What happened to the furniture and all the knick-knacks?' asked Erica.

'They stayed in the house. I suspect that most of the stuff disappeared over the years, considering all the tenants that lived there. We'll have to ask Ebba and Tobias about

357

that. There must have been at least a few things left when they moved in this spring.'

'By the way, Anna went out to see Tobias yesterday. She borrowed the boat. I wonder if she got back okay.'

'I'm sure she's fine, but you could phone Tobias if you're worried and find out when she left for home.'

'I think I'll do that.'

Erica took her mobile out of her handbag and tapped in Tobias's number. The conversation was brief, and after she ended the call, she looked at Patrik.

'Anna was out there for only an hour last night, and the sea was perfectly calm when she left.'

Patrik wiped his dusty hands on his trousers. 'You see.'

'Yes, I'm glad I called.' Erica nodded, but inside she felt a nagging doubt. Something didn't feel right. At the same time, she knew that she tended to worry too much, and she often overreacted, so she pushed the thoughts aside and went back to studying the items they'd taken out of the boxes.

'This is so odd,' she said, holding up a grocery list. 'Inez must have written this. It's hard to remember that she actually had a regular life that included things like grocery lists: milk, eggs, sugar, jam, coffee . . .' Erica handed the list to Patrik.

He glanced at it, sighed, and handed it back. 'We don't have time for things like this. We need to focus on finding something that might be relevant to the case.'

'Okay,' said Erica, putting the paper back on the table.

They continued their search.

'A very methodical guy, that Rune,' said Gösta, showing them an exercise book that seemed to contain an accounting of all their expenses. The handwriting was so neat that it almost looked as if the pages had been typed.

'Apparently no expense was too small to record,' said Gösta, leafing through the exercise book.

'That doesn't surprise me, considering what I've heard about Rune,' said Erica.

'Check this out. It looks like someone had a crush on Leon.' Patrik held up a page that had been torn from a notebook and was covered with scribblings.

'A heart L,' read Erica out loud. 'And she was practising her future name: Annelie Kreutz. So Annelie was in love with Leon. That also fits with what I've heard.'

'I wonder what Pappa Rune made of that,' remarked Gösta.

'Considering his need to control everything, it might have been catastrophic if they actually had a relationship,' said Patrik.

'The question is whether the feeling was mutual.' Erica sat down on the edge of the table. 'Annelie was in love with Leon, but was Leon in love with her? According to John, he wasn't, but he might have been keeping his feelings secret from the others.'

'The night-time noises,' said Gösta. 'You told us that Ove Linder said he heard noises in the night. Could it have been Leon and Annelie sneaking around?'

'Or maybe it was ghosts,' said Patrik.

'Right,' said Gösta, pulling over a bunch of receipts so he could go through them. 'Has Ebba gone back out to the island?'

'Yes, she caught a ride with the mail boat,' said Erica absentmindedly. She had picked up one of the photo albums and was studying the pictures intently. There was a picture of a young woman with long, straight hair, holding a child in her arms. 'She doesn't look very happy.'

Patrik peered over her shoulder. 'Inez and Ebba.'

'Yes, and these must be Rune's other children.' She pointed at three children of varying ages and heights, who seemed to be reluctantly posing in front of a wall.

'Ebba will be overjoyed to have these pictures,' said

Erica, turning the page. 'They'll mean so much to her. Ah, this must be her maternal grandmother, Laura.'

'That woman looks dangerous,' said Gösta, peering over Erica's shoulder.

'How old was she when she died?' asked Patrik.

Erica paused to think. 'She must have been fifty-three. They found her dead behind the house early in the morning.'

'Nothing suspicious about her death?' asked Patrik.

'No, not as far as I know. Have you heard otherwise, Gösta?'

He shook his head. 'The doctor went out there and decided that for some reason she must have gone out at night, suffered a heart attack, and died. There were no indications that her death was caused by anything but natural causes.'

'Was it her mother who disappeared?' asked Patrik.

'Yes. Dagmar disappeared in 1949.'

'An inveterate alcoholic,' said Gösta. 'At least, that's what I heard.'

'It's a miracle that Ebba has turned out so normal, considering her family history.'

'Maybe that's because she grew up on Rosenstigen instead of out on Valö,' said Gösta.

'You're probably right,' said Patrik as he went back to rummaging through the items.

Two hours later they'd been through everything, and they exchanged looks of disappointment. Although Ebba would undoubtedly appreciate having more family photos and personal possessions, they hadn't found anything of use to the investigation. Erica was on the verge of tears. She'd had such high expectations, but the conference room was cluttered with objects that were of no use to them whatever.

She glanced at her husband. Something was bothering

him, but apparently he couldn't put his finger on what it was. She'd seen that expression on his face before.

'What are you thinking?'

'I'm not sure, but something seems . . . fishy. I'm sure it will come to me later,' he said, sounding annoyed.

'All right then. Let's pack it all way,' said Gösta, and he began putting items in a box.

'I suppose there's nothing for it.'

Patrik started cleaning up too, while Erica stood there, making no effort to help. Her eyes swept over the room in one last attempt to find something of interest, and she was just about to give up when she noticed several black folders that she recognized at once. The family's passports, which Gösta had neatly stacked on the table. She squinted, then moved closer to examine them, quietly counting to herself. She picked up the stack and laid out the passports side by side.

Patrik stopped packing and looked at her. 'What are you doing?'

'Don't you see it?' She pointed at the passports.

'No. What do you mean?'

'Count them.'

Silently he did as she said. Erica noticed his eyes open wide.

'There are four passports here,' she said. 'Shouldn't there be five?'

'Yes, if we assume that Ebba was too young to have one.'

Patrik went over and picked up the passports. He opened them, one after the other, to check the name and photo. Then he turned to face his wife.

'Well? Whose passport is missing?' she asked.

'Annelie's. Annelie's passport is missing.'

FJÄLLBACKA 1961

Mamma knew best. That was a truth Inez had always taken for granted as she was growing up. She didn't even remember her father. She was only three when he had a stroke and died a few weeks later in hospital. After that, she had only Mamma and Nanna.

Sometimes Inez wondered if she loved her mother. She wasn't quite sure. She loved Nanna and the teddy bear that had sat on her bed since she was a baby, but what about Mamma? She knew that she ought to love her, just as the other children in school loved their mothers. The few times she was allowed to go home with another girl to play, she'd seen how mothers and daughters greeted each other with happy expressions and how the girl would throw herself into her mother's arms. Inez had felt a hard lump in her stomach when she saw her classmates with their mothers. Then she had done the same thing when she went home. She had thrown herself into Nanna's arms, which were always open to her.

Mamma was not a mean person, and she'd never raised her voice as far as Inez could recall. It was Nanna who scolded if she'd done something wrong. But Mamma was strict about the way things should be done, and Inez was not allowed to contradict her.

The most important thing was to do things properly. That was what her mother always said: 'Anything worth doing needs to be done right.' Inez was never allowed to be sloppy. Her lessons had to be written out neatly on the lines, and the numbers in her maths book had to be correctly formed. The faint impressions left by incorrect figures were forbidden, even if they had been carefully erased. If Inez was unsure, she had to write them down on a piece of scratch paper first, before entering the correct numbers in her notebook.

It was also important not to make a mess, because any sort of disarray at home would cause something terrible. She didn't know what that might be, but her room always had to be in perfect order. She never knew when Laura might peek inside. If anything was out of place, her mother would look so disappointed and say that she wanted to have a talk with Inez, who hated those conversations. She didn't want to make her mother sad, and that was usually the subject of such discussions – that Inez had disappointed Laura.

She wasn't allowed to make a mess in Nanna's room or in the kitchen either. The other rooms in the house – her mother's bedroom, the living room, the guest room, and the parlour – were all off-limits to the girl. She might break something, her mother explained. Children didn't belong in there. Inez obeyed, because that made life simpler. She hated quarrels, and she didn't like having that sort of conversation with her mother. If she did as Mamma said, she could avoid both.

In school she kept to herself, careful to do everything that was expected of her. And that clearly made her teachers happy. The grown-ups seemed pleased when children obeyed them.

Her classmates paid no attention to Inez, as if it wasn't worth the trouble to quarrel with her. On a few occasions they had jeered at her, saying something about her grandmother, which Inez found very strange, since she didn't have a grandmother. She had asked her mother about it, but instead of answering, Laura had decided they needed to have one of those conversations again. Inez had also asked Nanna, but she had unexpectedly

*pursed her lips and then said that it wasn't her place to discuss
such matters. So Inez didn't ask any more questions. It wasn't
important enough to risk yet another conversation, and besides,
Mamma knew best.*

❖

Ebba jumped on to the dock at Valö, offering effusive thanks for the lift. For the first time since she'd come here, she had a sense of anticipation and joy as she walked up the path towards the house. There were so many things she was looking forward to telling Tobias.

As she got closer, she was struck by how beautiful the house was. Of course it still needed a lot of work – in spite of all their efforts, they'd really only just begun – but it had potential. Like a white jewel, it stood there amidst all the greenery, and even though she couldn't see the water, she knew it was all around her.

It was going to take time for her and Tobias to find their way back to each other, and their life would never be the same. But that didn't mean that it would be worse. Maybe they'd be able to have a stronger relationship. She'd hardly dared think of such a thing before, but maybe they could also find room for a child in their life. Not while everything was still so new and fragile and they had so much work left to do, both on the house and on themselves, but maybe later Vincent could have a brother or sister. That was how she looked at it. A brother or sister for their angel-child.

And she'd managed to calm her parents' fears. She

had apologized for not telling them about everything that had happened and then persuaded them not to come rushing out to Fjällbacka. She'd also given them another call to say that she'd been learning about her biological family, and she knew they would be happy for her and understand how much it meant to her. But her adoptive parents didn't want her to go back to the island until the police worked out what was going on. So she had told a white lie, saying that she would spend another night at Erica's house, and that had seemed to satisfy them.

It scared her to think that someone was trying to harm them, but Tobias had chosen to stay, and now she had decided to join him. For the second time in her life, she chose Tobias. The fear of losing him was greater than her fear of some unknown person threatening them. It was impossible to control everything in life – Vincent's death had taught her that. And it was her destiny to stay with Tobias, no matter what happened.

'Hello?' Ebba dropped her bag on the floor in the front hall. 'Tobias? Where are you?'

It was very quiet in the house. She listened for sounds as she slowly went upstairs. Could he have gone to Fjällbacka on some errand? No, she'd seen the boat at the dock. There was another boat moored there too. Did they have visitors?

'Hello?' she called again, but she heard only her own voice echoing between the bare walls. Bright sunshine shone through the windows, lighting the dust motes that whirled through the air as she moved. She went into the bedroom.

'Tobias?' She stopped in surprise at the sight of her husband sitting on the floor, leaning against the wall, staring straight ahead. He didn't respond.

Ebba was instantly alarmed. She squatted down and

stroked his hair. He was haggard and worn out. 'What's wrong?' she asked.

He turned to look at her.

'You came back?' he said in a flat voice, and she nodded.

'Yes, and you have no idea all the things I want to tell you. I've had time to think while I've been staying with Erica. I realized something that I think you already know: that we only have each other, that we need to try. I love you, Tobias. Both of us will always carry Vincent here,' she placed her hand on her heart, 'but we can't live as if we're dead too.'

She fell silent, waiting for a reaction, but he didn't say a word.

'So many things fell into place when Erica told me about my family.' She sat down next to him and eagerly began recounting the stories about Laura, Dagmar, and the Angelmaker.

When she was done, Tobias nodded. 'The guilt has been passed down.'

'What do you mean?'

'The guilt has been passed down,' he repeated, his voice rising to a falsetto.

He ran his hand through his hair, making it stand on end. Ebba reached out to smooth it down, but he knocked her hand away.

'You've never been willing to admit your guilt.'

'What guilt?' An uneasy feeling settled over her, but she tried to shake it off. This was Tobias, her husband.

'Guilt for Vincent's death. How can we go on if you never will admit your guilt? But now I understand why. It's inside of you. Your grandmother's grandmother was a murderer of children, and you murdered our child.'

Ebba recoiled as if he'd struck her. And he might as well have done; that was how terrible his words were. He was accusing her of killing Vincent? Despair rose in her chest, and she wanted to scream at him, but she realized that something must be wrong with him. He didn't know what he was saying. That was the only explanation. Otherwise he would never say something so dreadful to her.

'Tobias,' she said as calmly as she could, but he merely pointed at her and went on:

'You're the one who murdered him. You carry the guilt. You always have.'

'Sweetheart, what are you talking about? You know what happened. I didn't kill Vincent. No one is to blame for his death, and you know that.' She grabbed Tobias by the shoulders, trying to shake some sense into his eyes.

She looked around and suddenly noticed that the bed was rumpled and had not been made. A tray on the floor held plates with leftover food and two glasses with dregs of red wine.

'Who's been here?' she asked, but he didn't answer. He merely stared at her with ice-cold eyes.

Slowly she began to slide away from him. She instinctively knew that she had to get out of here. This was not Tobias, this was someone else, and for a second she wondered how long he'd been this person that she now saw in front of her. How long had that coldness been in his eyes without her noticing?

She continued to back away.

Moving stiffly, and without taking his eyes off her, Tobias stood up. Terrified, she moved faster, trying to get to her feet, but he stretched out his hand and pushed her back down to the floor.

'Tobias?' she said again.

He had never laid a hand on her. Never. He was the one who always protested if she wanted to kill a spider, insisting instead that she carefully carry it outside. But that Tobias no longer existed. Maybe he had been destroyed when Vincent died. She'd just been too immersed in her own grief to notice, and now it was too late.

Tobias tilted his head to one side as he studied her, as if she were a fly caught in his web. Her heart was pounding, but she didn't have the strength to fight back. And where could she flee? It was easier to surrender. She would go to join Vincent. Death didn't scare her. Right now all she felt was sorrow. Sorrow that Tobias had fallen apart like this, sorrow that her hopes for the future had been so quickly shattered.

When Tobias leaned down and placed his hands around her neck, she calmly looked him in the eye. His hands were warm and their touch was so familiar. Those hands had caressed her skin so many times before. He pressed harder, and she felt her heart race. She saw flashes of light, and her body resisted, fighting for air, but by sheer force of will she made herself relax. As the darkness descended over her, she accepted her fate. Vincent was waiting for her.

Gösta was alone in the conference room. The excitement he'd felt when they discovered one passport was missing had now subsided. Maybe he was a cynic, but he couldn't help thinking that there could be many explanations for a missing passport. Annelie's passport could have been destroyed or lost, or it might simply have been kept elsewhere, separate from the others, and then disappeared when the house was emptied. It was still plausible that its absence was significant, but Patrik would have to work that out. In the meantime, Gösta felt an urge to go through everything one more time. He owed it to Ebba to be as thorough as possible. There might be something they'd overlooked, something they hadn't examined sufficiently.

Maj-Britt would never have forgiven him if he failed

to do all he could to help the lass. Ebba had gone back to Valö. Something dark and threatening awaited her out there, and he had to do everything in his power to prevent her from being harmed.

She'd held a special place in his heart ever since she'd clung to him on that day as she was about to leave their home. It had been one of the worst days of his life. Every detail of that morning when the social worker had come to take Ebba to her new family was imprinted in his memory. Maj-Britt had given the child a bath and combed her hair, tying it with a bow. Then she'd put the little girl into the dress with the ribbon around the waist, the dress that she'd sat up sewing for several nights in a row. Gösta had hardly been able to face the sight of Ebba on that morning, she had looked so sweet.

Fearing that his heart might break, he had planned to avoid saying goodbye, but Maj-Britt had insisted that they take a proper farewell from the lass. So he had squatted down and held out his arms, and she had come running to him, the bow in her hair fluttering and the skirt of her dress spread out like a white sail behind her. She had put her arms around his neck and held on tight, as if she knew that this would be the last time they saw each other.

Gösta swallowed hard as he cautiously took Ebba's baby clothes out of the box that Patrik had just packed.

'Gösta.' Patrik was standing in the doorway.

He gave a start and turned around. He was still holding a baby jumper in his hands.

'How did you happen to know where Ebba's parents live in Göteborg?' asked Patrik.

Gösta didn't reply. Thoughts whirled through his mind, and he tried to think of some explanation. Maybe he could say that he'd seen the address somewhere. He could probably make Patrik believe him, but instead he sighed and said:

'I was the one who sent all those cards.'

'So you're "G"?' Patrik asked. 'I can't believe that never occurred to me before.'

'I should have told you. I did try to bring it up a few times.' He bowed his head in shame. 'But I only sent cards to Ebba's parents. The last one that Tobias brought over here was not from me.'

'I realize that. To be honest, I've been wondering about that particular card. The message was so drastically different from the others.'

'And it wasn't a very good copy of my handwriting either.' Gösta put down the baby sweater and crossed his arms.

'No, it wouldn't be easy to copy your cramped style.'

Gösta smiled, relieved that Patrik had decided to be so understanding. He wasn't sure that he'd have been as magnanimous.

'I know that this case has special meaning for you,' said Patrik, as if he'd read Gösta's mind.

'I can't let anything happen to her.' Gösta turned around and began going through the contents of the box again.

Patrik didn't move, and Gösta turned to face him. 'It would change everything if Annelie is still alive. Or at least *was* still alive. Have you contacted Leon to say that we want to have another talk with him?'

'I'd prefer to surprise him. If we can catch him off guard, there's a greater chance that we can get him to talk.' Patrik fell silent, looking a bit uncertain about whether to go on. Then he said: 'I think I might know who sent that last card.'

'Who?'

Patrik shook his head. 'It's just an idea that occurred to me, and I've asked Torbjörn to check it out. I'll know more after I hear from him. Until then, I'd prefer not to say anything, but I promise that you'll be the first to know.'

'I truly hope so.' Gösta again turned away. There were still a lot of things to look through. Something that he'd already seen kept nagging at his memory, and he wasn't about to give up until he worked out what it was.

Rebecka probably wouldn't understand, but Josef had left her a letter nonetheless. At least she'd know that he loved her and he was grateful for the life they'd had together. He realized now that he had sacrificed both her and the children for the sake of his dream. The shame and pain had made him blind to how much they meant to him. Yet they had loyally stood by his side.

He had sent a letter to each of the children as well. No explanation was given to them either, just a few words of farewell and instructions about what he expected of them. It was important for them not to forget that they had a responsibility and a mission to fulfil even though he wouldn't be present to remind them.

Slowly he ate his lunchtime egg, boiled for exactly eight minutes. Early in their marriage Rebecka had been careless about the precise time. Sometimes seven minutes, sometimes ten. But it was years now since she'd failed to boil the egg properly. She had been a good and dutiful wife, and his parents had been fond of her.

But occasionally she was too indulgent with the children, which bothered him. They might be adults, but they still needed to be guided with a firm hand, and he wasn't convinced that Rebecka would be able to do that. He also doubted that she could keep their Jewish traditions alive. But what choice did he have? His shame would cling to them and ruin any chance they had of going through life with their heads held high. He was forced to sacrifice himself for their future.

In a weak moment the idea of revenge had occurred to him, but he had immediately pushed it out of his mind.

From experience he knew that revenge never led to anything good, it only brought more darkness.

After eating the last of his egg, he carefully wiped his mouth and got up from the table. As he left his home for the last time, he did not look back.

She was awakened by the sound of a heavy door opening. Confused, Anna squinted at the strip of light. Where was she? She had a terrible headache, and it took a real effort for her to sit up. It was cold, and she had only a thin sheet wrapped around her body. Shivering, she hugged her arms to her chest, as she felt panic creeping over her.

Tobias. He was the last thing she remembered. They had been lying in bed – his and Ebba's. They'd been drinking wine, and she was filled with an overwhelming desire. It all came back to her now. She tried to push the memory away, but the image of her naked body against his flickered in her mind. They had moved towards each other on the bed, the moonlight shining down on them. Then there was nothing but blackness. She couldn't remember anything more.

'Hello?' she called, facing the door, but there was no answer. Everything seemed unreal, as if she'd landed in another world, like Alice in Wonderland falling down the rabbit hole. 'Hello?' she called again as she tried to stand up, but her legs gave way and she collapsed on the floor.

Something big was tossed through the door, which was then slammed shut with a bang. Anna sat perfectly still. It was again pitch dark. Not a scrap of light from anywhere, but she realized that she needed to find out what had been thrown into the room. She started to crawl, using her hands to feel her way forward. The floor was so cold that her fingers went numb, and the rough surface tore at her knees. Finally she nudged something that felt like cloth. She kept on fumbling with her hands, recoiling when she felt skin under her fingertips. It was a person, a woman, judging by the scent and the hair. The eyes were closed, and at first she couldn't tell if the woman was breathing, although her body was warm. Cautiously she ran her hands over the neck until she felt a faint pulse. Without thinking, she pinched the woman's nostrils closed and at the same time tilted her head back. Then Anna leaned down and placed her mouth over the woman's. As she breathed into the woman's mouth, she had a vague feeling that she recognized her perfume.

Anna had no idea how long she continued the CPR. Intermittently she would place one hand on top of the other and press down on the woman's chest. She wasn't sure that she was doing it properly. The only time she'd seen it done was in the hospital dramas on TV, so she hoped that they'd presented the procedure accurately.

After what seemed like an eternity, the woman began to cough. It sounded like she might throw up, so Anna turned her on to her side and stroked her back. The coughing eased, and the woman breathed in air, taking long, whistling breaths.

'Where am I?' she croaked.

Wanting to reassure her, Anna ran her hand over the woman's hair. Her voice was so strained that it was hard to guess her identity, but she had her suspicions.

'Ebba? Is that you? It's so dark in here that I can't see a thing.'

'Anna? I thought I'd gone blind.'

'No, you're not blind. It's dark, and I don't know where we are.'

Ebba started to say something but was cut off by another coughing fit that shook her whole body. Anna continued to stroke her hair until Ebba made a move to sit up. Holding her arm, Anna helped her into a sitting position, and after a while she stopped coughing.

374

'I don't know where we are either,' Ebba said.

'How did we get here?'

At first Ebba didn't answer. Then she said quietly: 'Tobias.'

'Tobias?' Again Anna saw the image of their naked bodies. Feelings of guilt made bile rise up in her throat, and she had to fight back an impulse to vomit.

'He . . .' Ebba coughed some more. 'He tried to strangle me.'

'Tried to strangle you?' Anna repeated in disbelief. Then she realized that she'd had a vague sense that everything was not as it should be with Tobias – like an animal that can smell that another member of the herd is sick. But that had only increased his attraction. She was used to danger; it was something familiar, and yesterday she'd recognized her husband Lucas in Tobias.

Nausea surged up inside her again, and the cold from the floor spread through her body. She started shivering harder.

'Good Lord, it's cold in here. Where could he have taken us?' said Ebba.

'Surely, he's going to let us out,' said Anna, but she could hear the doubt in her own voice.

'I didn't recognize him. He was like a different person. I saw it in his eyes. He said . . .' She stopped and suddenly began to cry. 'He said that I murdered Vincent. Our son.'

Without saying a word Anna put her arms around Ebba and pressed her head to her shoulder.

'What happened?' she asked after a moment.

At first Ebba was crying so hard that she couldn't answer. Then her breathing grew calmer and she was able to speak.

'It was in early December. We were really busy. Tobias had three building projects that he was working on at the same time, and I was also working long days. It was obviously taking a toll on Vincent because he kept acting up and pushing our patience to the limit. We were totally worn out.' She sniffled some more, and Anna could hear her wiping her nose on her shirtsleeve. 'On the morning it happened, we were both about to leave for work. Tobias was supposed to drop Vincent off at the day-care centre, but then they called from one of the construction sites to say that he had to come immediately. Some sort of crisis, as usual. Tobias asked me to take Vincent so that he could go straight out there, but I had an important meeting that morning and I was furious that he thought his work should be given higher priority. We started quarrelling, and finally Tobias simply walked out the door, leaving me with Vincent. I realized that I was going to be late for yet another meeting, and when Vincent had another one of his tantrums, I couldn't take it any more. So I locked myself in the bathroom and sat down to cry. Vincent was crying too and pounding on the door, but after a few moments everything was quiet, so I assumed that he'd given up and gone to his room. I let a few more minutes pass as I dried my eyes and calmed down.'

Ebba was talking so fast that the words practically spilled from her lips. Anna wanted to put her hands over her ears so she wouldn't have to hear the rest. But she owed it to Ebba to hear the whole story.

'I had just come out of the bathroom when there was a loud bang from the driveway outside. A second later I heard Tobias scream. I've never heard a scream like that before. It didn't sound human, it was more like a wounded animal.' Ebba's voice broke as she went on. 'I knew at once what had happened. I knew that Vincent was dead. I could feel it in my body. But I rushed outside, and there he lay behind our car. He didn't have a coat on, and even though I could tell that he was dead, I kept thinking that he'd gone out in the snow without putting on his zip-suit.

And he was going to catch cold. That was what I thought as I saw him lying there – that he was going to catch cold.'

'It was an accident,' said Anna quietly. 'It wasn't your fault.'

'Yes, it was. Tobias was right. I killed Vincent. If only I hadn't sat there in the bathroom, if only I'd told myself that it didn't matter if I was late for that meeting, if only . . .' Her sobs became a wail, and Anna pulled her closer and let her cry as she gently stroked her hair and murmured consoling words. She felt Ebba's sorrow deep in her own body, and for a moment it pushed aside the fear about what was going to happen to them. For a moment they were simply two mothers who had each lost a child.

When Ebba's sobs subsided, Anna made another attempt to stand up. Her legs felt steadier now. Slowly she got to her feet, not sure whether she might bump her head on something, but she was able to stand up straight. Cautiously she took a step forward. Something touched her face and she shrieked.

'What is it?' said Ebba, clinging to Anna's leg.

'I felt something on my face, but it's probably just a spiderweb.' Trembling, she raised her hand and held it out in front of her. Something was hanging there, and it took several tries before she got hold of it. A string. She gave it a tug. The light that switched on was so bright that she had to shut her eyes.

When she opened her eyes again, she looked around in surprise. From the floor she heard Ebba gasp.

For so many years Sebastian had enjoyed having power, even in those instances when he'd chosen not to exercise it. Asking something from John would have been too dangerous. John was no longer the person that Sebastian had known on Valö. Though he managed to hide it well, he was so full of hatred that it would have been foolhardy to exploit the opportunity that fate had handed him.

He hadn't asked anything of Leon either, simply because Leon was the only person other than Lovart for whom he'd ever had any respect. After what happened, he'd quickly disappeared, but Sebastian had followed his career in the newspapers and via the gossip that had made its way to Fjällbacka. Now Leon had got entangled in the game, but Sebastian had already succeeded in getting what he could from it. Josef's ridiculous project was no more than a memory. The land and the granite were the only things of value, and he had converted them into a handsome profit in accordance with the agreement that Josef had signed without giving the document so much as a cursory glance.

And Percy. Sebastian chuckled to himself as he drove his yellow Porsche along Fjällbacka's narrow streets, waving to everyone he saw. Percy had been living a myth for so long that he'd failed to realize that he could lose everything. It was true that he'd been uneasy when Sebastian appeared like an angel to the rescue, but he'd never seriously believed that he might lose the birthright that was his. Now the manor was owned by Percy's younger siblings, and he had only himself to blame. He hadn't managed his inheritance properly, and Sebastian had merely seen to it that disaster struck a bit sooner than it otherwise might.

He had earned good money from the deal as well, but that was merely a bonus. Power was what gave him the most satisfaction. The funny thing was that neither Josef nor Percy seemed to have seen what was coming before it was too late. In spite of everything, they had counted on his good will and believed that he actually wanted to help them. What idiots! Oh well. Now Leon was going to put an end to the game. That was probably why he wanted all of them to meet. The question was how far he intended to go. Sebastian wasn't particularly worried. His reputation was such that people wouldn't be too surprised. But he was curious to see how the others would react. Especially John, who had the most to lose of any of them.

Sebastian parked the car but remained sitting in the driver's seat for a few minutes. Then he got out, made sure the key was in his pocket, and went up to the door to ring the bell. It was showtime.

Erica sipped her coffee as she read. It had been sitting for too long and tasted awful, but she didn't feel like making a fresh pot.

'You're still here?' Gösta came into the station's kitchen and poured himself a cup.

She stopped flipping through the folder and closed it.

'Yes, I got permission to stay and read through the file on the old investigation. So I'm sitting here wondering what it means that Annelie's passport is missing.'

'How old was she? Sixteen?' said Gösta as he sat down at the table.

Erica nodded. 'Yes, sixteen, and clearly head over heels in love with Leon. Maybe there was a quarrel and she decided to leave. If so, it wouldn't be the first time that a teenager caused a tragedy. But I have a hard time believing that a sixteen-year-old girl would single-handedly murder her whole family.'

'You're right, that doesn't sound plausible. She would have needed help. Maybe from Leon, if they were having a relationship. Maybe her father issued an ultimatum, they lost their tempers, and . . .'

'It's possible that's what happened, but it says in the file that Leon was out fishing with the other boys. So why would they give him an alibi? How would that benefit them?'

'I doubt they would have all colluded in Annelie's plan,' said Gösta pensively.

'I agree, I don't think they were sophisticated enough to do something like that.'

'Even if we assume this has to do with Annelie, and Leon, there still doesn't seem to be any credible motive to murder an entire family. Killing Rune ought to have been sufficient.'

'I was thinking the same thing.' Erica sighed. 'So I'm sitting here going through the interview transcripts. There must be something in what the boys said that doesn't ring true, but they all gave the same story. They were out fishing for mackerel, and when they came back, the family was gone.'

Gösta froze, his coffee cup halfway to his lips.

'Did you say mackerel?'

'Yes, that's what it says in the transcripts.'

'How the hell could I have missed something so obvious?'

'What do you mean?'

Gösta set down his cup and rubbed his hand over his face. 'It's amazing how you can read through a police report again and again without seeing what's right in front of your face.'

For a moment he fell silent, but then he gave Erica a triumphant smile.

'You know what? I think we just cracked the boys' alibi.'

FJÄLLBACKA 1970

Inez was keen to please her mother. She knew that Laura always wanted the best for her daughter and sought to make sure that she would have a secure future. Yet Inez couldn't help feeling a certain aversion as they sat on the good sofa in the drawing room. He was so old.

'With time you'll get to know each other,' said Laura, giving her daughter a firm look. 'Rune is a good and reliable man, and he'll take care of you. You know that I'm in delicate health, and when I'm gone, you'll have no one left. I don't want you to be as alone as I have been.'

Mamma placed her dry hand on top of Inez's. Inez could recall only a few occasions when she'd felt her mother's touch.

'I realize this may seem a bit sudden,' said the man sitting across from them, eyeing Inez as if she were a prize-winning horse.

It may have been unkind of her to think that way, but Inez couldn't help it. This was definitely sudden. Mamma had been in hospital for three days because of her heart, and when she came home, she had presented this plan: that Inez should marry Rune Elvander, who had been widowed a year earlier. Now that Nanna had died, the two women were all alone.

'My dear wife said that I should find someone to help raise the children. And your mother tells me that you're a clever girl,' the man went on.

Inez had a vague sense that this was not how things were supposed to happen. It was the early seventies, after all, and women had much greater opportunities for determining their own lives. But she'd never been part of the real world; she had only shared in the perfect world that her mother had created. And there her mother's word was law. If Laura decided that it would be best for Inez to marry a fifty-year-old widower with three children, she was not allowed to question that decision.

'I'm planning to purchase the old summer camp out on Valö and establish a boarding school for boys. I need someone at my side who will help me accomplish this. Are you a good cook?'

Inez nodded. She had spent many hours in the kitchen with Nanna, who had taught her everything she knew.

'All right, then it's settled,' said Laura. 'Of course we ought to have a proper engagement period, so how about a quiet wedding around Midsummer?'

'That sounds excellent,' said Rune.

Inez didn't speak. She was studying her future husband, noticing the wrinkles that had started to form around his eyes and the thin, resolute lips. Streaks of grey were visible in his dark hair, and his hairline was receding. So this was the man she was going to marry. She hadn't yet met the children; she knew only that they were fifteen, twelve, and five years old. She hadn't met many children in her life, but no doubt it would be fine. At least, that was what her mother claimed.

❖

Percy was still sitting in the car, staring at the approach to Fjällbacka, but he wasn't really aware of the waves or the traffic. The only thing he saw was his own fate, and how the past was merging with the present. His siblings had made an effort to be polite when he phoned. It was considered only proper to behave decently, even towards a man they had defeated. Percy knew full well what was concealed behind their deprecating words. That sort of malicious joy was the same, whether a person was rich or poor.

They told him that they had bought the manor, but he'd already heard the news. Attorney Buhrman had found out that Sebastian had gone behind his back. Using the same phrases that Sebastian had spoken, they explained that the manor was going to be turned into an exclusive conference centre. It was regrettable that things had turned out this way, but they wanted Percy to move out before the end of the month. Naturally the move would be over-seen by their lawyer to make sure that Percy didn't take anything that was included in the sale of the property.

He was surprised that Sebastian had actually decided to put in an appearance today. Percy had seen him drive past, heading up the hill to Leon's house. Suntanned, his

383

shirt unbuttoned, wearing expensive sunglasses and with his hair slicked back. He looked the same as always. And no doubt he wasn't feeling any different, either. It was just business, as he was fond of saying.

Percy cast one last glance at his face in the mirror on the visor. He looked like hell. His eyes were bloodshot from too little sleep and too much whisky. His complexion was ashen. But his tie was perfectly knotted. That was a matter of pride with him. He snapped the visor closed and got out of the car. There was no reason to postpone the inevitable.

Ia leaned her head against the cool pane of the window. The cab ride out to Landvetter airport in Göteborg would take just under two hours, maybe more, depending on the traffic, and she wanted to try to sleep during the drive.

She had kissed him before she left. He was going to have an awful time managing without her, but she hadn't wanted to be present when everything exploded. Leon had assured her that it would be fine. He said that this was something he had to do, otherwise he would never have any peace.

Again she thought about that day when they'd driven along the steep roads in Monaco. He had been about to leave her. The words had poured out of his mouth. He had rambled on, saying that things had changed and that he no longer had the same needs, that they'd had many good years together, but now he'd fallen in love with someone else, and that she was bound to find someone who would make her happy too. She had taken her eyes off the winding road to look at him, and while he continued to spew out platitudes, she had thought about everything that she'd sacrificed for his sake.

When the car swerved, she saw his eyes open wide and the flood of meaningless words stopped.

'Keep your eyes on the road when you're driving,' he told her. She saw a certain nervousness on his handsome face, and she could hardly believe it. For the first time in their life together, Leon was afraid. The feeling of power was intoxicating, and she stomped on the accelerator, noticing how the sudden burst of speed pressed her body against the seat.

'Slow down, Ia,' Leon pleaded. 'You're going too fast!'

She didn't reply, just stomped even harder on the pedal. The little sports car could barely stay on the road. It felt as if they were floating, and for one brief moment she was utterly free.

Leon had tried to grab the steering wheel, but that only made the car swerve all the more, so he let go. He kept begging her to slow down, but the terror in his voice made her happier than she'd felt in a very long time. The car was practically flying.

Up ahead she saw the tree, and it was as if some outside force seized hold of her. Calmly she turned the wheel slightly to the right, aiming straight for that tree. As if from a great distance, she heard Leon's voice, but then the rushing in her ears drowned out everything else. The next instant there was total silence. It was so peaceful. They were not going to be separated. They would be together for all eternity.

She was surprised to find that she was still alive. Next to her sat Leon with his eyes closed, his face covered with blood. The fire was swiftly gathering force. Flames began licking at their seats and reaching towards them. The smell of smoke filled her nostrils. She had to make a quick decision. Should she surrender and allow both of them to be engulfed by fire, or should she rescue herself and Leon? She looked at his handsome face. The flames had reached his cheek, and she watched with fascination as they scorched his skin. Then she made up her mind. He was hers now. And that was how things had been ever since, after she'd dragged him out of the burning vehicle.

Ia closed her eyes, feeling the coolness of the window-pane against her forehead. She didn't want to be part of what Leon was planning to do, but she longed for the time when they would once again be together.

Anna glanced around the bare room that was now revealed in the light from the single bulb. It smelled of earth and something else, harder to identify. She and Ebba had both tried in vain to get the door to open, but it was locked and refused to budge.

Along one wall stood four chests with metal mountings, and above them hung a flag, which was the first thing they'd seen when the light was switched on. It was dark with mildew and mould, but the swastika was still vivid against the red-and-white background.

'Maybe there's something in those chests that you could put on,' said Ebba, looking at Anna. 'You're shivering.'

'Sure. I'll take whatever we can find. I'm about to freeze to death,' replied Anna. She was ashamed of her nakedness under the sheet. She was the sort of person who never liked to be seen in the nude in a locker room, and after the accident, this feeling had intensified, thanks to all the scars criss-crossing her body. Although modesty was the least of her worries at the moment, her sense of embarrassment managed to outweigh both her fear and the cold.

'Those three are locked, but this one is open,' said Ebba, pointing at the chest nearest the door. She lifted the lid to find a heavy grey woollen blanket inside. 'Here,' she said, tossing the blanket to Anna, who wrapped it around herself on top of the sheet. It smelled vile, but she was grateful for the warmth and the protection it offered.

'There are canned goods in here too,' said Ebba, lifting

out several dusty tins from the chest. 'In the worst-case scenario, we can probably survive here for a while.'

Anna stared at her. Ebba's almost cheerful tone seemed oddly misplaced, considering their situation and her earlier emotional state. Most likely it was just a coping mechanism.

'But we have no water,' Anna pointed out, allowing the statement to hover in the air. Without water, they wouldn't last long, but Ebba didn't seem to be listening as she continued to dig through the chest.

'Look at this!' she said, holding up a garment.

'A Nazi uniform? Where did all these things come from?'

'Apparently there was a crazy old man who used to own this house during the war. These things must have belonged to him.'

'How disgusting,' said Anna. She was still shaking. The warmth from the blanket was slowly seeping into her body, but the cold had settled in her marrow, and it would take time for her to get warm.

'How did you end up here?' Ebba suddenly asked, turning to face Anna. It was as if she only now realized how strange it was for them to have landed here together.

'Tobias must have attacked me too.' Anna wrapped the blanket tighter around her body.

Ebba frowned.

'But why? Was it unprovoked? Or did something happen that . . .' She put her hand to her mouth and the look in her eyes hardened. 'I saw the tray in the bedroom. Why did you really come out here yesterday? Did you stay for dinner? What happened?'

The words slammed like bullets against the walls, and with each question Anna flinched, as if she'd been slapped. She didn't have to say anything. She knew that the answers could be read on her face.

387

Ebba's eyes filled with tears. 'How could you? You know what we've been going through, what things have been like for us.'

Anna tried to swallow, but her mouth was as dry as cotton, and she didn't know how to explain her actions or apologize for what she'd done. Her eyes brimming with tears, Ebba stared at her for a long time. Then she took a deep breath and let it out slowly. Calm and composed, she said:

'Well, let's not talk about this now. We need to stick together to get out of here. Maybe there's something in the chests that we can use to prise open the door.' She turned away, her whole body rigid with suppressed anger.

Anna gratefully accepted the offer of a temporary truce. If they didn't get out of this place, there'd be no reason to work anything out. No one would miss them for a while. Dan and the children were away, and it would be several days before Ebba's parents would start to worry. The only other person who might wonder what was going on was Erica, who usually became frantic if she couldn't get hold of Anna. Normally that would infuriate her, but right now she wished that Erica would start feeling anxious and begin asking questions with as much stubbornness as she usually displayed if she didn't get the right answer. Dear, sweet Erica, please be as curious and worried as you always are, prayed Anna in the light from the bare bulb.

Ebba had started kicking at the lock on the chest next to the one she'd already opened. The padlock didn't show any sign of budging, but she kept on kicking and at last got it to open.

'Come over here and help me,' she said, and together they pulled off the padlock. Then they leaned down and tried to raise the lid. Judging by the dirt and dust, it had been closed for years, and it took their combined strength to force it open. With a lurch, the lid finally yielded.

They peered inside and then stared at each other. Anna saw her own surprise mirrored in Ebba's expression. A scream bounced off the walls in the bare room, but she wasn't sure whether it came from her or from Ebba.

'Hi. Are you Kjell?' Sven Niklasson came forward and shook hands as he introduced himself.

'You didn't bring a photographer?' Kjell looked around the small space next to the luggage carousel.

'He's driving up from Göteborg. He'll meet us there.'

Sven pulled his small carry-on suitcase behind him as they walked out to the car park. Kjell had the impression that he was used to packing quickly and travelling light.

'Do you think we should inform the Tanum police?' asked Sven as he got into the passenger seat of Kjell's big SUV.

Kjell thought about this as he drove out of the car park and turned right.

'I think we should. But you need to talk to Patrik Hedström. Nobody else.' He glanced at Sven. 'I didn't think you usually worried about informing a particular police force.'

Sven smiled and gazed out the window at the passing landscape. He was in luck. Trollhättan Bridge was most beautiful in the sunshine.

'You never know when you might need a favour from somebody on the force. I already have an agreement with the Göteborg police, ensuring that we get to be present when they move in, since we've supplied them with information. Just think of it as a courtesy that we tell the Tanum police what's going on.'

'The Göteborg police probably weren't planning to offer the same courtesy, so I'll make sure that Hedström knows how generous you're being.' Kjell grinned. He was deeply grateful that Sven Niklasson was allowing him to ride along. This was more than a scoop for him as a journalist – this story was going to have reverberations in Swedish politics and shock the entire country. 'Thanks for including me,' he muttered, feeling suddenly embarrassed.

Sven shrugged. 'We wouldn't have been able to finalize things if you hadn't provided the information that you did.'

'So you were able to decode the numbers?' Kjell was practically bursting with curiosity. Sven hadn't told him all the details on the phone.

'It was a ridiculously simple code.' Sven laughed. 'My kids could have cracked it in fifteen minutes.'

'What do you mean?'

'One was "A", two was "B". And so on.'

'You're joking.' Kjell glanced over at Sven and almost drove off the road.

'No, I wish I was. It just shows how stupid they think we are.'

'So what did you find out?' In his mind Kjell tried to picture the numbers, but he'd never been good at maths in school. Nowadays he could barely remember his own phone number.

'Stureplan. It said Stureplan. Followed by a date and a time.'

'Jesus Christ,' Kjell said, turning right on to the round-about near Torp. 'That could have been disastrous.'

'Yes, but the police went in early this morning to pick up the people who were going to carry out the attack. Now they can't communicate with anyone to reveal that the police know all about the plan. That's why this is so urgent. It won't be long before the responsible individuals in the party notice that they haven't heard from the attackers, nor can they contact them. And then they'll be on guard, and we won't have another chance.'

'It was actually a brilliant plan,' said Kjell. He couldn't

shake off the thought of what would have happened if the plan had been carried out. The images were too vivid. It would have been tragic.

'I know. In spite of everything, we should be grateful that they're showing their true colours now. It's going to be a hell of an awakening for so many people who believed in John Holm. Thank God. I hope we won't see something like this again for a long time. Unfortunately, I think people have very short memories.' He sighed and turned to face Kjell. 'Would you mind ringing this Hedman fellow?'

'Hedström. Patrik Hedström. Sure, I'll do it.' Keeping one eye on the road, he tapped in the number for Tanum police station.

'So what's all the commotion?' said Patrik with a grin as he entered the kitchen. Erica had shouted his name, and he'd come running from his office.

'Sit down,' said Gösta. 'You know how many times I've ploughed through the old investigative materials, right? The boys all told the same story, but I've always had the feeling that something was odd.'

'And now we've discovered what it was.' Erica crossed her arms, a satisfied expression on her face.

'What is it?'

'It's the part about the mackerel.'

'The mackerel?' Patrik peered at her. 'I'm sorry, but could you possibly clarify that?'

'I never saw the fish that the boys had caught,' said Gösta. 'And for some inexplicable reason, it didn't occur to me during the interviews.'

'What didn't?' said Patrik impatiently.

'You can't catch mackerel until after Midsummer,' said Erica, enunciating carefully, as if speaking to a child.

It slowly dawned on Patrik what this could mean. 'And

all of the boys said that they'd been out fishing for mackerel?'

'Exactly. One of them might have been mistaken, but since all of them said the same thing, they must have discussed it. And because they didn't know much about fishing, they chose the wrong fish,' explained Erica.

'It was thanks to Erica that I worked it out,' said Gösta, embarrassed.

Patrik threw his wife a kiss. 'You're the best!' he told her, and he meant it.

At that moment his mobile rang, and he saw on the display that the call was from Torbjörn.

'I need to take this. Fantastic job, both of you!' He gave them a thumbs up, then went back to his office and closed the door.

He listened attentively to what Torbjörn had to say, jotting down notes on a scrap of paper that he found on his desk. No matter how odd, his suspicions had now been confirmed. As he listened to Torbjörn, he thought about what this might mean. By the time he ended the call, he had learned a new piece of information, but it left him more confused than ever.

He heard the sound of heavy footsteps in the hall, and got up to open the door. Paula was coming towards him, preceded by her enormous stomach.

'I can't bear staying at home and waiting. The girl I talked to at the bank promised to get back to me today, but so far I haven't heard from her.' She had to stop to catch her breath.

Patrik put his hand on Paula's shoulder. 'Breathe, for God's sake,' he said, and then waited for her to calm down a bit. 'Do you feel like sitting in on the meeting as we go over the case?'

'Of course.'

'Where the hell do you think you're going?' Mellberg

suddenly appeared behind Paula. 'Rita was so worried when you walked out the door that she made me follow you.'

Paula rolled her eyes. 'You don't have to keep worrying about me.'

'It's just as well that you're here. There's a lot we need to review,' said Patrik, heading for the conference room. He stopped on the way to ask Gösta to join them. After hesitating for a few seconds, Patrik turned and went back to the kitchen.

'You can come too,' he said, nodding at Erica. As he'd expected, she eagerly leaped up from her chair.

It was crowded in the room, but Patrik wanted to review the case there, surrounded by all the things that had once belonged to the Elvander family. The items served to remind them why it was so important to work out exactly what happened all those years ago.

Patrik briefly explained to Paula and Mellberg that the boxes had come from Junk-Olle's place and they'd already spent a lot of time going through the contents.

'A few pieces have fallen into place, but we need help to decide how to proceed. First, I can tell you that the mysterious "G" who sent the birthday cards to Ebba is Gösta Flygare.' He pointed at Gösta, who blushed.

'Gösta?' said Paula.

Mellberg's face turned beet-red, and he looked as if he might explode.

'I know I should have said something before, but I've already had a talk with Hedström about it.' Gösta glared at Mellberg.

'But the last card was not from Gösta. And the tone is very different to all the others,' Patrik went on as he leaned against the edge of the table. 'I had a theory about it, and I just talked to Torbjörn, who confirmed my suspicions. The fingerprint that Torbjörn lifted from the back of the stamp, which most likely belongs to whoever put the stamp on the card, matched a fingerprint on the plastic bag it was in. Tobias was the one who put the card in the bag before giving it to us.'

'But no one else would have handled the bag other than you and Tobias. So that means . . .' Erica turned pale, and Patrik saw the gears beginning to turn in her head.

Frantically she searched through her handbag for her mobile, and with everyone staring at her, she tapped in a number. No one spoke as the phone rang, then they all heard quite clearly the sound of someone's voicemail.

'Shit,' exclaimed Erica as she tapped in another number. 'I'll try Ebba.'

The phone rang and rang, but Ebba didn't pick up.

'Bloody hell,' cursed Erica, trying a third number.

Patrik made no attempt to go on with the meeting until she was done. He too was starting to feel uneasy about the fact that Anna hadn't answered her phone all day.

'When did she go out to the island?' asked Paula.

Erica was still holding the phone to her ear. 'Last night, and I haven't been able to get hold of her since. But I'm ringing the mail boat now. They took Ebba out to Valö this morning, so they might know something . . . Hello? Hi, it's Erica Falck . . . Exactly. You took Ebba out there . . . Did you happen to notice any other boats? A wooden *snipa*? It was moored at the summer camp dock? Okay. Thanks.'

Erica ended the conversation, and Patrik saw that her hand was shaking.

'Our boat, the one that Anna took out there, was still at the dock. So both Anna and Ebba are on Valö with Tobias, and neither of them is answering the phone.'

'I'm sure there's nothing to worry about. And Anna may have gone home by now,' said Patrik, trying to make his voice sound calmer than he felt.

'But Tobias said that she'd stayed only an hour. Why would he lie about that?'

'There must be a good explanation. We'll go to the island and check on things as soon as we're done here.'

'Why would Tobias send a threatening message to his own wife?' asked Paula. 'Does that mean that he's behind the murder attempts?'

Patrik shook his head. 'Right now we don't know. That's why we need to review everything we've found out so far and see if there are any gaps we can fill in. Gösta, could you tell everyone what you've discovered about the boys' testimony?'

'Sure,' said Gösta. He briefed his colleagues on how the mention of mackerel revealed the boys' statements to be false.

'It proves that they were lying,' said Patrik. 'And if they lied about that, they probably lied about everything else. Why else would they devise a story to tell us? I think we can assume that they were involved in the family's disappearance, and now we have further proof, which means that we can put pressure on them.'

'But what does this have to do with Tobias?' said Mellberg. 'He wasn't there back then, yet according to Torbjörn, the same gun was used in 1974 and in the shooting the other day.'

'I don't know, Bertil,' said Patrik. 'Let's take one thing at a time.'

'And then there's the matter of the missing passport,' Gösta continued, sitting up straighter in his chair. 'Annelie's passport is missing. This could mean that she was somehow mixed up in what happened and then fled abroad afterwards.'

Patrik cast a glance at Erica, who was looking very pale. He knew that she couldn't stop thinking about Anna.

'Annelie? The sixteen-year-old daughter?' said Paula,

395

just as her mobile began ringing. She took the call, listening with surprise. When she ended the conversation, she turned to her colleagues.

'Ebba's adoptive father told Patrik and me that an anonymous donor had deposited money in the bank for Ebba every month until she turned eighteen. They never managed to find out where the money came from, but naturally we thought it might be connected to what happened out on Valö. So I've been trying to find out . . .' She paused to catch her breath, and Patrik was reminded that Erica too had been short of breath during her pregnancies.

'Get to the point!' Gösta sat up straighter. 'Ebba had no relatives who were interested in taking care of her, so it's unlikely that any of them would have sent the money. The only person I can picture giving money to the lass would be someone with a guilty conscience.'

'I have no idea what the motive was,' said Paula, who was obviously revelling in delivering information that no one else knew. 'But the money came from Aron Kreutz.'

There was a stunned silence. Gösta was the first to speak.

'Leon's father sent money to Ebba? But why?'

'That's what we need to find out,' said Patrik. His mobile buzzed in his pocket. He took it out and checked the display: Kjell Ringholm from *Bohusläningen*. No doubt he wanted to ask some follow-up questions from the press conference. That could wait. Patrik put away his phone and once again turned his attention to his colleagues.

'Gösta, you and I will go out to Valö. Before we inter-view the boys, we need to make sure that Anna and Ebba are okay, and put a few questions to Tobias. Paula, keep trying to find out more about Leon's father.' He paused when he came to Mellberg. Where would he do the least damage? In reality, Mellberg preferred to do as little work as possible, but it was important that he didn't feel left out. 'Bertil, as usual, you're the best qualified to handle the media. Would you mind staying here at the station so you're available for any enquiries?'

Mellberg's face lit up. 'Of course I'll do that. I have years of experience dealing with the press. Nobody else comes close.'

Patrik sighed to himself. He had to pay a high price in order to keep things running smoothly.

'Could I go out to Valö with you?' asked Erica. She still had a tight grip on her phone.

Patrik shook his head. 'Not on your life.'

'But I really should go along. What if something has happened . . .'

'End of discussion,' said Patrik, hearing that his tone of voice was unnecessarily sharp. 'I'm sorry, but it's best if we handle this,' he added, giving his wife a hug.

Erica nodded reluctantly, and left the room to drive home. He watched her go, then got out his mobile and phoned Victor. After eight rings, he got the voicemail.

'No answer from the Coast Guard, as usual. And our boat is docked out at Valö.'

Just then he heard the sound of someone clearing their throat.

'I'm afraid I'm not going anywhere at the moment. The car won't start,' said Erica from the doorway.

Patrik gave his wife a sceptical look. 'That's odd. Gösta, could you drop Erica off at home, while I finish up a few things here at the station? We have to wait for a boat anyway.'

'All right,' said Gösta, avoiding Erica's eye.

'Good. I'll see you down at the harbour. Could you keep trying to reach Victor?'

'Sure,' said Gösta.

Patrik's mobile was buzzing again, and he automatically

glanced at the display. Kjell Ringholm. He might as well take the call.

'Okay, everybody, get started on your assignments,' he said and pressed the 'answer' button as the others left the room. 'Yes, this is Hedström,' he said with a sigh. He liked Kjell, but right now he really didn't have time for journalists.

VALÖ 1972

Annelie hated Inez from the very beginning. So did Claes. In their eyes she was worthless compared to their mother, who seemed to have been a saint. At least that was what it sounded like when Rune and the children talked about her.

Inez had learned a lot about life. The most important lesson was that her mother was not always right. Her marriage to Rune was the biggest mistake of her life, but she could see no way out of it. Not now, when she was pregnant with his child.

She wiped the sweat from her forehead and then continued to scrub the kitchen floor. Rune had high standards, and everything had to be polished and gleaming when the school opened. Nothing was to be left to chance. 'This is about my reputation,' he said, issuing new orders to her. She toiled from morning to night while her stomach grew, and by now she was so tired that she could hardly stay on her feet.

Suddenly Claes was standing in the doorway. His shadow fell over her, and she jumped.

'Oh, I'm sorry, did I scare you?' he said in that voice of his that always sent shivers down her back.

She could feel the hatred emanating from him, and as usual her whole body tensed, making it hard for her to breathe. There was no proof, nothing she could mention to Rune, and besides, her husband would never believe her. It would be her word *against his son's, and she had no illusions about Rune taking her side.*

'You missed a spot,' said Claes, pointing behind her. Inez clenched her jaw but turned to wipe the spot he was pointing at. She heard a clang and felt water dousing her legs.

'Sorry, I accidentally ran into the bucket,' said Claes, but his apologetic tone did not match the malevolent gleam in his eyes.

Inez merely stared at him. Her fury grew with every day, every abuse, every ugly prank.

'Let me help you.'

That was Johan, Rune's younger son. Only seven years old, but he had warm, intelligent eyes. He had clung to her right from the start. The very first time they met, he had slipped his hand into hers.

With an anxious glance at his big brother, Johan knelt down next to Inez. He took the rag from her hand and began wiping up the water that had spilled across the floor.

'Now you're going to get wet too,' she said, touched by the sight of his bowed head and the lock of hair falling into his eyes.

'It doesn't matter,' he said.

Claes was still standing behind them, arms folded. Anger flashed in his eyes, but he didn't dare reprimand his little brother.

'What a wimp,' he scoffed, and then left the room.

Inez sighed with relief. It was ridiculous. Claes was only seventeen. Even though she wasn't much older, she was still his stepmother, and she was expecting a child who would be his sister or brother. She shouldn't be so scared. All the same, for some reason she instinctively knew that she needed to keep out of his way and not provoke him.

She wondered how things would go when the students arrived. Would the mood be less oppressive when the house was filled with boys? Would their voices help to fill the void? She hoped so. Otherwise she was going to suffocate.

'You're a good boy, Johan,' she said, running her hand over his blond locks. He didn't answer, but she saw that he was smiling.

✣

Leon had been sitting at the window for a long time before they arrived. He gazed across the water at Valö, watching the boats passing by and the holiday-makers enjoying their few weeks away from their jobs. He could never have lived that sort of life himself, yet he envied them. In all its simplicity, it was actually a marvellous existence, although they might not realize it. When the doorbell rang, he rolled his chair away from the window after casting one last glance at Valö. That was where it had all begun.

'It's time to finish this.' Leon looked at them. The tension in the air had been palpable ever since they'd come in, one after the other. He noticed that both Percy and Josef were avoiding contact with Sebastian, who didn't seem the least bit bothered.

'What a fate, to end up in a wheelchair. And your face is completely ruined. You were always so handsome,' said Sebastian, leaning back against the sofa cushions.

Leon wasn't offended. He knew the words weren't intended to hurt him. Sebastian had always been blunt, except when he wanted to dupe someone. Then he had no scruples about lying. It was strange that people changed so little. The others hadn't changed either. Percy

401

seemed fragile, and Josef's eyes still held that serious expression. And John radiated the same old charm.

Leon had found out all about them before he and Ia came to Fjällbacka. He'd paid a lot of money to a private detective, who had done an excellent job and informed Leon of the various directions their lives had taken. But it was as if nothing that happened after Valö had any meaning now that they were all together again.

He didn't reply to Sebastian's remarks, merely saying: 'It's time for us to tell the story.'

'What purpose would that serve?' asked John. 'That's all in the past.'

'I know it was my idea, but the older I get, the more I realize what a mistake it was,' said Leon, fixing his eyes on John. He had surmised that it would be difficult to convince John, but he wasn't about to let that stop him. Regardless whether he was able to get all of them to agree or not, he had decided to reveal the truth. But his sense of fair play made him want to tell the others about his plans before he did something that was bound to affect them all.

'I'm with John,' said Josef in a flat voice. 'There's no reason to stir up something that has long been forgotten.'

'You're the one who always used to talk about the importance of the past. About taking responsibility. Don't you remember?' said Leon.

Josef blanched and turned his face away. 'It's not the same thing.'

'Yes, it is. What happened is still with us. I've been carrying it with me all these years, and I know that the rest of you have too.'

'It's not the same thing,' Josef insisted.

'You said that everybody who bore the blame for your parents' suffering should be held accountable. Shouldn't we be held accountable and confess our guilt?' Leon spoke gently, but he saw what a strong effect his words had on Josef.

'I refuse to permit it.' John clasped his hands in his lap as he sat on the sofa next to Sebastian.

'It's not for you to decide,' replied Leon, fully aware that he had just revealed his mind was already made up.

'To hell with it. Do whatever you like, Leon,' said Sebastian suddenly. He put his hand in his trouser pocket and pulled out a key. He got up and held it out to Leon, who took it reluctantly. So many years had passed since he'd last held that key in his hand, so many years since it had sealed their fates.

Utter silence descended over the room as they saw once again the images that had become etched in their memories.

'We need to open the door.' Leon closed his fingers around the key. 'I'd prefer to have the rest of you with me, but if you refuse, I'll do it alone.'

'And Ia—' John ventured, but Leon cut him off.

'Ia is on her way home to Monaco. I couldn't persuade her to stay.'

'Right. The two of you can always escape,' said Josef. 'Go abroad, while we have to stay here and deal with the whole mess.'

'I'm not planning to leave until everything has been settled,' Leon told him. 'And we're coming back.'

'No one's going anywhere,' said Percy. Until now he had listened in silence as he sat on a chair slightly removed from the others.

'What do you mean?' Sebastian was still indolently reclining against the sofa cushions.

'No one's going anywhere,' Percy repeated. Slowly he leaned down and rummaged in his briefcase, which he'd set on the floor next to his chair.

'Are you joking?' said Sebastian in disbelief. He was staring at the gun that Percy had placed on his lap.

Percy picked it up and pointed it at Sebastian. 'No. What do I have to joke about? You've taken everything from me.'

'But that's business. And you can't blame me. You're the one who squandered your entire inheritance.'

A shot rang out and everyone yelled. Surprised, Sebastian put his hand to his face, and blood trickled between his fingers. The bullet had grazed his left cheek and continued through the room and out the big picture window towards the sea. Their ears rang from the shot, and Leon realized that he was gripping the armrests of his wheelchair so hard that his fingers were practically locked.

'What the hell are you doing, Percy!' cried John. 'Are you out of your mind? Put down that gun before somebody gets hurt.'

'It's too late. Everything is too late.' Percy set the gun back on his lap. 'But before I kill every one of you, I want you to take responsibility for what you've done. On that point, I agree with Leon.'

'What do you mean? Aside from Sebastian, the rest of us are victims, the same as you.' John glared at Percy, but fear was clearly audible in his voice.

'We're all part of it. And it destroyed my life. But you bear the greatest responsibility, and you'll be the first to die.' Again he pointed the gun at Sebastian.

It was very quiet. The only sound they could hear was their own breathing.

'It must be one of them.' Ebba peered inside the chest. Then she moved away and threw up. Anna felt her stomach turn over, but she forced herself not to look away.

The chest contained a skeleton. A skull with all its teeth stared up at her from empty eye sockets. Short tufts of hair still clung to the bone, and she guessed that it was probably the skeleton of a man.

'I think you're right,' she said, turning to pat Ebba on the back.

Ebba uttered a few sobs before she crouched down and put her head between her knees, as if she thought she might faint.

'So they've been here the whole time.'

'Yes. I think the others are probably in there,' said Anna, nodding towards the two chests that were still closed.

'We need to open them,' said Ebba, standing up.

Anna glanced nervously towards the door. 'Shouldn't we wait until we find out if we're going to get out of here?'

'I need to know.' Ebba's eyes flashed.

'But Tobias . . .' said Anna.

Ebba shook her head. 'He's never going to let us out of here. I could tell by the look in his eyes. Besides, he probably thinks I'm already dead.'

Her words filled Anna with terror. She knew that Ebba was right. Tobias was not going to open the door. If they couldn't find a way out, they'd die here. Erica might have got worried and started asking questions, but it wouldn't do any good if she wasn't able to find them. This room could be anywhere on the island. And why would anybody discover it now if the police had missed it during their search for the Elvander family?

'Okay. Let's give it a try. Maybe there's something inside that might help us open the door.'

Ebba didn't reply but she immediately began kicking the lock on the chest to the right of the one they'd just opened. This padlock proved more stubborn.

'Wait a minute,' said Anna. 'Could I borrow your angel pendant? Maybe I could use it to unfasten the screws.'

Ebba took off the necklace and with some reluctance handed it to Anna, who began working at the screws. After removing the mountings from the two other chests, she glanced at Ebba, who gave her a brief nod, and then they each opened one of the chests.

'They're here. All of them,' said Ebba. This time she kept her eyes fixed on the remains of her family, which had been tossed inside like rubbish.

In the meantime Anna counted the skulls inside the three chests. Then she counted them again, just to be sure.

'There's one missing,' she said quietly.

Ebba gave a start. 'What do you mean?'

The blanket started to slip from Anna's shoulders, and she pulled it tighter.

'Five people disappeared, right?'

'Yes.'

'But there are only four skulls here. That means four bodies, unless one of them is missing its head,' said Anna.

Ebba grimaced. She leaned forward to count and then inhaled sharply. 'You're right. One is missing.'

'The question is: who?'

Anna stared at the skeletons. This was how she and Ebba were both going to end up if they didn't get out of here. She closed her eyes and pictured Dan and her children. Then she opened her eyes again. She refused to let that happen. Somehow they would find a way out of this place.

Next to her Ebba began to sob.

'Paula!' Patrik motioned for her to follow him into his office. Gösta and Erica had driven off to Fjällbacka, and

Mellberg had shut himself away to handle the media, or so he claimed.

'What's the matter?' Paula awkwardly sank down on to the visitor's chair.

'I don't think we'll get a chance to talk to John Holm today,' Patrik said, running his hand through his hair. 'The Göteborg police are raiding his house at this very moment. That was Kjell Ringholm who called. He and Sven Niklasson from *Expressen* are apparently on the scene.'

'Raiding his house? Why? And why weren't we informed?' She shook her head.

'Kjell didn't tell me any details. He just said it was a matter of national security, and that it was going to be big. You know how Kjell is.'

'Should we go out there?' said Paula.

'No. Especially not you, in your condition. If the Göteborg police have gone in, it's probably best that we keep out of the way for the time being, but I'm thinking of giving them a call to try to get some more information about what's going on. At any rate, it doesn't sound as if Holm will be available for quite some time.'

'I wonder what it's all about,' said Paula, trying to find a more comfortable position on the chair.

'I'm sure we'll hear soon enough. If both Kjell and Sven Niklasson are over there, the story will be in the papers any minute.'

'We could start with the others, in the meantime.'

'As I said, I'm afraid that will have to wait for a while.' Patrik stood up. 'I have to meet Gösta and go to Valö to find out what's been happening out there.'

'Leon's father,' said Paula pensively. 'How strange that the money came from him.'

'We'll have a talk with Leon as soon as Gösta and I get back,' replied Patrik. Thoughts were swirling through his

407

mind. 'Leon and Annelie . . . Maybe this has something to do with them, after all.'

He held out his hand to Paula, who gratefully accepted his help to get up.

'I'll see what I can dig up about Aron,' she said, and then plodded off down the hall.

Patrik picked up his summer jacket and left the office. He hoped that Gösta had succeeded in dropping Erica at home. He could picture her talking the whole way to Fjällbacka, trying to persuade Gösta to let her go with them to Valö. But Patrik wasn't about to give in. Though he wasn't as alarmed as Erica, he still felt that something wasn't right on the island. And he didn't want his wife out there if anything happened.

He had no sooner reached the car park than Paula called to him from the doorway. He turned.

'What is it?'

She was motioning him to come back, and when he saw the serious expression on her face, he hurried to comply.

'Gunfire. At Leon Kreutz's place,' she managed to gasp.

Patrik shook his head. Why did everything have to happen at once?

'I'll call Gösta and tell him to meet me there. Could you wake Mellberg? Right now we need all the help we can get.'

Sälvik lay spread out before them, the houses gleaming in the sunlight. From the bathing beach, which was only a few hundred metres away, came the sound of children playing and laughing. It was a popular place for families, and Erica had spent almost every day of the summer holiday out there while Patrik was working.

'I wonder what Victor is up to,' she said.

'Me too,' said Gösta. He hadn't been able to get hold

of the Coast Guard, so Erica had convinced him to come inside. She invited him to have a cup of coffee with her and Kristina while he waited to hear back from Victor.

'I'll try phoning him again,' he said, tapping in the number for the fourth time.

Erica studied him, trying to think of a way to persuade him to let her come along. Staying at home would drive her mad.

'No answer. Guess I have time to go to the toilet.' Gösta got up and left the room.

His mobile was on the table. Gösta had been gone only a minute when it started ringing, and Erica leaned forward to look at the display. It said 'Hedström' in big letters. She considered what to do. Kristina was in the living room, chasing after the kids, and Gösta was in the bathroom. She hesitated for a second and then picked up the mobile.

'Gösta's phone. This is Erica . . . He's in the bathroom. Shall I give him a message? . . . Gunfire? . . . Okay, I'll tell him . . . Yes, yes . . . I'll go get him right now. He'll be heading out in the next five minutes.'

She ended the call, and then a number of different options appeared in her mind. On the one hand, Patrik needed back-up; on the other hand, they needed to go out to Valö ASAP. She listened for Gösta's footsteps. He'd be back any minute, and she needed to make a decision before he appeared. She picked up her own mobile, and after a moment she tapped in a number. Martin answered on the second ring. In a low voice Erica explained the situation and what needed to be done, and he didn't hesitate for an instant. So that part was settled. Now all she had to do was give a performance worthy of an Oscar.

'Who was that on the phone?' asked Gösta.

'Patrik. He got hold of Ebba, and everything is fine out on Valö. She said that Anna was going to some country auctions today, so that's probably why she hasn't had time to call me back. But Patrik thought we should go out to the island and have a little talk with Ebba and Tobias.'

'We?'

'Yes. Patrik didn't think there was any danger now.'

'Are you sure?' Gösta was interrupted by the ringing of his mobile. 'Hi, Victor. Yes, I've been trying to get hold of you. We need a ride out to Valö. Preferably right now . . . Okay, we'll be there in five minutes.'

He ended the call and gave Erica a suspicious look.

'You can phone Patrik and ask him if you don't believe me,' she said with a smile.

'No, that won't be necessary. We might as well get going.'

'You're leaving again?' Kristina appeared, holding Noel in a tight grip. He was trying to get away, and from the living room came Anton's shrill scream at the same time as Maja began shouting: 'Grandma! Grandmaaaa!'

'I'll only be gone a short time, and then I'll take over,' said Erica, silently promising to think more kindly about her mother-in-law if only she were allowed to go out to Valö.

'Well, this is the last time I'm stepping in on such short notice. You can't assume that I'll give up my whole day like this, and keep in mind that I'm not really up to handling such a pace or such a noise level any more, and even though the children are lovely, I have to say that they could have better manners. And that's not my responsibility, that's something they need to be taught on a daily basis . . .'

Erica pretended not to hear as she uttered her thanks and slipped out to the front hall.

Minutes later they were on board the *MinLouis*, on their way to Valö. She tried to relax, telling herself that everything was fine, just as she'd told Gösta. But she didn't believe it. She knew instinctively that Anna was in trouble.

'Should I wait?' asked Victor as he smoothly brought the boat alongside the dock.

Gösta shook his head. 'No, that's not necessary. But we might need a ride back later on. Can we call you to come and get us?'

'Sure. Give me a ring when you're ready. I'll be making my rounds, checking out the area.'

Erica watched the boat move off, wondering whether it was a wise decision to let him go. But it was too late to change their minds.

'Hey, isn't that your boat?' said Gösta.

'Yes, it is. How strange.' Erica pretended to be surprised. 'Maybe Anna came back over here. Shall we go up to the house?' she said, starting off.

Gösta trudged along behind her, muttering to himself.

Up ahead they saw the beautiful, weather-beaten house. An ominous calm hovered over the building, and Erica felt herself go on high alert.

'Hello?' she shouted as they approached the wide stone steps. The front door stood open. No one answered.

Gösta stopped. 'That's odd, nobody's home. But Patrik said that Ebba was here?'

'Yes, that's what I understood.'

'Maybe they've gone down to the beach for a swim.' Gösta took a few steps to the side to peer around the corner.

'Maybe,' said Erica, going in the front door.

'I don't think we should just go in.'

'Why not? Come on. Hello?' she shouted again. 'Tobias? Is anybody home?'

Gösta reluctantly followed her into the front hall. It was very quiet, but all of a sudden Tobias appeared in the doorway to the kitchen. The police tape had been torn in half and was now hanging from the doorjamb.

'Hi,' he said dully.

Erica gave a start when she saw him. His hair hung in

411

lank strands, as if he'd been sweating profusely, and he had dark circles under his eyes. He was staring at them with a blank expression.

'Is Ebba here?' asked Gösta. A deep furrow had appeared between his brows.

'No, she went to visit her parents.'

Gösta gave Erica a surprised look. 'But Patrik just talked to her. He said she was here.'

Erica threw out her hands, and for an instant Gösta's expression turned stern, but he didn't say anything.

'She never came home. She phoned and said that she was taking the car and driving to Göteborg.'

Erica nodded but knew he was lying. Maria, who drove the mail boat, had said that she'd brought Ebba out to the island. Now she took a discreet look around, and her attention was caught by an object on the floor near the door. Ebba's bag. The one she'd brought with her when she came to stay for a couple of nights. That meant that she hadn't gone straight to Göteborg.

'Where is Anna?'

Tobias was still staring at them with that dead expression. He shrugged.

That settled it. Without another thought, Erica threw herself forward and grabbed the bag from the floor. Then she turned and ran up the stairs as she yelled:

'Anna! Ebba!'

No answer. She heard quick steps behind her, and she realized that Tobias was right on her heels. She made it to the top of the stairs and dashed into the bedroom, only to stop in the middle of the room. Next to a tray holding empty wine glasses and some leftover food was Anna's handbag.

First the boat, and now her handbag. Against her will Erica had to conclude that Anna was still on the island, just like Ebba.

She spun around to confront Tobias, but the words froze in her throat. There he stood, pointing a gun at her. Out of the corner of her eye, she saw Gösta come to an abrupt halt.

'Don't move,' snarled Tobias, taking a step forward. The muzzle of the gun was only a centimetre from Erica's forehead, and his hand was steady. 'And you – go over there!' He nodded to Erica's right.

Gösta obeyed at once. With his hands raised and his eyes fixed on Tobias, he moved over to stand next to Erica.

'Sit down!' Tobias said now.

Both of them sat down on the newly polished wood floor. Erica looked at the weapon. Where had Tobias got a gun?

'Put that down and we'll solve this together,' she ventured.

'How's that going to happen? My son is dead because of that bitch. How were you planning to solve that?'

For the first time there was a spark of life in his dead eyes, and Erica felt herself recoil from the madness she saw in front of her. Had it been there all along, behind Tobias's controlled facade? Or had this place on the island provoked it?

'My sister . . .' She was now so worried that she could hardly breathe. If only she knew that Anna was still alive.

'You'll never find them. Just like the others were never found.'

'The others? Are you talking about the Elvander family?' said Gösta.

Tobias didn't reply. He had squatted down, still pointing the gun at them.

'Is Anna alive?' asked Erica without expecting to get an answer.

Tobias smiled. Erica realized that her decision to lie to Gösta was the stupidest thing she'd ever done.

'What are you planning to do?' asked Gösta, as if he'd read Erica's mind.

Tobias shrugged but didn't say a word. Instead, he sat down on the floor cross-legged and continued to study them. It was as if he was waiting for something, only he wasn't sure what that might be. He seemed strangely calm. Only the gun and the cold gleam in his eyes ruined the effect. And somewhere on the island were Anna and Ebba. But were they dead or alive?

VALÖ 1973

Laura tossed and turned on the uncomfortable mattress. Why couldn't Inez and Rune have provided her with a better bed, considering how often she came to visit them? They needed to think about the fact that she was no longer young. And to top it off, she needed to pee.

She placed her feet on the floor and shivered. The November chill had set in, and it was hopeless trying to heat this old house. She suspected Rune of stinting on the heat in an attempt to keep costs down. He'd never been a particularly generous man. Little Ebba was sweet, at any rate, she had to admit that – but it was only pleasant to hold her for a short while. She'd never been fond of infants, and she possessed too little energy to spend much time with her granddaughter.

Cautiously Laura made her way across the wooden floorboards, which creaked under her weight. She'd begun putting on pounds at a distressing rate over the past few years, and the slender figure in which she'd always taken such pride was now a thing of the past. But why should she make any effort? She was usually alone in her flat, and the bitterness inside her grew with each day that passed.

Rune had not lived up to her expectations. It was true that he'd bought the flat for her, but she regretted not making a better match for her daughter. As beautiful as Inez was, she could have

415

had any man she liked. Rune Elvander was much too tight-fisted, and he made Inez work too hard. She'd become as thin as a rail, and she never had a moment to herself. If she wasn't cleaning, cooking, or helping Rune deal with the students, she was taking care of his children. The youngest was nice enough, but the two older ones were extremely unpleasant and quite shameless about it.

The steps creaked as Laura crept downstairs. It was a nuisance that her bladder could no longer make it through a whole night. It was especially miserable having to go outside to the privy in this cold. She paused. Someone was moving about on the ground floor of the house. She stopped to listen. The front door opened. Her curiosity was aroused. Who was awake, sneaking about in the night? There was no reason for anyone to go outside unless they were up to no good. Probably one of those spoiled brats involved in some mischief, but she would put a stop to that.

When she heard the door close in the front hall, she hurried down the rest of the stairs and pulled on her boots. She wrapped a warm shawl around her shoulders, opened the front door, and peered outside. It was hard to see anything in the dark, but when she stepped out on the stoop, she saw a shadow disappearing around the side of the house, on the left. This was going to take some subterfuge. She made her way down the steps, moving cautiously in case the frost had made them slippery. At the bottom she turned right instead of left. She would intercept whoever it was by coming from the opposite direction; that way she'd catch them in the act, whatever they were up to.

Slowly she slipped around the corner, keeping close to the wall. At the next corner she paused to see what was happening behind the house. Not a soul in sight. Laura frowned and peered through the darkness, disappointed. Where could they have gone? She tentatively took a few steps forward as she surveyed the property. Down to the beach? It was too risky for her to venture down there, she might stumble and fall. Besides, the doctor had warned her not to do anything strenuous. Her heart was fragile, and she wasn't supposed to overdo it. Shivering, she pulled the shawl tighter around her shoulders. The cold was starting to seep under her clothes, and her teeth were chattering.

Suddenly a dark figure appeared in front of her, and she jumped. Then she saw who it was.

'Oh, is that you? What are you doing out here, running around at this hour?'

The cold eyes made her shiver even more. They were as dark as the night. Slowly she began to back away, having realized her mistake. A few more steps. Only a few more and she'd turn the corner and be able to dash for the front of the house and the door. It wasn't far, but it might as well have been several kilometres. Terrified, she stared into those pitch-black eyes and knew that she would never enter that house again. She was suddenly reminded of Dagmar. The feeling was the same. She was powerless, caught, with no possibility of escape. Inside her chest, she felt something burst.

Patrik glanced at his watch. 'Where the hell is Gösta? He should have got here first.' He and Mellberg were waiting in the car, staring at Leon's house.

At that moment a familiar vehicle pulled up alongside, and Patrik saw to his surprise that Martin was behind the wheel.

'What are you doing here?' Patrik said as he got out of the car.

'Your wife rang and said there was a crisis and you needed my help.'

'What on earth . . .?' Patrik began but then stopped abruptly and pressed his lips together. Damn Erica. Of course she'd managed to dupe Gösta into taking her out to Valö. He was filled with both anger and concern. This was the last thing he needed right now. They had no idea what was happening inside Leon's house, which was what he needed to focus on at the moment. On the other hand, he was grateful that Martin had turned up. He looked haggard and tired, but in a crisis situation, even an exhausted Martin was better than a Gösta Flygare.

'So what's going on here?' Martin held up a hand to shade his eyes as he studied the house.

'Gunfire. That's all we know so far.'

'Who's inside?'

'We don't know that either.' Patrik felt his pulse quicken. As a police officer, this was the sort of thing he disliked most. They had too little information to assess the situation properly, and that was when things were most dangerous.

'Shouldn't we call for reinforcements?' said Mellberg from inside the car.

'No, I don't think there's time for that. We'll go over and ring the bell.'

Mellberg seemed about to protest, but Patrik spoke first.

'You can stay here, Bertil, and hold down the fort. Martin and I will handle this.' He turned to Martin, who nodded silently and took his service weapon from its holster.

'I drove past the station and picked up my gun. I thought I might need it.'

'Good.' Patrik took out his gun too, and then they cautiously approached the front door. He pressed the doorbell. The sound echoed inside the house, and then a voice called out:

'Come in. It's open.'

Patrik and Martin exchanged a surprised look. Then they went in. When they saw the group assembled in the living room, their surprise was even greater. There sat Leon, Sebastian, Josef, and John, as well as a grey-haired man whom Patrik assumed was Percy von Bahrn. He was holding a gun, and he refused to meet their eyes.

'What's going on here?' Patrik demanded to know. He was holding his service weapon down at his side, and he noticed that Martin was doing the same.

'Ask Percy,' said Sebastian.

'Leon summoned us here to put an end to the whole matter. I thought I'd take him at his word.' Percy's voice quavered. When Sebastian shifted position on the sofa, Percy gave a start and pointed the gun at him.

'Calm down, for Christ's sake.' Sebastian held up his hands.

'Put an end to what?' asked Patrik.

'The whole thing. Everything that happened. What should never have happened. What all of us did,' said Percy. He lowered the gun.

'What did you do?'

No one answered, so Patrik decided to help them out.

'During the interviews you all claimed that you'd been out fishing that day. But you can't catch mackerel at Easter.'

No one spoke. Finally Sebastian said with a snort: 'Typical city kids, to make a mistake like that.'

'You didn't offer any objections back then,' said Leon. He almost sounded amused.

Sebastian shrugged.

'Why did your father deposit money in the bank for Ebba while she was growing up?' Patrik asked Leon. 'Did you boys call him up on that day? A rich and powerful man with a network of contacts. Did he help you after you murdered the family? What happened? Did Rune go too far? Were you forced to kill the others because they were witnesses?' Patrik could hear how fierce he sounded, but he wanted to shake them up, get them to talk.

'Are you satisfied now, Leon?' jeered Percy. 'Here's your chance to put all the cards on the table.'

John Holm jumped to his feet. 'This is crazy. I refuse to get involved in any of this. I'm leaving.' He took a step forward, but Percy instantly turned to his right, pointed the gun at John, and pulled the trigger.

'What are you doing!' screamed John and sat back down. Patrik and Martin raised their weapons to aim at Percy, but lowered them when he continued to point his pistol at John. It was too risky.

'Next time you're the target. That's one legacy from

my father they can't take away. I used to begrudge the hours he forced me to spend practising my sharp-shooting. But I could shoot off that charming fringe of yours if I wanted to.' Percy cocked his head to one side and stared at John, whose face had turned ashen.

Only now did it occur to Patrik that the Göteborg police must have gone to John's house to find him. Most likely they had no idea that he was here.

'Take it easy, Percy,' said Martin calmly. 'We don't want anyone to get hurt. Nobody's going anywhere until we've settled this.'

'Was it about Annelie?' Patrik again turned to Leon. Why was the man hesitating if he really wanted to reveal what happened on that Easter weekend in 1974? Had he suddenly got cold feet? 'We think that she took her passport and fled abroad after the murders. Because the family were murdered, weren't they?'

Sebastian started to laugh.

'What's so funny?' asked Martin.

'Nothing. Absolutely nothing.'

'Was it your father who helped her disappear? Were you and Annelie sleeping together? Did everything fall apart when Rune found out? How did you get the other boys to help you and then keep quiet all these years?' Patrik motioned towards the group of middle-aged men. In his mind he saw the pictures of them that were taken after the disappearance. Their defiant expressions. Leon's natural air of authority. In spite of their greying hair and ageing faces, they were very much the same as back then. And they were still sticking together.

'Sure, tell them about Annelie.' Sebastian grinned. 'Since you're so keen on telling the truth. Tell them about Annelie.'

Patrik had a sudden flash of insight.

'I've already met Annelie, haven't I? It's Ia.'

No one said a word. They all turned to Leon with a mixture of fear and relief on their faces.

Leon slowly stretched his arms as he sat in his wheelchair. Then he turned towards Patrik so that the sun shone on the scarred side of his face, and said:

'I'll tell you about Annelie. And about Rune, Inez, Claes, and Johan.'

'Stop and think about what you're doing, Leon,' said John.

'I've already thought it through. It's time.'

He took a deep breath, but before he could say another word, the front door opened. And there stood Ia. She looked from one to the other, and then her eyes opened wide when she saw the gun in Percy's hand. For a moment she seemed to hesitate. Then she went over to her husband, put her hand on his shoulder, and said gently:

'You're right. It's impossible to keep running away.'

Leon nodded. Then he began to tell the story.

Anna was more worried about Ebba than about herself. Ebba's face was pale, and her neck was a fiery red with what looked like the marks from someone's hands. Tobias's hands. Anna's own neck did not feel tender. Had he drugged her? She didn't know, and that was the most frightening thing of all. She had fallen asleep in his arms, flushed with the feeling of acceptance and closeness, only to wake up here, lying on this cold stone floor.

'My mother is in there,' said Ebba, peering inside one of the chests.

'You can't be sure of that.'

'Only one of the skulls has long hair. It has to be my mother.'

'It could be your sister,' said Anna. She considered closing the lid, but Ebba had been wondering about her family for so long, and the contents of the chests provided some of the answers.

'What is this place?' asked Ebba as she continued to stare at the skeletons.

'I think it's some kind of air-raid shelter. And judging by the flag and uniforms, it must have been built during the Second World War.'

'It's so strange to think of them lying here all this time. Why didn't anyone ever find them?'

Ebba was starting to sound more and more preoccupied, and Anna realized that she would have to take charge if they were going to get out of here.

'We need to find something to prise open the door,' said Anna, giving Ebba a small shove. 'Why don't you have a rummage through the rubbish over there in the corner, and I'll . . .' She hesitated. 'I'll search the chests.'

Ebba gave her a horrified stare. 'But what if . . . what if they fall apart?'

'If we don't get the door open, we're going to die here,' said Anna calmly. 'There might be some tools in one of the chests. Either you have to do it, or I will. Take your pick.'

For a moment Ebba didn't move as she thought about what Anna had just said. Then she turned away and began rummaging through the rubbish heap. Anna didn't really think she'd find anything, but it would be good for Ebba to keep busy.

She took a deep breath and stuck her hand inside one of the chests. She felt sick to her stomach as she touched the bones. Dry, brittle hair tickled her skin, and she couldn't help letting out a shriek.

'What is it?' Ebba turned in alarm.

'Nothing,' said Anna. Then she steeled herself and continued her search. Her fingers scraped the wooden bottom of the chest, and she leaned forward to see if there was anything else down there. Suddenly she felt something hard, and she grabbed it between her index finger and thumb. It felt too small to be of much use, but she lifted it out all the same, to see what she'd found. A tooth. With a murmur of disgust, she dropped it back inside and wiped her hand on the blanket wrapped around her.

'Did you find anything?' asked Ebba.

'No, not yet.'

Anna forced herself to search through the second chest, and when she was done, she sank to her knees. There was nothing. They would never get out of here. They were going to die.

Then she made herself stand up again. There was one chest left, and she refused to give up, even though she shuddered at the thought of another search. Resolutely she moved over to the final chest. Ebba was huddled against the wall, crying. Anna glanced in her direction before she stuck her hand inside the chest. She swallowed hard as she reached for the wooden bottom, letting her fingertips move back and forth. She touched something. It felt like a stack of papers, although they seemed smoother on one side. She pulled out the bundle and held it up to the light.

'Ebba,' she said.

When she didn't get an answer, she went over to sit on the floor next to Ebba. Then she held out what she now saw were photographs.

'Look,' said Anna. Her fingers were practically itching to leaf through the pictures, but she suspected they were from Ebba's past. She should be the first one to see them.

With trembling hands Ebba took the Polaroids.

'What does this mean?' she said then, shaking her head.

She and Anna stared at the images, though they would have preferred not to. And they both realized that here was the explanation for what happened on that Easter weekend.

Tobias's attention was fading. His eyelids were heavy, his head drooped, and Erica saw that he was on the verge of falling asleep. She didn't dare look at Gösta. Tobias was still holding the gun in a tight grip, and it could be fatal to make any sudden move.

Finally his eyes fell closed. Slowly Erica turned her head towards Gösta as she held a finger to her lips. He nodded. She cast an enquiring glance at the doorway behind Tobias, but Gösta shook his head. No, she didn't think that would work either. If Tobias woke up as they crept past, there was a risk that he'd start shooting.

She paused to think. They needed to get help. Again she caught Gösta's eye and pretended to hold a phone to her ear. Gösta instantly understood and began rummaging through his jacket pockets, but then he gave her a resigned shrug. He hadn't brought his mobile. Erica scanned the room. Anna's handbag was a short distance away. Slowly she slid closer. Tobias twitched suddenly, and she froze for a moment, but he went on sleeping, his head bowed towards his chest. Then her fingers touched the bag, and she slid a few more centimetres to the side and managed to grab the handle. She held her breath as she picked up the bag without making a sound. Cautiously she searched the contents as Gösta watched. He suppressed a cough, and she frowned at him. They didn't need Tobias to wake up now.

Finally she found Anna's mobile. She made sure that the ringer was turned off, but then realized that she didn't know the four-digit code. All she could do was guess. She tapped in Anna's birth date. The word 'error' appeared on the display, and she silently swore. Anna might not have changed the code that came with the phone, but she couldn't think about that. She had two more attempts.

Erica thought for a moment and then tried Adrian's birthday. 'Error' again. Then she had an idea. There was one other date that was significant in Anna's life: the fateful day when Lucas died. Erica tapped in those four digits, and a green light miraculously welcomed her into the phone's world.

She glanced at Gösta, who sighed with relief. She had to act fast. Tobias could wake up at any moment. Thank God she and Anna had the same type of phone, so she easily located the menu. She began typing a text message, brief but with enough information so that Patrik would understand the danger. Tobias stirred restlessly, and just as she was about to send the message, she stopped and added a few more recipients. If Patrik didn't see it at once, someone else would and take action. She pressed the 'send' button and then put the bag back where she'd found it. She hid the mobile under her right thigh so she could get to it if necessary, but Tobias wouldn't be able to see it when he awoke. Now all they could do was wait.

Kjell leaned against the car, staring at one of the police vehicles as it drove off. The raid had failed. They had only John Holm's wife in the back seat.

'Where the hell is John?'

The area surrounding the house was still bustling with activity. The police were checking every nook and cranny, and the *Expressen* photographer was frantically trying to capture it all. He wasn't allowed to get too close, but with the lens he had at his disposal, that didn't bother him.

'Do you think he fled the country?' said Sven Niklasson. Sitting in Kjell's car, he'd already written the first version of his article, which he'd sent off to his editor.

Kjell knew that he too should be writing up his report. In fact, he should already be on his way over to the *Bohusläningen* office, where he would no doubt be heralded as the hero of the day. When he rang to tell them what had happened, the editor-in-chief had cheered so loudly that he nearly burst Kjell's eardrum. But he didn't want to leave until he'd found out where Holm had gone.

'No, I don't think he would leave without Liv. And she seemed surprised to see the police. If she didn't know about it, then John didn't either. They're said to be a very tight team.'

'But in a small town like this, rumours must spread faster than the wind, so even if he hadn't already taken off, there's a big risk he'll do that now.' Sven turned to gaze at the house with a grim expression.

'Hmm . . .' said Kjell, not really paying attention. In his mind he went over everything he knew about Holm, speculating where he might have gone. The police had already checked the boathouse without finding him there.

'Have you heard anything more about how things went in Stockholm?' asked Kjell.

'For once the Säpo security forces and the police seem to have successfully collaborated, and the raid went off like clockwork. All of the responsible parties were taken into custody without incident. Those guys aren't so tough when the shit hits the fan.'

'I guess not.' Kjell was thinking about the battle cries that would fill the newspapers over the next few days. And not just in Sweden; the rest of the world would once again voice incredulity that something like this could happen in Sweden, the country that so many people regarded as almost absurdly orderly.

His mobile rang.

'Hi, Rolf . . . Well, there's a bit of confusion here. They don't know where Holm is . . . What did you say? Gunshots? Okay, we'll be right over.' He ended the conversation and nodded to Sven. 'Hop in. There are reports of gunshots at Leon Kreutz's house. Let's go.'

'Leon Kreutz?'

'One of the boys who went to school with Holm on Valö.'

'I don't know. Holm might turn up here at any moment.'

Kjell leaned his arm on the roof of the car and looked at Sven.

'Don't ask me why, but I think Holm is at Kreutz's house. So make up your mind. Are you coming with me or not? The Tanum police are already there.'

Sven opened the passenger door and got in. Kjell got behind the wheel, slammed the door, and drove off. He knew he was right. The boys from Valö had been hiding something, and now it was going to be revealed. He definitely didn't want to miss it when the news exploded.

VALÖ 1974

Inez felt as if someone was always watching her. That was the only way she could describe it. She'd had that feeling ever since the morning when her mother was found dead. Nobody knew why Laura had gone outside in the middle of that cold November night. The doctor who came to examine her body concluded that her heart had simply given out. He had warned her that something like that could happen.

But Inez had her doubts. Something changed in the house after Laura died, and she could feel it, no matter where she was. Rune had become even more aloof and stern, and Annelie and Claes started defying her more openly. It was as if Rune wasn't paying attention, and that made them bolder.

At night Inez could hear crying in the boys' dormitory. Not loud, barely audible in fact. Someone seemed to be doing his best to muffle his sobs.

She was scared. It had taken several months for her to identify the emotion she had long been trying to put into words. Something was terribly wrong. They were all circling around it, yet she knew that if she mentioned her concern to Rune, he would merely grunt dismissively. But she could tell that he too was aware that things were not as they should be.

Fatigue was also taking its toll on her. She was worn out from all the work she did in the school in addition to caring for Ebba, and it was proving to be such a strain to keep silent about something that was supposed to remain a secret.

'Mammaaaaa,' whined Ebba from her playpen. She was holding on to the railing, her eyes fixed on her mother.

Inez ignored her. She had no energy left. The child demanded so much that she simply couldn't give her, and besides, she was a constant reminder of Rune. Ebba's nose and mouth were just like Rune's, and that made it hard for Inez to love the little girl. Inez tended to her needs, changing her nappies, feeding her, holding her and comforting her, but that was as much as she could do. Fear occupied too great a place in her heart.

Fortunately there was something else. Something that gave her the strength to hold out a little longer, that prevented her from running away, taking the boat to the mainland and leaving everything behind. In those dark hours when she toyed with the idea of fleeing, she never dared ask herself whether she would take Ebba along. She wasn't sure that she wanted to know the answer.

'Can I pick her up?' Johan's voice made Inez jump. She hadn't heard him come into the laundry room where she was folding sheets.

'Of course you can,' she said. Johan was another reason why she stayed. He loved her, and he loved his little sister. And the feeling was mutual. Whenever Ebba caught sight of Johan, her whole face would light up. Right now she was holding out her arms to him as she stood in her playpen.

'Come on, Ebba,' said Johan. She put her arms around his neck and allowed him to lift her out. Then she pressed her face close to his.

Inez stopped folding the laundry to watch them. She was surprised to feel a pang of jealousy. Ebba never looked at her with the same sort of unconditional love. Instead, there was always a mixture of sorrow and yearning in her eyes.

'Let's go out and watch the birds,' said Johan as he rubbed

his nose against Ebba's, making her laugh. 'Can I take her outside?'

Inez nodded. She trusted Johan and knew that he would never let anything happen to Ebba.

'Of course, you go ahead.' She went back to folding the laundry. Ebba began laughing and babbling merrily as they left the room.

After a while Inez couldn't hear them any more. The silence echoed between the walls, and she sat down on the floor, resting her head on her knees. The house held her in such a tight grip that she could hardly breathe. The feeling that she was a prisoner grew stronger with every day that passed. They were heading for a precipice, and there was nothing, absolutely nothing that she could do about it.

❖

Patrik wasn't going to answer his mobile when it started ringing. Percy looked as if he might fall apart at any moment, and since he still held a gun in his hand, that might be disastrous. At the same time, they were all mesmerized by Leon's voice. He was talking about Valö, about how the boys had become friends, about the Elvander family and Rune, and about how everything slowly but surely began to go wrong. Ia stood next to him, stroking his hand. After giving them the background for his story, Leon seemed to hesitate, and Patrik realized that he was approaching the event that had ended the boys' friendship.

Soon they'd hear the truth. But Patrik was so worried about Erica that he couldn't help glancing at his mobile. An incoming message from Anna. He quickly tapped on the display. When he read what it said, his hand started shaking uncontrollably.

'We have to go out to Valö! Right now!' he shouted, interrupting Leon in mid-sentence.

'What's happened?' asked Ia.

Martin nodded and said, 'Calm down and tell us what's going on.'

'I think Tobias was the one who set the fire and shot at Ebba. And now Gösta and Erica are out there with

432

him. Anna and Ebba have disappeared. Nobody's heard from either of them since yesterday . . .'

Patrik could hear that he was babbling, so he made an effort to regain his composure. If he was going to be of any help to Erica, he needed a clear head.

'Tobias has a gun, and we think it's the same one that was used on that Easter weekend. Does that tell you anything?'

The men exchanged glances. Then Leon held out a key.

'He must have found the air-raid shelter. That's where the gun was. Right, Sebastian?'

'Yes. I haven't touched anything since the day we locked the door. I don't understand how he could have got inside. That's the only key, as far as I know.'

'That doesn't mean there couldn't be others.' Patrik stepped forward and took the key. 'Where is this air-raid shelter?'

'In the basement, behind a secret door. It's impossible to find if you don't know where to look,' said Leon.

'Is that where Ebba might be?' Ia had turned very pale.

'That's a reasonable guess,' said Patrik, heading for the front door.

Martin pointed at Percy. 'What do we do about him?'

Patrik turned, walked straight over to Percy, and took away the gun before he could even react. 'That's the end of this nonsense. We'll straighten everything out later. Martin, you call for back-up while we drive, and I'll phone the Coast Guard to tell them we need a lift. Which one of you is going out there to show us where this air-raid shelter is?'

'I'll go,' said Josef, getting up.

'I'll go too,' said Ia.

'One person is enough.'

Ia shook her head. 'I'm coming too, and there's nothing you can say that will stop me.'

'Okay, come on then.' Patrik motioned for them to follow.

On the way out to the cars, he practically collided with Mellberg.

'Is John Holm inside?' asked Mellberg.

Patrik nodded. 'Yes, but we have to go out to Valö. Erica and Gösta are in trouble.'

'Oh?' said Mellberg, puzzled. 'But I've just been talking to Kjell and Sven here, and apparently the Göteborg police are looking for John. They don't know that he's here, so I thought . . .'

'He's all yours,' said Patrik.

'Where are you going?' Kjell Ringholm came over to join them, along with a blond man who seemed vaguely familiar.

'Another police matter. If you're looking for John Holm, he's inside. Mellberg is at your disposal.'

Then Patrik ran for the car. Martin was close on his heels, but Josef and Ia were slow to catch up, and Patrik impatiently held the back door open for them. It was against all regulations to take civilians along to a potentially dangerous situation, but he needed their help.

During the boat ride out to Valö, he paced restlessly in the bow, as if that might get them there faster. Behind him Martin was talking to Josef and Ia, instructing them to keep out of the way as best they could and follow directions. He couldn't help smiling. Over the years Martin had developed from a high-strung and tense cadet into a stable and reliable officer.

As they approached Valö, Patrik gripped the railing hard. At least once a minute he glanced at his mobile, but no more messages had come in. He had considered sending a reply to say they were on their way, but he decided not to, in case it gave away the fact that Erica had a phone.

He noticed that Ia was watching him. There were so many things he wanted to ask her. Why had she fled and never returned until now? What role had she played in the death of her father and the rest of the family? But those questions would have to wait. There'd be time enough later on to get to the bottom of things. Right now he needed to focus on the fact that Erica was in danger. Nothing else mattered. He'd been so close to losing her in the car accident a year and a half ago. That was when he realized how much he depended on her, and what a huge place she had in his life and his future.

When they jumped ashore, he and Martin both took out their service weapons, as if on cue. They motioned for Josef and Ia to keep behind. Then they cautiously started walking towards the house.

Percy was staring at some indefinable point on the wall. 'Oh well,' he said.

'What the hell's the matter with you?' John ran his hand through his blond hair. 'Were you planning to shoot all of us?'

'Hmm. Actually I was only thinking of shooting myself. I just wanted to have a little fun with you first. Scare you a bit.'

'Why would you want to kill yourself?' Leon looked at his old friend with a tender expression. Percy was so fragile in spite of his haughty manner, and Leon had noticed even back on Valö that he might fall to pieces at any time. It was a miracle that he hadn't. It had been easy to see that Percy would have a hard time living with the memories, but perhaps he'd also inherited a capacity for denial.

'Sebastian has stripped me of everything. And Pyttan has left me. I'm going to be a laughing-stock.'

Sebastian threw out his hands. 'Who uses the word "laughing-stock" these days?'

They were like children. Leon could clearly see that now. They were all suffering from arrested development. They were still out there on the island, living in their memories. Compared to them, he was actually much better off. He looked at these men and saw them as the boys they once were. And no matter how odd it might seem, he felt a kind of love for them. They had shared an experience that had shaken them to the core and shaped their lives. The bond between them was so strong that it could never be severed. He'd always known that he would return, that this day would arrive, but he hadn't thought that Ia would be at his side when it happened. Her courage surprised him. Maybe he had deliberately chosen to underestimate her so as not to feel guilt about her sacrifice, which was greater than anyone else's.

And why was Josef the one who stood up and offered to go along? Leon thought that he knew the answer. The minute Josef had come in the door today, Leon had seen in his eyes that he was ready to die. It was a look that he recognized. He'd seen it on Mount Everest when they got caught in a sudden storm, and in the life raft after the ship went down in the Indian Ocean. The look in the eyes of a person who had let go of life.

'I have no intention of taking part in any of this,' said John, getting up and straightening the creases in his trousers. 'This farce has been going on long enough. I'll deny everything. There's no proof; all they have is your word for it.'

'John Holm?' said a voice from the doorway.

John turned.

'Bertil Mellberg? That's all we need,' he said. 'What do you want? If you're planning to talk to me with that same tone of voice as before, you'll have to speak to my lawyer.'

'I have no comment about that.'

'Fine. Then I'm going home. Nice to see you.' John started for the door, but Mellberg blocked his way. Behind him stood three men, and one of them was holding a big camera, snapping one picture after another.

'You're going to have to come with me,' said Mellberg.

John sighed. 'What kind of nonsense is this? It's nothing but harassment, pure and simple, and I promise you there will be repercussions.'

'You are hereby arrested for conspiring to commit murder, and you will come with me immediately,' said Mellberg, smiling broadly.

Leon watched the whole scene from his wheelchair, while Percy and Sebastian also eagerly followed what was happening. John's face was now bright red, and he made an effort to push past, but Mellberg shoved him up against the wall and then clumsily brought his wrists together so he could put the cuffs on him. The photographer carried on snapping pictures as the two other men stepped closer.

'What do you have to say about the fact that the police have uncovered a plot that you and the Friends of Sweden call "Project Gimle"?' asked one of them.

John's knees buckled, and Leon watched with even greater interest. Sooner or later everyone was held accountable for their actions. He felt a sudden flash of worry about Ia, but he pushed it aside. No matter what happened, it was predestined. She needed to do this in order to be rid of the guilt and regret that had forced her to live all these years for his sake alone. Her love for him had bordered on obsession, but he knew that she had burned with the same fire that had driven him to take on each new challenge. And finally they had burned together, sitting there in the car on that steep slope in Monaco. They had no choice but to see this through to the end, together. He was proud of her, he loved her, and now she would find her way back home at last. Today everything would finally be over, and he hoped that it would be a happy ending.

Tobias slowly opened his eyes and looked at them.

'I was so tired.'

Neither Erica nor Gösta said a word. Suddenly Erica too felt overcome with weariness. The adrenalin had seeped out of her body, and the thought that her younger sister might be dead made her limbs feel as heavy as lead. All she wanted to do was to lie down on the wooden floor and curl up into a ball. Close her eyes, fall asleep, and wake up when this whole thing was over. One way or another.

She'd noticed that the display on Anna's mobile was blinking. Dan. Good Lord, he must be beside himself with worry after reading the message she'd sent. But there was no reply from Patrik. Maybe he was so busy with something that he hadn't yet seen it.

Tobias continued to study them. His whole body was relaxed, his expression indifferent. Erica regretted not asking Ebba more about what had happened to their son. His death must have set something in motion, until Tobias finally slid into insanity. If only she knew what happened, she might have been able to talk to the man. They couldn't just sit here, waiting for Tobias to kill them. And she had no doubt that murder was his intention. She had realized that as soon as she saw the cold look in his eyes. Gently she said:

'Tell us about Vincent.'

At first he didn't answer. She was aware only of Gösta's breathing and the sound of distant motorboats. She waited, and finally he said in a flat voice:

'He's dead.'

'What happened?'

438

'It was Ebba's fault.'

'Why was it Ebba's fault?'

'I never really understood it until now.'

'Did she kill him?' Erica asked, holding her breath. Out of the corner of her eye, she saw that Gösta was following the conversation intently. 'Is that why you tried to kill Ebba?'

Tobias was playing with the gun, shifting it from one hand to the other.

'I didn't mean for the fire to get so big,' he said, placing the gun on his lap again. 'I only wanted her to realize that she needed me. That I could protect her.'

'Was that also why you shot at her?'

'Ebba needed to understand that she and I had to stick together. But it didn't matter. I know that now. She manipulated me so that I wouldn't see the obvious. That she killed him.' He nodded, as if to add emphasis to his words, and his expression scared Erica so badly that it was all she could do to stay calm.

'She killed Vincent?'

'Yes, she did. And I finally understood everything after she went to stay with you. She inherited the guilt. That much evil can't simply disappear.'

'Are you talking about her great-great-grandmother? The Angelmaker?' said Erica in surprise.

'Yes. Ebba said that she drowned the children in a basin and buried them in the cellar because she thought nobody wanted them, that no one would ever come back to get them. But I wanted Vincent. I went looking for him, but he was already gone. She drowned him. He was buried with the other dead children and couldn't come back up.' Tobias spat out the words, leaving a trail of saliva trickling from the corner of his mouth.

Erica realized that it would do no good to try talking to him. Different realities had merged, creating a strange shadowland where he could not be reached. Seized with panic, she glanced across at Gösta. His resigned expression told her that he had come to the same conclusion. All they could do was pray and hope that they'd somehow survive this situation.

'Shh,' said Tobias suddenly, straightening up.

Both Erica and Gösta flinched when they saw him move.

'Somebody's coming.' Tobias grabbed the gun and jumped to his feet. 'Shh,' he said again, putting his finger to his lips.

He dashed over to the window and peered out. For a moment he stood still, as if considering his options. Then he turned and pointed at Gösta and Erica.

'You two stay here. I'm going now. I need to guard them. They can't be allowed to find them.'

'What are you talking about?' Erica couldn't stop herself from asking. The hope that someone was on the way to help them was mixed with the fear that Anna's life was in danger, if it wasn't already too late. 'Where's my sister? You have to tell me where Anna is.' Her voice rose to a falsetto.

Gösta placed his hand on Erica's arm to calm her.

'We'll wait here, Tobias. We're not going anywhere,' he said. 'We'll be here when you get back.' He kept his eyes fixed on Tobias.

Finally Tobias nodded, turned on his heel, and rushed downstairs. Erica wanted to jump up and run after him, but Gösta gripped her arm firmly and hissed:

'Calm down. We need to look out the window first, to see where he's going.'

'But Anna . . .' she said in despair, trying to pull her arm loose.

Gösta refused to yield. 'Stop and think before rushing into this. We'll check outside, then we'll go downstairs

440

and find whoever it is who just arrived. Probably Patrik and the others, and then we'll get them to help.'

'Okay,' said Erica, as she stood up. Her legs felt wobbly and numb.

Cautiously she and Gösta peered outside, trying to see Tobias.

'Do you see anyone?'

'No,' said Gösta. 'Do you?'

'No. He couldn't have gone down to the dock, because he'd run right into the arms of whoever's coming here.'

'He must have gone around to the back of the house. Where else could he have gone?'

'I don't see him, at any rate. I'm going downstairs now.'

Cautiously Erica made her way down to the front hall. The house was quiet. She didn't hear any voices, but she knew that they would be trying to approach as soundlessly as possible. She peered out the open front door and felt sobs rise up in her throat. There was no one there.

At that instant she noticed something moving among the trees. She squinted to get a better look and relief welled up inside of her. It was Patrik, and right behind him were Martin and two other people. It took a moment for her to recognize Josef Meyer. Next to him was an elegantly dressed woman. Could that be Ia Kreutz? She waved so that Patrik would see her and then went back inside the house.

'We'll stay here,' she told Gösta, who had come downstairs.

They took up position close to the wall so that they wouldn't be visible through the doorway. Tobias could be anywhere, and she didn't want to risk becoming a target.

'Where could he have gone?' said Gösta. 'Do you think he could still be inside the house?'

Erica realized that he was right, and she glanced around

441

in panic, fearing that Tobias might appear at any second and shoot them dead. But he was nowhere to be seen.

When Patrik and Martin finally came to join them, Erica looked into Patrik's eyes and saw both relief and concern.

'Tobias?' he whispered. Erica quickly told him what had happened when Tobias noticed that someone was coming.

Patrik nodded. Then he and Martin made a quick tour of the ground floor with their guns raised. When they came back to the front hall, they shook their heads. Ia and Josef hadn't moved. Erica wondered what they were doing here.

'I don't know where Anna and Ebba are. Tobias babbled something about needing to guard them. Do you think he's locked them up somewhere?' She couldn't hold back a sob.

'That's the door to the basement,' said Josef, pointing to a door down the hall.

'What's down there?' asked Gösta.

'We'll explain later. There's no time now,' said Patrik. 'Stay behind us. And you two stay here,' he said to Erica and Ia.

Erica was about to protest, but gave up when she saw Patrik's expression.

'We're going down there,' said Patrik, casting one last look at Erica. She saw that he was just as scared as she was about what they might find.

VALÖ, EASTER EVE 1974

Everything was supposed to be the same as usual. That was what Rune expected. Most of the students had gone home for the holiday, and she had timidly asked whether the remaining boys might have Easter lunch with them, but Rune hadn't even deigned to answer her. Naturally Easter lunch was only for the family.

She'd spent the last two days cooking: roast lamb, devilled eggs, poached salmon . . . Rune's wishes were endless, although 'wishes' was not the right word. They were demands.

'Carla always made these dishes. Every year,' he'd told her when he handed Inez the list for their first Easter together.

She knew there was no use protesting. If Carla had done it, that was how it had to be done. God forbid she should do anything different.

'Could you put Ebba in her highchair, Johan?' Inez said as she set the big roast lamb on the table. She prayed that she had cooked it properly.

'Does she really have to be here? She'll only make a fuss.' Annelie came sauntering in and sat down at the table.

'What do you suggest I do with her?' said Inez. After slaving away in the kitchen, she was in no mood for her stepdaughter's caustic remarks.

'I don't know, but it's disgusting to have her here at the table. It makes me want to throw up.'

Inez felt something snap inside of her. 'If it's that difficult for you, maybe you shouldn't eat with the rest of us,' she retorted.

'Inez!'

She jumped. Rune had come into the dining room, and his face was bright red.

'What did you just say? My daughter's not welcome at the table?' His voice was ice cold as he fixed his eyes on his wife. 'In this family, everyone is welcome at the table.'

Annelie didn't say a word, but Inez saw that her father's angry remarks, offered in her defence, made the girl so gleeful that she was about to burst.

'I'm sorry. I wasn't thinking.' Inez turned and then set the dish of potatoes on the table. But inside she was boiling. She wanted to scream out loud, obey her heart, and run away. She didn't want to be stuck in this hellish place any longer.

'Ebba spit up a little,' said Johan with concern as he wiped his little sister's chin with a napkin. 'She isn't sick, is she?'

'No, she probably just ate too much baby formula,' said Inez.

'That's good,' he replied, although he didn't sound convinced. He's getting more and more protective, thought Inez, wondering again how he could have turned out so different from his siblings.

'Roast lamb. I'm sure it's not as good as Mamma's,' said Claes, sitting down next to Annelie. She giggled and gave him a wink, but he pretended to ignore her. Those two should have been bosom buddies, but Claes didn't seem to care about anyone. Except his mother. He was always talking about her.

'I've done the best I could,' said Inez. Claes snorted.

'Where have you been?' asked Rune, reaching for the potatoes. 'I was looking for you. Olle unloaded the boards I asked him to get. I need you to help me bring them up from the dock.'

Claes shrugged. 'I was taking a walk. I can fetch the boards later.'

'Right after lunch,' said Rune, although he seemed satisfied with his son's explanation.

444

'It should be more pink,' said Annelie, wrinkling her nose at the piece of lamb that she'd put on her plate.

Inez clenched her teeth. 'Our oven isn't great. The temperature is uneven. As I said, I did my best.'

'Yuck,' said Annelie, pushing the meat aside. 'Could I have some gravy?' she said to Claes, since the gravy bowl was on his left.

'Sure,' he said, reaching for it.

'Whoops . . .' He was staring at Inez. The gravy bowl had landed on the floor with a crash, and brown gravy spilled all over, seeping down through the cracks in the floorboards. Inez looked him in the eye. She knew that he'd done it on purpose. And he knew that she knew. 'That was clumsy of you,' said Rune, peering at the mess. 'You'd better wipe it up, Inez.'

'Right,' she said with a strained smile. Of course it never occurred to him that Claes should clean up the mess he'd made.

'And could you bring us some more gravy?' said Rune as she headed for the kitchen.

She turned around. 'That's all there is.'

'Carla always had a little extra in the kitchen, in case we ran out.'

'But I don't. I put all of it in the gravy bowl.'

After she'd wiped up the mess, getting down on all fours next to Claes's chair, she went back to her seat at the table. Her food had gone cold, but it didn't matter. She no longer had any appetite.

'That was really good, Inez,' said Johan, holding out his plate for another helping. 'You're a great cook.'

His eyes were so blue, so innocent, that she almost cried. As she put more food on his plate, he fed Ebba, using her little silver spoon.

'Here come some good potatoes. Mmm, they're really yummy,' he said, and his face lit up when Ebba opened her mouth and swallowed a bite.

Claes laughed sarcastically. 'What a bloody wimp!'

'Don't talk like that to your brother,' snapped Rune. 'He gets the highest marks in all his classes, and he's smarter than the two of you put together. You haven't exactly been a model student, so I think you should speak politely to your brother until you show that you've got some brains in your head. Mamma would have laughed if she saw your marks and how incompetent you've turned out to be.'

Claes flinched, and Inez saw the tiny veins in his temples begin to throb. His eyes were as dark as could be.

For a moment no one spoke at the table. Even Ebba didn't make the faintest sound. Claes was staring at Rune, and Inez clenched her fists in her lap. She was witnessing a power struggle, and she wasn't sure that she wanted to see how it would end.

For several minutes father and son simply stared at each other. Then Claes looked away.

'Sorry, Johan,' he said.

Inez shivered. His voice was filled with hatred, and she knew that she ought to obey her instincts. There was still time for her to get up and flee. She should seize the opportunity, no matter what the consequences might be.

'Excuse me for disturbing you in the middle of lunch. But I need to have a few words with you, Rune. It's urgent.' Leon was standing in the doorway with his head bowed politely.

'Can't it wait? We're still eating,' said Rune with a frown. Having his meals interrupted was something he wouldn't tolerate, even under normal circumstances.

'I realize that, and I wouldn't ask if it wasn't important.'

'What's this all about?' said Rune, wiping his mouth on his napkin.

Leon hesitated. Inez glanced at Annelie. She couldn't take her eyes off the boy.

'There's an emergency at home. Pappa asked me to speak to you.'

'Oh, your father? Why didn't you say so.'

446

Rune got up from the table. He always had time for the wealthy parents of his students.

'Keep on eating. This won't take long,' he said, moving towards the doorway where Leon was standing.

Inez's eyes were fixed on Rune. She felt her stomach churn. Everything that she'd been through over the past few months settled into a hard knot. Something was about to happen.

He gazed out at the passing landscape. In the front seat that irritating fool Mellberg was having a heated discussion on the phone. It sounded as if he was refusing to turn him over to the police in Fjällbacka and instead insisted on driving the whole way to Göteborg. It didn't make any difference, one way or the other.

John wondered how Liv was going to handle this. Like him, she had staked everything on the plan. Maybe they should have been satisfied with what they'd already achieved, but the temptation had been too great to change everything in one fell swoop and accomplish what no other nationalist party had ever done before in Sweden: attain a dominant political position. In Denmark the Danish People's Party had carried out many of the things that the Friends of Sweden dreamed of doing. Had it been so wrong to try to speed up the process?

Project Gimle had been intended to unite all Swedes so that together they could finally restore the country. It was a simple plan, and for all that he'd occasionally worried about it, he had been convinced that it would succeed. Now everything was ruined. Everything they'd built would be torn down and forgotten in the after-shocks of Gimle. No one would understand that they had tried to create a new future for Sweden.

It had all started with a suggestion that was put forward in jest within the inner circle. Liv had immediately seen the potential. She had explained to John and the others that it might be possible to bring about a change swiftly, a change that would otherwise take more than a generation to occur. In the course of one night, they would start a revolution, mobilizing Swedes in a battle against the enemies who had wormed their way into the country and were in the process of breaking down society. She had presented a logical argument, and the price had been deemed reasonable.

A single bomb. Placed in the middle of the Sture Gallery during rush hour. Afterwards, all evidence collected by the police would point to Muslim terrorists. They had been working on the plan for more than a year, going over all the details and meticulously ensuring that it would be impossible to draw any other conclusion – everyone would believe that Islamists had carried out an attack in the very heart of Stockholm, in the heart of Sweden. People would be frightened, and their fear would make them angry. Then the Friends of Sweden would step forward, gently take them by the hand and confirm their fears. They would tell the people what they needed to do in order to feel safe again. In order to live as Swedes.

Now the plan would never be realized. John's worries about what Leon was about to reveal seemed ludicrous and absurd compared to the scandal that would now engulf him. He would be at the very centre of things, but this was not how he'd envisioned it. Instead of being his greatest triumph, Project Gimle was to be his undoing.

Ebba studied the photographs that she'd spread out on the floor. The naked boys stared blankly at the camera.

449

'They look so helpless.' She turned away.

'This has nothing to do with you,' said Anna, patting Ebba's arm.

'It would have been better if I'd never found out anything about my family. The only picture I'll have of them now, if we ever get . . .'

She didn't finish the sentence, and Anna knew that she didn't want to say out loud what she was thinking. That they might never get out of this place.

Again Ebba turned to the photos. 'They must be Pappa's students. If this is what he subjected them to, then I can understand it if they killed him.'

Anna nodded. The boys wanted to use their hands to hide their shame, but the photographer refused to allow it. Their anguish was so evident on their faces, and she could only imagine the rage that such humiliation must have fostered.

'What I don't understand is why all of them had to die,' said Ebba.

Suddenly they heard footsteps outside. They stood up and stared, wide-eyed, at the door as someone fumbled with the lock.

'It must be Tobias,' said Ebba, terrified.

Instinctively they looked around for somewhere to escape, but they were trapped like rats. Slowly the door swung open and Tobias came in, holding a gun.

'You're alive?' he said to Ebba. Anna was shocked to see how indifferent he was to whether his wife was alive or dead.

'Why are you doing this?' Ebba moved towards him, sobbing.

'Stop!' He raised the gun and pointed it at her, and she instantly stopped in her tracks.

'Let us out of here.' Anna tried to catch his attention. 'We promise not to say anything.'

'You think I'd believe that? It doesn't matter anyway. I have no wish to . . .' He stopped abruptly, peering at the bones sticking out of the chests. 'What's that?'

'Ebba's family,' said Anna.

Tobias couldn't tear his eyes away from the skeletons. 'Have they been here the whole time?'

'Yes, apparently they have.'

Anna hoped that Tobias would be so shaken that she'd be able to reach him somehow. She leaned down, which prompted him to gasp and swing the gun in her direction.

'I only want to show you something.' Anna picked up the photos and handed them to Tobias, who took them with a sceptical expression.

'What's this?' he said, and for the first time his voice sounded normal.

Anna could feel her heart pounding. The sensible, sane Tobias was still in there somewhere. He held the pictures closer so he could study them.

'My father must have done that to them,' said Ebba. Her hair hung in her face, and it was apparent from her posture that she had given up.

'Rune?' said Tobias, but then he flinched when they heard voices approaching. Swiftly he slammed the door shut.

'Who's there?' asked Anna.

'They're going to ruin everything,' said Tobias. His expression had changed, and Anna could see that there was no use hoping any more. 'But they're not getting in here. I have the key. It was above the doorframe here in the basement, long forgotten and rusty. I tried it in every lock, but it didn't fit. Then a week ago, just by accident, I found the entrance. It was so ingeniously constructed that it was practically invisible.'

'Why didn't you tell me about this?' asked Ebba.

'I was already starting to see the truth. That you were to blame for Vincent's death, but you refused to admit your guilt. You were trying to shift the blame to me. And in the unlocked chest I found this.' He waved the gun. 'I knew that I'd have a use for it.'

'They'll find a way to get in. You know that,' said Anna. 'You might as well open the door.'

'I can't open it. There used to be a knob on the inside, but someone removed it. The door locks automatically, and they don't have a key, so even if they do find the secret door, they won't be able to get in. Whoever built this cellar was paranoid – it'll withstand just about anything.' Tobias smiled. 'By the time they bring equipment over here to break their way in, it'll be too late.'

'Tobias, please,' said Ebba, but Anna could tell that it would do no good to try reasoning with him. Tobias had decided to die here, and they would too, unless she did something.

At that instant they heard a key being fitted into the lock. Surprised, Tobias turned his head. That was the moment Anna had been waiting for. She grabbed the angel pendant from the floor and threw herself at Tobias. She ripped a big gash in his cheek with the sharp edge of the pendant as she used her other hand to fumble for the gun. Just as she touched the cold steel, a shot rang out.

Josef had made up his mind to die today. It felt like the logical step after his failure, and the decision had actually filled him with relief. When he left the house, he still hadn't worked out how to do it, but when Percy began waving the gun about, it occurred to Josef that he might die a hero.

Now, strangely enough, it seemed like a rash decision. On his way down the dark basement stairs, his will to live seemed stronger than ever before. He didn't want to die, especially not in this place which had given him nightmares for so many years. He saw the police officers in front of him, and he felt oddly naked without a gun. There had been no question that he should accompany them. He was the only one who could show them the way. The only one who knew how to find hell.

The officers waited for him at the bottom of the stairs. Patrik Hedström raised an eyebrow enquiringly and Josef pointed to the far wall. It appeared to be an ordinary wall, with crooked shelves holding old paint cans. Seeing Patrik's sceptical expression, he stepped forward to show them. He remembered it all so well: the smells, the feel of the concrete floor underfoot, the musty air that he'd breathed into his lungs.

After a glance at Patrik, Josef pressed the right side of the middle shelf. The wall moved, swinging inward to reveal a passageway leading to a solid door. He stepped aside. The officers looked at him in surprise for a moment and then entered the passageway. At the door they paused to listen. They could hear a faint murmuring from inside. Josef knew exactly what lay behind the door. All he had to do was close his eyes for the image to be as clear as if he'd seen the room yesterday. The cold walls, the bare bulb hanging from the ceiling. And the four chests. They had put the gun inside one of them. That was where Ebba's husband must have found it. Josef wondered whether Tobias had opened the locked chests too, whether he knew what was inside. It didn't matter, because now everything was going to be revealed. There was no turning back.

Patrik took the key out of his pocket, stuck it in the lock, and turned it. He cast a glance at Josef and his colleagues, his face clearly showing that he feared what they were about to find.

Cautiously Patrik opened the door. A shot was fired, and Josef saw the officers rush inside, their weapons drawn. But he stayed in the passageway. All the commotion made it hard to know exactly what was happening, but he could hear Patrik shouting: 'Drop the gun!' There was a flash and a shot that reverberated loudly and painfully. Then came the sound of somebody falling to the floor.

In the silence that followed, Josef's ears were ringing, and he was aware of his own breathing, jagged and shallow. He was alive, he knew that he was alive, and he was grateful for that. Rebecka would be worried when she found his letter, but he would try to explain. Because he was not going to die today.

Someone came running down the basement steps, and when he turned, he saw Ia racing towards him. Her eyes were filled with fear.

'Ebba,' she said. 'Where is Ebba?'

Blood had sprayed over the chests and halfway up the wall. Behind her she could hear Ebba screaming, but it sounded far away.

'Anna.' Patrik took her by the shoulders and shook her. She pointed to her ear.

'I think my ear drum burst. I can't hear anything.'

Her voice sounded strangely muffled. Everything had happened so fast. She looked down at her hands. They were bloody, and she examined her body to see whether she was bleeding, but she couldn't find any wounds. She was still gripping Ebba's angel pendant in her hand, and she realized that the blood must have come from the gash on Tobias's face. Now he was lying on the floor, his eyes open. A bullet had torn a big hole in his head.

Anna turned away. Ebba was still screaming, and suddenly a woman came rushing in and threw her arms around her. Slowly she rocked her back and forth until Ebba's cries subsided to a whimper. Anna pointed mutely at the chests. Patrik, Martin, and Gösta stared at the skeletons, now spattered with Tobias's blood.

'We need to get you out of here.' Patrik gently ushered Anna and Ebba towards the door. Ia followed close behind.

When they were inside the main room of the basement, Erica came flying down the steep steps. She took them two at a time, and Anna moved fast to meet her halfway. Only when she buried her face against her big sister's neck did she feel the tears start to flow.

When they came upstairs to the front hall, they squinted in the bright light. Anna was still shaking as if she were freezing, and Erica read her thoughts and went to get her clothes from upstairs. She didn't say a word about finding them in Tobias and Ebba's bedroom, but Anna knew that she was going to have a lot to explain. Her heart ached when she thought about how upset Dan was going to be, but she couldn't think about that now. She would have to work that out later.

'I've phoned for reinforcements, and a team is on the way,' said Patrik. He helped Anna and Ebba to sit on the front steps.

Ia sat down next to Ebba, putting her arm around her. Gösta sat on the other side of Ebba, studying both women. Patrik leaned down and whispered in his ear:

'That's Annelie. I'll tell you more later.'

Gösta gave him a puzzled look. Then an idea flashed through his mind, and he shook his head.

'The handwriting. Of course – that's how everything fits together.'

He knew that he'd missed something when they were going through the contents of the boxes. Something that he'd seen and should have understood. Now he turned to Ia.

'She could have ended up living with us, but she had

a good life with the family in Göteborg.' Gösta noticed that the others were listening but had no idea what he was talking about.

'I couldn't bear to think about who might take her in. I couldn't bear to think about her at all. It was easier that way,' said Ia.

'She was so lovely. I was enchanted by her that summer, and we wanted to keep her. But we'd lost a child and had given up any idea of having a . . .' He turned away.

'Yes, she was lovely. A true little angel!' said Ia, smiling sadly. Ebba looked at them in astonishment.

'How did you work it out?' asked Ia.

'The grocery list. There was a handwritten list among the things that you left behind. And then you gave me the note with the address that you'd written down. And the handwriting was the same.'

'Would somebody please explain?' said Patrik. 'What are you talking about, Gösta?'

'It was Leon's idea for me to use Annelie's passport instead of my own,' said Ia. 'There was an age difference of a few years, but we were similar enough for it to work.'

'I don't understand.' Ebba shook her head.

Gösta looked her in the eye. In his mind he saw the little lass who had run around in their yard and left such an impression on his heart. It was high time for her to hear the news that she'd been waiting to receive for so many years.

'Ebba, this is your mother. This is Inez.'

Utter silence. The only sound was the wind rustling in the birch trees.

'But, but . . .' stammered Ebba. She pointed behind her, towards the basement. 'Then who is that in there, with the long hair?'

'Annelie,' said Ia. 'We both had long brown hair.' And she gently touched Ebba's cheek.

'Why haven't you ever . . .?' Ebba's voice was shaky with emotion.

'There is no simple answer. There's a lot that I can't explain, because I don't understand it myself. I forced myself not to think about you. Otherwise I'd never have been able to give you up.'

'Leon didn't finish telling us what happened back then,' said Patrik. 'I think it's time for us to hear the truth.'

'Yes, it is,' said Ia.

Boats had appeared out on the water, still some distance away, but coming towards Valö. While he welcomed the prospect that another team would soon take over, first Gösta wanted to hear, at long last, what happened on that Easter weekend in 1974. He took Ebba's hand in his. Ia took the other.

VALÖ, EASTER EVE 1974

'What's this?' Rune's face was white as he stood in the doorway to the dining room. Behind him were Leon and the other boys: John, Percy, Sebastian, and Josef.

Inez blinked at them in surprise. She'd never seen Rune lose his composure before, but right now he was so upset that he was shaking all over. He went over to Claes. In his hands he held a stack of photographs and a gun.

'What's this?' he repeated.

Claes didn't say a word, his face expressionless. The boys cautiously came into the room, and Inez sought Leon's eye, but he avoided looking at her. Instead, he stared at Claes and Rune. For a moment no one spoke. The air felt heavy and it was hard to breathe. Inez gripped the edge of the table. Something terrible was about to happen right in front of her, and no matter what it was, she knew that things were going to end badly.

A smile slowly spread across Claes's lips. Before his father could react, he stood up, grabbed the gun, and pressed it against Rune's forehead. He fell to the floor, lifeless. Blood gushed from the bullet hole, black with gunpowder. Inez heard herself scream. It sounded like it was coming from someone else, but she knew it was her own voice echoing between the walls, blending with Annelie's cries in a macabre duet.

'Shut up!' shouted Claes, still pointing the gun at Rune. 'Shut up!'

But she couldn't stop screaming. Terror forced the sound from her mouth as she stared at the dead body of her husband. Ebba was crying shrilly.

'I said, shut up!' Claes fired another shot at his father, making the body twitch. The white shirt slowly turned red.

The shock made Inez abruptly fall silent. Even Annelie stopped screaming, but Ebba was still crying.

Claes rubbed his face. In his other hand he held the gun. He looks like a little boy playing cowboy, thought Inez, but there was nothing boyish about Claes's face. Nor was there anything human about it. His eyes were empty, and he was still smiling that awful smile, as if his face had frozen into that expression. He was breathing hard.

Suddenly he turned towards Ebba and aimed the gun at her. She was still crying, her face bright red. As if frozen in place, Inez watched Claes's finger press the trigger as Johan threw himself forward. Then he stopped. With a look of astonishment, he looked down at his shirt, where a patch of red was spreading fast. Then he collapsed on the floor.

Silence once again descended over the room. An unnatural silence. Even Ebba was quiet, sucking on her thumb. Next to her highchair, Johan lay on his back. A lock of his blond hair had fallen into his eyes, which were staring, unseeing, up at the ceiling. Inez suppressed a sob.

Claes backed up so that he was standing against the wall. 'Do as I say. And be quiet. That's the most important thing of all.' His voice was eerily calm, as if he were enjoying the situation.

Out of the corner of her eye, Inez saw a movement near the door, and Claes seemed to notice it too. He instantly pointed the gun at the boys.

'No one leaves the room. No one's going anywhere.'

'What are you going to do with us?' asked Leon.

'I don't know. I haven't decided.'

'My father has lots of money,' said Percy. 'He'll pay you if you'll let us go.'

Claes uttered a hollow laugh. 'It's not money that I want. You should know that.'

'We promise not to say anything,' said John, but his plea fell on deaf ears.

Inez knew that it was pointless. She'd been right about Claes. She'd sensed that there was something missing inside of him. No matter what he'd done to the boys, he was going to cover up his crimes at all costs. He'd already killed two people, and he wasn't about to let anyone out of there alive. They were all going to die.

Suddenly Leon looked at her, and Inez realized that he was thinking the same thing. They'd never have any more time together other than those few stolen hours. They'd made plans and shared so many thoughts about how they were going to live. All they had to do was wait and have patience, and they'd have a future to share. Now that wasn't going to happen.

'I knew that whore was up to something,' said Claes suddenly. 'There's no mistaking those kinds of looks. How long have you been fucking my stepmother, Leon?'

Inez didn't say a word. Annelie turned from her to Leon.

'Is that true?' For a moment Annelie seemed to forget her fear. 'You bloody slut! Isn't there anyone your own age that you—'

Her words were cut off. Claes had calmly raised the gun and fired a shot through her temple.

'I told you to shut up,' he said tonelessly.

Inez felt tears welling up in her eyes. How long did they have left to live? They were powerless. There was nothing to do but wait to be slaughtered, one by one.

Ebba began crying again, and Claes flinched. Her cries got louder, and Inez could feel her whole body tense. She ought to stand up, but she couldn't make herself move.

'Make the kid stop.' Claes glared at her. 'I said, make the brat stop crying!'

She opened her mouth but no words came out, and Claes shrugged.

'Okay. In that case, I'll have to do it myself,' he said and again pointed the gun at Ebba.

As he pulled the trigger, Inez threw herself forward to protect her daughter with her own body.

But nothing happened. Claes pulled the trigger again. The gun didn't go off, and he stared at it in surprise. At that instant, Leon rushed forward to attack him.

Inez picked up Ebba and held her close, her heart pounding wildly. Claes was pinned to the floor under Leon, but he was twisting and turning to get free.

'Help me!' shouted Leon, and then he screamed when Claes punched him in the stomach.

It looked as though he was about to lose his hold on Claes, who was struggling ferociously. But a well-aimed kick from John struck Claes in the head and they heard a horrible cracking sound. His body went limp and he stopped fighting.

Leon quickly rolled away, landing on all fours on the floor. Percy kicked Claes in the stomach as John kept on kicking his head. At first Josef just stood and watched. Then he resolutely walked over to the table, stepped over Rune's body, and reached for the knife that had been used to carve the roast. He fell on his knees next to Claes and glanced up at John and Percy, who stopped kicking as they gasped for breath. A gurgling sound came from Claes's mouth, and his eyes rolled. Slowly, almost as if savouring the moment, Josef raised the big knife and laid the sharp edge against Claes's throat. Then he made a swift incision, and the blood began pumping out.

Ebba was still crying, and Inez held her even closer. The instinct to protect her child was stronger than anything she'd ever felt before. Her whole body was shaking as Ebba curled up like a little animal in her arms. She clung so hard to her neck

461

that Inez could hardly breathe. On the floor in front of them sat Percy, Josef and John next to Claes's ravaged body. Like a pride of lions surrounding its prey.

Leon came over to Inez and Ebba. He took several deep breaths.

'We need to clean this up,' he said in a low voice. 'Don't worry. I'll take care of it.' He kissed her gently on the cheek.

As if from a great distance, Inez heard him start to issue orders to the other boys. Scattered words reached her, about what Claes had done, about the evidence that had to be concealed, about the shame, but it sounded as if someone were speaking from far away. With her eyes closed, she rocked Ebba. Soon this would all be over. Leon would take care of everything.

❖

They felt strangely empty. It was Monday evening, and the events of the past days had slowly begun to sink in. Erica had gone over and over what had happened to Anna – and what might have happened. Yesterday Patrik had spent the whole day coddling her as if she were a child. At first she'd found it endearing, but by now she'd grown tired of his attention.

'Do you want a blanket?' asked Patrik, kissing her on the forehead.

'It's over eighty-five degrees in here at the moment. So, no thanks. No blanket. And I swear, if you kiss me on the forehead one more time, I'm not going to have sex with you for a month.'

'Sorry if I'm a little anxious about my wife.' Patrik went out to the kitchen.

'Did you see the newspaper today?' she called after him, but received only a mumbled reply. She got up from the sofa and went to join him. It was gone eight o'clock but the heat hadn't abated. She felt an urge for some ice cream.

'Unfortunately, I did,' said Patrik. 'I especially liked the front page: Mellberg posing with John Holm next to the police car under the headline: HERO IN FJÄLLBACKA.'

Erica snorted. She opened the freezer and took out a container of chocolate ice cream. 'Want some?'

'Sure, thanks.' Patrik sat down at the kitchen table. The children had gone to bed and a sense of calm had settled over the house. They needed to enjoy it while they could.

'I take it that Mellberg's quite pleased with himself?'

'That doesn't begin to describe it. And the Göteborg police are upset that he hogged all the credit. But the main thing is that Holm's plans were exposed and the attack was prevented. It's going to take a long time for the Friends of Sweden to recover.'

Erica wished she could believe that. She gave Patrik a sombre look.

'How did things go when you talked to Leon and Inez?'

He sighed. 'I'm not too sure. They answered all my questions, but I still don't understand.'

'What do you mean?'

'Leon explained what happened, but I have a hard time following his reasoning. It started when he began to suspect that there was something not quite right at the school. And finally Josef broke down and told him what Claes had done to him. And to John and Percy.'

'Was it Leon's idea to tell Rune?'

Patrik nodded. 'The boys didn't want to, but he persuaded them. I had the impression that since then he's spent a lot of time thinking about what would have happened and how their lives would have been different if he hadn't coaxed the other boys to talk.'

'It was the only right thing to do. He couldn't have known how insane Claes was. It was impossible for him to foresee what would happen.' Erica scraped the last of the ice cream from her bowl, keeping her eyes fixed on Patrik. She had wanted to accompany him when he went to see Leon and Inez, but he refused to allow it. So she'd had to make do with his report after the fact.

'That's exactly what I told him.'

'What about afterwards though? Why didn't they ring the police?' asked Erica.

'They were afraid that no one would believe them. And I think shock also played a part. They weren't thinking clearly. Plus, we can't underestimate the shame that they felt. The thought that people would find out what they'd endured probably made them go along with Leon's plan.'

'But Leon had nothing to lose by notifying the police. He wasn't one of Claes's victims, and he didn't take part in killing him.'

'No, but he did risk losing Inez,' said Patrik. He set down his spoon without even tasting the ice cream. 'If the details had been made public, the scandal would have been so huge that they probably couldn't have stayed together.'

'What about Ebba? How could they leave her like that?'

'That seems to be the thing that has bothered Leon the most over the years. He didn't come right out and say it, but I don't think he has ever stopped reproaching himself for making Inez leave Ebba behind. And I didn't want to ask. I think both of them have suffered enough from the decisions they made.'

'I just can't understand how he could have persuaded Inez to leave Ebba.'

'They were so in love. They were having a passionate love affair, and they were terrified that Rune would find out about it. Forbidden love is a dangerous thing. And Leon's father, Aron, also shares part of the blame. Leon phoned him to ask for help, and Aron made it clear that Inez would have to leave the country, but not with a small child.'

'Okay, I can see why Leon would agree to that. But Inez? Even if she was head over heels in love, how could she give up her own child?' Erica's voice quavered at the

465

mere thought of giving up any of her children with no hope of ever seeing them again.

'She probably wasn't thinking clearly either. And apparently Leon convinced her that it would be best for Ebba. I can imagine him scaring her by saying that, if they stayed, they'd end up in prison, and then she'd lose Ebba anyway.'

Erica shook her head. That didn't make sense. She would never understand how any parent could voluntarily give up their child.

'So they hid the bodies and then came up with that fishing story, right?'

'According to Leon, his father suggested that they dump the bodies in the sea, but Leon was worried that they'd float up to the surface, so he came up with the idea of hiding them in the air-raid shelter. They carried the bodies down to the basement and put them in the chests along with the photographs. They decided to put the gun back where Claes must have found it. Then they locked the room, counting on the fact that it was so well concealed that the police wouldn't find it.'

'And they never did,' said Erica.

'No. That part of their plan worked fine, except that Sebastian took possession of the key. Apparently he's held it like a broad-axe over their heads ever since.'

'But why didn't the police find any trace of what happened when they searched the house?'

'The boys scrubbed the dining-room floor and removed any blood that was visible to the naked eye. And you have to remember that this was in 1974, and it was the provincial police who did the technical examination. Not exactly CSI-calibre back then. Then the boys changed their clothes and went out on the fishing boat after making an anonymous call to the police.'

'And where did Inez go?'

'She hid. Leon said that was also his father's idea. They broke into an empty summerhouse on a nearby island. She stayed there until everything calmed down enough so that she and Leon could leave Sweden.'

'So the whole time that the police were searching for the family, she was in a summerhouse nearby?' said Erica in disbelief.

'Yes. The owners of the summerhouse probably filed a police report about the break-in later in the summer, but it was never linked to the family's disappearance on Valö.'

She nodded, satisfied that all the puzzle pieces had finally fallen into place. After spending so many hours trying to piece together what had happened to the Elvander family, she finally knew most of the story.

'I wonder how things will go for Inez and Ebba now,' she said, reaching for Patrik's bowl so she could eat the ice cream before it melted. 'I haven't wanted to bother Ebba, but I assume that she's gone back to stay with her adoptive parents in Göteborg.'

'You mean you haven't heard?' said Patrik, his face lighting up for the first time since they'd started talking about the case.

'No, what?' asked Erica.

'She's staying in Gösta's guest room for a few days to rest. Gösta said that Inez is supposed to come over and have dinner with them tonight. So I assume that they'll make an effort to get to know each other.'

'That sounds good. She needs it. The business with Tobias must have come as a horrible shock. Imagine living with somebody you love and trust, and then it turns out that he's capable of something like that . . .' Erica shook her head. 'But I bet Gösta is happy to have her staying with him. If only . . .'

'I know. And Gösta has probably had the same thought more times than we can imagine. But Ebba had a good childhood, and I have a feeling Gösta thinks that's the important thing.' He abruptly changed the subject, as if it was too painful to consider all the things that Gösta had missed out on. 'How's Anna?'

Erica frowned.

'I haven't heard from her yet. Dan drove straight home after he got the text message that I sent, and I know that she was planning to tell him everything.'

'Everything?'

Erica nodded.

'How do you think Dan is going to react?'

'I don't know.' Erica ate a few more spoonfuls of ice cream and then stirred what was left in the bowl so it turned into a runny mess. It was a habit she'd had since she was a kid. Anna did the same thing. 'I hope they can work it out.'

'Hmm,' said Patrik, but she could see that he was sceptical. So now it was her turn to change the subject.

She didn't really want to admit it, either to herself or to Patrik, but over the past few days she'd been so worried about Anna that she could hardly think about anything else. But she'd forced herself not to phone. Anna and Dan needed peace and quiet if they were going to have any chance of working things out. Anna would call eventually.

'Will there be any legal repercussions for Leon and the others?'

'No. The statute of limitations has expired. The only person who could have been prosecuted for anything is Tobias. And we'll have to see what happens with Percy.'

'I hope Martin isn't too upset about the fact that he killed Tobias. That's the last thing he needs to worry about right now,' said Erica. 'And it was my fault that he got involved in the first place.'

'Don't beat yourself up about it. He's doing as well as

can be expected, and he seems ready to come back to work as soon as possible. Pia's treatment is going to take time, and both sets of parents are helping them out, so he's talking to her about working at least part-time.'

'That sounds sensible,' said Erica, but she still couldn't help feeling guilty.

Patrik gave her a searching look. Then he reached out and stroked her cheek, meeting her eye. As if by silent agreement, they hadn't talked about the fact that he'd almost lost her again. She was here now. And they loved each other. That was all that mattered.

STOCKHOLM 1991

Two Carin Görings?

The Forensic Laboratory in Linköping has analysed the human remains that were recently found in a zinc-lined chest in the vicinity of what was once Hermann Göring's estate of Karinhall. The remains were said to belong to Carin Göring, née Fock, who died in 1931. The strange thing is that in 1951 a forest warden discovered some scattered skeletal remains that were presumed to belong to Carin Göring. Under great secrecy, they were cremated and then a vicar took the ashes to Sweden for burial in Lovö Cemetery.

That was the third time Carin Göring was buried. The first time was in the Fock family plot in Lovö Cemetery, then at the Karinhall estate, and finally in Sweden.

Now another chapter is being written in this peculiar story. DNA analysis shows that the latest discovered remains do indeed belong to Carin Göring. So the question is: Whose ashes are interred in Lovö Cemetery outside Stockholm?

AFTERWORD

I am writing this a week after the bomb explosion in Oslo,
Norway, and the shooting deaths on the island of Utøya.
I've been watching the news reports with a horrible feeling
in my stomach, just like everyone else, trying in vain to
understand how anyone could be capable of such evil.
The pictures of the destruction in Oslo made me realize
that the events in this book touch on that same sort of
evil. Unfortunately, it's true that reality is stranger than
fiction. By pure chance my story about people who use
politics to excuse their evil deeds happened to coincide
with what took place in Norway, but maybe it's an indi-
cation of the kind of society we live in today.

Yet there are other parts of *Buried Angels* that were
consciously based on real events. I want to thank Lasse
Lundberg who, during a guided tour of Fjällbacka, stirred
my imagination with his story about the Bohuslän granite
that Albert Speer supposedly chose for Germania, and
about the visit that Hermann Göring was said to have
made to one of the islands in the Fjällbacka archipelago.
I've taken the liberty of using these accounts to create
my own story.

I needed to do a lot of research about Göring in order
to write this story. Björn Fontander's book *Carin Göring*

skriver hem was a great resource, especially for all the information about the time that Göring spent in Sweden. It was in this book that I also discovered a genuine mystery that I could weave into the plot in that magical way that is sometimes granted to writers. And that's always wonderful. Thank you, Björn, for the inspiration your book gave me.

There is no Angelmaker from Fjällbacka, but of course there are similarities between the novel's Helga Svensson and Hilda Nilsson from Helsingborg, who hanged herself in her cell in 1917 before the death sentence could be carried out.

The summer camp on Valö does exist, and it has played a certain role in the history of Fjällbacka. I've spent many summertime weeks at the camp, and almost everyone who lives in Fjällbacka has some sort of relationship to the big white house. Today it's both a youth hostel and restaurant, and well worth a visit. I've taken the liberty of changing the dates and owners so that they fit into my story. As usual, I've had invaluable help from Anders Torevi regarding all the other details about Fjällbacka.

The journalist Niklas Svensson generously provided a great deal of expert help with the political parts of the book. A big thanks for that.

As usual, I've combined details from real life with my own imaginings. And any errors are entirely my own. I have also set the story at a time when the statute of limitations for murder was twenty-five years. That law has now been changed.

There are many people that I'd like to thank, including my publisher Karin Linge Nordh and my editor Matilda Lund, who have performed a Herculean task on the manuscript.

Thanks also to my husband Martin Melin, who is always

so enormously supportive of my work. Since he's now working on his own manuscript for the first time, we've been able to encourage each other as we've both spent many long hours writing. Of course it's also an incredible advantage to have my own police officer, and I can ask him everything between heaven and earth about police work.

Thanks to my children Wille, Meja and Charlie, who give me energy to pour into my books. And to my whole network: my mother Gunnel Läckberg and Rolf 'Sassar' Svensson, Sandra Wirström, my older children's father Mikael Eriksson, as well as Christina Melin, who stepped forward in an exceptional fashion when things started piling up. Thank you to all of you.

Nordin Agency – Joakim Hansson and the whole gang – you know that I'm incredibly grateful for the work you do for me in Sweden and the world. Christina Saliba and Anna Österholm at Weber Shandwick have put an enormous amount of work into everything that has to do with a successful author's career. You do an amazing job.

Thank you to my writer colleagues. None named, none forgotten. I don't get to meet with you as often as I'd like, but when we do see each other, I come away brimming with positive energy and the joy of writing. And I know that you're always there. A special place in my heart is reserved for Denise Rudberg, my friend, colleague, and supporter for so many years. What would I do without you?

And I couldn't write these books if the citizens of Fjällbacka didn't cheerfully allow me to make up all sorts of horrors about their small town. Sometimes I get a little nervous about what I'm doing, but you even put up with being invaded by a film company. This autumn it's going to happen again, and I hope that you'll be proud of the results when Fjällbacka has another chance to show off its unique setting to viewers around the world.

Finally, I want to thank my readers. You always wait so patiently for the next book. You encourage me in the face of adversity, you give me a pat on the back when I need it, and you've stayed with me for so many years now. I appreciate that. Tremendously. Thank you.

Camilla Läckberg
Måsholmen, 29 July 2011

www.camillalackberg.com